W9-AUS-676

—RALPH ARNOTE—

FALSE PROMISES

Emerald and Von Braun entered the Paragon Club and were met by Melanie, who hustled them upstairs, through the retracting wall panel and into the softly lit Blue Shark club. As their eyes adjusted to the light it became apparent that several nude young women were tangled together in a puzzling mass of hungry flesh.

"Captain Von Braun, I want you to meet Lord Hargraves—her majesty's ambassador." Emerald Lu smiled. "He very busy here. He starring in major motion picture, as they say in Hollywood."

Emerald Lu raised her arm and swung it in a circular motion. Almost at once, a huge screen high up on the opposite wall flashed on, and the x-rated gyrations of the diplomat and his three playmates came to life . . .

Books by Ralph Arnote
from Tom Doherty Associates, Inc.

Fallen Idols
False Promises
Fatal Secrets

FALSE PROMISES

-RALPH ARNOTE-

FORGE ®

A TOM DOHERTY ASSOCIATES BOOK
NEW YORK

FALSE PROMISES

Cover art by Joe DeVito

A Forge Book
Published by Tom Doherty Associates, Inc.
175 Fifth Avenue
New York, N.Y. 10010

Forge® is a registered trademark of Tom Doherty Associates, Inc.

ISBN: 0-812-55043-9

First edition: January 1995

Printed in the United States of America

0 9 8 7 6 5 4 3 2 1

To Tom Doherty

Acknowledgments

The support, advice and encouragement of these people make the world go around: Nancy Murphy, Bob Lofgren, Jolee Homestead, Bill Golliher, Linda Quinton, Roberta Yochim, John Del Gaizo, Monica Bartelone, Glory Roseman, Angelique Du Bois, Michael and Kathleen Gear, Yolanda Rodriguez, and the nonpareil Bob Gleason.

Sweet is revenge—
especially to a woman.

—LORD BYRON

1

Charles Clayfield sat behind the wheel of the Buick and watched. The narrow cardboard box in his lap held a dozen long-stemmed red roses, but for the moment he had completely forgotten them. In fact he had forgotten about everything except his black Mercedes and the activities now going on inside it.

The two occupants were clinched in an amorous embrace. Angela's long blond hair spilled down over the man's face, camouflaging the details of a prolonged kiss. They pulled ever so slightly apart for a moment, Angela sensuously stroking the man's face. Then they were together again, Angela's arms aggressively wrapping the neck and shoulders of her companion. The probing kiss began again, this time in full view.

Charles Clayfield adjusted the rearview mirror. His eyes ran over the license plate numbers again and again, as if the clear recognition of his wife were not enough.

It was a cloudy day and dusk was coming fast to the parking lot. He loosened the twine around the florist's box. Looking down, he removed the lid and began stroking the soft outer petals of the huge buds, each ready to pop into full splendor. When he glanced up again, only the man was visible in the Mercedes. Angela must have gone into one of the stores.

This day had started out innocently enough, he thought. He had completed his conference in Los Angeles a day early and decided to surprise Angela and the kids. Similar surprises in the past had always resulted in happy outcomes. His plane had landed right on time at Newark Airport. He had rented a car and stopped at the strip mall to buy the roses that now lay across his lap. Then, as he had turned on the ignition, the Mercedes, his Mercedes, had wheeled into the lot and parked two rows behind him, and his world had come crashing down.

Sixteen years, he thought. For sixteen years he had been married to Angela. Never once in all those years had there been the slightest hint of dissatisfaction. Jealousy was something he had left behind since their dating days. He could no longer find that emotion now. In its place, rage consumed him with an intensity that tightened his chest and turned his thoughts hard as stone.

He waited and waited until it was more dark than light in the strip mall. A full fifteen minutes must have passed. Then Angela's head rose to silhouette itself next to the man's. Angela had been in the Mercedes all that time.

Charles could feel the pulse pounding in his temples. His throat tightened and he could hear his own hard breathing. His hands roughly fingered the roses in his lap. One by one he crushed the burgeoning buds, twisting them from their long stems.

The door of the Mercedes opened abruptly, and the man got out. He was tall and well-dressed in a dark suit. Still in the car, Angela moved over the console to the driver's side and extended her hand out the window. The man brushed her hand with a kiss and then set off across the parking area, stopping once to wave and blow another kiss toward the Mercedes.

Charles looked down again at the roses. Only one rose had survived his anger. He carefully removed it from the box and set it aside on the front seat. He felt exhausted. He and Angela had been blessed with a life largely free from disappointments and troubles. But this was a turning point. Every feeling he had ever had for her was now changed.

Her familiar tossing and shaking of her long blond hair was as condemning as a fingerprint. She turned the ignition key and the sleek Mercedes purred to life. She drove slowly from the parking area, turning south on Chestnut Ridge toward their home in Saddle Hills.

Charles quickly turned his attention to the car her companion had now started. Still nervous, he fumbled for a pen and a scrap of paper and wrote down the license number of the black Oldsmobile as it left its parking space, made a right turn and passed in front of him. It was too dark to see the driver's face, though it was evident that he had a mustache.

Charles was torn between following the man and getting home as quickly as possible. But he had a compulsion to confront Angela as soon as he could. He wanted to look into those great violet eyes that would beg him to trust her. Making certain of the license plate number he had written down, he started his car and turned toward Saddle Hills. He wanted to hear the magic words that would explain away what he had just seen.

His thoughts ran to their children, Penny and

Chucky. She must be home already. What was she telling the kids about her day? It was to be a big weekend for the children. The housekeeper was to be away, and he and Angela had agreed to spend the three-day holiday doing only things the kids really wanted to do. Penny was to have some friends over for a slumber party. Chucky wanted to go see the Yankees.

Charles could think of no words she could say that would alter his feelings. Nothing could change what he had seen with his own eyes. After sixteen years, she did deserve a chance to explain herself. A day in court. But it would be meaningless.

He was sweating profusely in the air-conditioned car. Wild scenarios began to play through his mind. They involved complicated plots. Most of them revolved about two questions. Should he kill the man, or should he kill Angela?

Within minutes he was turning into his driveway. There was the black Mercedes. His eyes ran over the number on the license plate again, wishing pointlessly that by some miracle it had changed. Then Penny and Chucky came tearing out the door.

"Daddy! Daddy! You're home," and then, "Mommy! Daddy's home!"

Just as they tackled his knees, Angela appeared at the door. He looked at the violet eyes, the big smile. He thought of that beautiful face so recently buried in the lap of the tall stranger. She approached him and offered a brief kiss, flavored with a hint of minty toothpaste.

That's considerate, he thought, staring at the vivacious woman he had loved for every minute of their sixteen years.

"Hey! What a surprise! You're home a day early. Isn't that wonderful, kids? I've been thinking about you all day."

Angela took the single surviving rose from his hands. "Oh, how beautiful. I'll have to get this into a bud vase right away."

Charles had always given her a dozen roses, but Angela seemed not to notice the difference. She looked and acted toward him just the way she always did. He wished it could be that way, but he glanced toward the Mercedes and knew that nothing would ever be the same again.

2

"**B**usy day, I'll bet, with the board of directors meeting and all," ventured Charles. He eyed her closely, marveling at how casual and completely at ease she was. She had removed two frosted long-stemmed martini glasses from the freezer and placed them on the service bar between their kitchen and rec room. She had doffed her skirt and stood before him in a short clinging slip as she swirled the Tanqueray with a few ice cubes in a glass pitcher.

"Yes, it was a busy day. But it ended well. I've made Bradford Overstreet our new vice president in charge of just about everything that matters. It took a bit of doing. Some of the good old boys felt stepped on, I'm afraid."

Charles listened to her ramble on. She had returned to her job at ConCom Publishing six years ago, and since then she had picked her way stealthily through the corporate minefield to become president and publisher of the historic firm. Miraculously she had managed to do this and yet remain an attentive and caring parent. He had always wondered at her boundless energy and talent.

"Brad Overstreet really doesn't have much tact, you know. I'm afraid he'll ruffle a lot of feathers. But he's got more talent in his little finger than the rest of the board put together. ConCom needs him."

Charles continued to watch his wife closely as she ran on about her day. He wondered whether it had been Brad Overstreet in the Mercedes with Angela. If so, maybe she was misstating the part of his body that had all that talent.

"What's he look like?" Charles asked, realizing that he was being uncharacteristically curt. "I don't recall having met this chap."

"Tall fellow, wears a mustache, very dark. He came up though the ranks. He started as an editor about the same time I rejoined the company. You must have met him, perhaps at one of the holiday parties. We'll have to ask him over. You'd like him. Actually you're much alike." Angela stopped talking, seemingly lost in thought.

Charles let it drop. If Overstreet was the man he had seen that evening with Angela, he would know it soon enough after he checked the plates with Motor Vehicle. He studied Angela closely. Strange that he could know her for sixteen years and not know her at all.

Driving the rental Buick, they took Penny and Chucky with them to dine at the Hessian Barn that evening. Their conversation was animated as usual, the children filling him in on the details of their days while he had been away. Charles smiled at the way they both entered into conversation with adults with precocious ease. They were sure of themselves, and always brimming with youthful inquisitive persistence.

"Well, aren't you going to tell Dad about your big, big, big, big news?" Chucky leaned across the table to grin into Penny's face.

"Whatever do you mean? And quit grinning like that, Chucky. It makes you look like a moron."

Chucky persisted, his exaggerated grin a weapon of humiliation.

"Dad, make him stop!"

"She hates it, Dad, because I don't happen to look like Wilson Brewster the Third, Penny's big new boyfriend."

Penny flushed and shoved at her brother. "Make him stop, Dad. He acts so stupid!"

"Chucky! Quiet now!" Angela spoke firmly. "When your sister is ready to talk about her friends to us she'll tell us all about them."

"Can I say just one more thing?" Chucky said.

Angela brushed her hand over Chucky's curly hair and leaned over to give him a squeeze. "Okay, just one more thing, but only if you promise to be nice to your sister the rest of the evening."

Charles stared at the beautiful trio, a family to be proud of. Other diners were glancing their way and smiling understandingly at the classic sibling exchange.

Chucky elevated his voice just enough so everyone nearby could hear. "Just this morning Penny told Marsha on the phone that Wilson Brewster the Third is the only boyfriend she'll ever have in her whole life. She said she and Wilson Brewster the third are going to be just like you and Dad. Isn't that stupid? Wilson Brewster the Third being just like Dad?"

Angela pointed at Chucky. "That is quite enough, young man. Penny can say whatever she feels. She does have a right to change her mind someday. It's just fine that she thinks so highly of Wilson and that she has such a good friend."

"Yes, Chucky, women have the right to change their minds about the men in their life, especially when they are as beautiful as Penny and your mother." Charles watched Angela as he spoke, looking for some flicker of concern or guilt. There was absolutely no trace of either. "Of course, Angela, when a woman gets married, she no longer has the right to change her mind, does she?"

Angela extended her hand across the table to Charles. "Of course Daddy's right. And when two people get married, we hope they love each other, more and more each day, the way we do."

Charles looked steadily into his wife's moistening eyes as he lightly held her hand. If ever sincerity looked more convincing, he had never seen it.

"You're rather quiet, dear," Angela said thoughtfully. "Did everything go well in California?"

"It was a perfect trip, Angela. Everything went as planned. Maybe it's just a little jet lag."

As they left the Hessian Barn, the two children ran ahead to the car. Angela stepped in front of Charles and hugged him close to her, whispering the words he had always delighted in. "I know what's the matter, honey, and when I get you home I'll fix it all up." With that she placed a deep, probing kiss on his passive lips.

"Charles!" she said, backing away. "Are you really ill, or something?"

"I feel like a million bucks, Angela."

She stood back, looked at him questioningly and then broke into a broad smile. "Aha! You're playing your old game."

"What game is that, Angela?"

"The you-can't-make-me game! I've got news for you, baby. You are going to lose big. When I get finished with you, your nasty old jet lag will turn into ten hours of sleep." With that she hugged him tightly and forced another kiss on his reluctant lips. This time she stirred in him a faint response.

She smiled between kisses. "I've got you now, baby." Then she ran ahead after the children.

Charles followed along toward the car, watching as Angela hugged the kids. He realized again that he did not know her at all.

Charles Clayfield was technically a thermal engineer. His occupation was more that of an expediter and liaison between various government contractors involved in the specialized field of producing micro-detonators. Since the end of the cold war, budget cuts had taken wide swaths through the industry, but his specialization continued to be in demand. The search for tiny, portable means of creating massive explosions seemed to be a priority.

Actually Charles had long ago lost his technical cutting-edge know-how. He had become a politician, a good communicator who could give a lay person's explanation of his specialty to government intelligence and law enforcement units. His work and travels remained low-profile and quietly mysterious as compared to the glitzier business dealings of Angela Clayfield. In the past he had enjoyed her whirlwind career vicariously. But suddenly he didn't give a damn anymore.

Contemplating her gross infidelity was a strangely unemotional process. There had been no suspicions, no rumors, no guessing or wondering or hoping. He had seen it with his own eyes.

Angela was continuing on as if nothing had changed, walking toward the rental car, pausing to hug and giggle with Penny and Chucky. It was a perfect picture of an ideal family outing.

Charles got behind the wheel and turned on the

ignition, waiting for the others to finish playing around and get in. It was uncharacteristic of him not to open the door for Angela. When she glanced at him, he mumbled something to the effect that he wanted to get the air conditioner working quickly on this hot evening.

He looked, as if in a trance, across the steering wheel to observe another couple about their age getting into a car. They looked happy. Maybe, in this amoral world, he was being unfair to Angela and the stranger. Maybe in their minds a little oral sex in the front seat of the family car with a business associate was not to be taken so seriously. Maybe after a hard day's work such amenities had taken the place of "Have a nice day" or "See ya later!"

Angela leaned over to kiss his cheek. "Hey! Remember me? What is the matter? Tell us about it."

Charles turned to reward her with a mechanical smile. "Just tired, I guess. I stayed up all last night in California working on a contract." It was a lie, one of the first he had ever told her. He was surprised he felt so good about it.

He had actually spent the night at Los Alamitos racetrack with Willy Hanson. Willy was a former president of ConCom, someone Angela knew. He was the only one of her business associates Charles had actually befriended. Ordinarily his evening with Hanson would have filled their conversation. But now he would never tell her.

"Dad, are we going to see the Yankees tomorrow?" Chucky broke the lull in the conversation.

"We sure are! I got the tickets last week."

"Can I bring a friend? Paul wants to go."

"Absolutely! Mother would like Paul to join us, right, Angela?"

Now Angela was in deep thought. After a pause she said, "Why don't you just take Paul and make it

a male outing? You guys would all have a great
time."

"Hey, Mom, that's great!"

Angela laid her hand across the console to touch
Charles. He squeezed her hand affectionately, feeling good as he slipped deeper into dishonesty with
her. He found himself relishing the little plan that
was racing through his mind.

He turned toward Angela and gave her a warm
smile that couldn't have seemed more genuine.

That night, with tears in her eyes, Angela described their lovemaking as "brutal." Usually when
they were rejoined after an extended business trip,
they would spend hours exploring each other with a
sensitivity that gave more than it asked. But
Charles's behavior this time could be most accurately described as prolonged rape. He pounced on
her, consciously using his superior physical strength
to totally dominate her throughout their lovemaking, even slapping her at times as he insistently
moved around to use her body.

So out of character was his onslaught that at first
she cooperated, thinking it was just a new little
flourish he had worked out, a new little game to surprise her, a game that would soon end. Then she realized that he was purposely hurting her and she
struggled to end the ordeal.

"Shut up! Bitch!" He climaxed, then rolled from
the bed, slipped on a robe and went downstairs.

Charles slept on the couch for several hours before
daylight awoke him. He went back upstairs to find
that Angela had moved to the spare bed in Penny's
room. So much the better, he thought. It would be
easier for him to get a few things together and leave
for a while. He just couldn't stand facing her again
until he had decided exactly what he would do. Last
night had been crazy. He had deliberately tried to

punish her and she had put up with it longer than he had suspected she would.

He looked out the window and saw the Mercedes and the rental Buick in the driveway. He would take the Mercedes. He would buy a morning paper and drive over to Park Ridge and have breakfast at the diner. With a few cups of coffee under his belt, perhaps he could decide how to confront Angela with what he knew.

Charles sat in the Mercedes for a long time before starting the engine. He stared at their bedroom window upstairs. He thought about the ideals they shared. She had even adopted his religion readily and had become an active member of the congregation. They were of like mind about bringing up the children with a religious identity. The lawless disorder that permeated society concerned both of them, and they agreed that there was a paucity of ethical and moral values. Yesterday's behavior in the parking lot was so far out of character for Angela that it made rationality nearly impossible for him. He knew he would have to tell her everything he had seen. He just couldn't live with it in silence.

Charles put his hand on the ignition key for a moment, staring at the bedroom window where Penny and Angela were sleeping. Thoughts of Chucky came to mind. Today was the day he and Chucky were to go see the Yankees. Whatever the problems were with Angela, through it all they would have to work to keep this hell away from the children. He turned the key in the ignition.

The massive explosion took out windows all up and down the block. Fire belched from the windows of the Mercedes and roared skyward, shriveling the branches of a cottonwood tree overhanging the driveway. White heat engulfed the car. Then came another explosion as the gasoline tank erupted to send a boiling cloud skyward.

Charles Clayfield never had a chance. Indeed, very little would remain to identify and confirm that there ever had been a Charles Clayfield.

The explosion and towering pillar of smoke jolted the sleepy little town of Saddle Hills wide awake. By the time the firefighting equipment arrived on the scene, the sleek Mercedes was little more than a twisted lump of black metal. The firefighters turned their efforts to dousing the flames in a big Norway spruce that was threatening to burn the house.

3

The next morning Willy Hanson went to a marine store near the Marina at Dana Point, California. He was readying the ketch *Tashtego* for a trans-Pacific voyage that he and Ginny had been planning for months. They were getting down to final preparations now. Specifically, there were several lengths of line to be purchased for new sail sheets, and a few assorted pieces of hardware to bring the repair kits and tool locker up to snuff.

Willy Hanson was a bronzed, muscular, obviously fit man in his late forties, standing well over six feet in height. His thick, prematurely graying hair had been bleached white by constant exposure to the sun. He strode with a quick step this Saturday morning. Sailing time was drawing near, the day when their long-awaited dream of a Pacific crossing together would take place.

He had been with Ginny Du Bois a couple of years and they had been turbulent indeed. He had left

ConCom Publishing Company over two years ago, weary of guarding the bottom line and compromising his values. He desperately sought something more rewarding before time wore on.

The past two years, however, had been far from idyllic. He had become involved in an exposé of an international drug cartel, and that experience had nearly cost him and Ginny their lives. They had survived it after all, and Willy had published a highly successful book describing their experiences. But they were overdue for the sailing escape of a lifetime.

Willy crossed the small causeway that led back to the marina. Picking out the *Tashtego* from the others was a snap. The broad spreaders and taller than usual mainmast made her standout. In the distance he could see Ginny on deck looking his way. Her tall, well-toned, lithe figure and chestnut hair stood out strikingly in the clear morning air.

As he neared the ketch, though, he could see that something was on her mind, and whatever it was was unpleasant.

"Why all the unhappiness, doll? Did we spring a leak?"

"I'm afraid it's much worse than that, honey. I just got a call from your old publicist at ConCom."

"And?" Willy climbed aboard the *Tashtego* and moved toward her.

"Didn't you just have dinner with Charles Clayfield last week?"

"Yes, I met him at Delany's down at Newport Beach."

"Willy, he's dead."

"What!" Willy stepped back, eyes unbelieving.

"Katie Glover says he was killed in an automobile explosion in his own driveway yesterday morning. Katie said it looks like it was no accident."

Willy paced the cockpit slowly, trying to recall the details of his conversation with Charles Clayfield several days ago. "There's nothing I can recall that had indicated he was in any trouble at all." Then his thoughts turned to Angela Clayfield. "I didn't know his wife well but I do remember how aggressive she was during the years before I left ConCom. She was a striking blonde who always did her homework well and seemed to relish tough assignments. The fact that she became CEO of ConCom in such a short time had sent rumors flying. She stepped over and alienated so many people that there was a lot of nasty talk about her bedroom appetites."

"Did you believe them?"

Willy shook his head. "No. In fact I had imagined her at the other end of the spectrum. Charles was a churchgoer and had described Angela pitching countless hours of precious free time to work on youth projects."

His mind turned to Charles Clayfield's own career. Charles had revealed a little about his vocation to Willy, but always left much unsaid. "Charles marketed high-security systems involving sophisticated detonators for explosive devices, work that would attract the worst of clients."

"Any chance that he might have got done in by one of his own devices?"

"I doubt it. Did Katie say anything about the funeral?"

"She was a little uncertain but said there would probably be a service on Tuesday. There's an investigation slowing things down. There was also a problem identifying the remains. They'll have to use dental charts."

"I guess I'll have to go." Willy grimaced, deep in thought. "I suppose most of the ConCom people will be there to support Angela. It must be horrible for her and the kids."

"Kids?"

"Yes, I think they had two, a boy and a girl. God! It must be an ubelievable trauma for them."

"Willy, I think you should fly back. I can handle the rest of the preparation for the crossing. We can still leave in a week or so."

"Thanks, Ginny. Charles was a good friend. I'll take the red-eye both ways. Maybe I can help somehow."

Ginny followed Willy as he strolled up to the bow. It was a brilliantly clear day in Dana Point. The harbor, created by a system of massive jetties of boulder-size rocks, was a perfect haven for the serious sailor. It offered quick access to the Pacific Ocean for day sailing south to San Diego or north to the Los Angeles basin. Catalina furnished a snug getaway for weekends, and beyond beckoned the romantic lure of Hawaii, the South Pacific and the Orient.

Willy hugged Ginny tightly to his side as they stood before the bowsprit. "I hope that when we do sail, we'll be able to pick a day just like this." He turned to squeeze her to him and buried a lingering kiss in the hollow of her neck. "Don't you go hunting up another crew. I'll fly out Sunday evening. I could be back in forty-eight hours."

"Willy, take as long as you need. There's no point in me going with you. I don't know any of those people. And, by the way, you told me once that Angela Clayfield was a knockout. Let's not go overboard in consoling the widow, lover!"

"Ginny! What terrible taste."

"I'm sorry, Willy. I guess that was a terrible thing to say. It was meant to be funny. But I suppose under the circumstances, nothing much is funny. Those poor kids! What will that woman do?"

"Don't worry about Angela Clayfield. She's as hard as carbon steel. The way she took over that company was proof of that. Some very ambitious and aggressive people practically jumped out of her way to make certain she got the top job. Actually, I always felt Angela was a little too perfect. Maybe that's why Charles relished travel so much."

Ginny smiled as Willy pondered the life of his lost friend. "Well, baby, I'll make sure to keep my flaws intact. You can be certain that I will never become a perfect, carbon-steel bitch."

Willy grinned at her declaration, hugged her again and turned to go belowdeck to stow the line and tools he had bought at the marine store.

4

It was Tuesday morning before Angela Clayfield focused on the rental Buick Charles had driven home from the airport on the night before he had died. She was so taken up in the tragedy that she hadn't given the vehicle a second thought until one of the investigators from the district attorney's office came to the door to ask about keys for the car. They had already determined that it had been rented by Charles at Newark Airport.

She found the keys in a tray on Charles's dresser and walked outside to the Buick with the investigator, who began searching the car. He found a briefcase in the trunk embossed with Charles's initials. He tagged it and put it in a plastic bag so that it could be gone over later by the investigation team. Of course they were considering Charles's death a possible homicide.

Angela stood and watched as the investigator began to search the rest of the vehicle. He got down on his knees and pulled at something under the front seat, finally extracting a long narrow box bearing the label of the Chestnut Florist Shop. Angela remembered the single rose Charles had given her the night of his arrival. In fact it was still in a bud vase upstairs.

She watched as the investigator flipped open the loose lid of the box. Inside were what appeared to have been a dozen long-stemmed roses. The buds, however, had all been plucked from their stems and crushed into a pile of petals.

The investigator shook his head. "That's strange. Why would anyone do that?"

Angela shook her head too. She guessed that there were only eleven stems there, and wondered why Charles had given her only one rose.

"Where is the Chestnut Florist Shop?" the investigator asked.

"It's only about a mile from here. Charles used to buy me flowers there once in a while after returning from a trip."

"Maybe some mischievous imp working in the flower shop destroyed them as a prank. The world is filled with all kinds, you know." The man continued to probe under the seat.

Angela leaned against the Buick. Nausea swept over her. She thought back to the night when Charles had come home, trying to remember it in exact detail. He had reached the house within ten minutes or so after her. This would have put him at the Chestnut Florist Shop at the same time she had been parked there with Brad Overstreet.

He had seen them! He had to have been parked nearby. He had seen the whole thing, the oral sex and the good-byes. She couldn't suppress a gasp.

"Are you okay, Mrs. Clayfield?" The detective, still

on his knees, turned to study Angela, now steadying herself against the Buick.

"I'm okay. It's hard to stay in control. It's been a tough morning."

She again looked at the Buick. Miraculously it had been spared damage from the burning car nearby. "I guess I had better call Avis and have it returned. I wonder if they would send someone for it?"

"I'm sure they will, Mrs. Clayfield. I'm sure they will. Why don't you let me handle that for you? I'll call them when I finish."

"Thank you. Er . . . I don't believe I know your name."

"I'm Tom Price. I work out of the district attorney's office."

"Mr. Price." Angela was trying to tidy up her face. "You've been very kind. I'm afraid I'm not taking all this very well. I just don't know why Charles would take his own life."

The detective finally stood and looked directly at her. "Mrs. Clayfield, whatever would make you think that? I doubt very much that your husband took his own life."

"Oh, I hope not! You know . . . he was an expert with explosive devices."

"I would like to hear about that sometime, Mrs. Clayfield, when you feel up to it."

Angela walked backed into the house thinking about the roses. Charles must have been enraged. She tried to picture him in the car crushing the buds one by one as he watched her with Brad Overstreet. It had been totally her doing. She had convinced Brad that the secluded area between other cars at the end of the row of shops offered safety. He was to keep on the lookout while she pleasured him. Evidently he had been much too distracted by her amorous assault.

The words of the investigator ran through her mind. "I doubt very much that your husband took his own life," he had said. She thought about that. They had taken the rental car to the restaurant. The explosive device must have been planted in the Mercedes while they were at the restaurant. When they had returned he had pulled the Buick up past the Mercedes and parked it at the end of the driveway near the rear of the house.

Charles had come home a day early, a surprise to everyone. Whoever had planted the bomb might have known that Charles was supposed to be out of town. If that was the case, the terrifying conclusion could be made that the exploding Mercedes had been intended for her, not Charles.

Angela shuddered as she began to walk from room to room in the large house. All of a sudden she felt alone and afraid. She longed for Charles. It seemed impossible that she would never see him again.

She went to the phone to call Brad Overstreet. Gripped by fear, she had to talk to someone.

5

The exclusive Cottonwood Lake Country Club was known to be a stuffy, old-money club. Its aging membership was studded with the presidents, CEO's and board chairmen of a prestigious list of blue-chip corporations. No wonder, then, that Vinnie Lawson felt out of place as he teed off that morning. The bad luck of the draw for the annual membership tournament had placed him in a foursome with three aging members who could probably each spend his annual salary over a casual weekend. Though Vinnie was a vice president at ConCom, he was strictly middle management.

He could play a hell of a game of golf, though. All those years in the California sunshine had honed his game to a two handicap, and that talent had swung the members of Cottonwood Lake to accepting an otherwise marginal application.

All his life he had been a good athlete. Now, Vinnie Lawson, six feet tall and sturdily built, was thirty-eight years old, and still a hell of an athlete. With a little luck, he might even win the tournament.

The promotion and transfer from California had not been a popular one with his family. All the money realized from an increase in salary had been eaten up by the high cost of living in New York City, with no visible improvement in their standard of living. Friends left behind and strange new schools had been bitter pills for his kids to swallow. Sometimes he wondered whether Caron and the kids would ever forgive him.

Whap! Vinnie connected solidly on a long par five that sent the ball screaming along the stream edging the sixth hole. It bounced several times, bounding to a point almost three hundred yards from the tee.

"Young man, I'd give up my condo on Maui if I could just hit a golf ball like that," one of the aging partners said with a sigh. His partners all drove well, but to points perhaps a hundred yards shy of where Vinnie's ball had stopped. Two of them had sliced a little to the right. The other had driven his ball perilously close to the stream at the left of the fairway.

"Hey, that's a beauty, sir. You've cut the corner perfectly and saved yourself some distance." Vinnie waxed enthusiastic over his elderly partner's drive. He suspected that at one time he had been a hell of a golfer. Jerome Wheeler was a retired board chairman of Great Eastern Bank. Though he must now be in his late seventies, he had obviously retained a good measure of physical stamina as well as a sharp mind and incisive wit.

Wheeler looked at him with a squinty grin. "What a nice thing to say about a drive that I almost dunked into the water."

Vinnie returned his grin as they started down the

fairway. "You'll notice that I cut it pretty close, too. This is a long course and I believe in economizing on distance whenever you can."

Another partner was getting ready to make his second shot. Vinnie looked about ninety yards beyond to where his own ball had landed. Just across the small river was a heavily wooded area. A panel truck was parked among the trees and a man dressed in black sweatclothes was setting up a small easel.

It struck him as a little unusual.

Jerome Wheeler's second shot hooked wickedly to the left and bounced a couple of times before coming to rest a few yards ahead of Vinnie's ball. It was perhaps two paces from the fast-moving stream.

"How's that for economizing on distance?" The old man grinned broadly at the nearly disastrous shot.

"Hey, you have a good lie. You can't tell me you didn't play it that way on purpose."

"Young man, you should work for the State Department. They could use your diplomatic talent." Vinnie climbed into the golf cart with his partner and bumped slowly along the bank of the stream toward their lies.

Once again he noticed the panel truck almost directly across the stream from where he would take his next shot. The easel was now set up, the artist partially obscured by a large canvas. Vinnie wondered why he had picked this particular spot. It was nice, but other vantage points were much more scenic. He waved casually toward the artist, but the other man was evidently too wrapped up in his own project to wave back.

Vinnie selected a three iron from his bag as he stepped from the cart. He moved to address the ball nestled in the short rough next to the fairway. He paused to take a couple of practice swings, following through to picture the journey of the shot. Jerome Wheeler stared at the talented golfer.

Now Vinnie was standing motionless, addressing the ball, with a short waggle of his three iron. He drew the club back, nearly reaching the highest intended point of his backswing.

At that tense, motionless moment, the heavy Mauser hunting rifle steadied by the supporting easel cannonaded a shot some fifty yards across the narrow stream.

Vinnie Lawson, struck squarely in the back of the head with the hollow-point .30-.30 slug, pitched forward and dropped like a heavy stone.

Jerome Wheeler, frozen for the moment by the horror he had just witnessed, turned to see the sniper running toward the van. The engine roared to life and within seconds the van had disappeared into the woods beyond the stream. Wheeler stared helplessly at the trees for a second, then raced to the side of his prone golfing companion.

He took one look, then quickly turned his head away. He struggled back to the cart and sat down heavily in shocked silence. The other two golfers in their cart sped toward him across the fairway. One quick look at Vinnie Lawson told them there was nothing they could do to help.

Jerome Wheeler, slumped in his cart, gasped heavily. He pointed feebly across the river. "Don't let him get away."

The two golfers looked across the river to where Wheeler was pointing. Nothing was there but an easel and a canvas.

Wheeler tried to rise to a sitting position. "They shot Vinnie," he muttered. Then he slumped again and closed his eyes forever.

6

It was six-fifteen in the morning when the red-eye from Los Angeles set down on the runway at Newark Airport. For Willy Hanson it was a kind of homecoming. He hadn't been back east for several years. Nor had he visited ConCom since he had resigned abruptly from the company to pursue what he had regarded as more meaningful interests. It had taken the funeral of one of his closest friends to make it happen.

Willy checked in at the Waldorf shortly after 7 A.M. There were two messages for him, both from Katie Glover. The publicist was one of the few people who were still around from the days when he headed ConCom. He decided he would crash for two or three hours before facing the day. If things were still the way they used to be at ConCom, they wouldn't really get going until after ten o'clock anyway.

He had barely hit the sack when the harsh ring of

the telephone jarred him awake. It was Katie Glover.

"Willy! you old rascal! Where have you been for two years? I hope you've been saving up for me. I need a good shot of vintage Willy Hanson." Katie's low, raspy voice was the same as ever.

"Katie, you haven't quit puffing on those cigarettes. I can tell. Do you know it's only eight o'clock? Has ConCom changed its hours?"

"Willy, we've had a tragedy." Katie hesitated.

"Yes, I certainly agree with that. How's Angela Clayfield taking it?"

"Oh my God! You know, so much has happened in the past few hours that I temporarily put Charles Clayfield out of my mind. Angela is doing just fine, I guess. Or she was until she got the latest news. I'll pick you up for the funeral and tell you all about it. Obviously you haven't seen the morning papers."

"What's the latest, Katie?"

"Vinnie Lawson—do you know Vinnie?"

"Of course, I hired him myself, out in California. I understand he was brought in as a sales manager some time back."

"Willy, he's dead. He was murdered on a golf course up in Westchester yesterday."

"Katie, that's horrible. Who did it?"

"No one knows. He was teeing off when someone shot him from across a small river. Honest to God! It was unbelievable. One of the foursome was the old banker Jerome Wheeler. He had a heart attack and died right there on the tee with Vinnie. The other two guys in the foursome said someone took the shot and then climbed in a van and drove into the woods on the other side of the river."

Willy was quiet for several seconds, trying to picture the scenario Katie had described. "Katie, who in the world would want to kill Vinnie Lawson?"

"I don't know. But it sure isn't deer season. He was shot squarely through the head."

"It's crazy. Vinnie must have had some problem that no one knew about. How's Caron doing?" Willy was amazed that he could recall her name. He hadn't seen them in years.

"Her sister lives nearby. She's looking after her. The doctor prescribed a sedative. She can't talk about it to anyone yet. Of course, she isn't going to Charles's funeral today. I thought I would pick you up about eleven o'clock, okay?"

"Why don't you come on down as soon as you can get ready and I'll pop for breakfast?"

"In your room, Willy, like the old days?"

"Katie! For God's sake! People are dying all over the place and you're looking for a roll in the hay. I'll meet you in the Grill downstairs in forty-five minutes."

"Just testing, Willy. I guess I heard right about you being a one-woman man these days. She must be something!"

"You got that right, kid."

"Okay for now, then. I ain't going to quit trying, though. See you in twenty minutes."

When Katie hung up, Willy sat down and put his feet up and stared at the gleaming spire of the Chrysler Building a few blocks away. Two people he knew were dead by violent means. It was obviously a coincidence, though it was something to stir an old horse player's blood. The husband of the CEO of his old company and the sales VP of the same company had met foul play within days of each other. What were the odds against that? Prodigious, he thought.

Actually three people were dead, but he reasoned that the old banker didn't count. He'd taken his bad ticker to the wrong place at the wrong time. Willy thought about Vinnie, a real straight shooter. A great flair for financial stuff coupled with a classic sales personality. Well, he reasoned, it was a great way to go. Not many people were lucky enough to buy the ranch while staring down a lush green fairway alongside a river, and getting ready to whack the daylights out of a golfball.

Willy forced himself to complete a quick shower and shave. He seriously felt the lack of rest. Sleeping soundly on the red-eye was a knack he had never mastered.

He found Katie Glover walking toward the coffeeshop when he emerged from the elevator.

"Hello there, you old fossil." Katie greeted him with a hug and a quick kiss and walked on with him to the coffeeshop.

"Katie! you look like a million bucks." And she really does, he thought.

She filled him in on the few details she was aware of. The suspected homicides were being investigated separately, one in New Jersey and one in New York. There was little real information available beyond the original news reports. So far no one had even suggested that the homicides might in any way be linked. Only one newspaper had pointed out the coincidence of the tragedies' being linked to the same business firm.

"So, Katie, it looks like I'll have to hang around for two funerals, though I hardly know Caron. I'm not the best person in the world to offer condolences. Everything always sounds so inadequate." Willy paused as he thought about Ginny back at the marina. "Actually we were planning to leave on a trans-Pacific sail in a day or so. Sort of a vacation, though I plan to do a book about the whole thing."

"Willy, you really deserve it after all you've been through." Katie had obviously followed the story of his tribulations in the newspapers.

"Katie, tell me about this Overstreet guy who Angela just made your new prez."

For the first time Willy saw Katie's eyes light up. Katie had always been a world-class gossip, and he could see she had something juicy.

"I reckon I'd better let you ask Angela Clayfield that question. I'm sure Angela can tell you all there is to know about him." Katie's roots were in Texas and she had never quite lost her Panhandle drawl.

"I will if I get the chance. Why don't you fill me in just a wee bit, like you're dyin' to do?"

"Willy, I can't help it, but I think it's just scandalous how she crawls all over the landscape with the likes of Bradford Overstreet."

"Sounds like you think she is an earthworm or a slinky snake instead of the gorgeous dish she appears to be."

"Spoken just like a man, Willy. Let some bimbo strut around with that double-jointed wiggle, and you men start sniffin' up to 'em like polecats in heat. Hell! I can walk like that, too."

"Please don't, Katie. It would be more than this old guy could bear."

"Angela sank her fangs into Overstreet the moment he walked through the door four years ago. That was back when she was just an account executive and everyone thought she was such a smarmy little prissy-face." Katie paused as if trying to recollect the early days of Angela at ConCom.

"Katie! You shock me. It sounds like the old green-eyed monster's got a hold of you."

"Hey, you know me better than that. People's business is their own business as long as they keep it to themselves. But right from the beginning, they went public. First there were the long lunches, then the 'working dinners.' Then whenever either of them took a trip, the other would tag along for 'logistic support,' whatever that is. By the way, what is logistic support, Willy?" Katie winked and picked up the breakfast menu. Willy had once asked her to come along for that very reason.

"We did have our day in the sun, didn't we? What about Charles Clayfield, the one lying in the coffin? What did he think about all this?"

"He was a mysterious guy. Nobody ever got to know much about him. You got to know him better than anyone else in the company before you flew the coop."

"I guess that's because we lived near them out in Saddle Hills. I liked him, Katie. We became friends, although our friendship was not based on anything that had to do with ConCom. He was a fascinating guy. He was probably CIA."

"You're probably right there, Willy. He and Angela had totally separate careers. A lot of people said he was a spy, or some sort of munitions expert. All I know is that he traveled a lot. And it's a damn good thing for Angela. I guess it helped her pull the wool over his eyes."

"That's an incredible story, Katie. You know I had dinner with Charles in California just last week. He couldn't say enough about Angela. She's some kind of a wheel in their church. Works wonders with children. They have two of their own who evidently are just exceptional. All this and a CEO at ConCom. It makes you wonder how she does it, if you have her pegged right."

"Look, me and you, Willy, we're old buddies, right? I wouldn't tell anyone else in the world what I just told you. But something is haywire. Two people have been murdered, and that poor man died of a heart attack. And I have a strange feeling in my gut. Maybe I'm just a little hysterical. But you did ask me to bring you up to date. So there you have it. I've

told you what I know and what I think." Katie
shrugged. "I'm going to have a Belgian waffle, with
strawberries and whipped cream."

"Just to show you I still have a few weaknesses,
I'm going to join you. We have a long trip out to New
Jersey. It may be ages before we eat again."

"Just one more thing, Willy. And then I'll shut up
about the Clayfields. If Angela is somehow finding
the time to hang around the church, long enough to
become a big wheel in its activities, someone ought
to tell the minister's wife to keep her eyes peeled."

"Okay, Katie. That's enough. I can see you don't
like our new widow. But you don't think the woman
had a hand in any of what's happened, do you?"

Katie stared into her coffee cup in deep thought
for several seconds before answering. "No, Willy, I
don't. I don't think she has a moral bone in her body,
but no way can I imagine her lining up her husband
for a murder."

The drive to the Clayfield funeral would take
about an hour. Brief services were to be held in a
small chapel not far from the burial site. Most of the
ConCom executive team would be there, as well as a
healthy sprinkling of executives from other publishing houses and related businesses. Willy hoped he
would be able to say a few words to Angela Clayfield. After all, he had spent an evening with her
husband less than a week ago.

Willy signed the breakfast check to his room, and
then he and Katie walked the several blocks to the
ConCom offices on Fifth Avenue, where they would
join others in sharing several limos to New Jersey.

As they approached the lead limo, Willy heard Katie's name called out in a clear baritone. The voice
was that of a tall man made striking by a trim phy-
sique, with a mustache and jet-black hair that had

streaks of premature gray running through his side-burns.

"Katie, you and Mr. Hanson will ride with us." He extended a hand toward Willy. "I'm Brad Overstreet. Katie told us she was picking you up."

Willy nodded as he took stock of the tall man who stood squarely in front of him.

"Mr. Overstreet is our new president." The usually glib Katie seemed uneasy.

Willy shook Overstreet's extended hand. "I've been out of touch, but not unconscious. I've kept track. I've been impressed by all I've heard about you."

Overstreet seemed to regard Willy warmly. "Mr. Hanson, you, of course, are a legend around ConCom. I hope you will drop by your old digs and pay a visit when all this unpleasant business is over."

"Well, funerals are not my specialty, but I do hope I'll be able to see Angela for a moment."

"I'm sure she wouldn't miss the opportunity to see you. She speaks of you often."

"I had dinner with Charles only a week ago in California. He thought so much of his family. What a tragedy this is." Willy stared at Overstreet, trying to assess him in the light of what Katie had told him at breakfast. At first glance he was inclined to feel that Katie had probably let her imagination run away with her when it came to the handsome new executive.

"Charles was the salt of the earth. Poor Angela is in for some adjustment, but Angela Clayfield is as strong as they come. She has asked a few of us to drop by her home after the cemetery. She specifically mentioned you."

"Thanks, I'll do that. Katie, you'll come too?"

Katie nodded, betraying a hint of a smile. She was not about to miss such an important scene in her perceived mystery.

Overstreet was eager to continue the conversation. "Mr. Hanson, did you happen to know Vinnie Lawson in your days at ComCon?"

"Yes, but please call me Willy."

Overstreet nodded.

"As a matter of fact I hired Vinnie. It's absolutely terrible news."

"Then Katie has brought you up to date." Overstreet glanced toward Katie. "Did you tell him about how it happened?"

"I surely did."

"She also furnished me with a morning paper which is full of interesting speculation. From all appearances, it wasn't an accident or even a random killing. It appears that someone sought him out very carefully. Is there any inkling of who the killer was?"

"As far as I know, Vinnie Lawson didn't have an enemy in the world. He's going to be a tough man to replace."

Willy decided to probe further. "How about Charles? Any progress in that case?"

Overstreet shook his head. "One theory is that it was suicide. But don't suggest that to Angela." He paused to reflect. "Charles was always tinkering around with explosives, though. He had the knowledge. It could have been suicide."

Willy made up his mind at that moment. He didn't like Overstreet at all.

7

Kai-Tak Airport can be a challenge for any pilot. When the wind blows in from the South China Sea, the 747's must come in low over dense apartment buildings and approach a short runway that ends abruptly at the edge of the water.

Though he had been awake for over forty-eight hours, Captain Max Von Braun guided the lumbering jet over the rooftops of Kowloon with a steady hand. The touchdown was gentle, perfect, with several hundred yards of the short runway unused. The 747 turned toward Kai-Tak terminal, which had served the Crown Colony of Hong Kong for many years.

"Nice landing, sir." The young copilot always marveled at the expertise of Von Braun, though the captain had worried him a little this trip. Usually talkative, he had hardly spoken during the entire flight from California. Copilot Tommy Wing thought he looked incredibly tired.

Captain Von Braun had two hobbies he enjoyed discussing with the crew. He loved to play chess, and he collected maps and charts. During layovers, he would seek out museums and antique-book stores searching for authentic charts from the past. He displayed some and stored others in the condo he owned on the small island of Cheung Chau, where he spent most of his Hong Kong layovers.

The muscular Von Braun could easily have been mistaken for an ex-football or rugby player. His compact body stood about five feet ten. His arms were muscular, his neck thick, and overall he looked menacing. A meticulously maintained crew cut made him look like just what he was, a no-nonsense kind of guy.

The moment now facing him would be far more tense than landing the 747 had been. He had no control over what might happen at Hong Kong customs. He looked straight ahead. He had been through this routine hundreds of times. He tried to select a clerk who had passed him through easily many times in the past.

This time he had an extra chart case. Usually he carried only one. The few charts spread atop the contents would hardly bear close scrutiny. In all his trips, never once had an agent actually opened the case. He had seen it happen with others, though, and felt his heartbeat quicken as the clerk he had selected laid his hand lightly on the chart case.

"Good evening, Captain. Nice flight?" The agent stamped Von Braun's papers, then once again dropped his hand to the oversize briefcase, tapping it thoughtfully as if trying to guess its contents.

One of Von Braun's golden rules was always to have a backup plan ready in case something went wrong. This time, however, he had concocted nothing.

"The typhoon in the Philippines, will it come here, Captain?"

Von Braun shrugged. Everyone seemed to regard flight captains as weather experts. The agent's fingers continued to tap lightly on the briefcase.

"I think not. The storm appears to be tracking well north of here. Let's hope it continues that way."

"I hope so, sir. Enjoy your trip to Hong Kong." With that the clerk removed his hand from the case and motioned for the next person in line to step forward.

Affecting great nonchalance, Von Braun grasped his bags and sauntered toward the exit, even pausing to light up a cigarette, setting the heavy chart case at his feet while he did so. Then he strode through the door to seek a taxi. He told the crew he had commitments for the evening and would be unable to join them in the limo provided for their use.

The Mercedes taxi drove off swiftly into the gathering dusk. The captain stretched out his legs and contemplated the night ahead of him. Traffic was heavy as they neared the heart of Kowloon. The familiar smells of his chosen country began to make him feel at home. The narrow street was now filled with a stream of taxicabs, most of them Mercedes. He had always been puzzled about that. How could it be cost-effective? It was certainly a contrast to the ramshackle taxis back in the major cities of the United States.

Finally he wound up at the end of Nathan Road, paid his fare, and entered the prestigious old Peninsula Hotel to register. The Peninsula was a symbol of stability in his life. It had long offered luxurious shelter to the kings, queens, presidents, generals and statesmen who had carved out the future of the Orient. Now Von Braun liked to depend on it as they did.

It was reasonable to assume, however, that the old hotel had never before sheltered a scene like that which quickly developed in Von Braun's room. He set the heavy chart case on the large leather ottoman in front of the club chair; then he leaned back for a moment, relaxing as he scrutinized the worn piece of luggage. The trip through customs had been nerve-wracking.

He leaned forward to loosen two leather straps and lift the front flap of the chart case. He reached in to remove several charts that were folded across the top. He pulled out a *San Francisco Examiner*, now two days old, then removed the packets of money, one at a time.

The blocks of money built a pyramid seven levels high. Each carefully banded packet contained 500 hundred-dollar bills, twenty packets for a total of $1 million, all in U.S. currency. Von Braun slammed his broad fist down on the ottoman and began to laugh aloud. He glanced toward the door to make certain the deadbolt had been fastened. Then he loosened his shirt, pulled off his shoes, put his feet up on the ottoman and dropped off into a deep sleep.

8

The funeral was indeed brief, lasting no longer than fifteen minutes. It had been so at the insistence of Angela Clayfield. The minister read several pieces of scripture that he felt might be comforting to the family. Penny and Chucky sat to Angela's left, reaching for her hands frequently. To Angela's right sat an aging woman who was identified by Katie Glover as Angela's mother. Next to her mother sat Bradford Overstreet. The minister ended the service by proclaiming that the miracle of Charles's life had been passed on through his two beautiful children. Tears welled in the eyes of Angela Clayfield. Willy decided that if Angela wasn't truly griefstricken, she was a world-class actress.

Most of the people attending the funeral remained for the burial. Angela led the group up the slight rise to the gravesite. She was dressed in black from shoulders to ankles, her dress molding sleekly to her form, perhaps too sleekly for the somber occasion.

Katie nudged Willy and whispered, "She hasn't got a stitch on under that thing. Some of those old geezers over there are actually smiling."

"Maybe she's trying to cheer everyone up, Katie." Willy caught himself smiling as he noticed the supple, fluid action beneath the tight gown.

The austere gray steel coffin had remained closed during the service. What remained of Charles Clayfield had to be a grisly sight. Now it was in place over the gravesite. As the crowd hushed, the minister read briefly from scripture, ending with the Twenty-third Psalm. Willy felt compassion for the children and thanked God it would soon be over.

He scanned the crowd of a hundred or so people. Many of the faces he recognized from the old days. Some he knew but couldn't attach a name to. Then he noticed something that aroused his curiosity.

One man, rather tall and slim, was moving slowly along the fringe of the gathering. Every few feet he stopped, put his hands into his trouser pockets for a moment or two and then moved along several more feet. He continued in this way until he reached a point about ten feet away from Willy. Then Willy could see more clearly. When the man stuck his hands in his pocket, his unbuttoned jacket opened several inches, revealing the lens of a small camera. The man was taking pictures. In a quiet and unobtrusive manner he had managed to circle most of the gathering and apparently photograph everyone.

Willy studied the man as closely as he could without looking directly at him. He wore steel-rimmed glasses with circular lenses. His eyebrows were dark and heavy. A small slit of a mouth was in keeping with the plainness of his elongated face. His dark, uneven hair was slicked down to collar length. Willy decided he had never seen him before.

There was a slight stirring among the crowd and

Willy turned his attention back toward Angela
Clayfield. She had stepped forward to touch the coffin. Bowing her head, she moved her lips in some
unheard prayer. Then she turned abruptly away
from the casket and, dabbing at her eyes with a
handkerchief, strode back to the children. Without
another look back, she led them down the slope to
the waiting limo.

Willy, Katie and Overstreet followed and climbed
into the next limo, which followed the first back to
Angela's home in Saddle Hills.

When they arrived, Willy noticed the black spot on
the driveway. Nearby was an area of blackened
grass and a tall cottonwood that stood shriveled and
dying. Several dozen people, either family or top executives of ConCom, were led past the bleak reminder into the house, where they were offered
refreshments.

The children were put in the charge of a housekeeper, and Angela Clayfield joined the group almost
immediately. Willy thought she looked marvelous
considering the ordeal she had just been through.

Angela grasped Brad Overstreet's arm and led
him directly to where Willy stood, swirling three fingers neat of scotch in a tumbler.

"You two have met. I'm so glad." Overstreet nodded as Angela grasped Willy's hand. "We have the
legendary past and the promising future of ConCom
here together. Mr. Hanson, I want to thank you so
much for coming. I know you shared a good friendship with Charles."

Willy grasped her hand firmly. "I am sorry about
Charles, Angela. I will miss a very good friend. You
know, I had dinner with him only last week in California. All of this is hard to believe."

Angela looked stunned. "Oh, I had no idea he had
seen you only last week." She stared as if in a trance

through the window where the charred cottonwood
was clearly visible.

"Angela, are you okay?" It was Overstreet, jarring
her from her preoccupation with the tree. "Really,
you should keep those drapes closed until the land-
scapers have tended to all that."

"No, no, Brad, it's quite all right. Everything will
be all right." She turned toward Willy. "I'm so glad to
hear that you shared an evening with Charles. I con-
fess he didn't tell me about it, but I'm sure he would
have gotten around to it." She paused. "I do have one
favor to ask of you."

"I had planned to go back to California tomorrow,
but I'd be happy to help you in any way I can."

"I suppose you've heard all about Vinnie Lawson."

"Yes, Katie here and the morning papers have
brought me up to date."

Angela moved closer to Willy and took his hand in
both of her own. She stared at him as if searching
for the right words. The full blond mane and violet
eyes were dazzling. There was definitely a warm
aura about her. He pushed the word "sexy" out of his
mind. After all, it was the day of Charles's funeral.

"I've spoken to Caron Lawson. She wants Vinnie
buried in California. All of Vinnie's and her friends
and family are out there." Angela paused. "They
have a family plot there."

"What can I do?"

"I wonder if you could represent me and ConCom
at the funeral out there. Look in on Caron and let
me or Brad know if there is anything at all we can
do."

"Angela, I'd be happy to. I'm glad I can help." He
felt very good about Angela's request. It would put
him back on the same side of the continent as Ginny.
Now he could pitch in on the final preparations of
the *Tashtego*.

"Oh, one other thing, Mr. Hanson."

He fidgeted as Angela stared at him.

"I want to compliment and congratulate you on your best-seller. Who would have guessed that you would leave ConCom to uncover and bring down a major international drug baron?"

"You never can tell what's waiting around the next corner."

"Someday, when all this quiets down, I would like to talk to you about another project."

Willy nodded and smiled. "I'd be happy to." As he spoke, though, he wondered how a grieving widow could so easily switch gears and talk business at a funeral reception.

He watched Angela turn and undulate across the room to rejoin Brad Overstreet. Katie Glover had stood silently, listening in on the exchange. "Willy Hanson, you're getting out of town just in time. I think that wiggle of hers was just for you. It was her way of saying, 'Don't forget me, baby, cause I'm hot stuff.' "

"Katie, like the old song says, I think you've played around this old town too long. The woman is griefstricken. She's just handling it well."

"Oh Willy, do I have to teach you the facts of life all over again?"

"Please don't, my ticker couldn't stand it. Besides, Ginny just wouldn't like it at all."

9

Brook Laird was a talented young editor at ConCom who had distinguished himself through his work on the Willy Hanson best-seller. That success had landed Laird several other authors who were considered rising stars at ConCom. The editor had put his heart and soul into his job, particularly impressing Brad Overstreet. Even Angela Clayfield had taken him to dinner one evening to express her delight with his work. He hadn't been prepared for her extreme cordiality, or her lavish praise.

In fact, that night the young editor had become engulfed in the warmth of Angela Clayfield. All through the evening she had talked softly about different projects she had in mind for him, gazing at him intensely with those great violet eyes. Try as he did, he could not help repeatedly touching her leg with his own under the small corner table. Once he even excused himself for doing so, but his "pardon me" went unacknowledged. Several times when her conversation became more animated, her leg moved firmly against his own.

Before the evening was over he was aware of two things. One was that Angela Clayfield was not only beautiful, but also very intelligent. The other was that he was in love with her.

Of course he realized this must remain a private fantasy that he would treasure only within his mind. After all, she was a married woman with children. And though her husband was never seen around ConCom, Brad Overstreet certainly was. The rumors that circulated about Overstreet and Angela made any dim hope of his own an impossibility. Anyway, he didn't really want an affair. It just made him feel good to think about it. There was certainly no harm in that.

At the end of that evening they had hailed a cab. She had dropped him off at his place first. She had looked at him intensely, hugged him and given him a kiss right on the mouth. It was a quick kiss, probably meaningless, but he would treasure it nonetheless.

The very next morning Angela Clayfield walked into Laird's office shortly after he arrived at work. It was the first time she had ever done that. Morning coffee was usually reserved for her appointed president, Brad Overstreet.

"You know, Brook, I've been thinking about some of the things we talked about last evening and have come to a decision I would like you to consider."

Laird, more than a little taken aback, fished for words. "Fire away, Mrs. Clayfield."

"ConCom needs a new editor-in-chief, Brook. We need one badly. I want you in that position. All those ideas you talked about last evening, I want them in writing, so Brad Overstreet can review them."

Angela Clayfield had a way of sitting immodestly,

often with the spread stance of a male, or with one foot up on a chair. No matter how long her skirt, it always worked its way up to a level that exposed enough leg to distract any normal male she spoke to. Today she had actually put both legs up on Laird's desk.

He was listening to her and watching her. Suddenly he realized she was waiting for his reply.

"Of course, Angela." He hesitated for a second. Despite having had dinner with her the night before, this was the first time he had called her Angela. If she noticed it at all, she didn't let on. "I rambled a great deal, and you deserve all that in writing. I would like to flesh it all out. I'll try to have it for you this evening."

Angela betrayed a hint of a smile. "Brook! I have a great idea. Next week, we'll pick a day and spend it together on the *Lazy Dolphin*. We'll work together on the report so that all the thinking meshes together. You can present a thoroughly impressive report to Brad Overstreet before the end of next week."

The *Lazy Dolphin* was a fifty-foot Hatteras yacht that she and Charles kept in a marina near Rye, New York. The idea of going up there to work on a plan with the CEO for him to present to the president of ConCom confused him a little.

"Will Mr. Overstreet be there?" He realized his question sounded stupid and was sorry he had asked.

"Of course not, Brook. I think Brad would appreciate our putting our heads together. When you get to know me better you'll realize that I don't always do things by the book. I believe in keeping the pipeline open to all my managers. This frees up Brad to be task-oriented. Perhaps you feel that Brad wouldn't like you going over his head to work with me. Don't worry about that, darling. I will keep Brad up to date."

The word Laird heard most clearly, of all those Angela had spoken, was "darling."

"I'd love to do that, Angela. And by the way, I thank you for the promotion. I see some great years ahead for ConCom."

"Brook, you didn't ask about your raise."

"I guess I didn't."

Angela hesitated. "I suppose I should touch base with Brad on that. But I promise you I'll have it all squared away when we get to the *Lazy Dolphin*. I betcha we can find a nip of something up there to celebrate with."

She kicked her legs up and off Laird's desk, much to his delight, and stood to leave his office. "You are going to be fun to work with, Brook. We won't be able to spend a lot of time together, but it will be quality time. There's an old saying, Brook, something about working hard and playing hard. How do you feel about that, Brook?"

Once again he looked up into the intensity of her violet eyes. "It . . . uh . . . sounds good to me."

"It will be, darling, it will be." With that, she spun around and left his office.

Laird recalled that conversation as he sat through Charles Clayfield's brief funeral, staring ahead at the long blond mane of Angela Clayfield sitting several rows in front of him between her mother and Brad Overstreet. This was to have been their day on the *Lazy Dolphin*.

He was not one of those who were invited to Saddle Hills after the burial, so he took one of the limousines back to Manhattan. He decided to get out of the car on Twenty-third Street and walk to his apartment down on Ninth in the Village. It was a beautiful day in New York, a great day to walk and think. He again thought about Angela Clayfield. Then his thoughts turned to Vinnie Lawson. Too much had happened. Things at ConCom would probably take quite a while to get back to normal.

On Ninth Street, he opened the iron gate that closed off a small paving-stone patio in front of his door. As he stuck the key in the lock he noticed a folded brochure that had blown under the ironwork.

He picked it up and opened it to find a decorative map of Greenwich Village. A heavy pencil line started at Fourteenth Street, clearly marked in pencil as a subway stop. He followed the line, which led to Ninth Street, the spot where he was now standing. Printed clearly in tiny letters was his name, Laird.

He peered at the map carefully. It was an expensive-looking brochure, probably bought from one of the giftshops or bookstores in the Village.

He shook his head. Try as he would, he could think of no one who would need such a map to find him.

Once inside, he scanned the map again. Along the margin at the bottom was a row of what appeared to be handwritten Chinese characters. He tossed the map onto his kitchen table and decided to take it into the office the next morning to be translated. Perhaps it would reveal something about the owner of the map.

Brook Laird was thirty-four years of age, tall but slight of stature. Unruly black hair invariably fell down over his forehead. Bookish, erudite, introverted; all of those words generally fit his personality. However, when Laird was drawn out on a subject he really knew and passionately cared about, he could dominate a room full of people.

No one knew Laird better than Lily Langley. Lily was presently at Tulane working on a medical degree, and though there was no formal engagement it was understood that as soon as Lily completed her internship, they would be married and live happily ever after. For a man and a woman they were as much alike as two people could be. From the moment they had met there had been no doubt for either of them that they were made for each other.

They normally spent holidays and a rare weekend together. Lily would fly home from New Orleans, or he would fly down to meet her at Tulane for a couple of days. They handled the sexual tension well, intellectualizing that what they went without now would come back for them with double passion in the future. Never, despite long absences, did their trust in each other wane.

Now Laird couldn't get Angela off his mind. When he thought of Lily, visions of Angela always intruded. Those great, long, superbly curved thighs, the enigmatic smile, and the magnetic violet eyes pushed Lily Langley right out of his mind. The new infatuation just would not stop.

He went to Luigi's in the Village that night and had a pizza at the bar. Every woman he saw, he compared with Angela. He had suffered infatuations before, but none as provocatively disturbing as this one.

When he reentered his apartment, he paused for a moment to study the map he had thrown on the kitchen table. The cryptic Chinese characters piqued his interest. He held it up to the light. It seemed to be printed on a kind of parchment.

He entered the small room that served as his den and noticed the red light blinking on his answering machine. Figuring it was probably Lily, he flipped the playback switch.

"Hello, darling, this is Angela. I saw you today at Charles's funeral. Thanks so much for coming. Seeing real friends at such a time made the day so much easier. Today was to be our day on the *Lazy Dolphin*, wasn't it? We'll make it this coming Monday instead. I've discussed it with Brad and he thinks it's a great idea. See you then, darling. Come early and you can sample one of my omelets! There will be just you and me and all of our ideas. Thanks again, Brook, for coming. Bye now!"

He couldn't believe his ears. On the day of her husband's funeral, she had remembered their plans and had bothered to call. He felt intensely excited and played the short message again and again, increasingly convinced that it was purposely provocative.

He undressed, turned back the sheet and slipped into bed, totally forgetting that this was his regular night to call Lily in New Orleans. He thought of Angela Clayfield sitting in his office a few days ago. Memories of their dinner with legs touching under the table haunted him.

10

Vinnie Lawson's body was not released by the coroner for several days. His death had been ruled a homicide, so an autopsy report had been completed. Meanwhile Caron Lawson and their four-year-old twin sons had returned to California to the home of her parents.

Willy Hanson arrived in California to keep his commitment to Angela Clayfield. He would look in on Caron and represent ConCom at the funeral to be held near Riverside on Thursday. The remains of Vinnie Lawson were due to arrive the day before and would be met at Orange County Airport by Caron and her father. Willy had called and offered to join them, and Caron had seemed grateful for the offer.

As the casket was transported to the hearse from the plane, Caron Lawson was teary and red-eyed. Willy thought she looked terrible. She was a slight woman anyway, and the ordeal had taken its toll. She appeared nervous and frail and had difficulty

putting words together without breaking into tears.
Once she looked at Willy as they drove toward Riverside and asked, "Mr. Hanson, why . . . ?" and was
unable to say anything further.

The brief services were held the next morning at
the Canyon Hill Cemetery just west of Riverside.
Ginny offered to tag along and Willy was glad she
did. He could find little to say to any of the family
that offered any solace.

There were only about thirty-five people at the
service. As their minister offered his words of comfort, Willy looked across the casket and down the
gentle green swale beyond the gravesite. One man
persisted in moving ever so slowly to the rear of the
small cluster of people. Ultimately he reached a
point to one side and a little ahead of the group. He
jammed his hands into his pockets and forced his
jacket open just slightly.

Willy found himself staring into a small lens of a
tiny camera suspended from the man's neck. His
memory jolted back to the cemetery near Saddle
Hills, almost a week ago and three thousand miles
away. It was the same man with the same little camera. As the man turned and walked down the slope
toward the parked cars, Willy noted the black,
plastered-down hair that was jagged at the collar.

Willy quietly stepped away from the group. He
walked as smoothly as he could toward the parked
cars. A small black Mazda backed away from the
curb. ZAC-94711. He said the number to himself
over and over again until he was sure he would
never forget it. The Mazda moved slowly down toward the cemetery gates as Willy took a handkerchief from his pocket and coughed gently, then
worked his way back up to Ginny's side. He kept the
handkerchief at his mouth, creating the impression

that his movement had been made to suppress a cough.

The brief service over, Willy and Ginny walked slowly with the saddened group back to the parked vehicles.

"I'm really sorry, Caron. Earlier you asked why. I really don't know why. If you need anything at all, please call Katie Glover at ConCom. We'll be staying at the Marina at Dana Point for a few more days. I'll be in touch before we leave." He handed a card with the boat information on it to Caron's father, who nodded slightly, then put his arm around his daughter and led her to the waiting limousine.

"Gee, Willy, I hope she doesn't come all apart. She looked like a basket case." Ginny took his hand as they watched the limousine pull away.

"I couldn't think of anything to say that could possibly comfort her. No one in the whole group seemed able to find words."

"By the way, Willy, what's with the little stroll down the hill?"

"I wish I knew myself. It could be something or nothing. Did you notice the tall guy with plastered-down black hair and the lousy haircut? He left right in the middle of the service."

"I saw him drive away. Who was he?"

"He was ZAC-94711. That's the plate number on the Mazda. But the strange thing is, I saw that same guy last week back in New Jersey taking pictures at Charles Clayfield's funeral."

"You're kidding! I didn't notice a camera this time, though."

"It was there. Small and silent. He wears it on a thin line around his collar. He opens his jacket just slightly when he wants to take a picture."

"But of who, and for what?"

"He could be from law enforcement, I guess. Or

maybe it's ConCom that ordered a photographer. But why the same guy?"

"Willy, was there anyone at both funerals other than you? We could ask them if they saw him."

"No, not that I'm aware of. This fellow showing up in both places just doesn't make sense. He left the services early back in Jersey, too."

"It's over now, Willy. Why not give ourselves a break and forget about this one?"

"Because I think Charles Clayfield and Vinnie Lawson were both murdered. And I betcha Blackhead with the camera knows something about it. It just can't be dumb luck that the same person with a camera shows up to take pictures at funerals three thousand miles apart."

"Are you going to tell the police what you think?"

"I've got to at least give them the plate number. There has to be an explanation."

Ginny smiled her warmest smile. "Willy, when are we leaving on our trans-Pacific? The *Tashtego* is almost fully stocked."

"Soon, baby, soon."

"How about Wednesday? I don't see how we can help by hanging around. We'll check in from Hawaii or Samoa." She put her arms around him. "Do you think you'll be able to stand being all alone with me for a couple of months? We might drive each other crazy." She tilted her head and locked him in a long kiss.

"You know that's kind of what I had in mind. Maybe we better get out of the cemetery. We just might wake the dead."

For the moment at least, the anticipation of finally putting out on the *Tashtego* wiped the recent tragedies from their minds as they drove back to the marina. They decided to spend the upcoming weekend on a couple of short day sails to make sure the rigging was perfectly tuned for the crossing.

Ginny was carefully inventorying provisions. Every spare nook and cranny of the vessel was stowed with goods they would want to be able to put their hands on at a moment's notice.

That evening, Willy sat with his feet up on the transom, looking out at the orange ball of sun already half consumed by the ocean. For a moment his thoughts returned to the two funerals. The stark similarity of the two steel-gray coffins preyed on his mind. The frail, pathetic figure of Caron Lawson at Vinnie's funeral weighed heavily on him.

Willy relished the voyage ahead, but found it hard to escape the feeling that they were leaving unfinished business behind.

11

Captain Max Von Braun had decided not to go to his condo on Cheung Chau, since he had to pilot a return flight to San Francisco in just forty-eight hours. He hailed a cab at the stand in front of the Peninsula Hotel and gave the driver the address of the Paragon Club, deep in the heart of the once sleazy Wanchai district. Though Wanchai little resembled the hell pit of World War II days, it was still a place where just about any vice could be entertained. Von Braun had slept very nearly around the clock and was well rested for the strenuous night ahead. His Hong Kong tailor had furnished him with expensive copies of the best in Italian silk suits, one of which he wore now. There was nothing in his civilian clothes to connect him with Trans-Asiatic Airlines.

The Wanchai district was packed. Traffic inched along the narrow street that led to the Paragon Club. Blazing neon sang the praises of the delectable delights offered by the most exotic of all the sophisticated ladies in the entire Crown Colony.

The cabdriver dropped Von Braun at the alleyway straddled by a red neon sign that kept rewriting "Paragon Club" in continuous script over the alley. Von Braun strode down the alley about fifty paces before entering a doorway and ascending a flight of stairs.

A ticket vendor stood guard in a small foyer at the top of the stairs. After exchanging a few words with the vendor, Von Braun waited for a full minute before a door opened and a hostess in a snugly fitted evening gown appeared.

"Captain, you are here at last. Welcome!" The deafening beat of heavy metal surged out the doorway of the club, making the words of the hostess barely audible.

"I know I am a little late. I overslept."

"Pity, pity, but no real harm done. Your ladies await you." She moved close to Von Braun, the low-cut gown spilling a portion of her nipples into full view. "A gentleman did join your threesome a few minutes ago." The hostess held the captain close and whispered to make certain she was out of earshot of the other guests entering the foyer. "The girls were becoming anxious. Actually, he is a very nice man, no doubt compatible with you and the girls, if you know what I mean."

"Get rid of him!" Von Braun scowled menacingly at the hostess.

"Very well, Captain. No need to be excited. Sometimes our guests like to try a little something new. I will have no trouble finding the man other company."

"Melanie, Wanchai is a sewer. If I am going to crawl around in it, I will pick my own company. Always!"

"Of course, Captain. I have a message for you from Emerald Lu. She is leaving Cheung Chau on the late ferry, and will see you here about midnight."

"As soon as she gets here, show her to wherever I am."

"What if, Captain . . ." The hostess smiled faintly, running her tongue lasciviously along her lips. "What if you are erotically occupied at that moment?"

"She won't mind. Just show her the way to me. She just might want to join the party, you know." Von Braun peeled off several crisp hundred-dollar bills, U.S. currency, and stuffed them crudely into her cleavage.

"Not likely, Herr Captain! But we can try, can't we?"

Von Braun was shown to a dimly lit table in one of the darkened alcoves of the Paragon Club. He was quickly joined by two sleek and beautiful Chinese women and a tall statuesque blonde, the real attraction who had brought him to the Paragon club.

"Brigitte!" He put his hand on the shoulder of the blonde. "I haven't seen you in weeks. I have been back and forth to San Francisco a dozen times. All without seeing you."

"You have been here. You didn't call ahead. You should always call ahead to Melanie and tell her to be in touch with me."

"Where has my beautiful Brigitte been?"

"I've been in Brunei."

"The palace in Brunei, I'll bet."

"Max, you know better than to ask questions about my work. Do I ask you how to fly a plane?" Her hand softly caressed the back of his neck as she brushed his face with light kisses. Her free hand dropped to his thigh and began a casual exploration. The two other women giggled quietly at the aggressiveness of Brigitte, and pressed close to Von Braun, surrounding him with soft jasmine-scented attentiveness.

Busy hands and lips soon forgot about all else. The group began to draw the attention of other patrons.

"Excuse me, Captain Von Braun," Melanie said, interrupting them. "Perhaps it is time for the girls to show you our special game room. Pinball, sauna, billiards, all sorts of special lunacy goes on upstairs. The girls will show you the way."

The captain balked at first, but soon succumbed and followed Brigitte and the others. Melanie whispered to him, "Blue Shark Club is Emerald Lu's idea. She designed all of it after seeing the Acid Portfolio Club on Sixth Avenue in New York. Blue Shark is just like that, a copy. Everyone in Hong Kong wants to go to the Blue Shark, but no one knows how to get there. *Voilà!*"

At the end of a narrow hallway, she pressed a button that opened a panel door. The room inside was dimly lit. As their eyes adjusted, they made their way to a large circular bar and ordered drinks.

Von Braun scanned the large room. A maze of sofas and black leather booths surrounded a dance floor crowded with couples that groped as much as danced.

G-string–clad cocktail waitresses carried drinks through the maze of writhing bodies that found comfort on the sofas as well as the thick rugs on the floor. As Brigitte began to loosen his clothing, Von Braun started to chuckle and then broke into a heavy laugh.

Melanie had not yet left them. "What is so funny, Herr Captain?"

"I was just thinking, Melanie, about the old days." One of the sleek young women was now before him, loosening his shoes. "In the old days, the decadence of the Orient was imported to America. Now Hong Kong imports a pit like this from Sixth Avenue. Emerald Lu did a bang-up job of copying the Acid Portfolio. I'll have to tell her so if my ticker is still pumping after an evening with these young ladies."

"I told you you would like it here. Emerald really did fly to New York to copy this, you know."

"I do know, Melanie. I do know, because I flew her there. Now leave us alone. I think the time has come to do something besides talk, talk, talk ... Ah ... yes!"

12

Brook Laird had worked well into the night on Sunday, outlining his acquisition program in as much detail as possible. His computer, linked with the data supply in the ConCom office, had provided him with much of the information he would need for a convincing presentation to Angela Clayfield aboard the *Lazy Dolphin*. He tossed his finished report into an old leather briefcase, jammed in a couple of manuscripts, and left the Village at 6 A.M. He would take Angela at her word and arrive early. He should take advantage of every minute. He wasn't sure how much time he would have with the vivacious CEO once he became immersed in his new job.

As he drove north on the Saw Mill River Parkway into Westchester, he thought aloud, reviewing some things that were key to his publishing program. All at once his thoughts were interrupted by a vision of Angela. Her great violet eyes were looking right through him as he rattled on about books. In his

imagination he leaned over to kiss her and she ac-
cepted him hungrily. He tried to further explain his
program, but her response to him made that impossible.

There was a piercing screech of brakes as a car
trying to pass him on the narrow parkway swerved
off onto the shoulder. He whipped the wheel to the
right and came perilously close to rolling over. The
other driver regained control and passed, shaking
his finger as if scolding him. Laird cursed aloud at
his own carelessness, realizing that he had drifted
into the passing lane as he had indulged his sexual
fantasy.

Nevertheless, he continued thinking about Angela
as he drove on. She was smiling, something she did
rarely, and chuckling softly at his distress. But then
the mental image of Lily invaded.

Oh my God, I didn't call her the entire weekend.
He thought of pulling over to a public phone at the
first opportunity, but what could he say to her at six
o'clock on Monday morning that would make any
sense? Then he realized that he hadn't thought
about her all weekend.

He reasoned that he was overtired. Everything
would surely be all right when he got to the *Lazy
Dolphin* and he and Angela began seriously digging
into business. He forced himself to rethink the details of the report he had prepared. There were several points he had not developed completely, he
thought. He began to have doubts. Maybe the whole
thing was grossly incomplete. Maybe none of it
would make sense to Angela. Now, suddenly, he
could only envision her arching her back in peals of
laughter aimed at him.

The *Lazy Dolphin* lay motionless in her slip near
Rye, the water's surface a mirror with perfect reflec-
tion. The morning haze had not yet burned away.

The sleek Hatteras showed no signs of life. Laird began to wonder whether he had come on the right day or whether Angela had been joking. He glanced around the marina. There wasn't a hint of activity anywhere.

"Brook! Over here." He turned to see Angela just entering the dock behind him. "Good boy, Brook. Just in time. The ice maker jammed somehow. I figured I better pick up a couple of bags."

Laird set his heavy briefcase down on the dock and went to help her with the ice. Angela Clayfield was in the smallest string bikini he had ever seen. He took the ice from her and she went on ahead of him. Her figure was perfect, he realized. He wanted more than anything to put his hands on the curve of her hips and go from there.

As she climbed aboard the *Lazy Dolphin*, she turned to smile at him. She looked like no CEO in the world with those violet eyes and that disheveled blond mane.

"Mrs. Clayfield, you are beautiful." He heard himself saying the words, but he couldn't believe he had done it.

"Why, thanks, Brook. As you get a little older, the upkeep takes a little more time. But I'm glad you said that. It was such a nice compliment. By the way, I'm not Mrs. Clayfield. I am Angela. Okay?"

"I gotcha." He could see Angela eyeing the heavy briefcase.

"Wow! You came prepared. I like that! Maybe we'll get to it later. I'm sure we will. But I thought most of today we could just relax and get to know each other. We can just talk, and find out what's going on in each other's minds. Is that okay?"

"Sure, anything you say. I just pulled some stuff off the computer in case I needed some backup." Besides, he thought, he couldn't possibly tell her what was on his mind just then. Angela continued her delightful habit of sitting immodestly, even in the string bikini.

"Brook, did you bring shorts or a swimming suit? You're going to get awfully warm when the sun gets high."

"No, I didn't. I'll remember next time."

"You'll find some men's bathing suits hanging in a closet just off the shower. Change!"

Laird began to feel terribly warm and somewhat uneasy. He wasn't sure whether her order was titillating or disturbing.

"Sure. If you don't mind I'll do just that."

"What do you like in your omelets? You name it."

"How about some cheddar?"

"Sharp or mild?"

"The sharper the better."

"Good, I can make them both in the same pan. Then I want you to tell me all about your family, Brook." Angela stood in front of the small galley stove. She had put on a pair of very dark sunglasses and he couldn't tell whether she was looking at him or not.

He walked the narrow companionway and opened the small closet next to the shower. He selected a pair of swimming shorts from several hanging there and changed into them. The loose charcoal-gray trunks fit him perfectly. He walked back to where Angela was preparing to serve the omelets.

"My! You do keep yourself fit. I like that, Brook. You're a little pale, though." She pushed her bronzed leg next to his. We'll start doing something about that today."

"I jog, but that's usually early in the morning when there's no sun. I don't think I'll ever look like you."

Angela turned toward him and smiled. "Let's hope

not, Brook. Let's hope not." She extended her hand, which held a plate with a steaming cheddar omelet, complete with toast. "Here you are, sir."

They pulled stools up to a chart table. Angela flipped the dial on a small radio that was tuned to a station playing soft rock. Returning to the galley bar to pour the freshly brewed coffee, she undulated slightly to the beat of the music. Laird gaped at her. She hardly looked the part of a newly bereaved widow.

"Aha! You're staring at me! I caught you."

Then he remembered those damn dark glasses. She had been watching him the whole time.

"I'm sorry. I really am. But you're like no other CEO I've ever seen in New York."

"How many CEO's have you known, Brook?" She was sitting right next to him now, digging into her omelet. Her bronzed leg was touching his.

He smiled, trying to be as casual with the small talk as she was. "Well, actually, only two. There was Bill Harper before you, and a long time ago there was Willy Hanson, and I never saw either of them in a bikini."

Angela smiled along with him at his observation. "Well, Harper never aroused much interest in me, though sometimes I wish I had sampled some Willy Hanson."

"What!"

Angela, smiling broadly, turned to look directly at him. "Just a joke, darling, just a joke before we get down to brass tacks on that briefcase-load of reports you want to read to me."

She cleared the chart table of their dishes, then stooped to heft the heavy briefcase onto the table herself.

"First, Brook, we have some serious business to take care of. I must talk to you about your salary in-

crease. I have instructed Brad that the matter is to
be left completely in my hands, just between you and
me. Understood?"

"Certainly." There was her leg again, shoved right
up against his own. And now her hand was gripping
his thigh to emphasize each word. God, she was dis-
tracting!

"First of all, I want you to know that your increase
is richly deserved. The work you completed on the
Hanson book was just a beginning. Perhaps that
would have been a success no matter who worked
with it. But the other three best-sellers you had
since then were strictly the foresight and creation of
Brook Laird. Brook, you are a genius, and I need you
more than anyone else at ConCom."

"Angela, I think you're laying it on a little thick. I
had a lot of talented people working with me on
those projects."

"'And you should have those talented people
around you, and more of them. Brook, from now on,
you will maintain your own staff. Anything you want
to do, within reason." Angela was now pacing the
deck as she talked. The telephone started ringing,
but she continued pacing and talking without answering it. Finally it stopped and the muffled sound
of the recording machine could be heard aft in the
computer room.

Finally she paused to sit down on the chart table
in front of him. The string bikini and her immodest
posture made him too uncomfortable. Now it was
Laird who stood to pace the cabin while Angela
talked.

"I am going to double your salary, Brook. You
make sixty now. I am going to make it one hundred
twenty thousand. Do you like that, Brook?"

Laird didn't betray his shock. "I think that's wonderful. You'll get your money's worth."

"If it's so wonderful, then why are you pacing? Come back over here and sit down. I want to talk to you."

He walked back and sat down at the chart table. Angela reached out to run her fingers through the tangled forelock that had fallen over his eyebrows.

"Do you like me, Brook? I mean as a person, do you like me?"

"Angela, we hardly know each other. I don't know what to feel about you other than that you are the sexiest-looking person I have ever been alone with."

"Well! Now we're getting someplace! It took you a long time to get that off your chest, Brook."

Laird didn't know quite how to react to her aggressiveness. He reached uncertainly toward his briefcase and began to pull a file folder from it. Angela made a broad sweep of her arm and shoved the heavy case to the deck.

"Fuck the goddamn briefcase, Brook. First things first, darling. We'll get to that later. Now is the time to celebrate by taking care of what you have been staring at all morning long. Come with me!"

Angela took his hand, led him to the fore cabin and flung open the louvered door. A champagne bucket stood on a stand next to a queen-size bed that nearly filled the small cabin. It was covered with a satin sheet, with pillows at both ends of the bed. In an instant, Angela had dropped her bikini and scrambled forward to lie on the bed facing him. She pointed to the pillow at the foot of the bed. "That's your pillow down there, Brook; I suggest you put your head on it."

Laird moved slowly, more unsure of himself than ever before. He bent forward to slip off his sneakers while a nearby fax machine began to whirr. He sat

on the end of the bed and watched it spew out two
sheets of paper.

"Read them to me, Brook. For God's sake read
them to me and then go unplug the fax and the telephone."

Angela was now propped up on the satin pillow,
spread-eagled before him. He paused for a moment,
distracted by the unlikely scene. He started to read
the fax copy aloud and then fell silent as his eyes
raced ahead. He read the rest of the message in silence.

"Angela, it's terrible, just terrible."

"What's terrible?"

"An elevator fell fourteen floors in the ConCom
Building. Two people were killed and four others
badly injured. Here are the names." Laird leaned
forward to hand her the fax. The two people killed
were René St. Claire and Ryan Evans. Both worked
in the production department.

Angela closed her eyes. "This is absolutely unbelievable."

Laird bent over and picked up his sneakers.
Angela just kept staring into space. Then Laird
stood up and started to leave the cabin.

"Where in the hell are you going?"

"I guess we'd better get dressed and get back to
the city."

"Brook, that's crazy! There is absolutely nothing
we can do. We'll go back this evening."

Laird turned to face Angela, spread-eagled again
with her hands behind her head.

"Brook, come up here and put your head on me
and relax. You have to isolate the good from the bad.
It is a tragedy that we'll address our full energy to
later. Right now it's time for you to act like a man
who just got a sixty-thousand-dollar raise."

Laird fought himself. He hated himself for becoming aroused on the heels of such tragic news.

"Ah, darling, that's it, that's it. I knew you would get into the swing of things. Now don't hurry, we've got all day. You've been undressing me with your eyes all morning long, darling, and I like that attitude in my editor-in-chief so very much."

13

The next morning the scene at the ConCom Building was still hectic. Several police cars and pieces of firefighting equipment remained parked alongside the old art deco building. A police line barred entrance on one side of the lobby. Yellow tape blocked off a bank of four elevators on one side of the lobby.

Angela Clayfield arrived at about ten o'clock and was directed to a freight elevator that took her to the fourteenth floor.

Brad Overstreet, the building supervisor and the New York City police commissioner were waiting for her in the conference room. Timothy Doherty, the mayor of New York, arrived on the next elevator along with several members of the press. The mayor had asked that he be present when the investigators presented their report.

The police commissioner received a nod from the mayor and began to read.

"At approximately ten-thirty yesterday morning,

in the west elevator bank of the ConCom Building, there was an explosion either within or above elevator number four. Our explosive experts tell us that it was dynamite, perhaps a half to a whole stick. We suspect that the device was planted on top of the elevator cab's roof, or dropped into the shaft from above the cab. The elevator did not drop as earlier stated, but was heavily damaged and descended rapidly to the first floor.

"Because of the damage sustained, the door did not open. It took approximately eight minutes for firefighters to arrive on the scene and another minute to force entry into the cab. Five people were removed immediately. One died of injuries directly related to the explosion. One other suffered smoke inhalation and died on the way to the hospital. The other three persons were treated for smoke inhalation and have since been released from the hospital.

"Because of the ongoing intensive investigation, we are not prepared to take any questions at this time." The commissioner paused to clear his throat, then continued after skipping over several paragraphs in the report. "I can say that there are several important leads that are being followed up at this time. Obviously we cannot comment further for fear that the success of the investigation would be put in jeopardy. Also, during the investigation, the ConCom Building will be put on high-security alert. All persons entering and leaving the building must provide full identification. The cooperation of all employees is necessary. Many persons will be questioned in the process of the investigation. I know everyone will cooperate fully to help us find the fiend who did this. Thank you."

The police commissioner and the mayor came over to talk briefly to Angela Clayfield, who promised unqualified cooperation.

"Mrs. Clayfield, you have been through so much already," the commissioner said. "Were you anywhere near the explosion when it occurred?"

"No, Commissioner, I had pressing business out of the city yesterday, and was advised of it by fax. Last evening, Brad Overstreet came by my home to bring me up to date."

Overstreet stepped forward to join the conversation. "You know, Commissioner, this makes a total of four ConCom employees who have met with tragedy during the past two weeks."

The commissioner scratched his head and looked at Overstreet, "So far we have no indication that they are connected events. We will be exploring that angle, however. Mrs. Clayfield, I would appreciate it if you would talk to our investigative team later this morning."

"Of course, Commissioner, any time." Angela shook hands with the commissioner and the mayor.

Mayor Doherty looked deeply concerned as he left the room with the small pack of reporters at his heels. He had assured all that his office would not rest until the terrorists were brought to justice.

Angela Clayfield walked into her plush office, went to the window and stared out to watch a small freighter making its way up the East River a few blocks away. She was lost in thought about the string of disasters, and gripped by an unshakable fear. There was no question in her own mind that ConCom was under some sort of siege. She was convinced now that the bomb planted in the Mercedes had been meant for her. After all, Charles was supposed to have been out of town.

Her thoughts drifted to the long crumpled florist's box with the crushed rosebuds. She had thought about them a hundred times since Charles's death. She had been careless. The brief episode with Brad

Overstreet in the parking lot of the strip mall had been thoughtless and stupid. *Her* thoughtlessness and *her* stupidity—Overstreet had been unyielding until her persistent coaxing finally pushed him over the limit. She resolved to be more careful. There was just too much at stake for her peccadilloes to become public knowledge.

"Angela." She turned away from the window to find Brook Laird in the doorway. "Angela, I just wanted to tell you that yesterday was . . . was . . . incredibly exiting."

"Shut the door, Brook." Angela's voice had a sharp edge, much unlike yesterday's tone of provocative insistence. "Mr. Laird, I must warn you that if you can't keep your personal feelings to yourself around here, we can surely find someone else who can."

Laird was dumbstruck. "I . . . I . . . am sorry. I just thought . . ."

"Brook! For God's sake stop stammering. Be a man, Brook. I've just given you some advice. Now take it and get back to your office."

Reddening, he turned on his heel and walked toward the door.

"Brook!" It was Angela again. He fleetingly considered not paying any attention to her, but turned toward her again.

"Brook, Thursday is your day. Put it on your calendar, Brook. Block off Thursday for the next few weeks. Thursdays on the *Lazy Dolphin*. You'll just have to be happy with Thursday. Now get back to your office, Brook."

Only a little of the sharp edge had left her voice. Somewhere in her stern visage, he thought he saw the hint of a smile.

He walked back toward his office, feeling much like a scolded puppy. He glanced quickly around him, relieved to see that no one had heard their exchange. He entered his office and shut the door firmly behind him.

"I think I am absolutely sure now what the word 'bitch' really means," he said to himself. Then he broke into a broad smile. "Thursdays. Wow!"

14

The *Tashtego* performed magnificently. Willy and Ginny took her halfway to Catalina in a stiff fifteen-knot breeze, putting her through her paces. The big ketch had never been more finely tuned. On their return voyage all their conversation involved the reading they had done on places like Hawaii, Samoa, the Marianas, and Hong Kong. The days they had left in Dana Point were down to a very few, and the excitement they shared over the coming Pacific crossing on the *Tashtego* pushed everything else from their minds.

Both were reluctant to return to their slip, so they stretched the day out to take advantage of as much daylight as possible.

Ginny spotted the envelope first. Thumbtacked to the fire extinguisher box at the end of their dock was a white envelope marked PLEASE, URGENT, in large block letters. In smaller letters it was addressed to

William Hanson. After securing all lines, Ginny
handed the envelope to Willy.

He was gripped by a sharp, uneasy feeling. The
euphoria of the day at sea was completely swept
away. The events of the past few days had been most
unsettling and he couldn't shake the feeling that
there was still unfinished business ashore. If he
hadn't allowed them to be interrupted they would be
halfway to Hawaii by now.

Ginny stood silently as he read the contents.
"Well, what is it? Did we win the lottery?"

"No such luck. It's from Caron Lawson. Says she
would like to see us before we sail. Says she has
something to show me and asks that I call."

"That poor woman! She's got to feel so alone."

"I'll give her a buzz. Forget the galley, we'll have a
bite onshore. Maybe this will wait until morning."
Willy vaulted over the rail and headed for the public
phones at the head of the gangway to the floating
dock.

Just as he was about to pick up the phone, he
glanced at the windowed newspaper box next to
the telephone, and was startled by the headline in the
morning *Times*: CONCOM ELEVATOR PLUNGES 14 FLOORS.

He fished around for a couple of quarters, opened
the vending box and bought the paper. Forgetting
the phone for a moment, he scanned the story. Two
persons had been killed in the elevator's fall, which
had been caused by an explosive device in the elevator shaft. The article went on to point out that four
persons connected to the ConCom Publishing Company had been killed in the past ten days, including
the husband of ConCom CEO Angela Clayfield.

He tucked the paper under his arm and called
Caron Lawson. Perhaps this new tragedy at Con-
Com had sparked her urgent message.

"Hello, this is Caron."

"Hi, Caron, Willy Hanson here. Sorry it's so late. We've been out sailing and I just got your message. How've you been doing?"

"Very poorly, I think." The woman hesitated, searching for words. "Something has come up. Something I can't tell anyone in the world about, except perhaps you, Mr. Hanson. Please! I've got to talk to you tonight."

"Well, Ginny and I were just going out for a bite to eat. We'll come on up your way. We should be there in twenty or twenty-five minutes. Try and relax, Caron. You better refresh me on how to get there." Willy scribbled directions on the back of the envelope. "Caron, keep your chin up. We'll be there as soon as possible."

"Thanks, Willy." He thought he heard her quivering voice break just as he clicked down the receiver.

The drive took almost a half hour. Ginny read the article from the *Times* as they drove. "Perhaps this is what she wants to talk about. Maybe she knew one of the people who were killed. That woman must be devastated. Did you know either of the people, Willy?"

"I've racked my brain. I don't think so. So many people have left since I left. But I don't think this is what's on Caron's mind. Otherwise she would have come right out and said it. I think it is something personal, something about Vinnie. She said she couldn't tell anyone else in the world."

Caron was waiting in the driveway, idly spraying some flower beds with a hose, when they drove up.

"Hi, do you mind if we go somewhere else to talk?" Her voice quivered. "There is no need bringing my parents into this." She paused to pick up a manila envelope from a lawn chair, then climbed into the backseat.

"I'm sorry. You guys must be dead tired. I've done enough sailing to know it's hard work. I just have to talk to you. I'm afraid I'll go crazy if I don't talk to someone."

Willy turned into a Coco's Coffee Shop parking lot, then turned to eye the woman carefully. She was a nervous wreck and looked as if she hadn't eaten since Vinnie's funeral.

Finding a corner booth that offered privacy, they ordered coffee and asked for menus.

Caron slid the manila envelope across the table to Willy without saying a word. Ginny grasped her hand tightly just as she would have a small child's. "Caron, dear, please try to relax. We are your friends, just as Willy was Vinnie's friend."

Caron jerked her hand sharply away from Ginny's grasp. "That bastard. To think I loved that bastard!" Her eyes teared up and she quickly extended her hand again to Ginny. "I'm sorry I said that. You just don't know yet."

Willy opened the envelope and pulled out an American Airlines ticket folder. Inside were two tickets to West Palm Beach, with connecting tickets on a small commuter line to Grand Bahama Island. One ticket listed the name Vinnie Lawson and the other Angela Clayfield. Also included was a confirmation slip for a reservation at the Conch Cove Resort and Club on Grand Bahama for Vinnie Lawson and guest. As if that weren't damning enough, there was a short note from the travel agent: "I think you and your lady friend will find this place most charming. I got some special rates. I feel I owe you a good time after the dreadful experience you had at the place in Myrtle Beach."

Willy pushed all the material over to Ginny and stared off across the dining room, wondering what in the world to say to the disillusioned widow.

Ginny was the first to speak. "My God, these reservations are for this very day. Where did you get them, Caron?"

"They were underneath the mat in the trunk of Vinnie's car. I found them when I cleaned all his stuff out. There was also an envelope with a thousand dollars in it. I'll pay some bills with that."

Now it was Willy's turn. "Caron, ConCom used to cover executives with rather lucrative insurance policies. Has anyone been in touch with you?"

For the first time there was a hint of relief on the woman's face. "Yes, they called just today. There will be almost three hundred thousand dollars." Caron grasped Ginny's hand with both of hers. "And the way I feel right now, I would rather have the money than that sneaky bastard. And someday I am going to say my piece to that Clayfield woman. The only time I ever heard Vinnie speak her name was when he said he gave her a couple of golf lessons."

Ginny slid toward Caron and put an arm around her. Caron fell on her shoulder weeping and trembling.

Willy recalled the many comments Katie Glover had made about Angela Clayfield. It was beginning to look as if Katie had her properly pegged.

15

Captain Max Von Braun put the big Trans-Asiatic Airlines 747 into a final approach pattern for Kennedy Airport. He was now four days out of Hong Kong. The two-day layover in San Francisco had given him an opportunity to catch up on some much-needed sleep. He was going to have to be more careful. The copilot had caught him napping a couple of times on the run from Hong Kong. Of course, the fellow had given him the benefit of the doubt by saying, "Captain, if I didn't absolutely know better, I would swear you were getting a wee bit of a nap."

Emerald Lu had joined his party at the Paragon Club in Wanchai at 2 A.M. She had discovered the four of them, he, Brigitte and her two amorous companions, locked in a lazy circular embrace inspired by a teasing ritual Brigitte had imported from Brunei.

At that point he had been fighting exhaustion. His angina, unheard from for many months, had let him know it was still there. A vague soreness in his left shoulder and tingly fingertips had reminded him that the marathon with his three imaginative companions had probably gone too far.

Emerald Lu had persisted in watching the tantalizing exhibition for several minutes. Once, he thought she would join in and give the jaded participants some fresh inspiration. Von Braun smiled wryly at the thought as the lumbering 747 passed low over a succession of Long Island beaches. His right hand went instinctively to his left shoulder. It was a good thing she hadn't joined in, he thought. It might have pulled the last beat right out of his heart.

After dismissing the girls, he and Emerald Lu had enjoyed a discussion of her diabolical plan and its results thus far. Of all the people killed, only Vinnie Lawson had been on her list. The elevator "accident" had been ill-conceived. The fact that Angela Clayfield had not been in the Mercedes elicited a string of obscene invective such as he had never before heard.

"You were fully paid for your part, right?" she had asked him. "Next time, make certain we get the important people. And try to keep speculation away from any obvious connections between the events that were planned."

Von Braun frankly didn't know how that could be done. The press was already beginning to speculate, but he would pass along the instructions anyway. He would be an incredibly rich man if he could engineer the preposterous plan of wiping out the key personnel of a major corporation. What a vendetta! He thought only the sickest of minds could conceive of such unconscionable havoc.

The big airliner touched down with a hardly perceptible bump. It was one of Von Braun's patented landings, which drew unending admiration from all his colleagues. While taxiing to the terminal from the remote runway, Von Braun began to run over the extensive agenda he had laid out for himself over the next three days.

First, there was the business of his greatest endeavor on earth so far, *The Rare Chart Book*. His collection of rare antique maps and charts gathered from all over the world had been embellished by a brief explanatory text. A printer in Hong Kong had provided him with a high-gloss sampling of pages proposed for a massive book. Not only would it decorate the coffee tables of the affluent, it would of course be a technical extravaganza for any sincere collector or student of cartography. He had paid half a year's salary for one chart alone containing handwritten notations by Magellan. His hobby would thus win him a permanent place in academia.

ConCom had a division that specialized in such artistic volumes. Von Braun had in his pocket a letter from one editor who had seen several sample pages and was enthusiastic. The editor had agreed, in fact, to meet him and discuss the project this very evening at dinner.

Von Braun was a practical man. If ConCom was the best in the world at this type of publishing, they should be the ones to do it. The fact that Emerald Lu had actively engaged him in her vendetta to wipe out a few executives couldn't be allowed to affect the decision he had made concerning *The Rare Chart Book*.

The scheduled meeting with the Sino-Americo Personnel Development Company was secondary to him. In his luggage, he carried a handful of photographs developed and blown up in Hong Kong. The photos had been taken by an operative selected by

the Sino-Americo company. All the people who had
attended the ConCom funerals were identified ac-
cording to the degree of their importance. The photographs had been screened by Emerald Lu, who had
circled the faces of those she had selected for elimi-
nation.

Sometimes Von Braun wished he didn't know so
much about the business dealings of Emerald Lu. By
bringing him into her closed circle of accomplices,
she had made him a full partner in all the risk involved. She wanted their bond to be even tighter
than that, however. She had a graphic video record
of the many depraved evenings he had spent at the
Paragon Club. With this she thought she could
blackmail him. This rather amused the captain.
True, such a video might cost him his job, but so-
cially he was quite alone in the world, virtually im-
mune from blackmail.

Von Braun said his good-byes to the other crew
members and strode into the Trans-Asiatic terminal
after passing through customs. During the walk
through the arrival area he heard himself paged several times. Approaching the paging desk, he was
greeted by a tall, thin young man with tousled black
hair that flopped over his brow. The youth looked at
his uniform and the four stripes.

"I'll bet you are Captain Von Braun. Am I right,
sir?"

"You certainly are."

"I'm Brook Laird, ConCom Publishing." Brook
stuck his hand forward to be grasped in the strong
grip of Von Braun.

"Thank you for being so kind as to meet me here.
We have much to talk about, young man."

Dinner presented a wonderful opportunity for the
captain to show photographs of scores of rare charts
documenting man's explorative nature from Marco

Polo on. They were assembled in a superb way that could only be a labor of love.

The captain gave a delightful performance. Sixteen years with Trans-Asiatic had groomed a magnificent storyteller. Though the project would not likely be a significant money-maker, the captain acknowledged, it would be a prestigious and worthwhile undertaking.

"Captain Von Braun . . ."

"Please call me Max." He was folding his hands comfortably on the table after dessert. He studied Laird with more than casual interest. After all, his life's work was in this man's hands. He couldn't get over how young the man looked for one who held such an important position. Brook Laird must be talented indeed to rank so high on Emerald Lu's hit list.

"Captain, I know you are pressed for time. But I wonder if you might come over to the ConCom offices tomorrow. I would like you to meet a few people. I think we can nail a workable plan for your book."

"I will make the time. I have a two-day layover before returning to Hong Kong."

"Try to make it as early as possible tomorrow morning. I would like you to meet Angela Clayfield, our CEO. She has an appointment with me on some other matters at eight A.M. It would be a perfect time for you to meet her. I've already shown her the material you submitted previously, and she was impressed. Now, wait till she sees this!"

"I'd be happy to, of course."

"Oh, one other thing, Captain. You may have heard about the trouble we've had at ConCom. A few days ago there was a sabotaged elevator and two people were killed. The police have the building under high security. You will have to sign in, and I will have to come down to escort you upstairs. Of course there is no danger."

Von Braun tried to maintain a grave demeanor. He wisely decided to keep his distance from the whole subject.

"Oh yes, I read fragments of the story in the paper. Big cities like this have more than their share of psychotics. That will hardly stop me for furthering my book project. I will be there at eight o'clock sharp."

Von Braun showed up the next morning promptly at eight o'clock. He was met downstairs by Brook Laird, who escorted him up in the elevator and directly into the office of Angela Clayfield, who was leafing through the material the captain had left with Laird at dinner.

Laird was happy to see that Angela was thoroughly charmed by the captain. In fact she was very persistent in her suggestion that the captain join her for lunch or dinner on his next flight in.

"Captain, I so much want you to join me. You could describe a world to me that I do not have an inkling about. Now, please put me on your schedule." She extended her hand, which Von Braun brought to his lips.

"It will be my pleasure, Mrs. Clayfield."

Laird eyed the suave pilot. Why was Angela standing the way she was, with her hand on her hip and her sleek derriere cocked to one side. My God, what was that he felt? Was it jealousy? Just make it lunch or dinner on any day but Thursday, he thought as the captain left the office.

He glanced at Angela as he left to escort Von Braun to the elevator. She had already resumed the prim executive look. She should do a book on body

language, and illustrate it, he thought. She was such
a bitch. He could hardly wait until Thursday.

Just before he entered the elevator, Von Braun
turned to Laird. "You know, it is possible that I will
be held over another day. If so, that would give me
Thursday morning free. Would you pass that along
to Angela? I have just acquired another chart that I
would like to show her, hand-notated by no less than
Captain Cook. It contains revisions to the St. Law-
rence Channel."

"I'll certainly tell her, Captain. Thursdays are her
days for corporate think tanks on her yacht up in
Rye. But maybe she could find time."

Laird walked slowly back to his office, pausing
along the way to chat with several editorial associates who were fueling themselves for the day with
morning coffee. The big topic of conversation was
still the fallen elevator. Several had used the stairwell in their ascent to the fourteenth floor, but most
had trusted the usable elevators. Police still maintained a heavy presence in the building, and even
long-standing employees were being sent home for
ID badges that many had not bothered to wear
before the explosion. Speculation ran heavily toward the likelihood that the elevator bomb, Vinnie
Lawson's murder, and the bomb in Angela's car
were related. More than a few used the incident
as an excuse for taking a few sick days or vacation
days.

Opening his office door, Laird slipped off his suit
jacket and hung it on a hanger behind the door.
Sticking out of the jacket pocket was the unusual
map he had found in the doorway to his apartment.
There was a Chinese woman in the accounting department who could probably read the characters in
the margin of the fancy parchment map that had
pinpointed the place where he lived.

He dialed Lois Lin's extension. She was evidently not in yet, so he left a message for her to drop by his office when it was convenient. Damn! he thought. I could have shown it to the captain. He had lived in Hong Kong for many years and might have been of some help.

Laird was deep into the projects stacked on his desk when Lois Lin tapped gently on his partially open door.

"Oh, come in, Lois. It's nice of you to brave the elevators all the way from the sixth floor."

Lois smiled slightly. "Oh no! I'm not using the elevators for a while. Maybe that is good. I'll get some exercise."

"Hey. Maybe I should do that too. I need the workout a lot more than you do. Lois, please take a look at this." He pushed the map across the desk to her. "Look down in the corner. You'll see what look to me like Chinese characters and some numbers."

Lois fingered the stiff parchment, turning it to examine the script.

"Mr. Laird, this is the name and address of a gift shop."

"Wonderful. Will you please translate it for me? And I'll try to get there sometime today."

"Okay. I'll translate it, but you will not be going there today, Mr. Laird." She smiled impishly.

"Why not?"

"This gift shop is in Hong Kong. This address is probably in Kowloon."

"That's strange. I found it tucked under the gate to my patio."

Lois shrugged. "Maybe someone from the Village went to Hong Kong and bought these maps to sell in a store in the Village."

"I never really thought of that. It is a possibility. Well, thanks anyway, Lois. I'll keep your translation and check around a few places in the Village. Who knows? Maybe someday I may go to Hong Kong and check it out myself."

Lois grinned broadly, shrugged again and left the office. Laird tossed the map aside and returned to his manuscripts.

16

The Sino-Americo Personnel Development Company had no listed business address in New York City. The Great Eastern Gem and Artifact Company, however, had a small walk-up office on Mott Street. Pelly Kahn, a stocky South China mainlander in the United States on a temporary visa, headed the dingy office.

The lettering on the opaque-glass-windowed door had been applied with some sort of paste on letters that had obviously lost their adhesion with the passage of time. The door now cryptically read, THE GRE T EAS ER GE AND ARTI ACT CO. SUITE 211.

Pelly Kahn was a strapping man who appeared to be all torso. He was heavily muscled, his thick biceps and chest accentuated by a skintight black turtleneck sweater. His eyes were probably his most prominent feature. The large brown eyes were very dark, the pupils nearly merging with the iris. He seemed to blink only infrequently. Anything resembling a smile was not a part of his facial repertoire.

If Pelly Kahn had a title in his position at the helm of the Great Eastern Gem and Artifact Company, he did not know what it was. He was known to the few people who dealt with him just as Pelly, with one exception. The renegade aviator Max Von Braun called him Herr Kahn.

The room was sparsely furnished. There was an old leather couch and several worn caneback chairs that looked as if they might have been appropriated from some restaurant supply place.

One of the chairs was occupied by a slender, dark-complexioned man who sat nervously wringing his hands in his lap as Pelly talked.

"Afghanistan, you are from Afghanistan. Very difficult job bringing you to this country from Afghanistan. You must realize that others risked their lives to bring you here."

The man nodded in complete agreement and understanding.

"In fact, I am told you owe Sino-Americo thirty-one thousand dollars. Do you agree?"

"Yes." The man's voice was hardly audible.

"Do you have payment with you?"

"No."

"Very well, then, Mr. Ashtab, you know that it is required that you accept an assignment. You are very fortunate. The assignment will be all over within three days, and once it is completed your debt to Sino-Americo will be considered paid in full. You were born on a very lucky day, Mr. Ashtab."

The man was looking anything but lucky. His face was frozen in rapt attention, beads of perspiration forming on his brow. Pelly Kahn lifted a bright orange shopping bag from the floor beside his chair and sat it on the desk. He reached to the floor once again, produced a small metal fishing tackle box and placed it on the desk beside the orange bag. He picked up a pencil and a piece of yellow paper and pushed them across the desk.

"You make notes as I talk. There can be no mistakes."

Kahn paused a moment as the illegal immigrant grasped the pencil. "On this coming Thursday morning, you will drive to New Jersey across the George Washington Bridge. You will drive north on the Palisades Parkway past Exit 2 to the first scenic overlook beyond Exit 2. Plan to arrive there at 6 A.M." Kahn had to pause. The man was writing furiously but seemed to take forever.

"There will be a trash barrel positioned near the beginning of a row of parking places. Park and look in that barrel. You will see a shopping bag like this, and it will contain a metal box like this." Kahn pushed the two items across the desk.

Ashtab picked both of them up for a second. The tackle box felt empty.

"You will then drive north to the Tappan Zee Bridge in New York State and cross into Westchester. From there, you will proceed to Rye, to the marina you visited briefly last week. Did you have any difficulty finding it, Ashtab?"

He shook his head. "No. Very easy."

"You will take this card and place it in the slot at the gate." Kahn produced a plastic card and slid it over to Ashtab. "Once inside the marina, you will find very few people, perhaps no one. If you meet anyone, just be courteous. You are a smart man, Ashtab. Just use your wits."

The man was watching Kahn anxiously now. Kahn nodded toward his pencil and paper, a reminder that accurate notes were a priority.

"Walk out to gangway four. Climb aboard a 50-foot

Hatteras called *Lazy Dolphin*. There is an unlocked bait tank in the transom. Take the tackle box from the bag and put it in the bait tank. Then leave the marina." Kahn handed the man an envelope. "You will then drive to Newark Airport, where you will have about three hours to make your plane to Seattle. The ticket is in here. Your debt to Sino-Americo will be paid and you will then be free to enjoy a life in this magnificent country."

"That is all?"

"Yes. Wasn't that easy?" Kahn looked at Ashtab, who by now looked greatly relieved.

"Yes, I assure you that it will be done."

"One word of caution, Ashtab. I must warn you that you are not to open the metal box under any circumstances. Actually, it would be very difficult because it will be welded shut. If you did succeed in opening the box, something terrible would happen to you before you got aboard the plane to Seattle. Any questions?"

"I understand. Don't worry about anything."

"Good day, Mr. Ashtab. May you have a long and happy life in America."

17

Brook Laird had taken the doubling of his salary as a logical reason for an upscale shift in lifestyle. He began to look at the dingy apartment in the Village as temporary quarters. He found himself reviewing apartment listings carefully before he discarded the daily papers.

He found Lily's behavior particularly irksome. He had called to invite her up for the weekend to celebrate his new position. She had been noticeably unexcited about his promotion, and had pointed out that she needed the weekend to cram for exams. In his disappointment and anger he heard himself tantalizing her with news of his spending next Thursday on Angela Clayfield's luxury yacht.

Not a twinge of jealousy resulted. She had even encouraged him to have a good time. Also, she didn't even mention his not returning a number of her phone calls lately. Laird wasn't sure whether he should be relieved or worried.

He arrived home after 11 P.M. on Wednesday. He flipped on the answering machine, surprised to hear the voice of Angela Clayfield.

"Hello, Brook, dear. Captain Von Braun is meeting me for breakfast at the Waldorf. I suggest you go on up to the *Lazy Dolphin* in the morning and I'll join you as soon as I can. He said something about showing me a chart notated by Captain Cook. My! We're getting educated, aren't we! The more I have thought about his *Rare Chart Book*, the more possibility I see in it. I can imagine lots of prestigious promotional possibilities. Please forgive me for being late, Brook. And oh, yes! Since we are going to have a shortened day, please leave that heavy old briefcase at home. Sweet dreams, Brook."

Laird felt a rush of heat surge through him such as he had not felt since he was a teenager. It was sexual harassment, clear as day. She was actually ordering him about in his personal life, and to his great surprise, he found himself loving it.

He spent a restless night. The more he tried to sleep, the more Angela Clayfield filled the darkness of his room with tempting fantasies. Once the phone rang, but he did not pick it up when he heard Lily Langley begin to drone on about some new theory concerning the pituitary gland.

Finally she said, "Good night, Brook. By the way, Brook, you're never in anymore. Is everything all right? I've thought things over, Brook. There's no real reason we should get together before Thanksgiving. I can take a four-day holiday then. We'll have great fun, Brook. I've found a place where you can have all the blackened snapper you can eat for seven ninety-five. Bye-bye."

He backed up the machine so that he could play Angela Clayfield's message and Lily's consecutively. No question about it, Lily Langley was rapidly becoming a loser. Angela would certainly come up with something more appetizing than blackened snapper.

He remembered looking at the clock at 3 A.M. He woke up about seven and decided to try sleeping for a couple more hours before going to Rye. Finally he gave up. He arose, showered, and dressed for the day in swimming trunks, sweats and sneakers. A half hour later he was pointed north on the FDR Drive in his rented Grand-Am. When he crossed the Willis Avenue Bridge, he looked at his watch. It was nine-thirty. He should be at the marina before ten-thirty.

As he neared Rye, a towering pillar of black smoke climbed into the sky from somewhere near the waterfront. It was the only flaw in an otherwise perfect day. It was bright and sunny, the air unusually free of humidity. There was little wind, attested to by the smoke column, which soared skyward almost vertically. A perfect day for the water.

He looked at the briefcase on the seat beside him. He had dumped the contents onto his desk at the apartment, and had selected only a half dozen sheets of paper that contained a few items of mild urgency. The thinness of the briefcase was in stark contrast to the heavily laden one she had made so much fun of. He decided he would not bring business up at all unless Angela did.

He was now within a mile of the marina. The column of smoke was now white, apparently steam from water being poured on whatever was burning. As he turned off the Post Road and toward the marina, the white column rose directly ahead of him.

It was impossible to get closer than a couple of blocks from the marina. The streets adjacent to it were crowded with fire-fighting equipment. In the small harbor a fire boat was cannonading water into the base of the pillar of smoke, now rapidly dimin-

ishing. Clusters of people crowded along the board
walkway alongside the marina. Laird pushed his
way through to the gate and showed his plastic entry card to one of the policemen blocking his way.

"Not a chance, mister. The marina has been evac-
uated. It'll be several hours."

"I was meeting a friend on a boat out on gangway
four."

"Sorry sir, maybe tomorrow. There ain't nobody
out there." The broad-shouldered cop stood blocking
his path.

Laird began to work his way through the crowd
along the cyclone fence. He kept looking into the
base of the pillar of steam, trying to see the exact
location of the fire. As the haze cleared away, he
looked intently for the high profile of the big Hatteras yacht. All at once he realized it wasn't there.

He scanned the crowd around him and recognized
one man from his first trip to the marina.

"Hi. I was meeting a friend out there. Any idea
what's going on?" By now the steam and smoke had
virtually disappeared.

"Big Hatteras on gangway four blew sky high. A
couple of other boats went up too. I don't think there
is anything left on gangway four. I was still sleeping
out on pier two when there was this tremendous explosion. Never heard anything like it."

Laird scanned the crowd seeking other familiar
faces, but saw no one he recognized. He climbed atop
one of the wooden benches along the fence and
stared out across the water to where the *Lazy Dolphin* should have been. All he could see was an antenna and some electronic gear jutting out of the
water at a crazy angle. No question about it, whatever was left of Angela's classy toy was now on the
bottom.

He looked across the parking area behind him and

up the street where he had parked. Angela was due any minute.

Was it possible that she had already boarded the *Lazy Dolphin*? It was a question he didn't want to allow into his mind.

Then he spotted her. She was running down the block where he had parked. As she approached, he could see she was sobbing. She climbed the bench to stand next to him and look out across the marina.

"Oh Brook!" For just a second she clung to him tightly. "Hold me, Brook, I'm afraid."

"Cliff! Cliff!" Now she was shouting at someone inside the marina. "Brook, there's Cliff. He's the dockmaster here. Cliff!"

This time the man heard her and walked quickly toward where they both stood.

"Mrs. Clayfield. Am I ever glad to see you. You come out here sometimes on Thursday. I thought you might be aboard. Thank God! Was anyone aboard?"

"No, Cliff. Brook and I were both late this morning. We were going to work on the *Dolphin*."

"Good. I think we've accounted for everyone, then."

"Cliff, do you have any idea what happened?"

"Mrs. Clayfield, I haven't got an inkling. I suppose there will be an investigation. Did you have any problems aboard the *Dolphin* that you were aware of? The explosion seemed to center right there with her."

"Cliff, the *Lazy Dolphin* had no problems. Charles always kept her in tip-top shape. In fact I haven't had her out since Charles died." Angela rummaged around in a tote bag and produced a business card. "Cliff, if you can't reach me at home, please call my office when you learn anything about the fire. I hope Charles didn't leave the insurance policy aboard. We just spent a fortune putting in a new computer room."

"I'm sure sorry, Mrs. Clayfield. I'll keep you posted."

The dockmaster turned and walked over to join the fire chief and several men who appeared to be police officials.

Laird was amazed by Angela's demeanor. Though she had shed a few tears, the loss of the *Lazy Dolphin* was already being taken in stride. She climbed up on the beach and stared out over the marina at the lop antenna of the *Lazy Dolphin*, which jutted out from the water. Once, he thought she actually smiled for a second or two.

The dockmaster had concluded his conversation with the small circle of officials and turned away. He noticed Angela still standing on the bench and approached them.

"Mrs. Clayfield," he said, his voice a hoarse whisper. "They think the fire was started by some sort of explosive. The dock finger where the *Dolphin* was tied up was blown to bits. These guys have instructed me to close down the marina for several days while they make a careful search of all the vessels. I'll be in touch with you as soon as I get a report."

Angela shook her head, newly stunned, and grasped Laird's arm. "I can't imagine why anyone would want to blow up the *Lazy Dolphin*. I'll appreciate your staying in touch."

She led Laird by the arm as she turned to walk back across the parking lot and up the street to where they had parked. "Brook, if you don't mind, I'd rather not go back to the office. Do you mind following me back to my place? We can talk there and try to come up with some answers."

"Sure. After this I don't think I would accomplish much in the office anyway."

The drive back to Saddle Hills took about forty-five minutes. Angela drove aggressively, just the way she did everything else, Laird thought.

The large house was empty when they arrived. The children were off at school and Angela made a point of telling him that her housekeeper would not be back until late afternoon.

She led him to a large office that looked out over a pool and garden to the rear of the house. The office was luxuriously furnished. A massive sectional sofa wrapped around half the room and a heavy mahogany desk, complete with computer and fax machine, dominated the other half. He had a feeling it must have been Charles Clayfield's office. The room had a definite masculine imprint.

Angela removed her shoes, tossing them onto a chair next to the desk. "You know, Brook. Someone is trying to wipe us all out. First there was Charles, then Vinnie Lawson, the explosion in the elevator and now the boat. Until now, I tried to tell myself that the events were unrelated." She pulled her sweatshirt over her head and tossed it onto her shoes.

Laird gaped at her, entranced by the flimsy bra that didn't conceal the nipples of her ample breasts.

"But they are connected, Brook. Someone is trying to either slowly destroy the company, or kill me, or both. If we had been on time this morning we would be dead now. Have you thought about that, Brook?" She unzipped her slacks and, sitting on the edge of the desk, peeled them off and tossed them into the chair.

"I've thought about little else all morning. The succession of events could hardly be a coincidence. If Captain Von Braun hadn't called you for a breakfast meeting, we would indeed be dead. I think you'd better hire a private detective and a bodyguard as well.

Whoever is doing this has just barely missed you twice."

Angela walked close to him and put her hands on his shoulders. She pressed against him, the flimsy bra barely containing her.

"What else do you think, Brook? Is there anything else on your mind right now?" She began to move herself rhythmically against him. "I know there is, Brook. I can feel what you're thinking."

She leaned back and smiled at him, unsnapping the bra and letting it drop to the floor. Laird was awed by her ability to compartmentalize her thoughts and emotions. Tragedy had struck. Her life and career were seriously threatened. Yet she was able to turn off all that and stand in front of him naked, confident and insistent.

The telephone rang, but they waited. After a pause, the answering machine emitted the deep voice of Brad Overstreet. "For Christ's sake, Angela! The dockmaster at the marina tells me you're okay. Please call the office. It's a madhouse down here. They've put a police line around the building. Whoever these crazy bastards are, they are out to kill us, you especially."

"Brad, simmer down." The conference phone picked up her voice. "We'll talk later."

"Later! Angela, they're trying to kill you! Someone is. There may not be a later. I've just talked to a protection agency recommended by the police chief. He can have your house staked out by midafternoon. He insists on covering your every movement for a few days, or until these crackpots are caught."

"Okay, Brad. Go ahead with it. But tell them not to bother me until the kids get home from school. I was up late last night and the scene at the marina wore me out. I'm going to lie down and get some rest."

"Angela, I'll come over and—"

"Absolutely not. Brad, you are to stay right there in the office and handle what must be a chaotic mess. How did the people there find out about the boat?"

"Are you kidding? There has been nothing else on radio or television since it happened. They're tying it in to all the other events since Charles's death and drawing the logical conclusion. If these guys can find your boat it certainly won't be long before they find your home address."

"Okay, Brad, have the police, or whoever they are, come over here to cover the house as quickly as possible. But remember, they are not to disturb me until the children get home from school. I want the house covered, but I don't want to be disturbed."

"Angela, be careful . . ." Brad's voice trailed off. The gravity of the situation was obviously frightening to him.

"Oh, I will be, Brad. I have a nine-millimeter that Charles gave me. Believe me, I will use it if I have to."

"Atta girl! Talk to you this evening. The police want to shut down the building at three o'clock. They want to give the building one more search to make sure it's clean before opening it up tomorrow."

"Brad, did you see the material I left on your desk with all the maps and stuff?"

Laird, hearing both sides of the conversation, couldn't believe his ears. The world seemed to be burning around her, yet she was able to switch back to business.

"Yes, I glanced at it, but I—"

"Brad, it's wonderful. I want you to look at it and think of tying in a ConCom institutional campaign with it. The author is a real raconteur, a longtime captain for Trans-Asiatic. He has put his life into this book and a ton of his own money."

"Okay, Angela, I'll take a look and bring in advertising for a peek."

"Thanks, Brad. Brook Laird brought the project in. He can tell you all about the captain tomorrow."

"Good. Be careful now, doll."

"Hey, you be careful yourself. These nuts would probably like to nail the company president too. Bye!"

Laird was relieved when the conversation ended.

Angela was still sitting on the edge of the desk. "Come over here, Brook, and sit down."

He walked to the desk and sat in the massive leather chair. She brushed the errant locks of his hair back over his forehead and leaned forward to kiss him on the lips, her breasts brushing him when she pulled away.

"Did you bring that heavy old briefcase with you today?"

"Well, I did bring a briefcase. But I think it has about six pieces of paper in it."

"Really? Brook, I thought I told you not to bring it along today."

"Well . . . there really isn't anything important. In fact I left it in the car."

"Brook." She again leaned forward and drew her face very near to his. "I told you not to bring your work with you. You are going to have to get better at following instructions. Do you understand that, Brook?"

She again stroked his hair as she talked, then dropped her hand to gently massage the back of his neck.

"I'll never bring the damn briefcase with me again."

"Good, Brook, good! I think you finally know why you're here." She kissed him again, pulling away quickly to let her breasts brush his face. "Do you, Brook?"

"Yes."

"Yes what, Brook?"

"Yes, I know why I am here." The game she was playing had driven him to a level of passion previously unknown to him.

"Then begin, Brook. Begin making me feel good. You are going to have to hurry today. I guess we've only got a couple of hours."

18

EXPLOSION AND FIRE DESTROY CLAYFIELD YACHT. The
headline crossed two columns on page seven of *The
Los Angeles Times*. Willy Hanson read the brief account aloud to Ginny as she set about brewing their
morning coffee aboard the *Tashtego*.

The *Lazy Dolphin*, a luxury yacht owned by
Angela Clayfield, CEO of ConCom Publishing
Company, was sabotaged and sunk at its dock
near Rye, New York. No injuries were reported.
Experts on the scene believe the explosion was
caused by dynamite. ConCom CEO Angelo Clayfield had intended to spend the day working on
the yacht, but arrived at the marina late to find
the yacht destroyed. This was the fourth major
incident in recent weeks apparently targeting
ConCom Executives. Four persons have died; a
fifth, not associated with ConCom, suffered a fatal
heart attack while witnessing the execution-style

killing of ConCom sales manager Vinnie Lawson on a golf course several days ago.

Angela Clayfield's husband, Charles, perished in the explosion of their automobile in a driveway at the Clayfield estate two weeks ago. At first police were reluctant to connect the events, but New York City Police Chief Ryan Leary said they now have reason to believe that ConCom is being targeted by a group of terrorists. Police declined further comment.

"The New York papers must be going wild over this," Ginny said as she handed Willy his coffee.

"Ginny, someone is going to a lot of trouble without even indicating what it is they want. The automobile explosion, the hit on the golf course, the elevator incident and now the sinking of the *Lazy Dolphin* have all been highly technical schemes that cost somebody a lot of money. I'm going to call Katie Glover and find out if there's any other information."

Ginny sipped her coffee. "Honey, whoever is doing this doesn't seem to care who they kill as long as they're ConCom-related."

Willy stirred uneasily. Only two years ago he and Ginny had participated in the wiping out of a massive drug cartel, one of the largest on the continent. He had written a detailed account of their adventure that had sold over two million copies over the past year. ConCom, the company Willy had once headed, had made a fortune off that book. Now ConCom was being terrorized.

"Hong Kong." He said it aloud again. "Hong Kong."

"What do you mean, Willy?" Ginny looked at him steadily, afraid to match her thoughts with his.

"It's a gut feel, something I can't explain. It's as if there's some unfinished business."

Ginny walked around the chart table, stood behind Willy and began to gently massage the back of his neck. She knew exactly what he was thinking. Already the romantic trans-Pacific adventure was being shunted to the back burner. Her eyes became moist as she thought back two years to the night when Willy and Coley Doctor had led scores of federal agents into the milddle of the Sino-Americo drug cartel. Anyone who had escaped had undoubtedly packed off to Hong Kong.

"Willy, it doesn't make sense. Why would those hoodlums want to open an old wound? I can understand them wanting to do business in the United States again, but why would they risk calling attention to themselves with such a public and brutal vendetta?"

"Good question. But I think it can be easily answered. A year and a half ago we helped put their big trawler under the sea. Hell, some of it is still piled on the rocks down at Redondo. The head honcho, Logan Phipps, was shot through the head. Several others were killed, captured and sent to jail. Millions of dollars' worth of cocaine was seized. Every loose end was tied up neatly, except one."

"Okay, Willy, say it."

"Onyx Lu was never found. Everybody assumed that she was killed in the wreck of the trawler. It was a stormy night with heavy seas. Even if she fell overboard, I don't think she could have survived. But the body never turned up."

"That's not surprising, though, is it, considering the strong currents outside that jetty. I know you've thought about that, Willy."

"Of course. And now I've been thinking about all the crazy things that have happened at ConCom over the past few weeks. There is only one logical explanation. Onyx Lu is reawakening her insane vendetta."

Ginny walked back to the chart table and took a stool across from him. "Willy, I know it's a possibility, but do you know what the odds are against it? What about that Clayfield woman? Maybe she's the common thread in all these disasters. Caron Lawson told us that she has no scruples, and Katie Glover said she sexually harasses every executive in the joint. Maybe some angry spouse is fed up. Or maybe she has a lot of baggage that needs to be burned if she is to hold on to her reputation. Isn't it odd that she has survived three near misses absolutely unscathed? I don't think you have to go all the way to Hong Kong for an answer, Willy."

"Maybe not. But I can't understand how a woman in her position could pull off all these stunts. We're dealing with a cold, pragmatic killer, with unlimited resources. Angela Clayfield may be a cold, calculating bitch and she may have trouble keeping her thighs together, but she doesn't seem like a killer to me. I can look at her and read her like a book. I believe Katie. Someday, somebody is going to blow the whistle on her for sexual harassment. Right now they're all having too much fun."

"Or they're dead," Ginny said with a smile. She leaned forward to kiss him.

"There is one thing I want to do before we get on with the trans-Pacific," Willy mumbled through the kiss.

"And what is that, love?"

"Let's give old Coley Doctor a call and run this past him. I'd like to ask him to nose around a bit, just to make sure that we aren't on somebody's hit list."

"Tell him to come over. We'll feed him some of that tuna steak you caught the other day."

"Good. I'll call Katie first for any updates. When I'm finished on the phone, we're going to close all the curtains and I am going to make you number one on my own personal hit list."

"Why don't you do that first and then make your phone calls?"

"Is that an order, Skipper?"

"As a matter of fact, it is."

19

Coley Doctor was six feet six inches tall, but the slender black man was as agile as a cat. An all-American basketball player, he had forsaken what he felt would be a mediocre career in the NBA to become a lawyer, and now a private investigator. Willy Hanson and he had worked with the FBI to bring down Onyx Lu and her Hong Kong bosses. Coley had helped to piece together the workings of the massive drug cartel so that Willy Hanson could write his best-seller.

It was Saturday morning, the time Coley reserved for one-on-one scrimmaging with Stringbean Owens, a promising college junior who was beginning to make a name for himself in the Pac Ten. Coley knew the gutsy kid from his life back in his ghetto. Stringbean had talent equal to Coley's in his heyday, plus a little extra beef that would someday serve him well in the NBA.

Every Saturday and Wednesday at 7 A.M. they

scrimmaged together on one of the more obscure out-
door courts at Long Beach State. Coley had picked
up a gimpy knee along the way and he could no
longer beat the kid on raw talent, but once in a
while he could outwit him. The sessions were good
therapy for Coley and invaluable to Stringbean, who
was rapidly becoming the Pac Ten's top point guard.

Stringbean was driving around Coley toward the
basket when Coley noticed Willy Hanson sauntering
toward the court, hands jammed in his pockets. The
distraction was just enough to give Stringbean an
easy layup.

"Hey, man! You ain't even tryin' anymore. You
gettin' pooped already?"

Coley nodded toward Willy. "I see an old friend
coming. We'll have to cut this a little short this
morning." Then, in a quick spin, he headed toward
the basket for one last shot, but tripped over
Stringbean's extended leg to sprawl headlong on the
asphalt.

The youth extended a hand. Talking through a
sheepish grin, he said, "Hey, man, I knew you were
going to try that. You know better than to cut that
way on your gimpy leg. I'm sorry, pal."

"Don't worry about it, punk. I'll get you next time."
Coley grinned back at the future star and then
limped slowly toward Willy, who had watched the
whole thing.

"Coley, you're out of your league. You call that fun?
The kid could kill you." They both smiled as they
watched Stringbean arch gracefully through a private game of run and shoot.

"He's good, Willy. He's gonna be a pro. But what
brings you here? I know it ain't to get some exercise,
though you could sure stand it." Coley patted the
slight paunch that pushed against Willy's belt.

"You been reading the papers?"

"Yeah, I figured you'd show up sooner or later. I bet you think Onyx Lu is back in action and is doing her thing."

"What do you think?" Willy asked, wondering how much of the newspaper stories Coley had read.

"Hell, I don't know what to think. The ocean was a-boilin' and a-poundin' that night. It don't make any sense that she survived."

"That's what I thought, till the boat blew up."

"What boat?" Coley frowned.

"Angela Clayfield's yacht was dynamited in its slip a couple of days ago. The job burned out a whole finger of the marina in Rye."

"Angela Clayfield, the chick who runs ConCom?"

"Yeah. Nobody was hurt. Angela got to the marina late and missed the show."

"Wow!" Coley turned toward Stringbean, still drilling shots toward the basket. "Let's get a cup of coffee someplace." He called to Stringbean, "Gotta split, punk. You better work on that move to the left. The ref would have nailed you for that."

"Hey, old man. I don't think so." It was Stringbean's turn to grin.

Coley and Willy climbed into Willy's car and drove the few miles to Hof's Hut, where they both ordered breakfast. It turned out that Coley had followed the coverage of the ConCom story pretty well. He had even sought out the New York papers when the elevator had been sabotaged. The *Times* article had given a fairly complete summary of events to date. All he had missed was the ensuing story about the Clayfield boat.

"Coincidence, Coley? Could it all be coincidence?"

Coley knitted his brow as he chewed slowly on some hash browns with onions. "I sure don't think so. Somebody has it in for somebody. I think it's too much to suspect Onyx Lu, though. How the hell could she swing a deal like that? Besides, I really think she's dead. Maybe the Clayfield babe is the target."

"Maybe, but she certainly isn't the only target. What about Vinnie Lawson, the sales manager? Angela Clayfield was nowhere near that golf course. There are a couple of things I can add to what you've read in the papers."

"Hey, wait a minute," Coley said, holding his hands out. "It sounds like I'm being primed for a job offer. I might as well tell you I've got so much going that I hardly have time to shoot buckets with Stringbean anymore."

"Come on, Coley, what the hell. How much satisfaction can you really get from helping women nail their cheating husbands?"

"You think that's all private eyes do, don't you?" Coley paused. "Well, you're ninety percent right, but it pays good, and I get access to some of the finest stuff in town."

"Stuff?"

"Not drugs, you jerk. Pussy! Man, you think I've joined a monastery or something?"

"Ah! Well, speaking of that, did you ever get a good look at Angela Clayfield?"

"Yeah. I saw the pictures in the paper. Gotta be trick photography. Nobody looks that hot."

"Would you consider her for a client?"

"What do you mean?"

"I mean she calls the shots and you do the shooting. The woman needs help, Coley. Somebody is trying to wipe out her company. The body count has reached five already. I think I can get you on her payroll and the pay would be good. The 'stuff' is up to you."

"Sell me, man, sell me. What do you know that hasn't been in the papers?"

"I went to her husband's funeral in New Jersey. A few days later, I went to Vinnie Lawson's funeral here in California. I saw the same creepy-looking guy surreptitiously taking photographs with a miniature camera in both places. He moved around and must have gotten snaps of all the people who attended each funeral. Kind of weird, huh?"

"What did he look like?"

"'Aha! Old Coley's interested, isn't he?"

"Let's just say that right now I'm interested in that slinky soufflé, Madam Clayfield. What did he look like?"

"He was about five feet ten. Skinny. All bones. He had heavy straight black hair that looked like it had never seen a barber. He moved fast. I tried to catch up to him at the second funeral, but he got to his car and took off before I got close. I did get the plate number."

"Did he take your picture?"

"I'm sure he did. He probably got everyone."

"That's odd, but it probably doesn't mean anything. What else can you tell me?"

"Angela Clayfield is loose as a goose. She shacked up with Vinnie Lawson, her sales manager, at Myrtle Beach last summer. When she was cleaning Vinnie's car out, Caron Lawson found airline tickets to the Bahamas for this very week, for her and Vinnie."

"Hey, this is sounding juicier by the minute. What else?"

"Katie Glover, a PR person at ConCom, says Angela and her new president should buy each other knee pads before they wear out all their nylon and worsted. His name is Brad Overstreet. She also says that Angela spends a godawful amount of time with her editor-in-chief behind closed doors. He goes in with his tie on and comes out with his tie off, sweating bullets."

"Wow! Katie Glover's some source, huh?"

"Katie tends to be a gossip. Things might be exaggerated, but basically I tend to believe her."

"Hell, I can look at Angela Clayfield's picture in the paper and tell she wouldn't have anything to do with such goings-on. You know how you are an expert at boats and sailing. Well, my expertise is the human female." Coley pulled back on his counter stool and stared soberly at Willy, then broke into a big smile.

"Sure, Coley, that's why you're paying four alimonies."

"That's a cheap shot, pal, but I forgive you. What's the editor's name?"

"Brook Laird."

Coley looked at his watch. He watched the waitress undulate along the counter and then ordered another cup of coffee.

"Any chance these people were just in the wrong place at the wrong time?"

"Coley, someone set up an easel to serve as a tripod to hold a high-powered rifle. He blew Vinnie's brains out at the top of his backswing from across a river. It was deliberate. Maybe the people in the elevator were in the wrong place at the wrong time, but not Vinnie Lawson."

"Well, why don't I go to New York and poke around and see if I can take some of Angela's money? It's going to cost her two hundred a day plus a ticket to the big brickyard. I would charge any regular client three times that."

"Two hundred? Clip Angela for the six hundred a day. She can write it off her security budget. I'll call her and pave the way. She says she's read my book, so she may remember you."

The private detective nodded. He seemed to be smacking his lips over the upcoming employment.

"Ginny's fixing some tuna steak I caught the other day and wants you over tonight," Willy said. "We can eat on the yacht."

"Home cookin'! You got a date. I'll bring a couple bottles of Cabernet. Ginny as pretty as ever? I haven't seen her in a year."

"There's no stopping her, Coley. She'll be glad to see you."

20

Pelly Kahn was furious. He slammed the thick loose-leaf binder down on the otherwise bare desk with all the strength he could muster. It bounced, then tumbled to the floor, spewing pages from its opened metal rings.

"Bastards! Incompetent bastards!" He screamed the words in the barren office of the Great Eastern Gem and Artifact Company. Then he forced himself to sit motionless, with hands folded, ashamed of his lack of self-discipline. He quietly picked up the binder and spent several minutes reinserting the pages in their proper order. Then he sat quietly again, stonelike and contemplative.

His luck had been abysmal. The elevator incident had terrorized, but had killed no one of importance. The failure to catch Angela Clayfield aboard her yacht had been an unforgivable error in timing. He had been assured that the early-morning appointment on the yacht was a sure thing. Lois Lin, working within the ConCom office, had copied the information directly from Brook Laird's calendar.

Kahn opened the notebook to the top piece of paper. A typewritten notation on a piece of yellow foolscap had been taped to the blank page. The typed words were "Marston's Olde Oyster House, 41 St. near 5th. Reservation for two, 8:30 P.M."

This information had also come from Lois Lin, and unfortunately could not be easily double-checked. A call to the restaurant might be brought to the attention of the guests when they arrived. The plan had already been set in motion. Another new citizen would earn the right to live and prosper in America this very evening.

Kahn turned the page. It was important that the right person be terminated this time. He knew that Hong Kong Lady was a heartless taskmistress whose patience had already been taxed to the limit.

Kahn looked at his Rolex. It was 5:20 P.M., less than three hours to go. His selection of the Amoy Islander had been made after an intense screening. The man was brighter than most, had done time in a mainland prison camp, and relished his freedom in America because a return to the homeland would result in his execution. Also he spoke decent English and could handle the silenced .22 automatic as if it were an extension of his own body.

Kahn closed the notebook and lined it up evenly this time with the edges of the desk, taking time to straighten the loose pages so that none protruded from the edge of the binder. Then he pushed back from the desk and dropped catlike to the floor. He hooked his toes under the edge of the heavy sofa and began his evening ritual of 200 sit-ups. He did them slowly, counting softly aloud, changing languages after every ten sit-ups. He found that this routine pushed everything else out of his mind. After all, his plan was perfect. It was time to stop thinking about it.

Fifty blocks away, Angela Clayfield studied the slow-moving tableau reflected in the floor-to-ceiling mirror next to the king-size bed. The Eddingworth Arms, an elegant old brownstone, was a perfect trysting place. It was possible to use either a front or rear exit from the unmarked building. Most of the suites were held on retainer for corporate clients. ConCom used them to put up out-of-town bigwigs and for elegant small dinners and holiday parties. The company had retained the hideaway for years.

Soft music from a classical guitar wafted gently from a hidden sound system in the dimly lit room. Angela, lips parted, continued to stare in the mirror at the darkly handsome Brad Overstreet moving his full lips gently along her elevated thigh. She wondered why she found their reflections in the mirror so much more provocative than turning to face the actual erotic experience.

"Brad, darling. Brad! Damn you! You are never permitted to stop that. Do you understand? Never!"

Overstreet paused to smile up at her for just a second, then leaped from the bed and strode quickly across the room to a small couch. He took two overstuffed cushions and put them atop each other on the bed. He gathered the half dozen satin pillows already strewn about the bed and piled them on top of the two cushions.

The muscular Overstreet picked Angela up as easily as if she were a feather and tossed her onto the satiny mound, her head low and the rest of her body arched up over the pillows. He topped her with his own massive frame. Gently, rythmically, he engaged her in erotic abandon until finally their spasming bodies stopped, sated into exhaustion.

About an hour later they showered together and dressed for dinner.

"Brad, why do we always do it backwards?"

"Do what backwards?"

"I think most lovers go to dinner, have their champagne and caviar, or whatever. Then they go home, make love and go to sleep. We always make love first, work ourselves into a famished frenzy and then go out and eat too much."

"Frankly, I think the others are a little foolish. They have never discovered the ecstasy of love on an empty stomach. I'm not averse to having a little dessert later on, are you?"

"No, Brad, darling. In fact, it's a delicious idea."

It was about ten minutes after eight when they hailed a cab in front of the Eddington Arms. Overstreet cradled Angela loosely in his arms as the driver pulled away from the curb.

"Driver, take us to Marston's Olde Oyster House. It's on Forty-first Street near Fifth." On the short ride to the restaurant neither Angela nor Overstreet said a word, still lost in thoughts of their tryst.

Glenn Marston greeted them inside the landmark establishment and led them to the corner table that had become their favorite.

"Mr. Overstreet, we have pompano and blue marlin as specials this evening, flown in fresh, of course. Maxie will be with you in a moment to tell you about a few other things. In the meantime, I will bring your dry Rob Roy and a Tanqueray with olive."

"Glenn, your memory is perfect."

"Oh, no, Mrs. Clayfield. The only perfection I see right now is you."

Angela smiled and winked playfully at Marston. "Poor man," she said when he left the table. "He owns this wonderful restaurant and has to spend his life being an ass-kisser. How would you like a job like that, Brad?"

She turned to stare at him with her great unblinking violet eyes, demanding an answer to her rhetorical query.

Overstreet paused for a moment and then laughed in his soft baritone. "Do you really think there is a lot of difference, Angela?"

"I don't understand. Difference in what?"

"Angela, do you really think Marston is that much different from me? Is there really much difference between ass-kissing and pussy-kissing?"

Angela stared blankly at him for a moment, trying to calculate just how serious he was, then, grasping his hand, broke into a broad smile. "My, my. The magnificent Brad Overstreet is having an acute attack of low self-esteem. Tell me, Brad, do you want to switch places with Mr. Marston? Do you want me to buy you a restaurant? Are you getting weary of your job, Brad?"

"Of course not, dear, I can't even boil water. And Marston is much too old for you." Overstreet concocted a slight smile. "I'm sorry I said anything. Actually our lovemaking is sprinkled with dazzling reciprocity."

"Thank you, Mr. Overstreet. You really don't fancy yourself a slave, then?"

"Only when it is pleasurable to do so."

"Ah! I knew you were joking all the time. Here's Maxie with our drinks. Let's drink to our reciprocity, as you put it."

The dinner that was set before them deserved to be savored, mixed with soft conversation and much soothing eye contact. Overstreet and Angela were so ravished with hunger, however, that the beautifully prepared meal was gulped down with as much appreciation as a quick lunch on a workday.

When the waitress arrived with the dessert tray, she found Angela playfully sitting on Overstreet's lap. They were talking nose to nose and obviously enjoying it very much. It was Angela who looked up first, beaming at the waitress.

Maxie smiled. "Oh, pardon me. I'll bring the dessert tray back in a little while."

"Thanks, Maxie, but Brad and I have decided to have dessert at home."

Maxie winked. "Sounds like a great idea. I'll get your check."

Forty-first Street was devoid of traffic when Angela and Overstreet exited the restaurant. They started walking toward Sixth Avenue when a cabbie parked at the corner switched his lights on and pulled away from the curb. Overstreet walked to the edge of the sidewalk and raised his arm to hail the taxi.

When the cab drew even with them, the driver stopped, got out, and circled to the other side to open the door for his customers. Angela got in first and slid across to the other side of the rear seat. Such courtesy by a driver was certainly rare in this day and age, but Angela attributed it to the driver's quest for a big tip on a quiet night.

Once Overstreet had climbed in next to Angela, the cabdriver slammed the door, locking it, then circled the cab to get back behind the wheel. Before opening his door, he paused to let a car pass.

He withdrew the small .22 automatic from his jacket pocket. Even fitted with a silencer, it was still quite small. He quickly crouched by the door, steadied his hand on the open window glass and pumped five shots into Overstreet's chest before either of his passengers knew what he was up to.

Pff . . . pff . . . pff . . . pff . . . pff. All five shots were expended before Angela started screaming. The driver dropped the automatic and reached in quickly to slap the gearshift on the steering wheel. The cab lurched into motion and proceeded, driverless, down Forty-first Street, careening off parked cars as it picked up speed until it rammed solidly into a large van that was parked several feet from the curb.

The cabdriver strode quickly toward Sixth Avenue and turned the corner before anyone knew what had happened. He moved faster toward Forty-second Street, where he plunged into a late-night crowd at a busy intersection and was finally swallowed up in a steady stream of people disappearing into the subway.

Back on Forty-first Street, Angela Clayfield continued to struggle with the locked door, screaming at the stricken Overstreet to help her. Panicked, she scrambled over the top of the seat back and finally fell out of the cab through the driver's door.

Still screaming, she ran back toward Marston's through the small crowd of people that had begun to accumulate.

"Oh my God! Help me, help me!" She screamed again as she reentered Marston's. She tripped down a couple of steps into the sunken dining room and slumped onto a small couch in the foyer.

Glenn Marston rushed in and dropped to her side. "Madam, Mrs. Clayfield, what in the world has happened? Where is Mr. Overstreet?"

Angela stopped sobbing but continued to shake violently. "Oh my God, I think he's dead. He's been shot or something. Something terrible has happened . . . in a cab, out there." She pointed to the door.

Marston turned to his maitre d'. "Call the police, quickly. I'll take a peek outside and then stay with Mrs. Clayfield." Several **people had heard** his remarks and pushed out onto the sidewalk with Marston.

A couple of hundred feet down the street there was now a crowd of people. A police car had already stopped at the scene, and the whirling lights splashed the surrounding buildings with flashes of red and white. When the driverless cab had hit the van it had careened sideways to block all of Forty-first Street.

Marston pressed on down the street through the gathering crowd. Within what seemed only a couple of minutes police cars had filled the block and an ambulance wailed onto the scene. Marston stood by as they removed Overstreet from the taxi. His coat fell back, revealing a white shirt drenched with blood. Marston stepped forward to glimpse the face of the lifeless man.

"Back away! Everybody outta here!" A policeman grabbed Marston's arm. "You got business here?" the cop bellowed.

"Yes! I have got business here. A woman is in my restaurant, up the street." Marston pointed to the Oyster House. "She was with that man. She knows about the whole thing."

The policeman turned, and Marston saw the lieutenant's stripes. "Sergeant! Take this man back to that restaurant. He claims he has someone there who can tell us what happened."

Marston looked at the stretcher bearing the body of Overstreet. He turned to the sergeant. "He was my customer, he and the young lady back there." He motioned toward the restaurant.

One of the EMS workers overheard. "I hope you gave him a good meal, pal. It was his last."

Another policeman walked up to the sergeant. "We found a weapon. It's lying on the floor near the gas pedal. Looks like a small-caliber automatic with a silencer attached."

"Okay, seal off the area. We got work to do."

Angela Clayfield was still sitting on the couch in the foyer with the maitre d' and Maxie when Marston returned with the sergeant.

Marston squatted down in front of them. "Mrs. Clayfield, I'm afraid Mr. Overstreet didn't make it. I'm terribly sorry."

Angela stared glassy-eyed at the restaurateur. She shook her head slowly.

"Oh my God! What is happening?" She lapsed into silence again. Then, noticing the policeman for the first time, she rose to face him.

"The cabdriver! Did they get the cabdriver?"

"The cabdriver?"

"Yes! He killed Brad. He shot him while we just sat there helpless."

"Lady, I don't know anything about it. When the lieutenant gets here, he'll appreciate a statement."

Angela Clayfield sat down again on the couch, glancing far back into the restaurant as she did. She couldn't help noticing that the table they had occupied only minutes before was still cluttered with their dishes.

Only a few minutes had passed. And now he was dead. Brad Overstreet was dead! Just like the others. He was dead.

21

The hydrofoil had taken much longer than usual for the crossing to Cheung Chau. It was the day after a major storm and the South China Sea was still kicking up heavy surf against the outer islands. This made the trip from Hong Kong Central a miserable one for Von Braun. Several times during the voyage he had thought to himself that he would rather pilot the roughest flight imaginable than cope with the angry white sea. As he neared the slip on Cheung Chau he was still struggling to keep down the light snack he had eaten just before leaving Hong Kong.

As the ferry eased itself between the clutter of sampans and junks in the small harbor, he spotted a slender bicyclist in white shorts and halter making her way toward Juan's fishhouse at the north end of the small boardwalk. That would be Emerald Lu, he thought. Cycling in the sun with her long ponytail bobbing, she could have been, from this distance, any innocent young woman pedaling to market to buy fresh fish for dinner.

Dismounting the bicycle, she leaned it against one of the chair backs at Juan's. As she circled the table to sit where she could look out to sea, all vestige of innocence disappeared. Von Braun eyed the compact figure of the woman he knew so well. She moved with a fluid sensuality that captured every male eye along the waterfront. Women looked at her with envy.

This schoolteacher from the northern part of the small island was seen only rarely at the market-place. She taught English to young girls at the small private school in the north end. Thank God it wasn't young boys, thought Von Braun. They would have a tough time concentrating, just as he often did.

He directed a casual wave of the hand toward Juan's Fishhouse. No doubt she had spotted him and was eager to get to the business at hand. He wondered just what that would be. Rarely was he asked to see her on Cheung Chau. The office of the Paragon Club in Wanchai usually sufficed. As he drew near to her table on the veranda she flashed the slightest hint of a smile, which quickly disappeared as she turned her head to look out to sea.

"You look magnificent today, Onyx! The sea off the reef is no match for the green in your eyes."

The woman glanced quickly around the table to see if anyone had overheard Von Braun. "Captain, my name is Emerald. There is no Onyx here on Cheung Chau. In fact, there is no Onyx anywhere. If you persist in calling me anything other than Emerald you will not at all like the consequences. Is that clear?"

"I'm sorry." He looked around them. The nearest person was a waitress, fully fifty feet away, far out of earshot. "I guess I just like to think of the old days, before you went to California and got in all that trouble. Actually the emerald is a better match to your eyes. Emerald is a perfect name."

"Then make sure you use it. Someday you may slip at the wrong time. There are ears everywhere, Captain, even here on Cheung Chau. A few people read papers. News drifts in to residents who have friends on the mainland. I did not come to the end of the world to face recognition." She bent at the waist to tie a loose sneaker lace.

He watched her perfectly toned muscles ripple beneath the loose shorts and halter. As tired as he was, he felt himself respond to her. "My dear Emerald, I will not make that mistake again."

She motioned for him to join her at the table. When he sat down, Emerald pulled her chair uncomfortably close to him.

"We work well together, Captain, because you have the sense and talent to do whatever I want you to do, quickly and without stupid questions. Do you like pleasing me, Captain?" Her tiny waist and flaring hips were only inches away.

"Of course. Why else do you think I flew twelve thousand miles for this short meeting? I'm supposed to be on layover in New York, you know. I'm here as a passenger on another airline. I have a flight out of Newark for Amsterdam in less than forty-eight hours."

"Did I ask you to tell me your business?" Emerald waited as the waitress set two glasses of lemonade in front of them before she spoke again.

"Instead of talking about my green eyes and gawking at my body like an adolescent, I think you should tell me what in the hell is going on in New York. The whole thing has become a media circus. The crazy publicity has put everyone on guard. Now it may take months for us to complete our plan."

"Pelly says it won't. He assures me that it is impossible to connect any of the terminating events. He uses different people each time and then has the people done away with. It is an endless chain of events, impossible to stop once it has been set in motion. He says not to worry about the publicity. It will die down, although he may have to cool it for a few days. All of this is assured by the top dollar you are paying, dear. Believe me, the latest operation worked flawlessly. Overstreet is gone and they haven't a single clue."

"I don't want you to see Pelly anymore. Communicate our needs to him by public phone, and make our payoffs by regular mail. I don't ever want to hear of two of our people being together again in the United States." She put her hand over his and squeezed firmly. "Now that we have business straight, let's talk about tonight. I have a very special party planned for the Paragon Club. A former British ambassador will be there doing some very naughty things. It will be good relaxation before your flight. I insist that you be there."

"You mean you called me all the way from New York just to tell me to stay away from Pelly?"

"No, Captain. I have an important question to ask you. I was going to ask you tonight, but I will get it over with now. It is important that we are totally honest with each other."

Von Braun fidgeted with the straw in his lemonade. His old, worn ticker was getting a workout. Something came to mind, something Pelly Kahn had said. He felt tired, but now Kahn's words flashed like a warning beacon across his mind. "I have an operative right within the ConCom Building." He had mentioned it in passing, evidently to impress the captain with the thoroughness of his organization. If Kahn had told the truth, it was very possible that Von Braun's breakfast that day with Angela had been reported to Emerald Lu.

He had the sickening feeling that she was about to skewer him. "Emerald, of course you are right. If we are dishonest with each other, we open the door to failure. That is why I like to keep you posted about everything. Before you ask your question I would like to bring you up to date on a minor activity that you may not be aware of."

Emerald stared fixedly at the captain. He tried with all the confidence he could muster to continue the conversation in a casual, offhand manner.

"Emerald, you know of my fetish for antique maps and charts. Some time ago, before all this started, I submitted some material for a book directly to a young editor at ConCom. Lo and behold, they contacted me and expressed an interest in publishing it. They do very well with extravagantly ornate volumes that appeal to upscale collectors."

Emerald nodded, her expression unchanged. "They are the only publisher in the world for this kind of thing?"

"They are the best."

"So you went to visit them and in fact talked to Angela Clayfield in her office."

"Yes! A young editor named Brook Laird directed me to her. Believe me, I felt very strange in that building. I am surprised that you know about my visit, Emerald. Not only did it serve the purpose of getting my *Rare Chart Book* well on its way to publication, but it also gave me firsthand insight into the layout of that building. I intend to pass this information along to Pelly.

Emerald continued to stare at Von Braun. Finally she spoke. "I am glad you brought it up, Captain. Your visit to ConCom was reported to me by Pelly. I thought that he must have been mistaken, but now you have answered that question."

Von Braun nodded and studied her carefully. The contact within the building had reported his visit, but evidently nothing else. She began to smile and trace her finger along his thigh, through his trouser leg. She obviously did not know that he had diverted Angela from the boat that morning by suggesting breakfast. Thus Kahn's assault on the marina had missed its objective. Nevertheless, he had very nearly made a fatal mistake.

"What kind of a woman is she, Max?"

"Well, she is very interested in my book, so that makes her very interesting to me. Too bad her tenure at ConCom is so limited. But perhaps I can get things on their merry way so that the replacement will pick up the ball."

"That isn't what I meant, Max. I mean is she as striking and beautiful in person as the media make her out to be?"

"Ah, yes. She is that."

"Then perhaps I should save her for a toy, someone for me to play with."

"I think you might be disappointed, Emerald. I think she reserves her affection for the men in her life, and I do mean men, in the very plural sense."

"Too bad, Max. Ah well, there is always the Paragon Club." Once again she pulled her chair closer and let her hand fall into the captain's lap. Von Braun scanned the area quickly as she brazenly began her erotic probing. He decided that the tablecloth and his own body shielded her gentle caresses from everyone.

"Emerald, the next hydrofoil leaves for Central District in about forty minutes. I think we should be on it."

"I'll go back to my condo and change." Now Emerald was grinning broadly at his nervousness. "Do you want to wait here or come along with me?"

"I'll come with you."

"Same old Von Braun. I knew you would, you old lecher."

"Of course. Once you've sampled fresh creamery butter, you don't settle for anything less."

"We'll see about that, Max, won't we?"

Von Braun walked beside her as she wheeled her bicycle along the packed-sand path toward the row of condominiums near the end of the cove. Small lines, almost imperceptible, trailed from the corners of her eyes. How old was Onyx? he wondered. The tiny sensual figure was toned and flawless, but her eyes and provocatively parted lips hinted of an aging decadence acquired over many years. The evil bitch would become even more evil as the lines advanced, the captain decided. As they increased their pace along the sand, his hand brushed her backside frequently and he felt his maleness respond. Not many women could stir him that easily anymore.

But he felt something else as well. There was the twinge in his arm, and the hint of pain as the terrain turned slightly uphill. She would indeed kill him one day with her blatant passion, he thought. But better to end it all that way than to be in the cockpit and plunge forty thousand feet to end in an inferno against some mountain.

22

Willy Hanson bought a half dozen out-of-town newspapers. ConCom's terrorized company was the big national news story of the day. The *Daily News* headline blazed, CONCOM PREZ ASSASSINATED! The names Brad Overstreet and Angela Clayfield were everywhere.

A weapon had been found, but there were no other clues so far. A taxi driver had been picked up and released. The cab that had been at the scene of the crime had been stolen from where the legal driver had parked it about an hour earlier on the Lower East Side.

One thing seemed certain to Willy. There could no longer be any doubt that someone was methodically trying to wipe out the ConCom executive staff.

"Strange," he murmured to Ginny. "Strange that Angela wasn't killed, since she was sitting right next to Overstreet."

"The woman must be a basket case by now. First

her husband, then her sales manager, and now her president. And there were all those other people. Do you really want to send Coley into this mess? It's big, Willy. He could easily get himself killed."

"Look. Coley's well aware of the danger. But I doubt I could talk him out of it now. It'll be big money for him. Besides, he's intrigued with Angela Clayfield. Coley is actually turned on by her pictures in the newspaper. He wants to help the lady in distress."

"Help her do what?"

"Find out who's trying to blow up her building. If there is an orgasm or two along the way, Coley would consider that a nifty bonus." He pushed the stack of newspapers across the chart table toward Ginny.

"Willy! Angela Clayfield's lovers are dropping like flies. I don't know how you can even joke about it."

Willy reached across the table to grasp Ginny's hand between both of his own. "I guess I joke about it because I can't stand facing what I believe to be the truth. I think Onyx Lu is alive, insane, and will keep on killing until every last important person working for ConCom is dead. She is a woman who never gives up. ConCom caused her immense grief. She will not give up until she has gotten her complete revenge."

Ginny shook her head slowly. "How could that tiny woman crawl out of the ocean that stormy night, and put her life back together? How in the world could she assemble the resources to wage a vendetta that would cost thousands, even millions?"

"Do you know what disturbs me more than anything, Ginny? The elevator explosion. That had to be the work of a truly psychotic person. It killed people randomly without regard for their status within the company. Onyx Lu is totally evil. That act is as much her work as her own signature."

"If it is true, then we had better start thinking about ourselves, because we must be at the very top of her shit-list."

"I know. We could be next."

"Anybody home?" Coley's deep baritone voice boomed in through the open transom.

"Coley! Come on down here and talk some sense to us."

"You bet." Coley bent his six-foot-six frame to enter the hatch.

"Well, if it ain't my old pal, Ginny. Happy days are here again!" Coley set down a sack that obviously held several bottles of wine, then wrapped his arms around Ginny.

"Hey, Coley, not bad!" Willy had removed a bottle from the sack to read the label. "Where did an old ghetto runner get taste like that?"

"I learned it from the ladies. Classy ladies always appreciate fine wine. I betcha Angela Clayfield would like that bottle of wine."

"Have you read the newspapers today, Coley?" Willy asked.

"Nope. Not yet. I'd like to give that up. It ruins a person's digestion. I do read the scores when the Lakers are playing. Why?"

"Brad Overstreet was murdered last night in Manhattan. He was sitting next to Angela Clayfield in a taxicab."

"Wow!" Coley picked up the newspaper that Willy had shoved in front of him. When he finished the article, he paused, deep in thought. "It's that bastard Onyx Lu. I better get back to New York before she gets Angela. If I don't hurry, I won't have a client to pay me a lot of money. Man, that would be a shame."

Willy nodded grimly. "You think it's Onyx too."

"Has to be. There ain't nobody else that mean." Coley spoke matter-of-factly.

They were interrupted by a tapping on the hull of the *Tashtego*. "Ahoy there! Dockmaster's office has a telephone call for Willy Hanson."

Willy poked his head from the hatch and the messenger handed him a scrap of paper with a phone number on it. It was Angela Clayfield trying to reach him from New York.

"The lady said it was awfully important, sir. She said it may be a matter of life or death."

"Thanks, pal. I'll call her back in a few minutes."

The young man hesitated, apparently perplexed that the "matter of life or death" message didn't prompt a quicker reaction. "Sir, the lady was very insistent. I took the message myself. She seemed awfully nervous. I could hear a lot of people talking in the background."

Willy stared at the young man for a moment. If his intuition was correct, the trans-Pacific sail with Ginny was about to be wiped off their agenda for quite a while. He looked at his watch. "It's almost midnight back in New York. I'd better find out what's going on. Coley, open a bottle of wine while I go back to the dockmaster's office. The Clayfield woman must be desperate about something to call here in the middle of the night."

As he walked back to the dockhouse, the memory of Onyx Lu returned in full force. There was still no hard evidence to link the terrorist campaign to Onyx. Yet the incredible series of events back in New York bore the stamp of a degenerate genius, and in his lifetime he had met just one person in that category, and that was Onyx Lu. "That's nuts!" he muttered. "In this modern world riddled with terrorism, there must be a thousand Onyx Lus."

"What did you say, sir?" the messenger asked.

"Nothing. Really, kid, I was just talking to myself. You'll do that someday."

"Oh, I do that now, sir, especially when my girl-friend gets unreasonable."

"You ought to dump her, kid. Right now. Unreasonable women are the cause of most of the trouble a man has in his lifetime. Take my advice and dump her."

The kid grinned at Willy as he dug in his pocket for a key to unlock the dockmaster's office.

When Willy phoned the Clayfield residence in New Jersey, an answering machine responded after several rings. Willy paused, then identified himself. Immediately someone picked up the call. It was a male voice.

"Whom do you expect to reach, sir?"

"Angela Clayfield. I'm returning her call." There were some muffled voices in the background, and then silence while he waited for what must have been half a minute. It was obvious that some sort of security system had been set up and that the ensuing conversation would be monitored.

"Mr. Hanson, this is Angela. Thank you so much for calling back." The voice sounded crisp and clear, not at all the voice of a woman who had been going through hell.

"When you were back here attending my husband's funeral, you asked if there was anything you could do to help. Well, now there is." For the first time the voice at the other end of the line began to falter and hesitate. "You've read about Brad Overstreet?"

"Yes, it's all over the papers out here. Do they have any suspects at this point?"

"Absolutely no one. It is just hell back here. I've ordered the building closed for a few days to all but a few key people. We've set up a security perimeter here at the house. It will stay in place until there's some breakthrough in the case."

"So how can I help you, Angela?"

"Mr. Hanson, company business is not getting done. You ran ConCom so successfully for so many years. Would you consider coming back here and working with me on an interim basis for a few days or until all of this blows over? You name your fee, Mr. Hanson. The loss of Brad has created a big vacuum. You would be able to go over all his projects and keep things rolling."

"I gave all that up over two years ago, Angela. I'm afraid I wouldn't be much good to you."

"Oh, I'm sure you would. I need your advice more than anything else."

"Angela, I really didn't expect anything like this. I would have to think it over for a day or so. My partner and I had planned to leave on a long sailing trip. I would want to discuss it with her."

"Of course you should discuss it with her." Willy was certain he heard her voice falter. "Willy . . . Mr. Hanson . . . I just can't let these crazy bastards, whoever they are, destroy our company. I want to do everything I can to hold it together. You know how morale must be at ConCom. If people just knew that you were around, it would be a great boost."

"I hear you, Angela, but please don't get your hopes up. There is one other way I could possibly help you, though. I have a private investigator who has helped me a lot in the past. I want to sent him east. Tell him everything you know about what has happened and then turn him loose. He's sharp, and knows how to stay out of the hair of local police. Let him take a quick look at things first, and I'll give you an answer in a few days."

"I'll bet his name is Coley Doctor."

"That's right. You really did read my book."

"Of course I did. Every employee of ConCom has read it twice. Please consider my offer. Remember, you name your price."

"I'm more interested in Coley getting his price."

"Put him in touch with me right away."

"Better than that, I'll have him fly out in the morning." Willy hoped Coley would back him up on his commitment.

"That's fine. Let us know his flight number and we'll meet his plane. You have a deal, Mr. Hanson."

"That's between you and Coley," Willy said. "Though I think about six hundred a day would be fair for him."

"That's fine," Angela agreed. "But I think we have a deal too, Mr. Hanson."

"How do you know?"

"Because you haven't said no. That means yes, Mr. Hanson. You'll see."

Willy ambled slowly back to the *Tashtego*. Angela's request had struck a terrible chord in him. It was true that he had officially left the publishing business three years ago. But the drug war he had subsequently become involved in seemed increasingly to be related to the current bloodshed. He knew he could not in good conscience walk away from this trouble.

23

Angela Clayfield still felt ill at ease after hanging up the telephone. Her thoughts had turned to Willy Hanson immediately after the Overstreet killing, and she was disappointed that he wasn't prepared to drop everything and come running to her immediately.

The memory of the taxicab driver moving so swiftly and so unexpectedly to a position where he could fire the bullets into Overstreet at point-blank range would not leave her mind. The strange sound of the silencer-filtered shots echoed over and over within her head. She could not lose the monstrous fear that had paralyzed her into cringing inaction. She had expected to be shot immediately.

But why had the gunman stopped with Overstreet? Why hadn't he killed them both? She owed her life to the whim of that gunman, and didn't know why. Yet he had instilled in her a terror that grew with the sight of each passing stranger.

Angela made a decision to pack Penny and Chucky off to Vermont to stay with her sister, Michelle. They still missed their father terribly, and the presence of the security people and police had created an atmosphere that was far from reassuring.

Angela slept fitfully and rose to pace the house frequently. All the security people in and around the house made her very nervous. After all, they were strangers.

She took a brief walk through the garden at the rear of the house. The gardeners had removed the tall cottonwood that had been hopelessly charred by the explosion of Charles's car. Its absence was a painful reminder of Charles and all that had happened.

She paused and sat on a bench near a pool in the garden. A security man watched from the rear of the house. Her eyes began to fill with tears. Her life was in shambles. What would become of her children? Charles had always found time to spend with them that she was unwilling to allocate. Now that he was gone, it seemed clear that Michelle and Mrs. Lindsay, the housekeeper, would need to take complete care of Penny and Chucky for the foreseeable future.

She walked back toward the house. As she approached, the security man disappeared inside. Angela paused inside the door to scrutinize her image in a mirror. The simple black dress fit her provocatively well. She had been told many times that she had the figure of a twenty-three-year-old, and she knew it was true. She still had that second curve in the hip line so sought after by fashion models. No one would believe her thirty-six years.

She thought back to her days in college. Her MBA with all honors was a product of professorial sexual harassment. It had just come naturally to her. First the casual affair, then a short addictive phase, and then the subtle hint of blackmail. One philosophy professor had told her that her erotic persistence and expertise probably matched that of any of the grand courtesans and trollops of history. She made an A in the course.

Angela realized that her extracurricular shenanigans had only been temporarily sidetracked by her marriage to Charles. Charles Clayfield had been a challenge. He had a strength and magnetism that had held her on the straight and narrow until almost a year after Penny was born. But he traveled too much. There was too much time spent in church work with Pastor Cleveland Owens.

It had all been okay until the Christmas season of 1990. There was much late-night planning for the holiday festivities, and the good pastor began to nibble at her, casually at first. But soon his erotic demands began to take the place of the preparations for the good Lord's birthday.

His wife had actually confided in Angela. "Cleveland has been getting some strange ideas," she said. "He needs a long rest in some rural parish. He needs a small flock which will allow him ample rest. He just gets too wrapped up in the many problems offered by a large congregation."

The pastor applied for and was granted a transfer. Angela offered to come and visit them. The wife agreed with a hug and even tears. "You, of all people, have been Cleveland's friend. You are always welcome in our home!"

Such a fool of a woman, thought Angela. Someday, she might actually take her up on her offer.

She thought again of Overstreet, stone-faced in fear with the gun pointed right at him. What a waste! He had been such a good lover.

What in the hell is wrong with me? she wondered. The more fulfilling her lover, the more insatiable she became. Her psychiatrist had said her problem was not physical. He had told her that it was her drive for power, an urge to dominate everyone around her in both her business and her personal life. Her unique intelligence combined with her physical magnetism made conquests easy. Her complete domination of successive lovers produced a slavish allegiance from the people who worked for her. She was no different from the thousands of men before her who had climbed the corporate ladder by dominating people with a knowledge of their sexual proclivities. She had proven that when the tables were turned, rewards could accrue more quickly to the female than to her male counterparts.

The affair she had had with her psychiatrist, Dr. Brandt, served to verify that the erotic preoccupation that bedeviled her was not to be easily cured. She had dumped him summarily one afternoon after causing him to cancel a full schedule of appointments just to run the gamut of her personal version of the Kama Sutra.

But now her life was indeed in shambles. Charles, Vinnie Lawson, and Brad Overstreet were dead. All had been lovers. It was beyond belief that this was a chance occurrence.

She was left with the super-wimp, Brook Laird, for diversion, and of course that would never do. He was a poor substitute for the others. He was improving, but she was becoming weary of constantly playing teacher.

She turned again to look in the mirror. She now saw clearly the lines below her eyes that others refused to acknowledge. She thought for a moment that she might be crazy. Disaster was plaguing her life and she stood there wondering who her next lover would be.

Ah well, for now Brook Laird would have to do.

There was little likelihood of any more social life until the police came up with the madmen who were making her a prisoner in her own house.

She thought about calling Dr. Brandt. She would apologize for the past. She needed help. It wasn't normal to be breaking into tears as frequently as she was now doing.

Soon Willy Hanson would arrive to pick up the pieces at ConCom. Right now Angela was so depressed she wondered whether or not he would be of any help. She would have to do a lot of convincing as she briefed Coley Doctor.

And, oh yes, Captain Von Braun was to return to New York tomorrow. She realized that he had inadvertently saved her life by insisting that she have breakfast with him that morning. The charming, graying raconteur intrigued her. In spite of all that had happened, she looked forward to seeing him again.

24

Emerald and Von Braun entered the Paragon Club in Wanchai. Melanie hustled them upstairs, through the retracting wall panel to the softly lit Blue Shark Club. She touched her forefinger to her lips, cautioning them to make no noise; then she led them through a beaded curtain into a smoke-laden, dimly lit room. They could hear a great deal of grunting and soft giggling. As their eyes adjusted to the light it became apparent that three nude young women were tangled together in a mass of squirming flesh.

A man's voice called out from the center of all the activity. "Oh, for God's sake! Stop! Stop, I say. I've had quite enough."

His giggling companions were not at all deterred by his protestations.

"Lord Hargraves!" Emerald Lu's voice called out across the room. At once there was total silence.

A tall man struggled to his feet, wobbling on the

floor mattress, hastily pulling up a pair of boxer
shorts with some difficulty.

"Captain Von Braun, I want you to meet Her Majesty's former ambassador."

"Pleased, indeed, Lord Hargraves." The sight of
the nearly naked diplomat towering over his three
passionate attendants did not ruffle Von Braun at
all.

"Emerald . . . you surprise me. You've caught me
with my pants down, so to speak. Delighted to meet
you, Captain. I think we have some business to discuss."

"Mr. Ambassador, please don't feel a bit ill at ease.
Actually I envy you. Such lovely young ladies!" The
captain glanced nervously toward Emerald, who
seemed to be enjoying the discomfort of her guest.

Emerald stepped forward and grasped the waistband of Hargraves's shorts. "Max, our ambassador
has been very busy all afternoon. He starring in major motion picture, as they say in Hollywood."

Hargraves's face fell slack as he looked at Emerald, confused.

Emerald withdrew her hand from his shorts and
turned toward Von Braun. "Yes, Max. We make major motion picture just for Lady Hargraves. She
probably never know husband has so much talent.
He is very good, Max. I know."

"You . . . you're joking, of course." Hargraves
peered into the dimly lit corners of the room, trying
to see whether what she had said could possibly be
true.

"I am not joking. You know me better than that. I
have awful lot of fun but I never make joke. In a few
minutes you will see big show on big TV. Then we
talk."

Von Braun grinned at the disheveled and dis-
traught Hargraves. He too had been a surprise star

in one of Emerald's impromptu movies. But he had laughed when Onyx had suggested bribery. He was a loner in the world, with no wife to worry about. He was a man with a bum heart who didn't care one whit about tomorrow.

"Lord Hargraves," the captain said, "perhaps you would like to watch my tape after we watch yours. Then we could critique each other. I had only two young ladies for costars. You have three. I suppose my performance would not match yours."

"I—I don't know what you people think you are pulling," Hargraves stammered. "I might remind you that a crime against me is a crime against the Crown itself."

Emerald Lu started laughing and Von Braun joined her. One of the women on the mattress clasped her arms around the ambassador's leg and slid one hand under the leg of his shorts.

"Stop it! I'll have no more of this!" Hargraves turned red with anger as the other women joined in teasing him.

"All right, ladies, you may stop now. Our ambassador has had quite enough. I am sure that Lady Hargraves, and the Crown, will be amused by what we already have. Now, sir, maybe you had better put your clothes on. We have some talking to do. We have to talk about your yacht. That thing in your trousers has now made it my yacht!"

Hargraves shoved roughly at one of the persistent entertainers, who had been trailing kisses from his feet to a point midway on his inner thigh. She responded with a hiss very much like a cat's and dug at his leg with her ample fingernails, leaving a vivid streak of red as she fell back to the floor.

Emerald stepped forward quickly to slash out at Hargraves's face with a single open-handed blow. He now had a bleeding gash on his cheek to match the tear on his leg.

"Violetta, come here!" Emerald ordered. The young woman who had been pawed roughly by the ambassador rose and went to Emerald's side.

"Mr. Big Ambassador, you are a fool. If you dare treat my girls with any more brutality, you will learn the real meaning of pain. Now tell Violetta that you are sorry, and kiss her tenderly. Hurry, so that we can complete our conversation about our yacht."

Hargraves fidgeted and then leaned over to brush the young woman's lips with a quick kiss. "Violetta, I am sorry, but your scratching took me by surprise."

The young woman grinned and then looked questioningly at Emerald Lu.

"That wasn't much of a kiss, was it, Violetta? He was doing much better when we walked in and you had your legs wrapped around his noble head."

Violetta grinned and then backed away. She left the room with the other two women.

Emerald steered the two men to a dimly lit corner of the rectangular bar that served the scantily clad patrons of the Blue Shark Club. Von Braun and Emerald were the only ones fully clothed. The ambassador was still in his shorts, trying his best to salvage his dignity. His eyelids flickered nervously, anticipating what was to come.

Emerald raised her arm and swung it in a circular motion. Almost at once a huge screen on the opposite wall came to life with the X-rated gyrations of the diplomat and his three playmates. The other patrons of the sex club paused to watch.

Von Braun stared at the tableau for a couple of minutes and then leaned toward the ambassador. "Hargraves, shame on you. I'll bet Lady Hargraves has no idea how good you really can be in the sack.

This little flick will delight her! She will probably wish she could jump right into the picture."

The diplomat began to pale. Shaking, he reached for the tumbler of scotch on the bar and accidentally sent it rolling on its side. He looked pleadingly toward Emerald Lu. "Where are my clothes?"

Von Braun began chuckling aloud. "The former British ambassador has lost his clothes. That may be a first here in Hong Kong. But come to think of it, it probably isn't. Incidentally, what nation were you ambassador to? Perhaps your friends there would enjoy a print of this tape."

Emerald was staring at the action on the screen. "Lord Hargraves, someday, when you are thoroughly rested, I will take you home with me. But for now, you must tell me, where is the *Lantau Star*?"

Hargraves gulped. The *Lantau Star* was a small sleek ocean-going yacht, the property of his family. "It is not in Hong Kong. It is probably in Hawaii by now. Lady Hargraves had it taken there to await our holiday. I'm supposed to fly and meet her in a couple of days."

"Aha! How wonderful that it is in Hawaii. Perfect for my purposes. You are leasing the *Lantau Star* to Max. All for nothing. You can tell Lady Hargraves that your government requested it for a secret project. It will be returned to you within six months."

As she spoke, Emerald let her hand fall into the diplomat's lap, quickly and firmly wrapping her fingers around his testicles. He winced with pain, not daring to move for fear of something worse. Von Braun chuckled dementedly.

"Lord Hargraves, within an hour, a messenger will deliver a lease form for the *Lantau Star*. You will sign it. And then you will get your clothes."

The ambassador exploded. "This is insane! You expect me to agree to this?"

Emerald relaxed her grip and began to massage him. "Melanie," she called out. "Bring Lord Hargraves his clothes. But before you do that, send his wonderful tape out for copies, at least a thousand copies. I want one them sent to every member of Parliament in London, as well as to all the porn merchants here in Hong Kong."

Hargraves gave a nervous laugh. "You wouldn't dare do that. Do you forget who I am?"

"You are a fool. That's who you are." This time it was Von Braun who spoke. "We are the ones with the dirty pictures. You are the one sitting in his shorts. I say it again, Hargraves. You are a fool. You will be ruined forever if you refuse to sign this lease. Take it from me. Take it from this decadent old aviator. I have seen a lot of men under stress. Think about your life and all your friends back in London. You will either cooperate with us or you will probably go back to your hotel room and blow your own brains out." Once again Von Braun punctuated his remarks with a deep maniacal laugh.

Hargraves remained silent for several seconds, noticing that the damning videotape was being replayed.

"Okay, you win. You have the *Lantau Star*. Now please give me the tape."

"Lord Hargraves." Emerald watched his face as she slowly continued her massage. "You will get the tape back at the conclusion of the lease. Do not fear, it will be secured in a safe place."

"Oh for God's sake!" Hargraves stared again at the video screen, realizing fully now that he was at their mercy. "Okay! You've got a deal."

"Good, Lord Hargraves! I knew you were a reasonable man." Emerald moved her body even closer to the diplomat. "Our deal should be celebrated. Relax and enjoy yourself. I will think of something special."

Von Braun saw Melanie nearby and motioned for her to join him. His large deep laugh filled the room again as his arms encircled the girl. It would be healthy, he decided, for him also to do some celebrating!

25

Brook Laird stood at the door that connected to Angela Clayfield's bedroom. He turned the knob slowly, tenatively, almost hoping to find it locked. He had agreed to come to the Clayfield home in Saddle Hills, where Angela said she was setting up a command post for ConCom. She would operate the company from there until security in the Manhattan offices could be guaranteed.

He felt tense, wondering why he was hesitating to turn the knob to Angela's adjoining bedroom. He glanced at his watch, the only thing he was wearing besides a pair of silk boxer shorts. It was a full fifteen minutes before the time she had specified for him to come in and join her for some "high-quality relaxation."

Fifteen more minutes to enjoy, he reasoned. He had heard sounds from the room, and decided to surprise her.

He swung the door open and took a step into the

large bedroom. His heart jumped as he stared straight ahead at a small desk beyond the ornate canopy bed. A large, dark, frowning man sat there, a nine-millimeter piece protruding from a shoulder holster under his left arm. He stared silently at the minimally dressed Laird, a scowl dominating his face.

"Hello . . . I . . . I'm Brook Laird. I . . . I'm looking for Angela Clayfield. We have a few business matters to go over." Laird could see that the man's eyes were now focused on his shorts.

Still frowning, the man spoke. "I'm Grundy. Commercial Security Systems. Mrs. Clayfield will be along in just a few minutes. I'm just checking out the room." He turned toward the window and waved his hand. "About fifty yards over there is a window in the house next door. I'm going to recommend that the blind to this window right here remain closed."

Glancing again at Laird's shorts, he added, "That would be advisable in any case."

Laird caught the hint of a smile crossing Grundy's face. "I'll come back later when Mrs. Clayfield is in. I am glad to see that you guys are checking the place out."

"We have learned, Mr. Laird, that you can never be too careful. The people who are terrorizing Mrs. Clayfield are extremely resourceful and dangerous."

The man called Grundy rose and strode toward the bedroom door to the hall. "I'll be going back downstairs now." Just as he was about to step into the hallway, he turned again to look at Laird. With his peculiar scowl, he again contemplated Laird's shorts.

"Mr. Laird, I intend to keep our little meeting to ourselves. I don't think it would serve any purpose to bring my colleagues in on it."

"Thank you, Mr. Grundy. I appreciate that."

Grundy closed the door behind him.

Laird looked down at his flimsy shorts, feeling like an idiot. He wondered whether the man would, indeed, keep his conclusions to himself. He decided to retreat to his own room, put on a robe and wait until he heard Angela enter her bedroom. Next time he would knock.

26

Willy Hanson and Coley Doctor arrived at Newark Airport and took a cab directly to the ConCom Building in New York.

Willy had anticipated that they might have trouble getting into the building, but relaxed when he recognized Kevin, the chief security guard, standing inside the door.

"Sir, you are a sight for these sore old eyes!" Kevin greeted Willy with a handshake. "Welcome back. Mrs. Clayfield said I could expect you." As Willy grasped Kevin's hand, the guard turned to address Coley.

"You must be Coley Doctor. I've read all about you in the book. I want you gentlemen to autograph my copy."

"That would be a pleasure, Kevin. We'll pick up a copy upstairs for you. By the way, is Mrs. Clayfield in today?"

Kevin furrowed his brow. "Mr. Hanson, I ain't supposed to answer questions like that. When you get up to the fourteenth floor, maybe you better talk to Katie Glover. She's been expecting you. She'll bring you up to snuff."

"Good old Katie! She still thinks she runs the place, I guess."

Kevin grinned. "Maybe she does, Mr. Hanson. There ain't many of them left around here."

On the fourteenth floor they were met by another security guard, who had been alerted to their arrival. He escorted them around a barricade and unlocked the glass doors to the reception area. The guard quickly returned to a small table that had been placed near the bank of elevators.

"Willy!" Katie fairly screamed as she emerged from her office to greet him. "I hear you've come back to run the place. And you must be Coley Doctor. You're even taller and more handsome than Willy describes in his book. Hell, Willy could never write worth a lick anyway." Kate smiled broadly at Coley.

"Ms. Glover, I sometimes think that Willy's greatest talent is getting his friends into trouble. I'm here to keep him from doing that."

"Maybe I can help too, Mr. Doctor. Let's go back into my office where we can talk for a while."

"Call me Coley. Nobody calls me Mr. Doctor, except Peaches, my first wife. She calls me Mr. Doctor and I call her my first mistake."

Katie and Willy joined in a chuckle as Katie closed the door behind them and they seated themselves in her small office. Eyeing the ashtray and cigarettes on Katie's desk, Coley spoke first.

"Mind if I smoke?" he asked, extracting a miniature cigar from his jacket pocket.

"I just love a cigar. I'll join you if you have another" was her unexpected answer.

"Katie, I don't mind if you humor this guy a little,

but how about cracking the window a little, so I don't asphyxiate?"

Suddenly Katie became serious. She began to talk in a quiet confidential tone as if she thought someone outside the room might be listening. She leaned forward. "Willy Hanson, if you have the sense I think you do, you will turn around real quick and get straight back to California, and take your handsome friend with you. There is no point in allowing Angela Clayfield to drag any more of my friends into this mess."

She turned to face Coley directly. "Your friend and I go back a long way. Despite the fact that he can be a bastard once in a while, Willy here is the salt of the earth, and that Clayfield bitch will bury him." Katie paused to let her remark sink in.

Coley adjusted himself in the chair, allowing his jacket to fall back just enough to reveal the butt of his nine-millimeter jutting out from under his shoulder. "Ms. Glover, there are a lot of people getting killed. Somebody's got to put a stop to it." He paused to lean over the desk and light the small cigar he had given Katie, and then lit his own.

Willy watched the ritual with the cigars, glad to see that the two liked each other.

"Katie, the last time I saw you, before Charles Clayfield's funeral, we talked a lot about Angela's fast-lane lifestyle. Caron Lawson has reason to feel the same way. I've brought Coley up to date. Angela has certainly given a lot of women good reason to hate her. Is there anything concrete you can add to what you've already told me?"

"You bet! She's taken up with Brook Laird now, of all people! He's just about the wimpiest man alive and she's named him editor-in-chief. I just can't imagine the whole affair. The woman is positively sick. He was up in Rye with her the day the boat blew up. They both arrived after the blast."

Coley recalled the story he had read in the L.A. paper. "Did anyone ever say why they were late that day?"

"Oh, sure. Angela had a last-minute breakfast appointment with an author. I don't know why Brook got there late, unless Angela told him about breakfast. She probably just rolled over in bed and told him."

"Katie, do you remember who the author was that Angela had breakfast with?" Willy asked.

"Of course. It was Captain Max Von Braun. Sort of a Gregory Peck or a William Holden type, a dreamboat but much too old for that Clayfield snip."

"Katie, it sounds like you're pissed off that the old fellow had breakfast with Angela instead of you," Willy needled her. "You say he's an author. What did he write?"

"Well he's more of a collector than an author. Laird brought him in one day with the damnedest map collection you ever saw. I guess it's priceless. Each map is signed and annotated by different famous people from way back. I mean like Captain Cook, Magellan, John Cabot. I saw one with elaborate drawings on it done by Lewis and Clark. Laird suggested doing a fancy coffee-table book. Angela saw the promotional possibilities and turned the captain over to me to do a bio. So you see, I did have my time in the batter's box with the charming old goat!"

Willy stood up to stroll around the office, pausing to read the captions on some of the publicity shots mounted on the wall. "You say he's an airline captain. Who does he fly for?"

"Some outfit called Trans-Asiatic. They fly mostly in the Far East, but they do have a few flights to the United States."

Willy glanced at Coley, who was in the midst of expelling a long drag on the tiny cigar, staring at Katie as he did so. He turned his head slightly, and his eyes met Willy's. Coley spoke first.

"Katie, you say you did a bio on the captain. Where does he live?"

"Oh, he's quite an interesting man. He lives in Hong Kong."

Willy's heart skipped a beat. It was as if an evil hand had reached out and touched him from ten thousand miles away.

"Did he give you an address?"

"Oh, sure. Brook Laird bought his book, so we needed his address for the computer." Katie tapped on the keys of her small computer. "Here it is. He has asked us to forward all mail to the Peninsula Hotel in Kowloon, Hong Kong."

"That's all? A hotel?" Coley obviously wanted more.

Willy broke into the conversation. "The Peninsula is an elegant old hotel in Kowloon. This Von Braun must have megabucks if he makes the Peninsula Hotel his home."

Katie continued to read from the computer screen. "Von Braun said that he is well known at the Peninsula and that they would hold his mail for him when he's not there. He says he has a remote villa on a small island south of Hong Kong, but he spends more time at the Peninsula between flights than he does at the villa."

"What is the name of the small island?" Coley asked.

"I don't know about the spelling, but it sounded like Ching Chow. That's what I wrote down."

A prickly sensation raced down the back of Willy's neck. Ching Chow had to be Cheung Chau. And

Cheung Chau was the address Onyx Lu had given the court years ago in San Francisco.

Coley rose to walk over to where Willy was staring blankly at the promo photos on the wall. "What do you think, pal?"

"I think we have a real war on our hands."

"Could it be a coincidence? Everyone has to live someplace, you know."

"Coley, in view of everything we know, all circumstantial, we have to assume that this is a breakthrough."

"Hey, you guys look as if you'd seen a ghost." Katie was exiting from the computer file. "Come on, what we all need is a drink. They're having a barbecue rib special today at Lofland's. I'll pop!"

"Have to take a rain check, Katie. We have a date with Her Highness over in Saddle Hills."

"Ms. Glover, how many people have access to that information you just gave us?" Coley asked, blowing another billow of smoke toward the ceiling.

"Oh, anybody could get this data. However, I only put it in there a couple of days ago, and with all the excitement around here I'd be surprised if anyone has looked at it."

Willy leaned across the desk and grasped both of Katie's hands. "Katie, Coley and I need a printout of everything you have on Von Braun. Then, while we're still here, I want you to work over Von Braun's file in the computer. Leave the Peninsula Hotel as his only address and delete all the other stuff about Cheung Chau. Can you do that?"

"Of course I can. What's with Von Braun?"

"We aren't certain, Katie. But he could be a key bastard in this whole mess."

Katie left the office and returned a few moments later with a desk calendar in her hand. "If Von Braun is up to no good, maybe someone should roust

Brook Laird out of Angela's sack and tell him. Laird
has an appointment with him in two days that will
probably be in Saddle Hills."

"Thanks, Katie. Please do me a favor and don't tell
anyone else about Von Braun. By the way, where
does he stay when he's in New York?"

"At the Waldorf."

Coley whistled. "Big money, even for an airline pilot."

Willy nodded and spoke to Katie again. "Did the
police ask for any of this information?"

"Nope. As far as I know they hadn't checked him
at all."

Coley mulled this over for a moment. "Of course,
they didn't know the right questions to ask."

For the first time Katie seemed frightened. "Are
you guys going to the police with this information?
Let me know if you are and I'll take a nice long vacation."

"Katie, don't worry. The police don't value circumstantial evidence from rank amateurs like us. Just
let us know if they start asking questions." Willy
checked his watch. "Coley, maybe we've got time for
those barbecue ribs after all. Now that we've rattled
Katie's nerves, the least we can do is keep her company for a while and let her pay for our lunch."

Coley nodded. "I was going to stay here with Katie
all along."

Katie was beaming. "Hey, just like old times, huh,
Willy?" Then she looked down the long hall along the
executive floor. "Except that some of my favorite big
wheels are six feet under."

27

Captain Max Von Braun left his station on the flight deck and made his way through the darkened cabin to the stairwell that led to the Business Class section in the old 747. It was well after midnight. Trans-Asiatic Flight 11 was about an hour out of Amsterdam bound for Kennedy Airport.

Von Braun quickly spotted Jocelyn, standing provocatively in her familiar nonregulation short skirt. She was chatting with a passenger in the forward part of the cabin. He walked forward and brushed by her, then sauntered back down the aisle. He glanced back and saw that Jocelyn had finished her conversation and was now starting up the stairwell. After a moment, Von Braun walked back through the Economy cabin and quickly ascended the stairs. Midway he stopped and clutched the handrail as the familiar dull ache returned to his left shoulder. He noted his shortness of breath as the numb feeling proceeded down the length of his arm. Then came the prickly feeling in his fingertips as he stood like a statue, trying not to move a muscle. Slowly he moved his right hand to his shirt pocket to grasp the small amber vial. Resting a moment, he twisted the cap from the vial and dropped two of the tiny white tablets of nitroglycerin into his hand and poked them under his tongue. He remained stationary for another couple of minutes, then finally breathed deeply and easily as the medication took effect.

Feeling more comfortable now, except for a dull headache that was the usual aftereffect of such an episode, he made his way to one of the lavatories a few steps away. Casting a quick glance around him, he tapped lightly on the door. The latch clicked and the panel opened a crack to reveal the statuesque Jocelyn, his playmate on many trips across the darkened sky.

"I thought you were never coming," the tall blonde said as she pulled him into the room and flipped the latch on the door. He embraced her eagerly, glad that the cramped confines of the room limited his exertions. Jocelyn's energy was feverish and he felt himself drifting into her consuming passion. Soon he slumped to sit on the closed commode as Jocelyn, facing the door, lowered herself carefully into his lap. On and on she ground herself against him until both slumped in blissful exhaustion.

"Jocelyn, that was wonderful." Von Braun was thinking of his angina and the enormous risk he had just taken.

"Oh, Captain! Someday we'll have to try this at sea level. Where do you stay in New York?"

"It's no use, dear. I have business there and will be going on to Hong Kong tomorrow." The captain flipped the latch to peek outside, paused briefly to kiss his amorous partner, then abruptly left the lavatory.

Back on the flight deck, the mild headache again reminded him of the problem on the stairwell. The pins and needles in his fingertips told him it was still not settled. He nevertheless insisted on taking over the controls from his copilot. Tommy Wing was a young Chinese pilot recruited by Trans-Asiatic in Singapore. He had learned to fly with the Peoples' Republic Air Force. Rumor had it that he was well connected on the mainland. He had been given a sweet appointment to a trade mission to Singapore, and then he applied to Trans-Asiatic. Mysteriously, the Peoples' Republic never made an issue of this, and Wing was still free to move in and out of China without restriction.

"Captain, you look tired. I would be pleased to stand watch into Kennedy." Wing studied Von Braun closely. He looked pale and washed out. Von Braun was certainly not his robust self.

"Nonsense, Tommy! If anything, I am too well rested. I need to get back to my running regimen. I'd like to avoid these short hops to Amsterdam. My life was well adjusted to the Hong Kong–San Francisco run for several months."

Wing continued to eye the old pilot closely. "Just asking, Captain. You say you are relaxed. I thought you looked tired. You must know which it is." The two gazed into the clear, starry night. The developing glow in the sky to the north would be Newfoundland. Both fixed their eyes on it for a moment and then instinctively checked their bearing. Wing gave a quick thumbs-up to the captain and rose from the copilot's seat to stretch.

Leaving the flight deck for a few moments, Wing paused at the galley, where Jocelyn was fussing with the coffee.

"Hello, my beauty," he murmured, making certain that no one overheard him. He moved closer to her, letting his hand drop to rest lightly on the curve of her hip.

"I think Tommy Wing had better be careful where he puts his hands. He could easily start a fire aboard this aircraft."

Wing grinned at the remark and removed his hands.

"Jocelyn, have you taken a close look at Von Braun this trip? He looks very tired. In the light of the cockpit he looked absolutely ashen. I think our hero needs a vacation."

Jocelyn turned to address Wing, studying him closely. "Why tell me about it? Talk to the captain. I think he might listen to you. He likes you, you know."

"I did talk to him, but he insists he's okay."

"In that case, I would believe him."

"Thank you for the coffee, my beauty." Wing smiled at Jocelyn and lightly brushed his free hand along the curve that so enticed him as he passed her to return to the flight deck.

"Here, Captain. Coffee, from Jocelyn. She just made it. Perhaps it will pep you up."

Von Braun said nothing but took the cup in his hand and began to sip from it. They both watched silently as they approached the glow far ahead of them that would be metropolitan New York.

Von Braun straightened up in the cockpit, responding to a twinge somewhere within his left shoulder. He froze, trying to pinpoint the location. Actually it seemed lower, more toward the middle of his chest. He toyed with the idea of turning the landing over to Wing.

Nonsense! he thought. He had landed the big 747's a thousand times. The excitement stirred by this routine procedure would certainly be something he could endure without incident. Still, he felt ill at ease.

As he stared ahead into the night sky toward New York, his thoughts turned to Pelly Kahn. That bastard had betrayed him to Angela. Von Braun actually welcomed Angela's instructions to stop dealing with Kahn in person. Of course, it would create a few problems. They would have to arrange a drop point for money. That would be done in the morning during his last face-to-face visit. Maybe that was what was making him nervous now and causing the pain in his chest. Pelly Kahn was intelligent, unscrupulous and a karate expert. Von Braun decided he would take a weapon along to their meeting.

Trans-Asiatic Flight 11 was now well along on its approach into Kennedy. They had dropped below 10,000 feet and the Long Island shoreline sparkled with lights in the clear air. Von Braun persisted in his decision to make the final approach and landing.

The flaps were now fully extended as the massive jet lumbered across the sandy beaches now only a few hundred feet below. Momentarily Von Braun tried to reach inside his left shirt pocket for the amber vial. It wasn't there. He must have jammed it into his trouser pocket in his haste to meet Jocelyn. The pain and numbness in his arm began to dominate his thoughts as the jet raced over the beaches far short of the well-lit runway ahead. A quick burst from the throttle goosed the giant craft to the runway, where it slammed down with a jolt that brought screams from the passengers.

Copilot Wing stared at his captain, whose face was twisted into an almost maniacal grin. Both were silent as the jet slowed rapidly in its course down the runway. They were evidently okay. Miraculously, the 747 had survived the rough landing.

Von Braun, white-knuckled at the controls, began to breathe more easily.

Wing spoke first. "Captain, that was hardly one of the patented Max Von Braun gentle landings. However, now you have proven that you are human, just like the rest of us." Then he gave Von Braun a forced smile and an A-OK salute with his thumb and forefinger.

"All's well that ends well, Tommy. I'm sorry I gave you a little spasm there. Actually we made it with a few feet to spare!" Von Braun now actually felt pleased with himself. "These things are marvelous pieces of machinery, you know. One learns to respect them more every day."

Wing merely nodded. He continued to watch Von Braun closely whenever he could sneak a glance. It was the captain's eyes that disturbed him. He seemed to have trouble staying awake, even after all that had happened. The copilot decided he would have to have a conversation with him on land somewhere, when they were both well rested.

Von Braun sat quietly until the jet was empty before deplaning. He passed through customs after the others, and went directly to a cabstand, where he asked to be taken to the Waldorf.

The long ride into the city was relaxing in the light predawn traffic. Still, he was unable to doze. He thought about tomorrow's meeting with Brook Laird in New Jersey. Then he thought about Hawaii, and the *Lantau Star*, the luxury yacht now leased in his name. His mind raced on. Willy Hanson, Ginny Du Bois and the *Lantau Star* all ran together in his thoughts. And then there was Onyx Lu, a madwoman, obsessed with killing. When would it stop? No wonder he had trouble resting!

28

"Where is the map?" Pelly Kahn asked the question of the slender Hunan native in a barely audible voice. As usual his desk was clear of all papers. His hands were folded, giving him an almost priestly appearance.

The man looked at him in fear and then turned his eyes toward the floor without saying a word.

"Where is the map?" This time Kahn raised his voice, separated his clasped fingers and slammed his two fists on the desk for emphasis.

Steve Lo winced and looked up, his eyes pleading. "I tore it up. I destroyed the map. I no longer saw any use for it."

Once again the menacing Pelly Kahn folded his hands on the desk. In a voice that did not totally conceal his rage, his piercing eyes scathing the terrified Lo, he proceeded. "It would be so wonderfully comforting if true. You are a liar!"

Kahn screamed, both fists crashing down again.

"The map is in the hands of Brook Laird. You left it conveniently in his doorway. Why, liar, did you do that?"

Lo sighed heavily, then whimpered, "No reason. I just lost it, that's all. I just lost it. Once I had located the apartment, I wanted to get out of the neighborhood quickly. I must have dropped it. I am sorry. Does it really matter?"

"Matter? I'll tell you how much it matters, liar. This matters so much to me that it has bought you your passage back to Hunan. You have managed to bungle the simplest of assignments. You may leave now."

"Leave? I was expecting money."

"There is no money for liars or bunglers. And you are both." Kahn opened the drawer in front of him, withdrew a nine-millimeter Ruger and placed it on the desk. "We will be in touch when the arrangements have been made for your return to Hunan. As I said before, you may now leave."

Lo stood and backed nervously toward the door. He turned, opened the door and bounded down the flight of steps to the street. For the moment he was free. He walked swiftly for several blocks until he got to Bowery and then turned north.

Looking behind him and seeing no one, he turned down a street packed with lunch-hour pedestrians and mingled with the crowd. Lo was not a fool. He knew they wouldn't go to the trouble and expense of sending him back to Hunan. People who failed assignments just disappeared. No one ever saw them again. He turned to look back into the crowds behind him and then started to tremble. He imagined that everyone was looking at him.

At that point, Lo made a decision. He would seek help from Brook Laird. He really didn't know much about what was going on, but Laird would be grate-

ful to know that someone was trying to kill him. Lo
pointed himself west on Ninth Street. He knew just
where the apartment was. He would wait for Brook
Laird there.

The iron gate to the small patio in front of Laird's
apartment was locked this time. The doorbell within
the patio was out of reach. Lo looked at his watch. It
was not yet six o'clock. If Laird worked late, he
might not be home for many hours. He decided to
walk the streets or see a movie and return later.

Backing away from the patio gate, he bumped unexpectedly into someone standing behind him in the
gathering darkness.

"Tell me, liar, do you want the key to the lock?" Lo
turned abruptly to stare into the eyes of the squat
Pelly Kahn.

"Why did you follow me here?" Lo's voice was nervous, high-pitched. He was sweating, fully aware
that Kahn would follow him for only one reason.

"After you left my office, I said to myself, I bet
that lying sneak Steve Lo will run to Brook Laird
and try to save his skin. But Steve Lo will have to
wait in Brook Laird's doorway for many days. Brook
Laird is not living there now." Kahn pressed himself
against Lo, forcing him back against the iron gate.
Lo could feel the hard steel of the Ruger that was
pointing into his abdomen.

"Here, take the key." Kahn pressed the key into
Lo's hand and prodded his belly with the weapon.
"Now, unlock the gate."

Lo bent over to fit the key in the small lock, and
let the chain fall loose to the sidewalk. Kahn pushed
him inside the gate to the small patio, now shrouded
in the evening darkness.

Kahn quickly glanced up and down the street outside the gate. "Now, liar. I am going to give you one
more assignment. I want you to stay right here in

this patio until Brook Laird returns, no matter how many days it will take. How do you like that assignment?"

"Oh, I like it. I will do it," Lo gushed nervously, fearful of Kahn's kindness.

Kahn again glanced up and down the street. "Now, turn around and face the door. Are you carrying a weapon?"

"No."

"I'm afraid I must check. Stand very still while I frisk you."

Kahn delivered a vicious karate chop that severed the slender Lo's spine at the base of his skull. "Now, fool, you can wait forever for your new friend, Brook Laird."

After emptying Lo's pockets, Kahn pushed the body into the darkest area of the patio. In all likelihood it would not be discovered until morning.

He then bounded up the stairs to the street and closed the iron gate behind him. By the time he had walked to Bleecker Street, he felt quite good about this accomplishment and broke into a rare smile. A dangerous loose end had been eliminated. His victim was a faceless, nameless person without friends or identity, except back in Hunan on the other side of the world.

29

Grundy eyed the visitor closely. His tall, athletic frame stretched nearly to the top of the doorway. He was well dressed, his camel's hair jacket bulging suspiciously under his left shoulder.

"You must be Coley Doctor."

"You got that right. Your boys at the gate were pretty thorough. You would think they would have told you the black guy was Coley Doctor. By the way, this white guy here is Willy Hanson."

Grundy forced an uncomfortable smile. This was getting to be a house full of real characters. The woman of the house was a nympho, now upstairs with a house guest who ran around in silk shorts. Now here was this smart-ass giant. He wondered what Willy Hanson's angle would be.

Willy stuck out his hand to shake Grundy's. "We're here to see Angela Clayfield. I guess we're a few minutes early."

Grundy shook Willy's hand while frowning at

Coley Doctor, who was giving the room a careful once-over. "I'm Grundy, I run the security operation here for Mrs. Clayfield. I'll tell her you're here. She's expecting you, though I'm afraid she didn't say anything about your friend."

"Don't worry about Coley here. He goes everywhere I go. Just tell that to Mrs. Clayfield."

Grundy walked across the room and spoke quietly into a small intercom. Angela Clayfield's voice answered and suggested that the two guests be served coffee, since it would be fifteen or twenty minutes before she was ready to meet them. She sounded sleepy.

"I'll have some coffee brought in from the kitchen," Grundy said.

"That'll be fine. Coley here takes three lumps of sugar. I take mine straight."

Grundy was about to call the kitchen when a car screeched to a stop in the driveway. Two doors slammed and a moment later two policemen burst into the room. One of them started to speak to Grundy, but noticed Willy and Coley, then grabbed Grundy by the arm and led him outside to the driveway.

When Grundy reentered the room he walked straight to the intercom and connected with Angela. "They found another body. Looks like an Asian. No identification. He was found with a broken neck, locked in Brook Laird's patio."

"Oh my God!" Angela's exclamation rang through the intercom. Grundy lowered his voice and spoke privately with her before hanging up and turning to face Willy and Coley.

"Any suspects?" Willy asked Grundy.

"Not a one. We don't even have an identification. Hell, a lot goes on in the Village. This thing may not have anything to do with our problems."

"I bet it does," offered Coley. "From what I can see there are bodies all over the place. You can bet your ass there is a connection."

"But this man was not a ConCom employee like the others."

Angela Clayfield entered the room and nervously grasped the extended hand of Willy Hanson. Her long blond hair hung loosely around her shoulders. She wore a yellow jumpsuit that covered everything but was tight enough to prove she was well-toned underneath. Willy noticed Coley rubbing his chin, eyeing her.

"Willy, you've heard the latest? My God, this is terrifying."

Willy put his arm around Angela's shoulders and felt her lean into him. "Hold yourself together, Angela. We'll get to the bottom of this."

"I know, but how many more . . ." Her voice trailed off and she stepped away as Brook Laird entered the room.

Laird looked as if he was fresh from a shower. His hair was slicked back, and he reeked of men's cologne. Willy couldn't help glancing at Angela. The same aroma had come from her when they were close a moment ago.

"Angela, this is Coley Doctor." Angela extended her hand. "I would like for your security people to bring Coley up to date on everything that has happened. Perhaps Mr. Grundy can talk to Coley while you tell me what it is you expect from me."

"Of course, Willy. Let's go into my office. Grundy and Coley can talk here." Angela led Willy into the large den, which had been converted into an office. It was complete with computers, fax machines, telephones and a printer. A pair of lavender panties hung over a light cord plugged in by a window. Angela broke into a smile as she noticed Willy's eyes briefly come to rest on the light cord. She said nothing.

"Angela, I feel a little like a fish out of water here. It's been a long time since I've had anything to do with the company. Frankly, I don't know whether I am even qualified at this stage of the game. What is it that you would have me do?"

"I want you to take Brad Overstreet's job. I want you to be the hands-on person until this mess is over with. You've done it all before. Things don't really change that much, though in a big way they have changed completely. Right now ConCom is falling apart. The employees are panicked. On many days half of them do not come in. Now, with this business in front of Laird's apartment, more people will be scared away."

"You can hardly blame them."

"I know. But you could rally them through this crisis."

"Angela, maybe you don't know. I left ConCom because I hated being here. It was a conscious decision on my part. I wouldn't get back into this rat race for anything. The only reason I came back was because I thought maybe I could help find out who is responsible for the terrorism. Charles was a friend. Vinnie Lawson was a friend. A number of people who still work there are friends. Coley and I want to help get to the bottom of this."

"Charles would really appreciate your coming back to help, Willy. Don't you think that part of your helping should be to hold ConCom together until we solve the terrorism problem?"

"I'll make a deal with you, Angela. I'll serve as CEO for ninety days, without compensation. I'll take care of some of the important day-to-day business. But I must also be totally involved in the investigation." Willy tried to penetrate the stare of Angela's violet eyes to see how she was taking his request.

"You can write your own ticket, Willy." Angela walked over to where he was sitting on the edge of the desk and grasped his hands. She shook her head. "This whole thing is driving me crazy, Willy. Whatever you want you've got."

She moved closer. Again he noticed a faint trace of Laird's cologne in her hair.

"I want Coley Doctor to be the key inside investigator," Willy said. "Coley will work with the police and he will oversee Grundy and your security unit. He will also stick to you like glue. We are not going to let anyone else be killed if we can help it. For the ninety days, if it takes ninety days, I will work for nothing, but Coley Doctor's fee will be a thousand dollars a day. He's worth twice that much."

Angela looked into Willy's eyes. "You've got a deal, Willy. If he is worth it, pay him twice that much. You're the boss for ninety days." She moved closer and sealed the deal with a kiss full on his lips. Willy received the kiss, immobile.

"I think you'd better tell Grundy out there about the new pecking order. I'm not sure he's going to like it. He and Coley have been measuring each other like a pair of wounded grizzlies."

"No problem." She stepped back. "We can get started on an important piece of business this afternoon. I'm expecting a visitor. I asked him to join me in Saddle Hills rather than go into New York. He's a charming old airline pilot who is doing a map and chart book the likes of which no one has ever seen. It will be an outrageous coffee-table book that we are giving a big institutional play."

"That's hardly ConCom's cup of tea, at least the ConCom that I remember."

"Oh, this one is. I think you'll agree once you've

met Captain Max Von Braun and have seen what a collection he has."

"Angela, I wouldn't miss him for anything. Who found him?"

"Brook Laird stumbled upon him. It was an amazing piece of luck."

Maybe it wasn't luck, Willy thought. And he wasn't ready to share his information on Von Braun with anybody. "Angela, I'd like your people to search him thoroughly before they let him enter this house. You and I will talk with him in the living room. I'd rather not have him or any other outsider see the layout of your house."

"Why on earth . . . ?"

"Angela, remember. I'm the boss for ninety days. Sealed with a kiss."

30

"I still don't understand how you could agree to such a thing. And I really don't understand why in heaven does everything have to happen so fast." Lady Hargraves was pacing the floor, stopping once in a while to stare at Diamond Head, only a mile or so from their exclusive beach club on Waikiki.

"My dear Margaret, I realized that you never really feel comfortable aboard the *Lantau Star*, especially during this season when one storm seems to follow another in the South Pacific. This will give you the opportunity to remain here in Hawaii and enjoy the bridge tournaments. I'll fly back from San Francisco and we'll stay here through the holidays. We'll simply have a ball. They will be using the yacht for three months or so and then it will be ours again."

"Who precisely are 'they'?" Lady Hargraves looked skeptical.

"The government of Hong Kong wants to use it in

a special project with a Chinese trade commission
making a special effort to attract wealthy American
business leaders to Hong Kong. I suppose they are
preparing for 1997. Actually, it will be a feather in
our cap if we come to their aid. We will need friends
in high places on both sides of the ocean once they
lower the flag."

Margaret Hargraves looked sternly at her husband. Secretly she was glad. The *Lantau Star* was a
monumental expense and it would be delightful to
have it taken off their hands for a while. But she
was determined to make it seem to her husband that
she was greatly disappointed.

"You must know that I have made elaborate plans
to entertain many of our dearest friends aboard the
Star over the next few weeks. What do I tell them?"

"Simply tell them it is a great privilege for us to
accommodate the Hong Kong government in their
cooperation with China. We want to do everything
we can to see that the transition in 1997 goes well."
Lord Hargraves felt pleased with himself. He could
see that Lady Hargraves was buying his clearly
stated logic.

"John, I suppose you are right." She approached
him with a tear or two in the corner of her eye. "You
always are so right in business matters, John."

Hargraves clasped his arms around her shoulders.
His mind drifted from their conversation now that she
had given in to his proposition. His thoughts returned
to Emerald Lu and the orgy at the Paragon Club back
in Wanchai. He had thought seriously about killing
himself after seeing the tape. Thankfully, everything
seemed to be working out.

"You know, my dear, I don't like to bother with financial matters. But the *Star* costs us a bloody fortune to maintain. It will actually be nice for someone
else to pick up the tab on her for a few months, and

pay us for the privilege. It is not quite like it used to be, you know, being on pension and all."

Margaret Hargraves pulled away from him and returned to the window overlooking Diamond Head. She didn't like it when he mentioned money. When the crises had come in their lives, she had always been the one to come up with the money. The wealth left to her by her father was considerable and they had dipped into it frequently, even when John had been an ambassador.

"You know best, John. When will you be leaving?"

"We are sailing tomorrow. The new crew has been familiarizing themselves with the *Star* the past two days. They seem quite professional. There is really nothing to worry about."

"It's such a shame that they couldn't use our crew, or at least some of them."

"Yes, but their own people have worked together before. It's all part of the deal that we are being paid handsomely for."

"Very well, John. You are the seaman in the family. I will enjoy the season here on Waikiki and hope you will return as quickly as possible so as not to miss the bridge tournaments. Everyone at the club would miss you terribly."

"I wouldn't miss it for the world, dear. It is one of the great excitements of my life, you know." As he said it, his mind wandered again to the orgy in Wanchai. Emerald Lu had developed his addictions to lecherous levels. He wondered whether he would ever really be entertained again by sitting at a bridge table with the old crowd.

Hargraves poked his hand deep into his jacket pocket. He could feel the flat glass vial tucked into an inner pocket. It had been a gift from Emerald and contained enough cocaine to get him to California and back if he was careful.

Lady Hargraves sat down at the desk and picked up the telephone, eager to confide the latest news to her friends. The ambassador retired to their bedroom to complete packing for the voyage that was to begin tomorrow.

Emerald Lu had insisted that he be on board the vessel as it cruised to California from Hawaii. Since he was the listed owner of the *Lantau Star*, this would assure smooth entry into U.S. ports, and his political status would circumvent potential problems.

Her real interest in taking the *Lantau Star* to California, however, remained a mystery. He reasoned that there could be some truth to the story about the trade development program. Emerald Lu was probably trying to legitimatize some business operation foreseen for 1997.

In truth, Hargraves didn't really care about Emerald's scheme, whatever it was. He did have hope, however, that she might supply the *Lantau Star* with some of her entertainers from Wanchai. That would certainly make the voyage pass swiftly.

31

Pelly Kahn fingered the small envelope thought-fully. It had been handed to him by Max Von Braun that very day. Kahn was puzzled by the request that they no longer communicate with each other in person. He thought it foolish. He was skittish about using the telephones at the Great Eastern Gem and Artifact Company for anything other than the bit of legitimate business that came along. He had therefore arranged a callback system with Von Braun that would involve communicating by public phone only.

The curiosity of the press was not dying down at all. Each day the papers ran follow-up stories concerning the families involved in the tragedies. As far as he could tell, the authorities had nothing to go on. He believed he had left no footprints anywhere.

Kahn took a magnifying glass from his desk drawer and scanned the heavily taped small envelope. Under the transparent tape he found the single strand of black hair just where it should be, criss-crossing the flap several times, barely visible. The hair came from the head of Emerald Lu, and in effect it was her signature. He was to take no communication seriously unless the fine hair was there and intact. If it was truly from her, there would also be a tiny fragment of a single hair inside the envelope.

Using a small knife, he slit the tape along the end of the envelope and withdrew a single page. Peering inside the empty envelope, he saw the expected half inch of fine black hair. He read the message, several paragraphs typed on white paper.

On October first there will be a reception at the Sports Bar in the La Reine Sheraton at Los Angeles International Airport at seven P.M. Come prepared for a week or two of diversion.

Come equipped for all eventualities, darling. An exciting time will be had by all.

"Of course this takes precedence over anything on your schedule and must be kept a secret. The reception will be for you alone.

Kahn looked at his watch. It was September 28th. Of course, he would have to fly. This meant picking up weapons out on the Coast. The weapons would be no problem, given the considerable talents of Emerald Lu. But he hated to fly.

One thing was certain. Something very big was happening. He decided he would shut down the Great Eastern Gem and Artifact Company and place a vacation sign on the door. Chances were it would be closed for good.

He read the short letter several times, then burned it in a small ashtray on his desk. He stirred the ashes until they were powder, then too them to the washroom, where he flushed the powder down the commode. He considered his schedule. There were only two full days before he had to leave and he still had to complete a major part of his assignment. He again looked at the tiny hair in the envelope, shook it onto the desk and brushed it onto the floor. Emerald Lu! Was it too much to hope that she would be there herself? An involuntary stirring in his loins made him furious.

He slammed his fists on the desk and then scrambled to lie face down on the hardwood floor. He began to do push-ups until he could do no more. Then he hooked his toes under the edge of the desk and did sit-ups until he fell back in exhaustion.

Kahn stared at the ceiling, conjuring up the image of Emerald Lu. She was a woman with an iron will. She was beautiful and deadly. She was the only female in the world who gave him a feeling of weakness. And he, Pelly Kahn, sometimes killed people just because they were weak.

32

The New York City taxicab pulled to a stop in front of the command post at the gate of the Clayfield estate. Its driver rolled down his window and looked up at the guard.

"Tell your fare we are not permitting vehicles beyond this point." The guard pointed to the heavy chain across the end of the driveway.

Max Von Braun rolled down his window and spoke. "My name is Max Von Braun. Angela Clayfield is expecting me."

The guard nodded and spoke a few words into a hand-held telephone, then turned back to Von Braun. "Okay, you can go in alone, but the cab must stay out here."

Von Braun shoved a hundred-dollar bill at the cabdriver. "I'd appreciate it if you would wait for me."

The cabdriver pulled onto the shoulder and turned off his engine. Von Braun climbed out of the cab and allowed the guards to inspect the large flat portfolio he was carrying. It enclosed a small manuscript and several large maps and charts wrapped neatly in transparent plastic, stowed carefully between rectangular sheets of posterboard. Von Braun reluctantly allowed himself to be frisked. At last he began the long walk down the driveway past the guards.

Angela Clayfield met Von Braun at the door with a warm handshake. He responded by kissing her hand lightly.

"Captain, I'm so sorry for the trouble out there at the gate. Under the circumstances, our people are being very cautious."

"That's quite all right. Really, under the circumstances, I take no offense at all. Let's hope they catch these scoundrels soon, so we can get back to business as usual." Angela led Von Braun into the house.

Brook Laird thanked the captain for braving the cab ride to rural New Jersey.

Von Braun responded by putting his arms around Laird's shoulders. "I want all of you to know that it is this young man who first saw the value in my pet project. I look forward to working further on this project with Brook."

"Captain, Brook is as excited about this as you are."

Angela introduced Willy to Von Braun as the president of ConCom. He grasped Willy's extended hand warmly. If the name Willy Hanson meant anything to him, he didn't show it. But when Angela introduced Coley Doctor, Willy thought he noticed some hesitancy in Von Braun. If he indeed was connected with Onyx Lu, it was very possible that he would recognize one or both of them.

Willy got down to business. "Angela tells me you have ancient maps and charts that would have great appeal to an affluent market."

Von Braun seemed pleased with Willy's summary. "This material is the result of a hobby I've had for many years. It has been a labor of love, as they say. If I can share it with the world, it will make me very happy. It all started over thirty years ago when I was quite young. I was visiting Australia when I stumbled upon a chart used and annotated by Captain Cook. In fact, his initials are written on it next to several of the notations. I paid well over a month's pay for it, a lot of money in those times. That was the beginning."

"Angela tells me you are a pilot with Trans-Asiatic," Willy said.

"That is correct. Spending my life piloting around the world made it rather easy for me to pursue the collection of maps as a hobby. Mr. Hanson, I am aware that you are also quite a traveler."

Coley Doctor looked sharply at Von Braun. It was a surprise to hear him say he knew of Willy's travels.

"Aha! You've read my book," Willy exclaimed. "That is flattering. But I'm afraid most of my travel has been quite local as compared to all your globe-circling."

Von Braun chuckled and cleared his throat. "From what I see in the newspapers, you have quite a best-seller there. It should come as no surprise to you that I have read your book. You describe with such passion all those fiends who sour my adopted part of the world. I found it fascinating, absolutely fascinating!"

Coley spoke up. "Where do you make your home, Captain?"

"Actually I don't live in any one place. Where I hang my hat, as they say. But because of my commitment to Trans-Asiatic, I find myself spending a lot of my leisure time in Hong Kong."

"Captain," Angela broke in, "let's move into the

next room. My colleagues are anxious to see the material you've brought." With that she moved into a large dining room, opening the drapes to let in the maximum light by which to view the charts.

The charts were spectacular. Captain Cook, Vasco da Gama, Magellan, Lewis and Clark, Pizarro, John Cabot—the list went on and on. The collection was carried right into the twentieth century with annotated hand-drawn maps by Admiral Byrd and Charles Lindbergh. The materials they were shown were expertly photographed color copies. Von Braun assured them that the pricey originals were in a bank vault in Hawaii. Angela suggested that the originals should be assembled for a heavy-security press party at some prestigious museum upon publication of the book.

"Good idea, Angela. I'm sure that could be easily arranged." Willy seemed genuinely interested in the project, trying to slip back into the role of publisher for the moment.

Coley was paying small attention to the conversation, taking the time to scrutinize Von Braun. He noticed the pilot's ashen complexion and the dark circles around his sunken eyes. His face was a map of deep lines and scars. There was a certain rugged, almost decadent, handsomeness about him. But he just didn't look physically fit. Coley pictured the watery-eyed captain at the controls of a 747 and shuddered.

"Captain, are you going to be available for the next few days?" asked Angela.

"No, I must leave for Hawaii tomorrow, and from there return to Hong Kong. I can leave all this material with you, though. If there are any questions that are absolutely urgent, leave a message at the Peninsula in Hong Kong. They know how to reach me."

Von Braun, preparing to leave, paused for a moment and looked searchingly around the room. "Will someone be kind enough to show me to a bathroom?"

"Of course, Captain," offered Brook. "Straight down the hall there, third door on the left."

Von Braun started down the hallway as the others huddled around the charts still spread on the table. Coley backed away from the group to watch Von Braun, who walked right past the third door on the left and continued to the end of the hall, looking into the rooms on either side. Having done that, he turned to see Coley watching him.

Von Braun shook his head and shrugged, as if to say, "Whoops! I missed it." He walked back to the bathroom door and entered it.

Coley was becoming very nervous. He wondered how thoroughly Von Braun had been frisked at the gate. He had missed the bathroom door on purpose and was casing the first floor as well as he could. Coley would bet on it.

Within a couple of minutes, Von Braun returned to find the others still perusing the charts. He was all smiles, and the others responded with smiles of their own. All except Coley, who left quickly to explore the bathroom Von Braun had just vacated.

Angela touched the captain's arm as he moved to the front door. Outside, they could see his cabdriver slumped behind the wheel reading a newspaper.

"And where will you be staying while you're in Hawaii, Captain? It's one of my favorite places. I wish I were going with you."

"I've always liked the Moana Surfrider on Waikiki. It is quiet, yet in the middle of everything, if you know what I mean. However, I'll only be there for a night, so it doesn't matter much where I stay."

"Have a good flight, Captain," Angela offered, a

firtatious look in her eye. "I'll bet all of your flights are good."

"Yes, they are," he lied, thinking back to the nearly disastrous landing only yesterday at Kennedy.

Captain Max Von Braun walked alone down the long narrow driveway to his waiting cab. The others, with the exception of Coley, continued to study the charts left on the table. Coley stood at the window in the living room watching every step Von Braun took until he opened the door and climbed into the cab.

Willy, pulling away from the others, sidled over to Coley at the window. "Our suspicions may be wrong, Coley. The captain looks just like what he says he is, an old flyboy with an unusual hobby."

Coley turned and frowned at Willy. "I think that old bastard is straight from Cheung Chau. I'll bet he could give you Onyx Lu's birthmark count. While all you guys were drooling over all those old maps, I watched him walk down the hallway. You remember when Brook told him loud and clear, third door on the left? Well, he walked five doors to the end of the hallway and took a long look at every room. Believe me, Willy. He was casin' the joint. Not only that, he didn't even use the john and he didn't flush it."

Willy and Coley stared out the window, focusing on the two security guards at the end of the driveway.

"Are you sure, Coley?"

"Yep, I just wish I would have hit him with Cheung Chau. I should have asked him, 'How are things in Cheung Chau these days?' I would have liked to have seen the expression on his face. Willy, Jesus! He's slipping away from us!"

"Well, we can't go to the police with an expression on someone's face."

"Yeah, I know, but Onyx Lu used to live on

Cheung Chau. I think one of us has to go there and see if she's alive and kicking."

"Coley, sometimes you forget you're six feet six and black. You would stand out like Ambrose Light on that little island. I would be just as visible. Either one of us would be nailed."

"I guess you're right. I'm going to check out the bathroom again."

"What in the hell for?"

"That friendly old guy who looks like everybody's favorite uncle might have put some plastique in there and I don't want to be in this house when it blows up."

"Not likely, Coley."

"It wasn't likely that the elevator would get blown up either."

"Coley, let's go say our good-byes to Angela. Brook Laird is starting to drool. Let's get the hell back to the city so they can get it on."

"You noticed that too."

"Yep."

"I just can't believe that wimp knows what to do with all that female machinery."

"Coley, you're jealous. You know, sometimes you've got to pass right by a candy store. You just can't stop at all of them."

As they turned away from the window, Angela entered the living room carrying the short manuscript that had been included with the charts. She sat on the sofa, tucking her long legs under her, and began to turn the pages.

Willy studied her for a few moments. If the woman had any physical flaws, he couldn't find them.

"Not a stitch on under that jumpsuit," Coley mumbled.

"Probably not, Coley, but neither of us will ever know for sure, will we?"

"Brook," Angela called, startling Willy and Coley. "Will you come here for a moment?" Laird was still in the adjoining room leafing through the charts.

"Brook, this needs work badly. Your captain is a great collector and organizer but he can't write worth a lick. Why don't you to take this into the study right now and work through a few pages? If you can't straighten it out easily, we'll hire a ghost to do it."

"Oh, really? I thought the material he showed me some time ago was quite good. I'll spend some time with it first thing in the morning."

"Brook, I wish you would do it right now. It just seems as if nothing is getting done around here. Just look it over enough so that we can determine our next step. I'm going to have to spend some time with Mr. Hanson here, before he returns to the city."

"Sure, Angela, I'll be glad to."

Coley winked at Willy. "Willy, I'm going out to the gates with Mr. Grundy, the security man. I want to know exactly what procedures are being taken."

Willy nodded and Coley headed out the door with the sour-faced Grundy.

"You have a lot of confidence in Coley, don't you, Willy?" Angela asked.

"Confidence in Coley? Yes, I do. He's the best. He's the bravest man I know. He could be playing ball in the NBA. Pure guts would have made him a great player."

"Why didn't he?"

"Coley wanted to be a lawyer. He has the degree, you know. He just got sidetracked by the system. It's been my good fortune to have had him on my side for a while. Someday he'll be a great lawyer."

"And what about you, Willy? Does it feel good to be back?"

"Absolutely not. My life is in a sailboat back in

California. I'm here because this is a big dirty mess
that is affecting a lot of old friends. Keep looking for
a replacement for Overstreet. I'll be out of here the
day this riddle is solved."

Angela looked at Willy with those violet eyes and
walked over to him. "That is too bad. We would
make a great team."

She stood face to face with Willy before grasping
his hand. "Thank God you're here, for however long."
She put her arms loosely around his shoulders. "I
need somebody strong right now. Brook is talented,
but he is not strong."

Her arms tightened and Willy felt her warmth. He
began to feel uncomfortable. He began to feel chal-
lenged. Then he caught another whiff of Laird's cologne. He patted her shoulder gently and moved
away.

"Angela, leave it to Coley and me. We'll put the
company back on course. We'll get to the bottom of
this, as a favor to you, for Charles."

Angela took a step backward and looked at Willy
with her eyes wide and innocent. "I miss Charles
terribly. In some ways he was like you. He was deci-
sive, strong and confident. So am I. So we clashed
and fought a little, but never let any dispute become
too serious. No one could ever really come between
us."

"I know what you mean. I was married once and
we let just about everyone come between us. It was
a life of hell. Now I know what it is when two people
are good for each other. I have that now with Ginny.

"Angela," he continued, "if I'm really to help you, I
need to ask some questions that may be difficult for
you."

"Oh please," Angela said, shaking her head. "Ask
away. I don't think there's any question I haven't already been asked a dozen times."

"Tell me, then. Is there anyone in the world who is terribly upset with you?"

"The answer is absolutely no. Who could possibly be upset enough with me to commit murder?"

"Oh, maybe someone like Caron Lawson."

Angela looked sharply at Willy. He glanced out the window, watching Coley talk to the security men.

"Why in the world would a sweet person like Caron Lawson be upset with me? Caron is a perfect jewel."

"Oh come on, Angela, you and Vinnie Lawson were messing around in resorts all over the East Coast. If I know, she must know. Now, Caron isn't the type to go killing people, but if there are other paramours . . . who knows?" Willy shrugged and looked directly at her. Now he knew what she looked like when she was furious.

"Mr. Hanson! That will be enough for today. You were hired to put ConCom back on course, not to ask me perfectly bizarre questions about my personal life." Hard as nails as she was, she was actually showing a few tears.

"Angela, if you don't like my style, fire me. There are a lot of young phenoms around who would relish this job." Willy moved toward the door. "I turned Coley and myself into targets by taking this job. If you find my first tough question off limits, that's just too damn bad!"

Angela was wringing her hands now, trying to stop more tears from coming. "Okay, Willy. I will tell you all about it some other time. It was a single mistake. Did you ever make a mistake?"

"Lots of them."

"Can we go on from here?"

"You're the boss. Coley and I are going back into the city. Shall we see you here tomorrow afternoon?"

"Yes . . . yes, I think that's a good idea. I'm sending

Brook back to his place in the morning. He can't possibly function here."

"Good idea. I don't think he should stay in his apartment, though. Let him check into some hotel under another name for a while."

"I'll tell him." Angela paused. She didn't feel comfortable about her clash with Willy. "Willy, I'm sorry . . . Caron Lawson has every right to feel bad about me. It was a mistake. You had every right to ask that question. In fact, I thank you for making me be honest, Willy." She stepped forward again to give him a hug. He kept his arms at his side. "Can't you stay this evening? I would feel so good if you were in the house."

"Angela, Coley and I have a lot of work to do. We can't waste a minute. I want to show up at ConCom before they close. I think it would build up morale a little if they saw some management around." He gave Angela a quick squeeze and then turned and walked toward the door.

"Of course that makes sense, Willy. Please keep me posted. I feel as if you and Coley are all I've got going for me right now."

Willy waved, then went out and strode rapidly down the driveway to meet Coley. He felt like a heel for confronting Angela about Caron Lawson. But it had been an important first step, he knew. Like breaking in a wild horse. Maybe it would provoke her to be honest with him in the future.

33

Willy and Coley arrived at ConCom about 3 P.M. and went directly to Brad Overstreet's old office. Overstreet had been dead for five days now. Detectives had been through his personal files and his desk. If anything of significance was found, the police were not letting anyone know. Katie Glover told them that the detectives had removed two small sealed cardboard boxes from the office that morning and informed the office manager that the company could resume use of the office.

Willy made a quick tour of the floors that housed the ConCom offices and said hello to the employees who remained from the old days. The news of Willy's return had spread rapidly, and everyone seemed genuinely buoyed by his presence. The office manager, Derrick Harrison, was especially warm. They walked back to Willy's office together.

"Willy, in my thirty years at ConCom, I've never seen such jubilation as this morning when Katie

Glover circulated the media release about you coming back. I think everyone here is encouraged by seeing a firm hand on the tiller again."

"Thank you, Derrick. I'm here for the very short haul, just to pitch in until this mess is over with." He sat down at his desk. "From your point of view, how far away from normal are things now?"

The slender, graying Harrison fidgeted with a pocket watch that he pulled from a vest pocket by a gold chain. His specialty was getting things done, putting through requisitions for supplies, and generally making everyone as efficient as they could be in their offices. He rarely offered opinions on company policy or personalities.

"I would say, sir, that only about sixty percent of our employees are showing up for work. The elevator incident frightened so many of them. A few more come in each day."

"Willy! God, you look great there at your desk." Katie Glover entered the room with Coley, who was reading a piece of paper as he walked.

"Katie, I wish I could say I'm glad to be here, but under these circumstances, I'm not. What's this I hear about a media release?"

"Here you are," Coley volunteered, handing the paper to Willy. "It's just the usual thing, telling everyone you're back, and what a hotshot you are."

Willy glanced at the headline. "Leave it to Katie to lay it on a little thick. When are you sending it out?"

"It's already out, Willy. It will be in all the morning papers. Angela wanted it that way."

Coley was scowling, looking very upset. "It's a bad mistake. We just don't need stuff like this."

"What!" Katie Glover frowned at Coley.

"We're already target enough. You trying to get us killed?"

"Coley! We'll just have to live with it. Katie was

only following Angela's instruction." Willy turned toward Katie, who looked dumbfounded by Coley's accusation.

"The news would have gotten out anyway, Katie. We just weren't quite ready."

Willy stuffed the media release into his pocket. He knew exactly why Coley was upset, and he shared Coley's concern. Ginny was back at the marina in Long Beach. Now others would know she was there alone.

Willy looked at his watch. It had been three hours since he had seen the captain. "Coley, let's get out of here. We've got things to do." He turned to Katie. "From now on, I must approve all press releases. If you have any trouble with Angela, you let me know."

Within minutes they had left the building and hailed a cab.

"Take us to the Waldorf," Willy instructed.

"Five will get you ten that our decadent old aviator ain't at the Waldorf."

"I'll take that bet, Coley. It would be a pleasure to lose."

It seemed as if they waited an eternity at the front desk of the Waldorf. At their insistence, the manager checked every possibility. Max Von Braun, Brown, Max Braun, Captain Braun. There was no one registered who remotely fit the name.

"Okay, Coley. You win. The old bastard is a liar. Let's get to the Buchanan Park. Ginny is supposed to call me there at five-thirty."

"It can't happen too soon to suit me. You've got to get her off the *Tashtego*. I'd say pronto, old pal! Has she got a place where she can hole up for a while?"

"Ginny's a bit of a loner, but she does have a couple of close friends she could call on. At worst she can stay in a hotel out of the L.A. basin for a few days. Coley, I should get back there within the week."

"That's okay, pal. We'd be stumbling over each other anyway. Besides, you cramp my style. Did you see all those little cuties back at the Waldorf?"

"It's that cutie back in Saddle Hills I'm worried about, Coley. Every time Angela Clayfield wiggles, you start to drool."

"I'n not sure she's my kind of a woman if she hangs around with a nerd like Brook Laird."

"She's a woman in need, Coley. After all, Brook Laird is at least a fourth-stringer. Charles Clayfield, Vinnie Lawson, and Overstreet are all dead. She's just flat run out of manpower."

The Buchanan Park was a small hotel near Gramercy Park. Willy and Coley took adjoining rooms, unlocked the door between them and chatted nervously as the time approached when Ginny was to call.

Nobody knew where they were staying except Angela Clayfield and Ginny. Now Willy was sorry he had told Angela. He had no confidence in her discretion.

"By the way, boss, before I walked into your office today Katie told me that the coroner was releasing Overstreet's body. His mother requested that he be shipped to Miami for burial. There ain't gonna be a funeral, just a memorial service for the immediate family."

"That's a shame. I was hoping for a funeral just to see if the same clown would show up with a camera who was at Charles and Vinnie's funeral. I guess that makes sense, though. Overstreet had no wife or kids."

It was 5:33. The two men kept up idle conversation, trying not to think about the time. Willy was drumming his fingers on the small writing desk when the phone finally rang.

"Hi, lover."

"Hi, sweetheart," Willy answered, breathing a sigh of relief at the sound of Ginny's voice.

"What's happening in the big city? Hey, I miss you. In fact the *Tashtego* is pretty spooky without you."

"Ginny, I have no news that's good news. Coley and I are just sitting here trying to make sense of all this. If the police are on to anything they're not telling anyone. But I might as well tell you that we have reason to believe our old friend in Hong Kong is engineering all this."

"Have you told the police what you think?"

"We can't come close to proving it. The papers are making a circus out of this. I think the authorities would love to get off the hook by blaming it all on some person ten thousand miles away, even if she didn't exist."

"Tell them anyway, Willy. I'm scared stiff. Maybe it's too big and complicated for you and Coley . . . You need help. Willy, I just can't make myself go back to the *Tashtego*. I'm locking her up and will go to stay with Ingrid in Pasadena."

"You have her number?"

Ginny gave him the phone number and he jotted it down on hotel stationery. "That's a good idea, going to Pasadena. Coley and I were going to ask you to stay away from the *Tashtego* anyway. Don't tell Ingrid the gory details. We don't want any more innocent people brought in on this. Also don't leave word with the marina. Call them from a public phone once in a while to check on the *Tashtego*."

"Willy, I've got an idea. Why don't you tell Mark Whitcomb what you think?"

"You might have something there. I'll run it by Coley. But I have got some good news for you. Coley and I are splitting up. I'll be back within a week and he will stay here as ConCom security chief."

"That's what I call real good news. Hey, are you behaving around that Clayfield dish?"

"She's bad news, baby. I'm leaving her to Coley, who doesn't know any better."

"Tell him to be careful. He might catch something . . . Like instant death. I love you, Willy."

Willy hung up the phone.

Coley had followed most of the conversation but not all of it. "Okay, what are you supposed to run by me?" he asked immediately.

"Ginny said that if we can't trust the police, we should run it by your old friend, Mark Whitcomb."

Coley stared out the window into Gramercy Park. Whitcomb was the FBI agent who had led the final assault when Onyx Lu's drug operation was shut down. Everyone had been sent to prison or died in the mop-up except Onyx.

"I think maybe Ginny is right. We trusted him once before. Maybe we should do it again. Let's sleep on it. Maybe something will pop wide open in a day or two. Who is Ingrid?"

"She's an old college pal of Ginny's. I think she's president of a bank in Pasadena. I don't think there's any risk in Ginny's being there. She's going tonight. She's scared stiff. I have to get back soon."

"I'll see if I can locate Whitcomb tomorrow while you're at ConCom."

"You know, Coley, Ginny is the best in the world."

"You're lovesick, old man. I hope I never catch that disease. It must be hell."

34

It was about nine that evening when Grundy fielded a telephone call. A man identifying himself as Lenny Maguire asked for Angela. Grundy put the call on hold and walked into the next room, where Angela was huddled with Brook Laird over the material she had earlier requested him to review. Grundy noticed that she had changed the yellow jumpsuit for what looked like tennis shorts and a bulky sweatshirt emblazoned "Amelia Island Tennis Club." She was sitting very close to Laird, one arm around his shoulders, both of them reading the same page of the Von Braun manuscript.

"There's a guy on the phone. Says he is Lenny Maguire. He says you're expecting his call, Mrs. Clayfield."

Angela hesitated for a moment, looking at Grundy with her wide, unblinking violet eyes. She stood up. "As a matter of fact, I have been expecting his call. I'll be back in just a minute, Brook."

Angela walked into the next room to pick up the phone. Grundy followed and sat on a sofa, where he had been going through a stack of newspapers. Angela spoke quietly, but Grundy could hear most of what she was saying.

"Lenny, you're calling awfully late. You keep a gal waiting, I see." Thirty seconds of silence went by before she spoke again.

"Oh, it's going to be difficult. Until all this stuff blows over, I'm practically under house arrest." There was another long pause.

Then Grundy heard what amounted to a soft giggle.

"Look, if it is absolutely necessary, I suppose I can come into the city for a few minutes in the morning. One of our editors is making the trip. I'll go with him."

Grundy frowned. His orders were that Angela Clayfield was to go nowhere unless elaborate security precautions were taken.

Angela glanced at the glowering Grundy. "I'll have to bring a bodyguard with me, but that's okay. I wouldn't think of doing otherwise. We'll have breakfast at the Plaza, like the last time, okay?"

There was another long lapse in her end of the conversation.

"Don't worry, Lenny. Everything will be fine. See you at nine o'clock at the Plaza." She hung up then, but stood with her hand on the phone for some time, as if in deep thought. Finally she returned to Brook Laird.

Grundy followed her into the other room. Angela was explaining to Laird that she had arranged a morning meeting with someone from the West Coast. They needed to discuss a movie deal tied in to one of ConCom's books.

"Mrs. Clayfield, I don't want to butt in or anything, but I am under strict orders to not let you out of my sight." Grundy knew she was strong-willed, and he didn't expect his job to be easy.

"You can come along with Brook and me. You've got four other people on the job here now. They can keep this place secure."

"Okay, Mrs. Clayfield. But I got to stick to you like glue."

"Grundy, I wouldn't think of going anywhere without your protection. Just make sure that machine gun of yours is loaded. Brook and I will feel safe for sure."

"It ain't a machine gun, ma'am. It's just a nine-millimeter."

"Whatever you say, Grundy. You'll love having breakfast at the Plaza. I think we're all going stir-crazy around here."

Angela walked over and picked up the material she had been reviewing with Laird. "Brook, you've done a good job. I'll go over the rest of it before I fall asleep. Good night, guys, see you in the morning."

With that she turned and went up the staircase to the second floor. Neither Laird nor Grundy could resist turning to watch the sleek legs and short pleated tennis skirt as she mounted the stairs.

"Do you think it's safe?" Laird asked as soon as Angela was out of earshot.

"Don't worry, kid. Your father will take care of you."

"My father?"

"Yeah, his name is Nine-Millimeter." Grundy patted the weapon now jammed under his belt.

Laird smiled sheepishly. Grundy continued to scowl as he watched Angela disappear down the second-floor hallway.

Laird arose from the dining room table where they had been working and went into the living room with Grundy. He just didn't feel comfortable about going upstairs so soon after she had left.

"Mind if I catch up on the latest?" Laird pointed to the pile of newspapers.

"Not at all, kid, help yourself."

Upstairs, Angela locked her bedroom doors before going to her walk-in closet. She reached back into a second row of hanging clothes and found an old winter coat she seldom wore. She reached into a deep pocket and slipped out a small flat satin purse. It was embroidered with red silk thread in the shape of a capering dragon. Inside was a row of heavy dark plastic vials. She extracted one and took it over to the dresser, where she opened it carefully. She rummaged for a moment in a jewelry box that sat on her dresser and finally extracted a tiny golden spoon. The handle of the spoon was also embellished with a tiny prancing dragon, with a chip of ruby for an eye.

Taking great care, she scooped a level spoonful of the fine powder. Closing one nostril with an extended forefinger, she inhaled the cocaine into the other nostril. She didn't waste a particle of the dust. Practice makes perfect, she thought as she returned to the closet to hide the satin purse again.

She went to the small refrigerator in one of the nightstands, withdrew a bottle of champagne and set it on the dresser. After pulling the loose sweatshirt off over her head, she tossed it to the floor. Moving to the side of the bed, she piled all the silk-encased pillows up against the headboard.

She walked to the door that opened to the guest room and unlocked it. She kicked off her shoes and sprawled across the bed, propping herself up against the pillows. She stared at her image in the mirror across the room and waited.

When Laird closed the door in the next bedroom,

Angela closed her eyes and feigned sleep. Laird opened the door to her room almost immediately.

"Angela, I'm sorry. I didn't think it would look right to rush right up here. I thought I should spend a little time with Grundy."

Angela opened her eyes. "Brook, sometimes you say the stupidest things. Grundy is a fool." She stared at him blankly. "Brook, you've been wearing those clothes all day. Take them off and use my shower. For God's sake, hurry, Brook. Sometimes I think I haven't taught you very well."

Laird emerged from the shower five minutes later and walked to Angela's bedside, mopping himself dry with a thick bathtowel.

She opened her eyes and giggled softly. "You really did take a shower, didn't you? Why, Brook?"

"You asked me to, Angela."

"I know. But a lot of men wouldn't have done it."

"I guess you're right about that, but I thought you wanted me to."

"Will you always do everything I want you to do?"

"You know I would, Angela. Are you going to take off that tennis skirt?"

"I hadn't thought much about it, Brook. Does it bother you? Does it present some great obstacle that you can't contend with?" Again she giggled softly.

"I think I can contend with it, Angela. Actually it—"

"Turns you on. That's it, Brook. I'll bet it turns you on."

Again there was that soft giggle. She was laughing at him. But he didn't seem to care at all. She bent her knees toward her chest and slipped off the skirt and tossed it across the room. He was becoming incredibly aroused.

"There, Brook, do you like me better now? Turn around. See that bottle of champagne over there on the dresser? I want you to pop the cork and bring it over here with you."

He walked over to the dresser. Angela watched him in the mirror. He took the bottle and unwound the wire mesh over the cork. He put his thumb under the edge of the cork and pushed as he twisted the bottle. It came off with a resounding pop.

"Well, Brook darling, bring it over here."

"I was just looking around for glasses. Do you have a couple of glasses around here?"

"Of course I do. But we won't need them."

"We won't?"

"What did I tell you, Brook?" Again that soft laugh as he walked toward her.

"I am going to teach you a few things so that when you get together with your lady friend in New Orleans . . ."

"Lily and I broke up."

"Oh, you did, did you? Well then, I've got you all to myself. I like that, Brook. Come over and sit on the edge of the bed and give me the bottle."

He did exactly as she asked. She took just a sip from the bottle and asked him to do the same.

"I'm crazy, Brook. Do you know that?"

"You're beautiful. You're hot."

"You've got that right. I'm hot and beautiful. Now, Brook, I am going to teach you how to drink champagne. I am going to teach you how to drink champagne without glasses or the bottle."

Angela started dribbling champagne along her bosom, the clear bubbly liquid trickling down her body. Laird watched spellbound.

"Well, Brook, what are you waiting for? It's a sin to waste champagne."

"Angela, you are crazy."

"And you love it."

"Yes, you've got that right."

35

Emerald Lu wasn't fearful of much in life, but the ordeal of passing through airports bound for another country concerned her, especially at Kai-Tak. The fabricated passport had served her well so far, but common sense told her that somewhere, someone might identify her as Onyx. For the flight to Hawaii, she picked a time when Kai-Tak would be crowded. She also had arranged for several of the pupils in her English class in Cheung Chau to accompany her to the airport. One of the other teachers had offered to join them as chaperone, agreeing that a visit to Hong Kong's airport would be a great field trip.

The children were well scrubbed and handsomely dressed. Emerald herself made an effort to look as matronly as possible.

The short ferry ride from Cheung Chau to Kowloon was delightful. The South China Sea was like

a mirror that day, and the air was clear. It was a
perfect day for pointing out landmarks of interest to
the curious children.

She recalled the last crossing on the afternoon she
and Max Von Braun had set out for the Paragon
Club to meet Lord John Hargraves. Emerald valued
Von Braun greatly. He had served her well as a cou-
rier, but she wondered how long he would last. Between his bad heart and crazed lifestyle, his days
had to be numbered.

He had recently told her the story of a rough landing he had made at Kennedy. Someone had turned
him in. Von Braun suspected his copilot, a brash
young flyer named Tommy Wing. Emerald had filed
that name in her mind. She didn't want anyone up-
setting the applecart. Tommy Wing might have to be
taken care of.

In Kowloon, the four children, their chaperone
and Emerald Lu piled into a taxicab for the short
drive to Kai-Tak. At the airport, the children
were awed by the bustle and the enormous aircraft.

Emerald checked in without difficulty and boarded
the 747. Several rows behind her she saw Brigitte.
They did not allow their eyes to meet.

The big 747 roared down the infamously short
runway at Kai-Tak and took off with only a few hundred feet to spare. They were headed due east toward Hawaii, where the *Lantau Star* was, nestled in
a slip near downtown Honolulu.

She paged through the complimentary copy of *The
Wall Street Journal*. A small article on page three
mentioned that Willy Hanson had been named pro-
visional president of ConCom. Emerald smiled. Lois
Lin had already told Pelly Kahn about that. Dimin-
utive Lois, a tigress who behaved like a lamb. Emer-

ald put on a black satin eyeshade to remove herself from the others in the cabin. She wanted to think only of Willy Hanson and how sweet her revenge was going to be.

36

Grundy was conducting a security meeting with his men when Laird came downstairs in the morning. He looked exhausted and unsteady on his feet. He had cut himself several times shaving, which didn't help the overall picture.

"Good morning, Mr. Laird. You look like you've had better nights." Grundy grinned.

"Yeah. I guess I didn't sleep a wink. Lots on my mind, I suppose. I'd really rather not go into the city, but Angela insists."

"Whatever Mrs. Clayfield wants, Mrs. Clayfield gets. Right, Brook?" Grundy was leering at Laird now.

"CEO's of companies usually do have a way of calling the shots, Grundy." Laird poured a cup of coffee, wondering how much Grundy might have overheard the night before. The bastard had probably eavesdropped.

Angela Clayfield came into the room right on time,

looking like a princess in a dark green form-fitting suit that set off her eyes. The mane of blond hair bounced and tossed perfectly as she moved. In contrast to Laird, she looked as if she had just returned from an exhilarating vacation. She carried a large briefcase and an even larger matching handbag.

"Okay, guys, let's go. We'll take my new Mercedes. Brook, I think you should drive. That way Grundy can be free to look around and see to it that we all get there alive."

Grundy nodded. "Mrs. Clayfield, you would make a fine bodyguard. Rule number one is that you always free up the eyes of the protector." He turned to Laird.

"Mr. Laird, Mrs. Clayfield and I just hope you don't fall asleep while driving. As I mentioned before, you look like hell this morning."

They arrived at the Plaza at ten minutes before nine, a bit early for the meeting with Lenny Maguire.

"Brook, Grundy stays with me. You can catch a cab and go on downtown to ConCom. You can leave the Mercedes with valet parking here. Grundy, you are welcome to join Lenny and me for breakfast, unless you would rather just sit somewhere and watch over us."

"I'm hungry, Mrs. Clayfield."

"Good. See you in a day or two, Brook. Say hello to Willy and Coley for me." She waved him off.

Inside the Plaza, Angela asked the maitre d' for Lenny Maguire's table. The maitre d' was studying the seedy-looking Grundy. He managed to look scroungy even when he tried to dress well.

"Ah yes, he does have a reservation, but has not arrived as yet. Perhaps you would like to be seated."

Angela surveyed the dining room. "I would appreciate that table over in the corner. It would be quiet there."

The maitre d' scanned his seating chart for a moment. "Of course, it is our pleasure."

Once seated, Angela surveyed the dining area to see whether she recognized anyone. She did not. Then she turned to Grundy. "Order me some grapefruit juice and some coffee. We deserve an eye-opener while we wait for Lenny. You'll have to pardon me for a couple of minutes. I have to use the ladies' room."

She pushed the briefcase toward Grundy. "Here, guard this with your life." She rose to leave the table, taking with her the large handbag.

Grundy nodded and signaled the waiter.

Angela walked a few steps toward the front of the dining room before stopping to take a careful look behind her. Then, moving swiftly, she exited the hotel, said a few words to the doorman and waited while he hailed a taxicab. Within seconds she was moving away from the Plaza down Fifth Avenue. About six blocks from the Plaza she shoved a ten-dollar bill at the driver and climbed out of the cab.

She waited for a few moments, then hailed another cab. "Driver, take me to Kennedy Airport."

The cabbie shook his head. "Lady, I don't make that trip this time of day."

"Here's a hundred dollars. Take me to Kennedy Airport."

"Why didn't you say so in the first place, lady?"

Angela read the name of the driver on the posted license. She would love to turn him in. But on this day she would not.

The driver veered over to the East Side Drive going north. "The bridge will get us there quicker than the tunnel at this hour. Okay?"

"You're the driver."

Entering the Trans-Asiatic terminal, Angela walked up a flight of stairs and was confronted by a giant wooden dragon mounted on a heavy glass door. Gold letters on a panel next to the door proclaimed it the Trans-Asiatic Mandarin Club.

Angela pushed the buzzer mounted over the panel. The door opened into a lavishly furnished room designed for the comfort of VIP's as they awaited Trans-Asiatic planes or passengers. A hostess sat behind a small reception desk.

"I'm looking for Max Von Braun."

"Oh yes. He is expecting a guest. You are Ms. Schilling?"

"Yes."

"You will find Captain Von Braun in the next room. He asks that you join him for a light breakfast."

Angela entered the other room and quickly found herself face to face with the captain.

"My dear, I was afraid you would get cold feet, as they say in your country. Welcome to our little bit of Asia here at Kennedy." Von Braun stood and hugged her warmly.

"Max, I wouldn't miss this trip for anything in the world. Where will we be staying in Hawaii? I've told no one."

"I'll let that remain a surprise for you," Von Braun said. "It may be on a boat, a fabulous yacht. We'll talk about it later. Do you have your luggage?"

"I brought very little, Max. I'll buy a wardrobe there."

"Good! That's my kind of woman. Let's celebrate before we fly." From an inner jacket pocket, Von Braun produced a small black satin pouch with an embroidered red dragon.

37

Grundy looked up from the newspaper. His coffee was gone and he had downed Angela's as well. He looked at her briefcase, overstuffed with papers, sitting in the chair next to him. He looked at his watch and gave a start. It was 9:34.

Grasping the heavy briefcase, he walked to the maitre d's podium. "Did Mr. Lenny Maguire ever show up?"

"I'm afraid not, sir. Do you wish to take care of the check?"

Grundy looked around. "Well, I'm really waiting for the young lady to rejoin me."

"Oh . . . she left some time ago. I thought you knew." Grundy felt his pulse quicken as a waiter came forward with a check.

"Nineteen dollars!" Grundy looked at the waiter in disbelief. "For two cups of coffee and a grapefruit juice!"

"I'm sorry about your companions, sir. Perhaps

there is some misunderstanding." The maitre d' ignored his protest.

Grundy shoved a twenty at the man and headed for the entrance of the hotel, toting the heavy briefcase. Seeing the doorman, he fumbled for the claim check for Angela's Mercedes. Cursing, he realized Laird had taken it with him. The doorman confirmed that the Mercedes was still with valet parking and that the beautiful young lady had requested a cab.

It was late morning before Grundy showed up at ConCom. He found Coley and Willy together in Willy's office. They listened to his story in disbelief, pausing now and then to ask pertinent questions.

"Why in the hell didn't you call us right away?" Coley demanded.

"I was looking for her. I thought maybe I could find her." Grundy set the heavy briefcase on Willy's desk. "She left this with me when she went to the ladies' room. I was sure she would come back for it."

Coley groaned. Up to this point, Willy hadn't said a word. "Grundy, it's possible that we may never see Angela Clayfield again. Who was supposed to meet her for breakfast?"

"Some movie guy from L.A. Lenny . . . something."

"Oh Jesus!" Coley exclaimed in exasperation. "Of all the stupidity! Let's get Brook Laird in here and see if he remembers anything."

Laird paled when he heard the story. He recalled that the man's name was Lenny Maguire, but said he had never heard of the guy until he had called the Clayfield house yesterday.

"Who took the call?" asked Willy.

"I did," admitted Grundy.

"What did the guy say? Come on, Grundy, think!" Coley pleaded.

"He asked to talk to Angela. Said his name was Lenny. I handed her the phone. That's all."

"Did you listen to her end of the conversation?"

"Not really, except she seemed to know the guy well. It sounded like a friendly conversation."

Laird spoke up. "I was in the next room. I could hear enough to know that it wasn't a very private conversation. I would agree that whoever she was talking to, she knew rather well."

Coley eyed Laird closely. "Brook, you look like hell today."

"Thanks, Coley."

Grundy was eager to let the spotlight turn to Laird. "I think Mr. Laird here can tell us a lot more about Mrs. Clayfield than he would have us believe."

"What in the hell do you mean by that?" Laird shouted.

Willy pulled the contents of Angela's briefcase out onto his desk. He glanced through a few loose papers. The Von Braun manuscript and a large chunk of another manuscript were in separate boxes. There didn't seem to be anything that would shed light on where Angela was.

Laird asked the inevitable question. "Shouldn't we call the police?"

Willy shrugged his shoulders. "And tell them what? That we have a person missing for two hours? She left voluntarily. There is no evidence of foul play at all. You couldn't even file a missing persons report based on that. For all we know, she might be somewhere in the hay with somebody."

Coley laughed. "I'd let the police know. They might be interested considering everything else that's happened at ConCom."

"Be my guest," Willy said quietly. "Then let's clear out of here. Brook, I want to talk to you for a few minutes before you leave the office. You are not to go back to your apartment. The company will put you up in a hotel. You choose the hotel and don't tell anyone which one it is. We'll pick up the tab later."

Willy turned to Grundy. "Grundy, you get on back to Saddle Hills and keep an eye on that house. One thing about a house, it can't run away from you."

Laird grinned at the sullen Grundy as they both left the room.

Coley sat at the desk, jotting notes on yellow paper.

"Willy, you knew Angela Clayfield's husband real well. Did he ever indicate to you that his wife had problems other than her obvious wandering eye? In all your conversations with Charles, did any inkling of misbehavior ever come out regarding Angela?"

Willy was quiet as he thought back to the times he had spent with Charles Clayfield as a friend. "I've tried to remember every word he ever said to me, Coley. Charles Clayfield idolized his wife and their children. He marveled at the way she was able to juggle the big job, the heavy dose of church work, the kids, and all the other family things. He thought Angela was perfect."

"You know, Willy, a lot of people around here feel the same way about Angela. Despite all the rumors along the executive corridor, most of the working stiffs really like her. This one little gal down in accounting, Lois, met me on the elevator and asked if I knew how Angela was taking all this. She said she was a nice lady."

"Why did she ask you?"

"Oh, I guess she had seen me around the building with you and figured I had connections."

"Any conclusions you've come to from that pile of yellow paper? Anything more to discuss before we call Mark Whitcomb?"

"Well," Coley said, "there are two things I can't

reconcile. One has to do with the children. It just
doesn't make sense to me that a woman as devoted
to family as her husband claimed she is could just
dump off her children as easily as she did. She
seems perfectly content to let her sister and housekeeper keep them. When we were at the house in
Saddle Hills, I saw photographs around the house,
but none of Charles or the kids."

"You said you had two things that bothered you.
What's the other one?"

"The woman's willing to have an affair with anyone. There were Vinnie and Overstreet that we know
about. And now there's Brook Laird. Did you take a
good look at Brook today? I never saw a guy so
pussy-whipped."

"He did look like he needed a long vacation."

Coley went on, "Did you ever look into Angela's
eyes and notice the way she stares at you without
hardly ever blinking? The big violet eyes are so
beautiful, but they just aren't normal. And maybe
her nympho behavior is fairly recent. It could all tie
in to some sort of addiction."

"Coley, you think she's on cocaine or something
worse? That would be too simple."

"If I could have got her in the sack one night, I
would know for sure what's eating her."

"Coley Doctor, always generous in offering his diagnosis."

"Hell, man, I am the diagnosis and the cure, all
wrapped up in one big package."

The two of them laughed and headed for the elevator.

38

Brook Laird felt miserable. By the end of the day Angela had not shown up. At five o'clock he left ConCom and started walking toward Broadway, where he turned north. He decided he would walk to the Highlander, hoping the exercise would clear away his persistent hangover.

Angela Clayfield's disappearance didn't alarm him as much as it did the others. Given Angela's behavior the night before, he had decided that she was certifiably crazy. He had been expecting a wild evening but what had gone on was far beyond that. The all-night sexual escapade had left him exhausted and scarred, with bruises and bites that he felt with every step he took. Her disappearance didn't really surprise him. Nothing she did now would surprise him. He felt certain that she would probably show up the next day. She was probably out on a toot with Lenny Maguire, whoever he was.

Just short of reaching the hotel, he heard someone

call his name. He turned to see Lois Lin rapidly approaching from behind.

"Mr. Laird! Wow! You are almost running. I have been trying to catch up with you for a long time."

"I'm sorry, Lois. I had no idea." He was surprised. He knew the woman only casually. A few words in the hall or elevator once in a while constituted their entire relationship. The only exception had been when he asked her to translate the Chinese characters printed on the map left in his doorway.

"I have some news for you. I know you were curious about the map I translated for you. It seemed to worry you."

"Lois, I was puzzled at the time, but really, I had forgotten about it. I hope you didn't go to a lot of trouble." He looked closely at the petite woman. She was as cute as hell, with dark eyes and jet-black hair that tossed with every movement. Lois was a welcome contrast to the voluptuous Angela.

"Oh, it was no trouble." The rush hour crowd jostling past them on the sidewalk made it hard to talk. She glanced around. "Can we talk about it for a minute? I think you will be relieved."

"I'll tell you what. Let me buy you a drink. We'll go into the hotel here. There's a great lounge up at the top. We can relax and you can tell me all about it."

"Oh, that would be so nice of you, Mr. Laird."

"Please call me Brook." He followed Lois into the hotel, noting that her petite figure moved saucily inside the tight, short skirt. He had never really paid much attention to her around the ConCom office.

Lois ordered a glass of Cabernet Sauvignon. Laird ordered a martini. He felt momentarily removed from the troubles that had plagued him all day. He hoped Lois would hang around awhile.

"So tell me all about it. What is the news about the map that I found in my doorway?"

"Well, I found the same map in a travel shop and in a bookstore in the Village. The man at the bookstore tells me he gets them from a supplier in Hong Kong who sells them all over the world."

"Oh. Then anyone could have bought it, anyone who was looking for my apartment."

"Oh yes. He said even messengers buy them sometimes because of the detail." She took a long sip from the glass of wine, which was already half gone.

"Well, I'll just forget about it, then. It really doesn't bother me anymore." He had very nearly forgotten about the map anyway, with all the excitement of the past couple of days. "It was nice of you to bring me up to date. And nicer to have you join me for a drink. It has been a long day. Looking at your beautiful face has made me forget all the bad things."

"Bad things?"

He caught himself. Up to this point Angela's disappearance wasn't public information, and he decided he wouldn't say anything about it. "Oh, it's really nothing. Just a difficult day at the office. Sometimes things just don't seem to go right."

He noticed that her wine glass was empty. "Do you have time for another? I need another martini."

"Oh yes, I have lots of time. I don't get to talk to the big mucky-mucks very often." She broke into a full smile and crossed her legs. He didn't know which he enjoyed more.

"I am hardly a big mucky-muck, as you put it."

"Oh yes you are. Everyone at ConCom knows how important you are."

Laird flushed as he affected a laugh at her flattery. "Angela Clayfield is the boss. Everyone knows that."

"And Mr. Willy Hanson?"

"I suppose he is another boss, but only for a little while."

"Really? Is he a nice person?"

"Nice? I guess he is, as long as you stay out of his way. I really don't know him that well. I know one thing. There is nothing as nice about him as there is sitting here with Lois Lin."

"Oh, that is so flattering." She took a long sip of the second glass of wine and grew more serious. "What are you doing uptown? I don't want to keep you from anything. I know from the famous map that you live in the Village."

"I'll tell you a secret if you promise not to tell a soul."

"How exciting! What is it?"

"I'm home. I'm living in this hotel for a while. So you are not keeping me away from anything."

"Really! In this hotel? Why? It is farther from your office than your apartment." Her eyes grew serious. She crossed her legs again. It seemed to be a sort of nervous ritual with her. He liked it.

"With all the trouble around the office, everyone is sort of hiding out. You're the only one who knows where I am, so don't go telling anyone."

Lois beamed. "You've got a deal, but only if you buy me one more glass of wine. The Cabernet is very good here."

"Good. I'll join you with another martini." Laird glanced at his watch. They had been there only a half hour or so and were ordering a third drink. He decided Lois was just what the doctor had ordered.

He was really not a drinker. He had long ago decided that his system was not made for it. Every time he had tried it he had paid for it with horrendous hangovers. But sexy little Lois Lin was more than he could resist. An hour later she had moved next to him in the booth, drawing him out about the workings of the publishing world and particularly the inner workings of ConCom. The martinis kept coming and the legs under the short skirt kept crossing and uncrossing.

"Brook, you are a devil. I'm going to see you to your room. You've got to get some rest. Okay?"

"You're coming up there with me for a while to make sure it's safe?" He slurred out the words and lurched against her.

"I wouldn't miss it for anything," she said as he ran his hand along her thigh. "But first I must use the ladies' room. I'll be right back."

She twisted away from him and walked toward the rest room. She stopped in the vestibule to use a public phone. The conversation lasted only a minute.

When she returned, Laird was staring glassy-eyed at the lights of Manhattan below.

"Here, give me your key. We don't want any fumbling around when we get there." He grabbed for her leg. "Now, Brook, behave yourself or I won't go!"

"Okay, okay! I hear you." Surprisingly, he was able to walk fairly steadily to the elevator. Once inside, he crushed her against the wall in an embrace.

Lois pressed the floor number.

"Baby, we need a bottle of champagne." He was out of control.

"I don't think you do, Brook. Whatever for?"

"I'm gonna show my baby how we can drink without glasses."

"Then you'll have to call room service, Brook. We'll order two bottles."

"Two bottles! Good idea! One for you and one for me."

Lois unlocked the door and maneuvered Laird to the bed, onto which he fell heavily. She began rubbing his neck and massaging his shoulders. Almost instantly, he fell into a drunken sleep.

Lois waited a minute or so to make certain he was truly passed out. Then she surveyed the room thoroughly, careful not to touch anything. When she left the room, she took the key with her.

About an hour later Laird winced in pain as his head was jerked around roughly so that the intruder could see his face.

"What in the . . . Who in the hell . . ." Laird opened his eyes to see a stocky man with piercing, unblinking eyes. "Who in hell are you?"

"Pelly. My name is Pelly. A fat lot of good it will do you to know."

"Where? . . . Who?"

"Pelly. I told ya before. Hey, punk, I'm the last man you'll ever know."

He released Laird's hair, letting his head fall to the bed. Then a powerful right hand chopped into the back of Laird's neck. The blow would have split heavy lumber.

39

Mark Whitcomb sat silently, listening for over an hour to the incredible theory concocted by Coley and Willy. The FBI agent had been tipped off and guided by the pair in the biggest drug bust he had ever made. It was Whitcomb who had actually engineered the massive raid in California that had wiped out the drug cartel run by Onyx Lu and her Hong Kong associates. It was only because of his past association with the two men that he now gave them the courtesy of hearing them out.

Whitcomb shook his head in disbelief. "You are asking me to believe that Onyx Lu survived being tossed overboard in that raging storm over two years ago. Somehow you believe she was able to walk away with nothing but the skimpy dress she wore that night, and then miraculously rebuild her life and resources to a level high enough to wage a massive secret vendetta against the people who destroyed her empire?"

Coley nodded. "Look, I spent a lot of time with Onyx. The woman was insanely vindictive. She would routinely have people knocked off for wearing the wrong color socks."

Whitcomb again shook his head. "Look, you don't have to convince me. I was there. I saw firsthand how ruthless she was. But your theory is preposterous. Think about it. Put yourselves in her position. There was Charles Clayfield, Vinnie Lawson, and then Brad Overstreet, all killed by experts. From the mode of their death, I would judge that different killers were involved. I say that because so far they haven't left a shred of evidence behind that the police have found."

Willy smiled at Whitcomb. "Aha! You've been following the case."

"Of course I have. I read the papers. But tell me, if you really believe your own theory, why put yourself in jeopardy by returning to ConCom? Onyx would rather nail you than all the others put together."

"I came back to help Angela Clayfield. To tell you the truth, if our suspicions are right, I feel sort of responsible. The least I can do is help out."

Another agent walked in and handed Whitcomb a fax that ran for two full pages. Whitcomb groaned as he read the message.

"Gentlemen, there is a shocking new development. How well did you know Brook Laird?"

Now it was Willy's turn to groan, hearing Whitcomb referring to Laird in the past tense. "Not well at all. Why?"

"He has just been found with his neck broken. He was discovered by a housekeeper at the Highlander Palace."

Coley smacked his fist into his palm. "Oh no! We told him to check into a hotel because we thought it would be safer than being at home. Somebody must have been right on his tail."

Whitcomb fingered the fax for a moment, then shoved it across the desk for Willy and Coley to read. "Actually, this gives us our first indication of a common killer. The Asian found in the patio of Laird's apartment also had a broken neck."

Coley looked at his watch. Angela Clayfield had been missing less than twenty-four hours. It was his guess that the chances of finding her alive had been reduced from slim to none.

Mark Whitcomb stood up from his desk and began to pace the office. "Willy, where is that beautiful Ginny Du Bois right now?"

"She's stashed away with a friend in California. Coley and I haven't told anybody where. Thank God! It doesn't look like this stuff is going to stop."

"Willy, I want to give you some advice." Whitcomb cleared his throat and pointed at Willy. "If I were you, I would get my ass back to California and stick to her like glue."

"I planned to do that. Coley's staying here to help security at ConCom."

"Willy, why don't you hole up someplace and write another book? I strongly advise that you leave the investigation to the professionals. We have a maniac on the loose who is proficient at breaking necks. I'd hate to have you and Coley drop out of my fax machine like Brook Laird did."

He turned to Coley. "Take a look at every single ConCom employee. I'd bet my life that there is a mole inside. And let me know the moment Angela Clayfield shows up. Leave the rest to me."

"What about finding Onyx Lu?" persisted Coley.

Whitcomb grimaced. "I think she drowned in the Pacific Ocean off Redondo Beach. That's what I think." There was a thoughtful pause. "However, in view of the latest killing, I will keep your theory in mind. Every horse player has to play a long shot once in a while, when he has absolutely nothing else to go on."

"Thanks. That's all Coley and I expected. We'll keep in touch. I hope to hell we're wrong."

40

Max Von Braun had stowed his uniform and donned a pair of jeans and a leather jacket for the American Airlines flight to Hawaii. He had taken a three-week vacation from Trans-Asiatic. Angela Clayfield, alias Jane Schilling, flew next to him in the last row of First Class next to the cabin divider. Angela had done her best to tone down her appearance by wearing loose slacks and a bulky sweater. She tried to sleep while Von Braun buried himself in the latest Richard Wheeler Western he had purchased at Kennedy. The Old West had always intrigued him. He hoped one day to travel the Western high country and perhaps unearth some long-lost maps annotated by the early explorers and settlers.

When they changed planes in San Francisco, Von Braun had a tense moment as a flight crew he knew passed within a few feet of Angela and him. He wanted to make it all the way to Hawaii without being recognized.

He wondered whether he would ever again captain another flight out of Hong Kong. He doubted it. Tommy Wing's accusations had attracted too much attention. He would be questioned. The thing he feared most was another physical. He was experiencing the symptoms a couple of times a week now.

Angela opened her eyes and turned to him. Without makeup and under a floppy gray beret, she still looked beautiful. "Captain, you look tired. Can't you sleep?"

"If I slept, I couldn't enjoy looking at you, my dear."

"Maybe you could use a drink. I could stand a scotch."

Von Braun fidgeted in his seat and then reached deep inside his jacket pocket. "I have something much better than that. We're at forty thousand feet. This will put us up to eighty thousand." He grinned broadly as he fingered the satin pouch. He wanted her pretty well out of it by the time they reached Hawaii.

"You scoundrel! Do you really think we should do that up here?" Angela, her eyes wide, obviously thought they should.

"No problem, my dear. In fact, we can do anything we want to up here." He thought of Jocelyn for a moment. "Someday I'll show you."

He slipped the small pouch into her hand. "You use the lavatory first. I'll be waiting there for the pouch when you come out. Then when we're both back here and feeling good, I'll tell you all about Lord Hargraves's fabulous yacht."

"Lord who?"

"Hargraves. He was an ambassador to several sultanates in Southeast Asia. Married a lot of money and latched on to this magnificent yacht. I think you'll like it."

"You must think I'm insane to do something like this on the spur of the moment. Max, I want to thank you for such a great idea. I was petrified by all the violence around ConCom. I just can't handle it. But I can handle this." She caressed the miniature satin purse. "You know, Max, I've been thinking that I should call Willy or Brook when we land. Just a few seconds to tell them I'm okay, so they don't worry."

Von Braun's heartbeat picked up and he felt the twinge of angina in his upper left arm. He reached slowly for the vial of nitro in his shirt pocket, and then remembered that he had packed it with his shaving kit.

"Something wrong, Max?" Angela was puzzled as Von Braun sat motionless for a few seconds.

"No, just thinking, my dear. Wait a few days before you call them. If you called, I think our little vacation would suddenly be overrun by a large assortment of constabulary types. That hardly goes along with our little passion, does it?" He touched the small zippered purse packed with vials of cocaine.

"You're right. I'll wait a couple of days. Actually, it will be quite a publicity coup. I'll call Katie Glover from the ambassador's yacht. The whole world will know the next morning."

"Angela, that is a marvelous idea. Lord Hargraves will relish all that publicity."

Von Braun brushed a kiss on her hand as she rose to go to the lavatory. He sat quietly for a few moments, hoping the twinge in his arm would go away, before he followed her. He ogled her voluptuous figure as she walked forward. He felt more relaxed already. Once she was aboard the *Lantau Star*, she would be so preoccupied that a phone call to New York would be the last thing on her mind. Anyway,

that wouldn't be his problem anymore, it would be
Onyx's. His responsibility would end once they
reached the gangplank of the *Lantau Star*. That
thought put him at ease and his anxiety passed.

By the time the 767 touched down in Honolulu,
Angela's spirits were soaring.

As they taxied along the apron she leaned on Von
Braun's shoulder. "How old are you, Captain?"

Von Braun never liked that question. "I am old
enough to relish all the excitement that the world of-
fers."

"And how old is that?"

"I'm fifty-five," he said, barely audible.

"Oh! You look older." Angela saw him wince. "I'm
sorry. I really believe that you look exciting . . .
worldly. A man like you is a gift to a woman like
me."

"A gift? That's nice. I've never been called a gift."
He winked his approval at Angela. She was becoming a little giddy.

"Will there be anyone else aboard Mr. Ambassador's yacht?"

"Oh yes. There will be a lot of my friends. They
should be quite amusing to you. They will certainly
find you charming. There will be bridge, backgam-
mon, movies, and lots of parties." Von Braun
squeezed her hand. "Just relax. If you tire of this old
aviator, there will be others."

"Oh Max! Who could ever tire of you?"

Since neither of them had checked luggage, they
were able to walk swiftly to the curb outside the bustling terminal in Honolulu. Angela quickly donned
sunglasses when the dazzling afternoon light hit her
eyes. "Oh Max, I feel wonderful. I feel as if I have
slipped into another world."

"Oh, you have, my dear," Von Braun responded. It

was, indeed, a different world, he thought, one from which she probably would not return. He was beginning to feel tense again. He hoped the next hour or so would pass without major incident.

Taking Angela's arm, he crossed the street and they made their way to a roped-off area set aside for livery vehicles. A stretch limo with darkened glass blinked its lights and slowly approached them. A young chauffeur with sun-bleached blond hair jumped out and held a rear door open for them.

A striking woman of Asian extraction was already sitting inside. She wore dark sunglasses that couldn't conceal her classically beautiful features. Lustrous jet-black hair fell well below her shoulders. She wore a silk dress brightly patterned in an island motif. The dress, short to begin with, was hiked up to expose the full length of her legs. She beamed at the couple knowingly from behind the dark glasses.

"Aloha. My name is Emerald. I will be your hostess aboard the *Lantau Star*. Lord Hargraves himself insisted that I meet you here." Her soft, low voice had a tinge of British accent.

"Aloha, Emerald. I am Max Von Braun and this is my companion, Angela Clayfield, as you are no doubt already aware." Von Braun breathed a sigh of relief once the limo had left the airport and began moving rapidly toward a downtown wharf in Honolulu.

"Ah, Mrs. Clayfield, it is my pleasure to introduce you to the *Lantau Star*. She is a most exquisite vessel, perfect for slipping away from all your cares. It is my duty to take care of your every need and make all the guests of Lord Hargraves happy in every way. Please remember that, Mrs. Clayfield."

Angela removed her sunglasses for a moment to study this woman. There was something imperious in her manner. A perpetual soft smile played about her lips. Angela wished she could see her eyes. Max was unusually quiet, as if he already knew the woman and the usual introductory platitudes were not needed. Of course, Max did look extremely tired. Maybe he needed this getaway as badly as she did.

"Emerald, perhaps there is something you can do for me. I left New York rather unprepared. I need to buy clothing. Is that possible before we sail?"

The handsome woman hesitated for several moments. "I'm sure we can manage that. I will be happy to take you." Emerald took off her sunglasses for a moment.

Angela was startled by the beauty of the woman. Her intense green eyes enhanced the rest of her.

"Max, isn't she lovely to take me shopping? Do you want to join us?" Angela turned to find Max staring at the woman. Again she felt uneasy. She wondered whether something was going on between them.

"No, my dear. I think I'll skip that. I think I will take your advice and have a little nap." Max closed his eyes as if to illustrate his sincerity.

"That's all right, Angela." It was the first time the woman had called her by her first name. "You and I don't need Mr. Von Braun. We will do everything together." The smile again played about her lips as she put on her sunglasses.

The limo pulled alongside the sleek *Lantau Star*. The gangplank ran up to the deck under a sundodger emblazoned with the Hargraves coat of arms. The oceangoing yacht sparkled in the warm sunshine. A small helicopter was lashed to an aft deck constructed for that purpose.

"Oh Max, how beautiful!" Angela's eyes swept along the gleaming yacht. "It's even more magnificent than you described."

Two hands stood waiting to grasp the small pieces of luggage they carried. One walked quickly toward the bow of the first deck, with Max Von Braun following. "Good-bye, ladies. I'll see you after your shopping."

"Max seems awfully tired. I hope he can get some sleep," Angela said, trying to make conversation. Emerald remained quiet as she led the way toward an inner cabin amidship. The other crewman followed them, carrying Angela's small bag. In the distance Angela could see bustling activity along the wharf. A Chart House restaurant was clearly visible.

Emerald unlocked the cabin and walked in. The sailor followed them and set the tote bag on a small vanity table, then turned and took his station outside the open door.

Angela looked around the cabin. It was small, and almost spartan in its furnishings. There was a berth, a club chair and a small dressing table and vanity stool. A tiny porthole faced dockside near the low overhead of the cabin. It was a far cry from the quarters Von Braun had described. She turned around to face Emerald, suddenly sensing that something was wrong. The sailor, now standing in the doorway, was watching her every move.

Emerald doffed her sunglasses. "Mrs. Clayfield, I know that—"

"Please call me Angela," she said anxiously.

"Mrs. Clayfield, you are a business executive. You no doubt grasp complicated situations quickly. For your own sake I will not mince words."

Angela began shaking. "Wha ... what in hell is going on here! Where is Max?"

"Mrs. Clayfield, you will enjoy the comfort of this cabin until we get well out to sea. Max Von Braun is no longer of any consequence to you. He works for me. I am the skipper of this vessel. My name is Onyx Lu."

Angela gasped, then rushed toward the door. The

wiry seaman grabbed her roughly and wrestled her to the berth.

"Matsu! That's enough!" ordered Onyx.

The cocaine, the scotch and the imprisonment all combined to render Angela immobile. She breathed heavily and gaped at her two captors as they backed out of the door, closing it and locking it from the outside.

Angela twisted the knob, which turned freely but failed to open the door. Pounding at the metal door, she screamed, "Max! Max! Max! You miserable bastard. Max, you miserable bastard."

She tried to look out the tiny porthole. She could see nothing but several buildings and the Chart House down the wharf. She pounded on the wall until her hands were too sore to pound any longer. Her voice rasped from screaming. It was obvious no one heard or cared.

Angela slumped on the berth, too weakened to continue her useless tirade.

"Onyx Lu." She shuddered as she said the name aloud. She had read Willy Hanson's book a long time ago. Now she wished she had read it more carefully.

41

The unexpected demise of Brook Laird shook Con-Com to its foundation. The city newspapers were afire with the brutal but scant details of the latest major executive to meet with foul play. The disappearance of Angela Clayfield had yet to be made public.

During a brief staff meeting that morning, Willy announced that the entire company would be shut down for two weeks. Those with personal computers and workstations at home could continue working on projects, but the majority of employees would enjoy a two-week paid vacation.

Coley toured the building with the personnel director, who was trying to reassure employees. Many seemed to feel that the historic company was on its last legs, and were clearing personal belongings from their desks to take with them.

On his way up a stairwell, Coley ran into Lois Lin.

He seemed to be bumping into her frequently since their meeting on the elevator.

"Hello, Mr. Doctor. How are you going to spend your vacation?" Lois, bright-eyed, spoke as if she was happy to have the days off. Her attitude was quite a contrast to the mood of the office in general.

"I'm afraid I don't get the time off." He eyed her appreciatively. He liked the way the little woman moved.

"Oh, that's too bad." She seemed genuinely concerned.

"So what are you going to do for the next couple of weeks?"

She shrugged, looking thoughtful for a moment. "Well, I have been trying to rustle up a cheap air fare to California. I have a sister I haven't seen in a while near Lake Tahoe."

"Hey, that's nice. I wish I were going with you," he joked.

"Why don't you come along?" She laughed like a little bell tinkling.

"No. Even if you meant it, I couldn't go." Coley winked and started to leave her at the top of the stairwell, then added, "I'll tell you what I will do. I'll pop for a quick drink if you hang around here for a few minutes."

"Okay, you've got a deal," she agreed. "The scuttlebutt is that you were a basketball whiz. Maybe you can tell me all about that."

"I sure will. I like to brag about how great I was." He grinned at her as she started to walk down the hallway. "You know, Ms. Lin, you walk very nicely."

"Well, thank you, Coley. No one ever told me that before." She grinned and gave him a wink and a wave.

Lois Lin was certainly upbeat, Coley thought. A welcome relief these days, considering all the gloom

and doom in the building. He needed a morale
booster, that was for sure. And who knows . . .
maybe six foot six ex-basketballers turned her on.

Coley spent the next few minutes comparing notes
with Willy, who would be heading for Newark soon
for a flight to Los Angeles.

"So, boss, do I detect a lack of a battle plan?" Coley
and Willy had been through hell together and neither of them had ever run from a fight.

"Relax, Coley. I'm not running away." Willy began
tossing papers into a small briefcase. "I find it impossible to believe that in all these crimes, there
isn't a clue pointing to someone. But I have to get
back to Ginny for a while. Let Whitcomb and the police work on it for a few days."

"They have a pretty good lead on Laird, Willy. His
blood alcohol count showed pure white lightning.
Tom Price, NYPD, told me just a little while ago."

"So?"

"He spent his last hours in the Highlander Palace
roof lounge, drinking at least seven martinis, some
of them doubles. He had a female companion, who
drank three glasses of Cabernet while he was trying
to fly like a bird. The police have a copy of the
check."

"Any ID on the woman?"

"Nope, but they've got a crew up there now making composite sketches. Several people say they
would know her again in a minute."

"Sounds good, maybe we'll get a break. Keep me
posted, Coley. I'll call you every day. You know Ginny's P.O. box out there." Willy grasped Coley's hand
with both of his own and squeezed hard. "You know,
Coley, if they've killed Angela, you and I must be
next on their list."

"Especially you, boss. When you get out to the
Coast, I want you to chuck that peashooter you carry

and get a nice nine-millimeter. Then get married to it."

Willy grinned at Coley as he walked out the door with his briefcase and a carry-on bag on his shoulder. The scarred-up old thirty-eight he carried around had always been a subject of Coley's ridicule.

Alone now, Coley found his thoughts turning to Lois Lin. He made a pact with himself. No nonsense. He would have a quick drink and maybe a slice of pizza. Any frivolity would have to wait for another day.

By four in the afternoon, the building was virtually empty. Coley decided to poke around Angela Clayfield's office before the police began the investigation that would surely come if Angela didn't surface.

A leather-bound appointment calendar lay at the corner of a very orderly desk. He opened it and started leafing through the past few weeks. It was heavily annotated with phone numbers, lunch and dinner dates. He decided to photocopy the whole thing so that he could study it later. He would make an extra copy for Willy, who might be able to make something more of it than he could.

Standing at the copy machine, he watched it belch out two sets of collated copies. Several times he noticed Von Braun's name. Then his eye caught a notation on August 7th. It was written in Angela Clayfield's tiny handwriting. "Call Lois Lin today!" ConCom was a fairly large company. He wondered what business Angela could have with a remote clerical employee.

The calendar would bear a lot of study. The police would no doubt check through it carefully. He finished the copying and returned the leather binder to Angela's desk. None of the drawers were locked, so he took the liberty of looking through their sparse contents. He found nothing that he thought would be useful.

He did discover one item at the rear of the top drawer that made him stop for a moment: a small black satin purse embroidered in red with a curled dragon. The purse was empty. Coley fingered it thoughtfully for a moment and then tucked it back where he'd found it.

He walked back to Willy's office and was surprised to find Lois Lin waiting for him. She was standing at the window looking down a stretch of Broadway that trailed all the way to Times Square.

"I just love New York in the fall," she commented. "It is so hard to believe that we are having all this terrible trouble here."

"It is beautiful." Coley joined her at the window. "Are you a native New Yorker?"

"Oh no. I'm an Army brat. My father was stationed in the Philippines for years. That is where he met my mother. I have been in New York for only about three years."

"Well, personally, I'd take Tahoe over all of this. I'll bet you get out there with your sister and never come back."

Lois shook her head. "No, I'm a big-city girl. I even liked Manila, and that takes a bit of doing."

"What is it you do for ConCom? You've got to do something besides walk around and look beautiful. Or maybe they pay you for that."

There was that little tinkle in her laugh again. "I'm afraid not, Mr. Doctor. I do very boring things down in accounting. I am very low on the totem pole here, even in my own department."

"Then somebody's making a big mistake. Let's get out of here."

They walked toward midtown, where Coley found

a trendy new microbrewery and negotiated for a secluded booth.

"So, Lois, what is it you want to do with your life?"

"I want to marry a tall rich basketball player," she said with a sparkle in her eye.

"Well, that sure keeps me out of your plans. It's way too late for me and the NBA."

"I heard you were awfully good. Why didn't you turn pro when you could have?"

"You have been reading Willy Hanson's book. You gotta be careful about that. He exaggerates a lot. Besides, I like being a lawyer. I'll make some bucks someday."

It was when Coley ordered their third beer that he felt her nyloned knees touch his legs under the narrow table. His legs were long, but she had avoided them until now. He didn't flinch and she persisted. Coley began to feel the old juices flow. It didn't take much. It was great to be alive, single and out on the town in New York City. Of course, Lois Lin was a no-no. Or was she?

"So what brought you to ConCom?"

"The accounting department, believe it or not. Accounting was my major. In fact, I am going back for my MBA this fall if I can swing it." She had apparently crossed her legs under the table and was now swinging one leg against the cuff of Coley's pants.

Coley sat silent for a moment and finally decided nothing ventured, nothing gained. "Why are you doing that?"

"Going for my MBA?"

"No, shining your shoes on my trousers."

She stared at him unblinking. "I'm sorry. I was just being comfortable and you didn't seem to mind."

"Oh . . . if that's all you meant, be my guest. I had an old dog once who got comfortable rubbing against people's legs. Be my guest."

"Coley! That was vulgar. I wouldn't expect you to say anything like that." She continued brushing her leg against his.

"Don't you have a boyfriend to run home to?"

"No. Are we having dinner together? Or would you rather be alone?"

"I think we ought to have dinner and talk about your future in the financial world." Coley slumped down and groped under the table with his long arm, finally grasping the crossed leg just above the knee. He uncrossed it, letting his hand linger on her thigh for several seconds.

"Coley, you are just too hot. Do you treat all of your ladies like that?"

"Nope, I've never done anything like that before," Coley lied, as she extended her hand across the table to grasp his own. Her big brown eyes continued to challenge him.

All at once he realized that he was not picking her up. She was actually hitting relentlessly on him.

He raised her hand to his lips and kissed it lightly. "Let's ask for a menu. Let's have dinner and I promise you that I'll be good."

She withdrew her hand and moved against the back of the booth, breaking all contact. "Good idea. I'm famished."

"You know, I've only been in New York for a few days. All those ConCom people are a mystery to me. How well do you know Angela Clayfield?"

He thought he noticed her stiffen slightly before falling back again into a relaxed mode. "Angela Clayfield?" She shook her head. "I don't know her at all. She is always courteous on the elevator. She always speaks. Once I took some papers up to her office. She had some people in, so I just dropped them off. She is a beautiful woman."

Lois smiled at Coley and again extended her hand across the table. Coley decided to let her play with his fingers. What she had said didn't explain the note on Angela's calendar.

"Where are you and Mr. Hanson staying in New York?"

The question was natural enough, Coley thought, but still it set off an internal alarm.

"The Waldorf," Coley lied.

"Hey, that's nice. That is, I suppose it is nice. I have never been there." She continued exploring Coley under the table with her foot.

"Young lady, if you keep that up, I'll have to accommodate you up to the Waldorf."

"Oh, you're getting vulgar again."

"I think you like that."

"You are perceptive, Mr. Doctor." She lifted his hand to her lips and planted a lingering, moist kiss on his palm.

He continued to let her play with his hand while he surveyed the menu. "I think I'm going to have some pasta. Perhaps we'll get a bottle of wine with that. What are you going to have?"

"You."

"I mean right now. As an appetizer, so to speak."

"You order for me. I'm sure it will be fine." Lois glanced around the bar. "Do you see a telephone anywhere? I should call my roommate and tell her I'll be very late. She worries."

"There were several near the door where we came in." Coley watched her fishing around in her purse for change. He felt distinctly uncomfortable. What if Lois Lin was the mole inside ConCom? What if she was setting him up right now? Something like this could have happened with Brook Laird.

He watched her move through the restaurant. She certainly did walk nicely.

The place was not crowded. He began to isolate people in the bar and restaurant and study them. Paranoia engulfed him. If Lois Lin, that hot, classy little chick, was one of the terrorists, they could have been tailed to the restaurant. One of the several dozen customers now sitting around the room could be an accomplice. Or perhaps she was on the phone calling a hit man right now.

"Coley, that is preposterous," he whispered to himself. He slipped the nine-millimeter from its shoulder holster, careful to keep it under his jacket, and stuffed it into his pants where he could keep his hand on it.

He looked at his wristwatch. Lois had been gone about five minutes. Abruptly he asked the waiter for the check. It arrived about the same time Lois slid back into the booth. She looked at Coley with disbelief as he pushed several bills at the waiter.

"Coley, dear, we haven't eaten yet."

Coley noticed that since her return, he had become a "dear." "I guess I've lost my appetite. If you don't mind, we're getting out of here." He watched her closely. She glanced at her watch, then broke into a big smile.

"You know what? I've lost my appetite too. Why don't you take me on a little tour of the Waldorf, and then we'll eat later, if we still want to."

Coley stared back into her unblinking dark eyes. Relentless wasn't the word for it. The brazen bookkeeper was issuing a command.

As they left the restaurant, Lois walked ahead. Coley scrutinized the other patrons along the way, but nobody seemed to be paying any attention to them. Outside, a taxicab was starting to pull away. Coley yelled just in time to stop it. Lois climbed in first. When Coley sat down, Lois slid over as close to him as she could get.

"Eighteenth Street," Coley advised the cabdriver.

"Eighteenth Street?" Lois shouted, even though she was right next to him. "The Waldorf is up in the fifties!"

"You got that right. But what's the hurry? I found this place last night, Pete's Tavern. They make a great corned beef sandwich and I'm hungry as a bear." He watched her stiffen like an iceberg.

"Coley, you can't be serious. I thought we were going to the Waldorf to have some fun. Now you're trading me for a corned beef sandwich? Not on your life. I'll get out here, if you don't mind." She made a move toward the door handle as the cabdriver slowed down.

"Okay! Okay! You win." Coley put both hands up in front of him. "Driver, take us to the Waldorf."

"You are a tease, Coley." Suddenly she was all over him. "I have a special punishment for men who tease me like that." Her lips explored his face as her hands burrowed into his clothing.

Their arrival at the Waldorf came too quickly for Coley. Lois fairly ran up the steps to the lobby ahead of him.

"Let's have one nightcap, doll." Coley steered her into the lobby bar. "This has been one hell of a day. Besides, they have these big bowls of mixed nuts with lots of cashews. I'm famished."

"All right, Coley. But will you order me a double Bailey's on the rocks while I go to find the rest room? You made a mess out of me in the cab!"

"I did what! You were like a wild animal in heat!"

"You ain't seen nothin' yet, baby," she whispered as she turned and left the room.

Coley watched until Lois had rounded the corner of the lobby lounge. He stood up then, strode rapidly through the hotel, and ran down the stairs to the

Lexington Avenue entrance. He hailed a cab and sped off southward toward the Buchanan Park.

He smacked his fist into his hand, thinking of the hot little package he had dumped in the lounge. I guess I'm just a coward, he thought.

"Oh well," he mumbled to nobody, "Willy Hanson would be proud of me."

42

$\mathbf{W}$illy was still adjusting to the idea of being a target. He ran over the plan again and again in his mind. As CEO, however temporary, he had to be a target. Whoever was terrorizing the company would have him at the top of the list. He would stand out in the open and see who came after him. Whitcomb would use all his resources to provide cover. It should be easier around a marina than most places. Most of the nearby boats would have agents aboard.

Katie Glover had promised to plant the story in the morning newspapers. Willy Hanson, ConCom's new CEO, would toss a gala at the yacht club to celebrate the opening of ConCom's West Coast office. The real eye-opener would be the news that ConCom planned to move its entire operation to the West Coast in the near future. Meanwhile Willy would keep himself tantalizingly visible, living openly aboard the *Tashtego*.

Only one thing really bothered him. On the phone

that morning, Ginny had insisted on riding out the ordeal with him.

The big jet touched down right on time at John Wayne Airport, near Newport Beach. Ginny was waiting for him. God! she was beautiful, he thought. He held her close for several moments, wishing they did not have such an ordeal ahead of them.

"We'll stay the night in the Sheraton. Whitcomb won't have the stakeout in place until tomorrow evening."

"I'll stay anywhere, Willy, as long as we're together." Ginny touched his cheek, then held his hand. "I didn't like our separation much."

"Good," Willy answered with a smile and a squeeze of her hand. "Me neither. Let's get checked in and I'll fill you in on everything."

They had dinner at a little fish place on the Lido in Newport. Halfway through the main course Willy told her Angela had disappeared. They sat close and watched the lights shimmering off the water.

"Willy, are we ever going to make our Pacific crossing?" Ginny grasped his hand and rubbed her head against his shoulder.

"Of course we will, someday."

Ginny smiled.

"Let's get back to the hotel, honey. I don't think I've had a good night's sleep since I left."

"Sleep? You're thinking about sleep? Willy, that's not very nice."

Willy buried a kiss in her neck. "I'll remember the other things as soon as we close the bedroom door."

They were lying in each other's arms, wide awake, watching the morning sun move shadows across the wall, when the phone rang.

"That has to be Coley." He glanced at his watch. It was 10 A.M. in New York. "Hi."

"Hi yourself," Coley said. "Glad to hear you're

alive and kicking. That's more than I can say for my date last night."

"Coley, admit it. You have an almost flawless knack for picking losers."

"That ain't what I mean, boss. I took that pretty little Lois Lin out for a drink last night. They found her in an alley on Third Avenue this morning with a broken neck."

"Oh Jesus."

"That makes number five, boss. I think it was supposed to be me. I think she was trying to set me up last night. I ducked out and I think she took the heat."

"What makes you think that?"

"She was trying to get me into a hotel room, and she did everything but jump my bones in public to get me there. I felt like Brook Laird. I actually felt like that white dude! I think she was the mole we were looking for. I also found her name on Angela Clayfield's desk calendar. I'm sending you a copy of the whole calendar."

"Has anyone heard from Angela?"

"Nope. I figure she's number six. Goddamn it, Willy. I screwed up. I had Lois Lin in the palm of my hand last night. My paranoia was working overtime. I actually knew she was one of them. How many times do you think I've turned down a piece of tail? But I played goody-goody just like my boss told me to."

"It's a good thing, Coley, or you would probably be the one with the broken neck. We can't worry about Lois Lin. She was too far down in the pecking order to know very much."

"I guess. How's Ginny doing?"

"Ginny's doing great. She's right here on my shoulder."

"Hi, Coley."

"Ah, I should have known. You've been eavesdropping. You heard the whole story."

"Yes, Coley. It's ghastly. It could have been you."

"She was a pretty little thing, Ginny."

"Coley! She was rotten!"

"Yes she was . . . Hell, I guess we're all a little rotten. Oh well . . . You two guys take care of yourselves out there. I'd rather be out there with you."

"Soon enough, Coley. Hold the fort."

43

Max Von Braun turned toward Copilot Tommy Wing and winked. The new 757 was locked in on the southern approach to San Francisco International Airport. They had just flown over the San Mateo Bridge, and the hotel complex in Burlingame was off to the left. This was his first flight with Wing since the horrendous approach to Kennedy a couple of weeks before. Most of the passengers this trip didn't even know when the wheels hit the runway. The touchdown was perfect.

Wing smiled his approval as he initiated the post-landing procedures.

"Tommy, I don't think we'll be flying together much anymore. I've put in for some short runs out of Kai-Tak. I want to stay closer to Hong Kong in my old age." To himself, the captain cursed the man for reporting him. He wasn't looking forward to the hearings in Hong Kong next week.

"Captain, I'll miss you. I hope everything works out for you."

Silly bastard, Von Braun thought again. If he had kept his mouth shut there would have been no hearing in Hong Kong next week.

"I am going to stay around California for a while, and then hitch a ride back to Hong Kong for the hearing." His stare bored straight through the young copilot. "Somebody didn't like my approach to Kennedy a couple of weeks ago."

Wing shrugged as if he didn't know anything about it. "Sorry to hear that, Captain. I'm sure everything will be all right. You're the best."

Von Braun strode rapidly through the concourse and made his way to the courtesy rental car lane outside the terminal. He reached into his breast pocket and fingered the envelope that Onyx had given him, with orders to mail it from some small community in Northern California. Then he was to wait for further instructions. Von Braun felt reduced to an errand boy. He didn't like the change in stature.

Exiting the airport, he drove south along the road to San Jose, then east across the San Mateo Bridge. He felt a certain pang of sorrow. He prided himself on being without conscience, but he had actually developed a genuine affection for Angela Clayfield, and he felt a certain concern for her. Part of it was the enthusiasm she had shown for the chart book. Now, with Laird dead and Angela on the high seas for God knows how long, the whole publishing project was in limbo. But beyond that, the woman appealed to him, addicted as she was to the offerings of Lois Lin. A few days aboard the *Lantau Star* and Angela would just become another one of Onyx Lu's expendable zombies. What a waste, he thought.

The exit sign read "Hopyard Road." He was in

Pleasanton. That was far enough, he decided. He pulled off the freeway and into a gas station and asked directions to the local post office.

He pulled the envelope from his jacket pocket. The stamp was already affixed. First-class mail. No special handling or priority postage, yet he had flown several thousand miles just to mail it from an obscure place.

Von Braun fingered the envelope thoughtfully. Curiosity was killing him. Not only was it sealed, but a line of transparent tape protected the contents. It was addressed to Willy Hanson, of ConCom Publishing Company, to a post office box in New York. Something big must be happening, he thought, and the diabolical Onyx Lu had planned every step herself, even this simple little side trip to the California countryside.

He thought of all the dead bodies Onyx was responsible for and gave up the idea of opening the letter. He walked into the post office and dropped it into the slot marked "Out of Town."

Von Braun felt weary. The flight from Hawaii with Tommy Wing and the subsequent freeway driving had taken their toll. Finding Hopyard Road again, he came upon a cluster of roadside motels. He pulled into one that looked comfortable and checked in. Outside his sliding door was a large swimming pool nestled in an elaborately landscaped garden. Several young women were splashing in the pool, while others were sunning.

All of a sudden he felt invigorated. He fetched the little satin purse from his jacket and rubbed the embroidered dragon thoughtfully. There's no fool like an old fool, he thought. And I am an old fool.

44

Angela Clayfield stared at the ceiling above her berth. She felt weak, reluctant to move. It was as if she were drugged. The small cabin seemed to move with a gentle rocking motion. Then she remembered the *Lantau Star*, and realized that they were no longer in port. She looked down at herself. Where were her clothes? She wore a flimsy nightgown that covered almost nothing.

"You look lovely, Angela. You look like a motion picture star. I envy you."

The voice startled her, rousing her from her stupor. She turned her head abruptly, and the small cabin seemed to reel around her. Sitting in a small club chair, Onyx Lu watched her.

Angela struggled to sit erect on the bunk, then fell back against her pillow helplessly.

"Where is Max? I want to talk to Max." She tried desperately to get her mind working. The last thing she could recall was Max sitting next to her on the way from the airport.

"Max is not here, darling. He had other business to attend to. I assured him that I would take good care of you."

Angela's vision began to focus on Onyx. She sat in the lotus position wearing only a tiny bikini. She was well bronzed and not the least bit shy about her near nakedness. A paperback book lay open, pages down, on the overstuffed chair arm. She had apparently been there for some time.

Angela winced as she again struggled to sit up. Her arms ached terribly and she saw that they were badly bruised. Then it all came back to her, the pounding on the door.

"You have no right to keep me here." She made a move to stand up, but gave up as the room began to spin again.

"Relax, my pet, the door is not locked. You are free to join us any time you wish."

"Join who?" In an all-out effort, Angela stood up and stumbled to the cabin door. The door opened easily and she gaped outside. Then she remembered the nightgown that left her virtually naked and quickly closed the door. Fighting nausea, she tripped back to the berth.

"As fetching as you look, and as much as everyone would appreciate you, perhaps you had better change before going on deck. I have brought some other things for you to wear." Onyx pointed to a swimsuit hanging on the door to the lavatory.

Angela slumped back onto the berth. "Where are we? Why do I feel like this? What have you done with my clothes?"

"One question at a time, dear. We have no secrets out here. You are our guest, and the guest of Lord John Hargraves, who is dying to meet you."

"That's stupid. I was kidnapped. That bastard, Max . . ."

" 'Kidnapped' is a very unpleasant word. Relax. You have complete freedom on the *Lantau Star*. I emphasize the word complete. You will have more fun here than you could ever imagine. It's up to you."

Angela was getting more cogent by the moment now. Her thoughts went back to Max's strange aloofness during the trip from the airport in the limo. "Where are we now?" Her voice was getting stronger.

"We are perhaps three hundred kilometers out of Honolulu. It is a gloriously sunny day and there is scarcely a ripple on the sea." Onyx stood and walked over to take the swimsuit off the door. She tossed the pieces on the bed and then walked closer to run her hand across Angela's tousled blond hair.

Angela cringed. "Don't touch me!"

"Sorry, my dear. You will get over that. I understand that you feel hostility now. But I feel certain that will turn to affection. That is the way it works with people who fancy themselves victims."

"Never!"

"We'll see . . . we'll see. As for your clothes, I decided they were not appropriate for our voyage. I am sorry that we didn't have time for that shopping trip. It would have been such fun. But Lord Hargraves was in a hurry to get going."

"Lord Hargraves? What has he got to do with all this?"

"This vessel belongs to him. He is the owner of the *Lantau Star*. He is responsible for everything that happens aboard her." Onyx smiled and then again tried to run her fingers through Angela's hair. "At least, my dear, we try to keep him convinced of that."

"Don't touch me!"

"Lord Hargraves will find you charming, and I

think you will find him very appealing, and comforting. British diplomats have a knack for that."

Angela stood again, finally feeling as though she had control over her own body. Onyx was ogling her nakedness.

"Please, if you don't mind, I would like some privacy. I would like to pull myself together and change."

"Certainly. That's much better. Go with the flow. This voyage can be a very pleasant experience for you. For all of us."

"I doubt that. Why do I have this sick feeling? What have you given me? What drug?"

"Perhaps you are a little seasick."

"I don't get seasick. I've been around boats all my life."

Onyx leered. "Yes, I know all about that. But the *Lazy Dolphin* can hardly compare to the *Lantau Star.*"

"You bitch! You're the one who had her sunk!" The emotional outburst caused Angela to almost lose her balance again. "What in the hell have you done to me! Why do I feel like this?"

"Maybe it's the heroin," Onyx said softly.

"The what!"

"It's a dangerous drug, darling. From now on, you will be given the choice to take it or not. We'll see how you do."

45

Coley Doctor drew the nine-millimeter from its holster and placed it on Angela Clayfield's desk in front of him. He had been given his choice of all the offices in the building, and decided that he would be happy here. With the door open, he could see down a long hallway almost the length of the building. Only six people had access to the upper floors of the building, so Coley felt his position was secure.

At noon today Willy Hanson and Ginny would be moving aboard the *Tashtego*. Coley was expecting a call almost any minute to brief him on the security precautions at the marina.

Coley picked up the composite sketch of Brook Laird's drinking companion. It was unmistakably Lois Lin.

He had already checked out her desk down in accounting and found it empty. She had obviously not intended to return to ConCom after her night with Coley.

The only personal property she had left behind was a winter coat hung on the back of her office door, probably overlooked. The pockets were empty, except for one item: a small satin purse, about three inches by four inches. It was handsomely embroidered with a coiled red dragon, an exact duplicate of the one Coley had found in Angela's desk. The purse was empty.

Coley opened Angela's top drawer again and fished out the small purse there. Why should Angela and Lois Lin have duplicates?

He cursed himself as he tossed the purse onto the desk. If only he had gotten a room at the Waldorf and carried through on the date with Lois Lin, he would have a lot of answers by now. Or he would be dead.

Coley looked up and saw Derrick Harrison, Con-Com's aging office manager, walking the long hallway toward him.

"Mr. Doctor. You'd make a fine executive, sitting so tall in that chair."

"Derrick, please call me Coley. There's no need for any formalities around here."

"Coley it is, then."

"I'll tell you, Derrick, how people allow themselves to get chained to one of these desks has to be one of the great mysteries of mankind."

Harrison leaned across the desk as if there were somebody who might hear. "I think it has something to do with money."

"I guess that's why I never have enough," said Coley, nodding. Of course, he thought, those big alimony checks every month don't help any.

Harrison glanced down at the desk and picked up the brightly colored satin purse. "That's a pretty thing. Mrs. Clayfield's, I imagine. She has lots of pretty things."

"By the way, have you seen any other purses like this around here?"

"No." Harrison fingered the soft purse thoughtfully. "I suppose that was a gift to Mrs. Clayfield. By the way, I haven't seen her around for a few days. I hope she's okay. I feel so sorry for that woman. It seemed like everything was rolling along real smooth-like. Then this terrible trouble started."

Coley decided not to tell him about Angela's disappearance yet. It would be newspaper headlines soon, anyway.

Harrison stared out the window, deep in thought. "You know, I did see another purse something like that one. I remember now. I used to play a couple rounds of golf with Vinnie Lawson each summer. Now there was a fine young man. A great golfer, too. Taught me a lot. Anyway, he had a purse like that. He carried it in his golf bag. Kept it full of tees."

"Really?" Coley asked.

Harrison grinned. "Yep, I kidded him about it once. Told him it looked kind of sissified. His purse was pink, but it had the same dragon on it."

"How long ago was that?"

"Well . . . let me see. It must have been last June. I think that was the last time we played."

"If you see any more of them, let me know, will you?"

"Why, sure." Harrison eyed the colorful purse silently for a moment. "Oh, I almost forgot why I came here. Mr. Hanson told me to give all his mail to you. There hasn't been much, but there are a few letters in here." He laid a manila envelope on the desk.

"Thanks, Derrick. I'll pass them along." Coley emptied the contents of the envelope on the desk. There were half a dozen letters addressed to Willy Hanson.

Harrison walked toward the door. "I promised

Harry Hills down in operations I would drop by. If there is anything else I can do, let me know. The place is as quiet as a morgue."

"Thanks, Derrick," Coley said, as he began opening the first envelope. The first letters were congratulatory notes from people outside the company. Coley tossed them aside.

The fourth envelope was postmarked Pleasanton, California. Scotch tape had been used to carefully seal the seams of the standard white envelope. It was addressed to Willy Hanson and marked "Personal." Following Willy's instructions, Coley carefully slit the end of the envelope with the letter opener. A Polaroid snapshot fell out onto the desk. It was a picture of Angela Clayfield in a peignoir. She looked either intoxicated or half asleep. Coley's heart skipped a beat. He took two sheets of white paper out of the envelope, unfolded them and began to read.

Dear Willy,

Long time no see! I think of you so often. I promised myself that I would never contact you again until I had some very big news.

Well, the time has come. I have some momentous news. I am sorry to have to tell you this way. I would have preferred the old days when we communicated so intimately.

Angela Clayfield is enjoying her vacation so much, although she does miss her old friends. Those that are left must miss her. Hey! she is a knockout.

In fact, she has an assessed valuation of one million dollars, plus one Willy Hanson. I will require cash, and your body. You will be glad to know that I want you alive.

I'm giving you a few days to get the money to-

gether. I am sure that the ConCom board will cooperate.

It's the second part of the deal that interests me most, Willy. I want you. I want you day and night, lover. I have big plans for you.

Enclosed is a picture of Angela. Doesn't she look beautiful! My nightgown is a little small for her, but we don't mind, do we?

You'll be hearing from me in a few days. Meanwhile, get the million together in hundred-dollar bills. And, lover, don't get any heroic ideas. Unless you do as you are told, Angela Clayfield will join Charles in the churchyard back in Saddle Hills.

> *Your soulmate,*
> *Onyx Lu*

Coley studied the photograph. Angela was lying on a narrow twin-size bed set against a light blue wall. There was absolutely no clue to her location. The letter was typewritten, and that didn't help either.

He picked up the telephone to call Willy.

"You're getting some wild fan mail back here in the office," Coley said when Willy picked up the phone. "You're a real popular guy. Nice friends. That's what always impressed me about you."

"Okay, Coley. Get your tongue out of your cheek and tell me what's up."

"It seems you have a letter from your soulmate." Coley described the picture and then read the letter. "It's typewritten. Anyone could have sent this. Anyone who has read your book and knows the background."

"No chance. The letter came from Onyx. I recognize her style. She evidently has three objectives: to destroy ConCom, to ransom Angela, and to get rid of me."

"So what do we do with the letter?"

"I hate to do anything. Was it registered?"

"No, just plain first-class mail. Do we tell Whitcomb and get the feds working on it?"

"Tell him to handle it as a missing persons thing, not a kidnapping. Tell him to keep the ransom note away from the press. I'm already a highly visible target out here. Onyx should have no trouble communicating with me."

"Okay. Hey, one other thing. I found a little red satin purse with a dragon stitched on it in Angela's desk, and one like it in Lois Lin's office. Now, Harrison says he saw one in Vinnie Lawson's golf bag, too."

"That's the clincher, Coley. We're dealing with Onyx. Those purses come packed with cocaine."

"A lot of ConCom employees are holding these bags. Sounds like a little corporate perk?"

"ConCom has lots of housekeeping to do."

"Onyx is doing a good job of that already."

46

The *Lantau Star* was plowing her way through swelling seas caused by a distant storm.

In a luxurious aft stateroom, Lars Svenson was moving in a slow, rhythmic tempo over the small woman beneath him. His massive, athletic frame completely covered her. Guttural gasps from the woman urged him on. He had been at this work for over an hour. Finally a long deep moan came from the woman.

She dug a fingernail into the bronzed shoulder of the first mate. "Stop! Stop it, you fool. Rest for a while, just a little while." Then Onyx Lu managed to raise herself on one elbow, laughing as she sank her teeth into the first mate's neck.

"Where did you acquire such stamina? Ohh . . . And you are still there. Just wait a few moments and then I will show you how much I appreciated that." Onyx cajoled and maneuvered her way on top of the muscular seaman and lay perfectly still, staring into his unblinking blue eyes.

"Where did I acquire it? I think it comes naturally. I may have embellished it by exploring women in Honolulu, Adelaide, in Wanchai, and other places. I have been first mate for Lord Hargraves for over ten years and I guess we've gotten around a bit. But of all the women I've known around the world, you are the most beautiful. You have the sexiest mouth I've ever seen."

Svenson had come to her cabin to go over the fine points of the oceangoing yacht. The original blueprints of the boat lay on a table in her cabin, along with two cups of coffee that were now quite cold.

Onyx had included Svenson in the crew with some reluctance. He had been with the boat since its launching, and Hargraves had been insistent. The *Lantau Star* had its secrets and eccentricities. He feared making an extended voyage with the green crew Onyx had brought from Hong Kong. Now Onyx felt more comfortable with her decision.

"Lars, you are a talented mate, both professionally and personally. Just don't forget who the real captain of this vessel is." She brushed her hand through the sun-bleached hair of the handsome Swede. "I'm yours to enjoy, for now. Welcome aboard."

"Happy you feel that way, Miss Onyx ... ahh ... oh, that's it. Don't stop that. I won't permit you to stop."

Onyx paused and smiled provocatively at the first mate. She would let the comment go for the moment. In due time she would teach him that only she spoke with such authority aboard the *Lantau Star*.

Toward the bow of the vessel, in her tiny cabin, Angela Clayfield eyed the swimsuit that still lay on the bed where Onyx had tossed it the day before. She stood up to peek through the tiny porthole. It

was blue water and a light chop as far as she could
see. The tiny opening did not permit any lateral vision.

She picked up the swimsuit and put it on, surprised that it fit her tall figure well. She studied her
features in the small mirror, and decided that she
looked a hell of a lot better than she felt.

Angela examined the tiny red mark on her arm.
Heroin, Onyx had said. She wondered if it was true.
She knew her desire for cocaine had been kindled
one night when she had met Lois Lin at a club in the
Village. She wished Lois was around now. Maybe
that bastard, Max, was still on board. He would
have cocaine.

Angela tried the door. It was unlocked. She
stepped into the companionway and walked a few
paces to the main deck. She held the handrail and
quickly sized up the *Lantau Star*. She estimated it
was about 140 feet long. The small helicopter lashed
to an aft flight deck dominated that part of the
yacht. The vessel was polished and sleek, obviously
kept in top condition. A deckhand passed by, the
only person visible at that moment. He nodded,
smiled pleasantly and continued making his way aft.

Angela look a deep breath and decided to explore
the bow of the boat. When she was about halfway
forward, a tall, distinguished man, probably in his
fifties, but exceedingly fit, left his stateroom and
turned in her direction. He appeared to be as startled as she was.

"Aha! You must be Angela Clayfield," he exclaimed. "I am John Hargraves. Emerald has been
worried about you. Said you were not feeling well."

"Emerald? You must mean Onyx."

"Oh yes, I keep forgetting. In Hong Kong, I knew
her as Emerald. Mrs. Clayfield, you look spectacular.

You should have ventured on deck before. You en-
hance the appearance of this drab vessel."

Angela was confused by the gentleman's manner.
He acted as if she were actually a guest, not a hostage. "I take it you are Lord Hargraves, the owner of
this yacht."

"Yes, I am. However, I have her under lease to Ms.
Lu at the moment. So you see, I am a guest on my
own vessel. I'm afraid I have no control over the
Lantau Star on this voyage. And by the way, please
call me John."

"Well then, John, you're a guest and not a hostage
as I am?" The headway of the boat caused Angela's
blond mane to blow into her eyes. She could see Hargraves staring at the line of her bikini top.

"Mrs. Clayfield, 'hostage' is a harsh and dismal
word. We do have freedom aboard this boat. Might
as well enjoy it for a short time."

Angela decided that he was an old lecher. "A short
time? What is a short time? Where are we going?"

Hargraves turned his palms up and shrugged. "I
thought we were going to San Francisco, but right
now we don't seem to be on that heading." He
glanced at the noon sun and the shadows cast by the
rail stanchions. "I would reckon that we are headed
more toward the Mexican coast."

"What are they going to do with me? You must
have heard them talking."

"I could ask you the same question. We are both
peas in this same pod, so to speak." As if to comfort
her, he patted her arm lightly. "Ah, poor thing, we'll
have to try to support one another."

Angela pulled away from him, at the same time
fixing on the man's eyes. His pupils were dilated,
though they should have been contracted in the
bright sun. His fixed stare became annoying. "John,
perhaps we'll talk another time. Right now neither

one of us seems in a position to help the other." With
that she strode quickly toward the bow. There was a
row of deck chairs there. She decided to sit for a
while, hoping she would be left alone.

She closed her eyes, trying to concentrate and remember clearly the past few days. So much had happened since she had walked out on Brook Laird and
Grundy at the Plaza. She silently cursed herself.
Max had made it sound so romantic. They would escape for a few days and then pop up in Hawaii. She
would arrange a press party to announce the discov-
ery of a whole binder of Captain Cook's original
charts. It had sounded like a dynamite idea. But the
suave old aviator was a con artist. His charm and
the cocaine had blinded her. She remembered his silence when they had been joined by Onyx. She
should have followed her instincts and jumped out
right then.

Von Braun had done his job well. She doubted the
authorities would ever be able to pick up the trail of
her trek from the Plaza to the *Lantau Star*. She felt
tears trail down her cheeks.

She thought of Brad Overstreet, slumped over
next to her in the taxi. She missed Brad terribly. He
had been strong. She had gone off the deep end that
night after the shooting. The pills, the booze and the
cocaine had taken over.

"Hi!"

Angela was startled by a voice at her side. She
turned to see a tall slender woman with platinum-
blond hair.

"Mind if I sit with you a while? My name is
Melanie." The young woman was studying Angela,
obviously noticing the tears. "Wow, you are beautiful.
Lord Hargraves certainly didn't exaggerate about
that. He simply raved about you when I saw him a
few minutes ago."

"Tell me, Melanie, are you a hostage too?" Angela asked the question matter-of-factly, amused by her own tone.

"Oh, no. I am here because I want to be. Onyx invited me along. I think she did that because Lord Hargraves is fond of me. Of course he's fond of just about anyone in panties."

"Yes, I gathered that." Angela forced a faint smile, trying to be pleasant with the young woman. Perhaps she would be able to fill in some of the blanks. "Where are we going, Melanie? Lord Hargraves was a little vague about it."

"We're going on a cruise." Melanie giggled. "Really, that's all I know. Try to relax. Just go with the flow, as they say, and everything will be okay."

Angela nodded dejectedly and sensed that Melanie wanted to make her feel better.

"I would guess that only Onyx and Lars Svenson know where we're going."

"Lars Svenson?"

"He's first mate, the brains at the bridge of this fancy boat. And he is a dreamboat, the only dreamboat on board. You'll know him the minute you see him. There must be a half dozen deckhands. A couple of them are kind of cute, but nothing compared to Lars. Why don't you join us for dinner this evening? You might as well meet everyone. Onyx always plans a little surprise."

One of the crew passed by. He stopped near the bow and seemed to be inspecting the rigging that suspended one of the lifeboats.

"Excuse me." Melanie stood up and started to walk toward the crewman, then looked back over her shoulder toward Angela. "Remember, join us tonight. Live for each day. We do have fun."

She went to speak to the crewman. She reminded Angela of the tall showgirls in Las Vegas revues who sometimes dance poorly but look great just strutting around.

The water had flattened out. The *Lantau Star* moved effortlessly, with a scarcely perceptible roll, across the long swells, leaving a wake that stretched for miles. Angela, feeling slightly better in the warm sun, decided to circle the main deck. Leaning over the bow pulpit, she looked at the gentle spray created by the boat knifing through the sea. Under any other circumstances, the cruise would be idyllic.

As she walked toward the stern she again saw the helicopter lashed to the specially constructed flight deck. A swarthy, slender man, probably Chinese, opened the hatch on the bubble and climbed down onto the deck. His face crinkled in a friendly smile and he waved casually toward her.

"Good day, Mrs. Clayfield. They call me Gyro. I fly the copter. I like to go up on the pad and check things out now and then."

"You must be a very good pilot, Gyro. The landing pad looks very small."

"It is small, but adequate, if one is experienced. I'll show you one day."

Angela decided to be friendly. "That would be nice. How about Honolulu right now?"

The man frowned. Then the crinkly grin came back to his face. "Oh no. That is much too far away for today. Someday, maybe." Gyro gave her a quick salute and walked rapidly forward.

She decided she liked him. He seemed out of character with the others. She wondered what quirk of fate had made him a partner in this nefarious voyage.

Finally she returned to the narrow passageway that led to her cabin. She found lunch waiting for her; a seafood salad and a thermos of coffee sitting on the small table. Stretched out on the bed was a dress, or more accurately a sarong. There was a note from Melanie again beseeching Angela to join her at dinner. Angela held the sarong up in front of her and knew it would fit.

Sitting down to the seafood salad, she decided to take Melanie up on her offer. Who knew? Maybe something useful would be gained by it. Maybe someone else aboard was as miserable as she was.

Angela dozed for a while, relaxed by the salt air and warm sunshine. The nap was her first drug-free rest since she had come aboard. There was a gentle knock at the door. It was Melanie.

"It's cocktail time, princess." Melanie glanced at the sarong, now tossed over a chair. "I bet you look dynamite in that."

Angela looked at her watch. It was not 6 P.M., unless they had changed time zones. "It's nice, Melanie. Thanks. But how can I be civil to people who are holding me prisoner?"

Melanie sat on the bed next to Angela. She crossed her hands in her lap and looked pensively. "Princess, all of us aboard the *Lantau Star* are in some way prisoners of Onyx. All for different reasons, different debts and commitments. All of us sort of play a role for her. In return, she rewards us and protects us. We live a life much better than most of us have ever known before."

"But I'm not like that. To me, this isn't the good life. My good life is thousands of miles from here."

"I don't know anything about that, but Onyx always has her reasons. In your case, she needs you for something. Whenever that something is achieved, she won't need you anymore. You'll leave her and go back."

Melanie spoke with sincerity, but Angela couldn't help thinking of all the people back in New York who were now dead.

"What did Onyx ever do for you? Why are you better off aboard the *Lantau Star*? What is your role? What is your debt to her?"

"She rescued me from a brothel in Wanchai. She got me out of there while I was still beautiful and still healthy. She has been like a mother to me."

"And in return?"

"It is my job to make all of Onyx's friends happy, to cater to their pleasures, make life in this ugly world more pleasant for them."

"Melanie, in other words she rescued you from being a low-class whore to turn you into a high-class whore."

"Those are terrible words, Angela. You don't understand. But you will. Now, please get dressed so we can go to dinner."

Angela shook her head. "Sorry, I don't believe I'm up to playing any kind of role tonight."

"I wish I could change your mind." Then, boldly, Melanie took her forefinger and traced a gentle line down Angela's breast. "Do you want me to make love to you before we go?"

"Melanie!" Angela sprung to her feet. "For God's sake, no! I like you, Melanie. Just be my friend. Okay?" Angela picked up the sarong from the chair and began to put it on.

"Of course I'll be your friend." Melanie watched Angela dress and then reached into a small beaded handbag she carried. She pulled out an even smaller satin purse embroidered with a tiny laughing dragon. "Here. Help yourself. This will get you through the evening. I'll join you, if you don't mind."

Angela shook her head at first, but then reached for the purse. The compulsion was just too great.

The *Lantau Star* had a small but ornate dining room. A few years back, Lord Hargraves had entertained the social elite all over Southeast Asia. On this night it was like a miniature cruise ship. At first glance, the dozen people in the dining room appeared to be having a delightful time, drinking, chatting and enjoying the guitar-strumming balladeer. He was the deck-hand Angela had passed early in the day.

Dinner was a lavish seafood buffet. It was prepared by a chef known as Kelly. Melanie whispered that Onyx had "saved" him from paying the penalty for a hopeless gambling debt to a casino in Macau.

Onyx and Lars Svenson arrived later than the others. Onyx was dressed in a floor-length black turtleneck gown that molded to her flawless figure like black paint. Svenson wore an officer's jacket, but wore it casually open at the neck.

Svenson made his way straight to the table Angela was sharing with Melanie and Gyro. "You must be Angela. I am Lars Svenson. I must say that you and Melanie light up the whole room." He smiled broadly. "Perhaps you will come to the bridge tomorrow. I would love to show you about the *Lantau Star*." He sat next to Angela and leaned over to whisper so that the others couldn't hear. "Please do that. I must talk to you."

He leaned back then and laughed, as if they had exchanged some pleasantry.

Svenson was certainly every bit as impressive as Melanie had described in their morning conversation. He was well over six feet, young and boyishyly handsome. She noticed that Onyx, who had sat down to dine with Lord Hargraves, could hardly keep her eyes off the first mate.

"I would be happy to tour the bridge with you, Mr. Svenson." Lars went over then to join Onyx.

Angela leaned over to whisper to Melanie. "What is his great debt to Onyx?"

"He belongs to the boat. He came with Lord Hargraves. Isn't he a doll!"

Angela was elated. There was at least one other person aboard who perhaps didn't want to be there.

Soon after the main course it became apparent that this occasion was like no other party. The little dragon purses began to appear here and there and were used openly. She was feeling her own high from the hit shared with Melanie in her cabin.

After most people had visited the dessert table, the guitar player launched into a dramatic classical solo, and a statuesque young blond woman, costumed only in a bejeweled belt, entered the room. She began an exhibition of erotic dancing that soon had most of the guests clapping and cheering her on. The dance was savagely erotic. The dancer approached Lord Hargraves, her belly inches away from his leering face. Then she abruptly turned and ran from the room before Lord Hargraves was provoked to participation in her finale.

"That was Brigitte," Melanie whispered to Angela. "She dances up a storm, doesn't she?"

"And now . . ." Onyx rose to speak. "And now we have a very special treat. We have a very special home movie. I think you will recognize some of the players, and that will make it all extra fun."

Gyro got up from the table, walked over to Angela and leaned over her shoulder. "I don't think you will enjoy this. I need some fresh air. Care to take a walk around the deck?"

"Gyro, get lost! We're just having fun." Melanie didn't want her new friend to leave.

Angela looked at Gyro and decided to stay. Her curiosity wouldn't permit her to leave. She looked at Melanie, who shrugged and began watching the videotape projected on a screen at the end of the room.

The quality of the tape was poor, but it was unmistakably Lord Hargraves participating in an all-out orgy with three women. One of them was Brigitte.

Recognizing the tape from the Paragon Club in Wanchai, Lord Hargraves rose from his table, face livid, and stormed out of the room. The pornographic tape ran on for twenty minutes, though the repetitious gymnastics were all but ignored by most of the group long before it was over.

"Why did she embarrass Lord Hargraves like that?" Angela asked.

"It's all just good fun. The party's just getting started," Melanie explained.

Lars Svenson grasped Angela's wrist. "I agree, it is all crude as hell. Even if you didn't know the people in it, it would have been crude."

Angela excused herself and left the room, expecting Svenson to follow her. He didn't.

Halfway to her cabin, Melanie caught up with her. "You should say good night to Onyx, don't you think?"

"Look, Melanie, I am a prisoner on this stinking boat. All the cocaine in the world won't let me forget that."

"Then we've got to find something that will." Melanie followed Angela into the cabin and closed the latch behind her.

Angela flung herself on the bunk, for the first time fully aware of her hopeless situation.

"You poor doll. I think it is time for us to share another hit." She began slowly massaging Angela's tense shoulder muscles. "I feel terrible for you, Angela. It is not right for such a beautiful person to feel so badly."

47

The fact that a missing persons report had been filed for Angela Clayfield hit the newspapers on the fourth day after she had disappeared. Her photograph dominated the front pages of all the dailies. The stories rehashed ConCom's recent tragedies and urged readers with any information to contact the police or the FBI.

The NYPD actually got an early break on the case. Two employees of the Trans-Asiatic Mandarin Club at Kennedy Airport positively identified Angela as the companion of Max Von Braun, a Trans-Asiatic captain. The guest register listed the companion as Ms. Jane Schilling, who bore a striking resemblance to newspaper photographs of Angela Clayfield. Angela and Von Braun had met for a light breakfast while they awaited an American Airlines flight to California. The hostess at the Mandarin Club told police Von Braun came there frequently to await flights, but had never before waited with a guest.

A check with American Airlines revealed that the couple had made a connecting flight to Hawaii from San Francisco.

When Coley Doctor walked into Angela Clayfield's office about 9 A.M., the message light was blinking on her phone. There was an urgent request from Whitcomb for him to call, another from Tom Price of the NYPD, and still another from Willy.

Coley called Whitcomb first, as he scanned the morning dailies.

"Coley, I guess you've read the morning papers."

"Yep. Angela is all over the place."

"We've got an ID on Angela. So far the press is in the dark. But who knows when some politician is going to pop off. There's a good chance she is in Hawaii, or at least was four days ago. She made the trip with Max Von Braun."

"Oh hell." It was all Coley could say. He and Willy had mentioned Von Braun to Whitcomb, but had not told him that Von Braun had failed to check into the Waldorf as planned.

"Look, you mentioned that Von Braun was doing some sort of fancy book for ConCom. I think this smells like some sort of publicity scam. I've got our Honolulu office working on this, but I hope we aren't going to end up looking like fools."

"Not a chance. We'd know about it if it were."

"Willy agrees," Whitcomb said. "I talked to him a few minutes ago. He said Katie Glover would know about it if it were a publicity stunt."

Coley felt his adrenaline start to pump. This was the first real lead they'd had. "Mark, I think I had better get my ass out to Hawaii."

"Stay out of it, Coley! Our guys over there don't need any distraction."

"If you've agreed to set Willy up as bait in California, why can't I do the same thing in Hawaii?"

"We can't spare the manpower to give you cover, Coley. Willy and Ginny are taking the *Tashtego* down to San Diego. There's a small marina on Harbor Island where we can do a better job of covering them. We'll see that the trip down there gets publicized. As for you, Coley, I want you to stay in New York and read a good book. It was hell the last time you and Willy decided you could do a better job than us."

"Just thought I could help. You know, Angela and Von Braun got a four-day jump on us."

"Coley, I can count. Everyone in the FBI can count. We make sure of that before we give them a badge." Whitcomb hung up.

Coley wanted to tell Whitcomb he was going to Hawaii anyway, but didn't have the chance. He decided to call Willy.

Before he could pick up the phone, he saw Derrick Harrison making his way down the hallway toward him. The office manager was spending a lot of time on his floor. With only six people in the building, Coley figured Harrison must get lonely.

"Coley, I'm glad I caught you in. With all the rigamarole around here, I've been postponing a lot of personal errands. I have an appointment in traffic court this afternoon and a doctor's appointment later. I wonder if I can just call it a day after lunch."

"Hey, be my guest. That makes one less person I'll have to worry about this afternoon. What sort of a crime did you commit?"

"Oh, just a couple of minor traffic tickets. You stand a chance of getting them dismissed if you bother to show up. Sometimes the policeman doesn't show."

"Good luck! Whenever I get in trouble, everybody shows up and starts pointing fingers. 'That's him! That's him!' "

Harrison gave a little chuckle. "I take it you've read the morning papers. Seeing Mrs. Clayfield's picture all over the papers brought tears to my eyes. She is such a beautiful woman. I guess you haven't heard anything yet, have you? Has anybody identified her yet?"

The pointed question caught Coley a little off guard, and he came close to blurting out Whitcomb's news. "No . . . actually no one has heard anything, as far as I am aware."

There was an awkward pause. Harrison looked as if he wanted to say something, but didn't.

"Derrick, I sure will let you know if something breaks."

"Thanks. I worry a lot about Mrs. Clayfield." The manager left the office.

Coley watched him walk the length of the hallway. He felt uncomfortable about their conversation. The man seemed to know more than he was letting on.

The conversation with Harrison reminded him of something else. He checked Caron Lawson's phone number on the back of his calendar and dialed.

"Caron, Coley Doctor here. How are you doing?"

"It's been rough, Coley. I guess it will take a long time. What can I do for you?"

"Do you know where Vinnie's golf bag is?"

"Why, sure. It's out in the garage where he always kept it."

"When you get time, I want you to check and see if something is in there. I'm curious to know if you find a small satin purse filled with golf tees. The little purse is embossed with a dragon."

"I'll check right now if you hold. It's not far away."

Coley waited. It was a couple of minutes before she came back to the phone.

"Coley, I've found the purse, but there are no golf

tees inside. There are a couple of little amber-colored medicine bottles and nothing else."

"Caron, will you hold on to the purse until you can give it to Willy Hanson? And don't open the bottles."

"What's in them?"

Coley paused, thinking the woman had gone through so much grief, he didn't have the heart to tell her. "I'm not sure, Caron."

"It's cocaine, isn't it?"

"It might be. Any reason why you would guess that?"

"Vinnie had a small problem once, but I don't want to talk about it right now."

"I understand. Keep your chin up, Caron."

"I try to." With that she hung up.

Coley left Angela's desk and walked quietly down the long hallway. He turned toward the foyer at the end of the hall. Derrick Harrison was sitting as if in a trance at the reception desk, one hand on the phone and the other on the desk.

"You okay, Derrick?" The man jumped, startled by Coley's voice.

"Oh sure. Just thought I would sit here for a moment and make a couple of phone calls."

"Help yourself. I wish you would use another phone, though. You're an easy target to anyone who gets off those elevators."

"I guess you're right. You guys cover every angle, don't you? Thanks for looking out for me." Coley watched as Harrison punched a couple of buttons on the telephone and then stood up.

Coley looked at the myriad buttons on the receptionist's telephone. "I guess this is sort of a central control panel, right?"

Harrison hesitated and Coley noticed his hand trembling. "Well, actually the whole system is automatic. But this station is equipped to handle calls manually as well. If a caller exhausts the menu in the computer, he finally gets to talk to the human being who sits at this desk."

"Tell me. If a person were just a little curious or just plain nosy, I bet he could tap into ongoing calls here. Is that right?" Coley stepped forward until his six-foot-six frame was inches away from Harrison.

"Now . . . now . . . that . . . that wouldn't be ethical. I suppose it's possible, though." Harrison was shaking as Coley blocked his path to the elevators.

"You know what I would do if I ever caught anyone listening in on one of my conversations?"

"You . . . you'd be upset, I'll bet."

"Upset! I'd whip his eavesdropping ass! So don't ever do it."

"Well now, Mr. Doctor, we don't talk to each other like that around here. That sounds like an accusation. I think you owe me an apology."

Coley let him brush by him to exit the foyer. "Mr. Harrison, I want you to stay in your office. You don't need to play mailman tomorrow. I'll handle the incoming mail. Got that?"

Harrison didn't bother to wait for an elevator. Without responding to Coley, he ducked into the stairwell, out of sight.

Coley felt convinced that Harrison had listened in on his calls to Whitcomb and Caron Lawson.

The question was, did that mean anything or was it just idle curiosity? Coley kicked at a wastebasket, sending it tumbling down the hall. He didn't enjoy giving an old fogey like Harrison the third degree. Then he smiled. For two thousand bucks a day, he could put up with it.

He decided to call back Inspector Price of NYPD. Price didn't mention the breakthrough, and he decided not to reveal that Whitcomb had brought him up to date.

"Mr. Doctor, I am looking through a personnel file turned over to us by Ms. Glover. The file contains information about Lois Lin, the ConCom employee found with the broken neck. There is very little here of help." The policeman paused, apparently glancing through the file as he talked.

"I'm sorry to hear that." Coley said matter-of-factly. "Nothing at all?"

"There is a letter of recommendation attached to her original application for employment. It is from a man listed as ConCom's office manager, a Mr. Derrick Harrison."

Coley's ears perked up. "What does Mr. Harrison say in his recommendation?"

"He states that Ms. Lin did some private tax work for him and impressed him as being extremely capable. The letter is very brief, that's about it. I have been trying to reach Mr. Harrison, but have been unsuccessful so far. We know so little about the deceased that we feel he may be able to tell us something."

"He was just here. I'll have him call you, as soon as I can find him."

"No rush. Tomorrow's okay."

"I'll go look for him right now."

Coley hung up the phone and made a beeline straight to Harrison's office. Harrison was not there. Coley had the distinct feeling that he would never see Harrison again.

48

The radio shack of the *Lantau Star* was small, but packed full of sophisticated communications gear. Lord Hargraves was a hobbyist in that area, and whenever something new was publicized he always made a point of updating the boat's equipment. Onyx Lu had met Lars Svenson in the small room for a conference with a man named Sharky.

Sharky, a native Burmese, was a member of the crew that had come from Hong Kong with Onyx. He was muscular, barrel-chested and usually wore a turban. He generally remained aloof, rarely joining the others in the dining area or speaking unnecessarily to anyone, with the exception of Onyx.

The radio shack was off limits to everyone other than Onyx, unless Sharky had invited them. Onyx, Svenson and Sharky had been in serious discussion for almost an hour. Lord Hargraves had approached the room once, but had been waved away by a gesture from Sharky.

"Well, then it is decided." Onyx spoke with finality. "Our destination is San Diego. How long will it take to get there, Lars?"

"Eighty to eight-five hours, depending on weather, of course."

"I don't like it," Sharky said, furrowing his brow as he studied a chart Svenson had placed in front of him. "We have made elaborate plans. Now they all have to be changed."

Onyx nodded. "Of course they do, Sharky, but we have over three days. You and I will talk, and we will change them. Pelly is in California now. He can take care of matters on land."

Svenson felt out in the cold, unaware of what specific plans they were talking about. "Perhaps I can help," he volunteered. "I know the harbor area in San Diego well. The *Lantau Star* has been there twice before."

Sharky looked at Svenson, showing no feeling. "We know that. Your knowledge will be very useful in due time. For now, I suggest that you return to the bridge and concentrate on getting us to San Diego on schedule. Onyx, you and I will continue this conversation soon."

Svenson left the radio shack, perplexed by the situation Lord Hargraves had put them in. This was certainly not the kind of mission he had bargained for. It was becoming increasingly obvious to him that he and the ambassador were prisoners aboard the ship, as Angela Clayfield was.

The former ambassador was usually on deck long before now. Svenson hadn't seen Lord Hargraves since he had left the party in a fury during the showing of the videotape last evening.

That had been a real shocker for Svenson. He had long realized that Hargraves was a fool, but he felt sorry for the man. He must have been mortified in front of the Clayfield woman and the strangers among the diners.

Onyx Lu was proving herself to be a woman without conscience. His sexual marathon with her the previous day worried him. He had to wonder if there might have been a hidden camera. He doubted that Onyx would include herself in a videotape, but still he would have to be on his guard next time—if there was a next time.

Onyx emerged from the radio shack, spotted Svenson and joined him at the ship's wheel. She stood beside him for a moment, then moved behind him, encircling him with her arms and taking the wheel from his grasp as she pressed against him.

"Lars, you weren't a naughty boy with any of my other guests last evening, were you?"

"Hardly."

"I saw you talking to Angela Clayfield. She is beautiful and very sexy I hear. At least Melanie says she is sexy."

"I'll never know."

"You always say the right things, Lars. I think that is something you have learned from the ambassador. I will be taking a little nap at about two o'clock. Do you want to share that with me?"

He felt his libido soar out of control as Onyx moved one hand down his chest. "Of course." He wondered whether Sharky could see them from the radio shack.

Without another word, Onyx left the bridge and went aft to where Gyro was climbing up to the copter. Svenson looked quickly back toward the radio shack. Sharky was huddled over the receiver, earphones on, facing the other direction.

Svenson had already set the *Lantau Star* on its new course. They were moving into a headwind that created an annoying roll for the beamy yacht. But this was the only course that would get them to San Diego in eighty hours.

Angela Clayfield appeared on deck dressed in slacks and an oversized shirt tied at the waist. Her hair was loose, blowing free in the wind. Svenson decided that she was a gorgeous woman, no matter how she dressed. No spring chicken, but still a "ten." He motioned to her, inviting her to enter the confined area of the bridge. She responded immediately.

"Good morning, Lars. I guess it's still morning. I thought I would follow your suggestion to visit the bridge." She looked beyond him toward the radio shack and then looked questioningly at him. "Who's he?"

Without glancing back, Svenson answered, "Sharky, don't worry about him."

Her thoughts drifted back to the *Lazy Dolphin*, now on the sound's bottom in Rye. It had been a luxurious coastal cruiser, but nothing as seaworthy as the *Lantau Star*, which could be pointed toward any destination in the world.

"This yacht is beautiful. Too bad she's involved in a felony. It doesn't become her. How can Lord Hargraves consent to the *Lantau Star* being used like this? And what about last night? I felt as if I was trapped in one of New York's sex clubs."

"It was a sordid show, wasn't it? I hope you realize that I had nothing to do with it. I'm here to look after the *Lantau Star*."

"And Onyx Lu."

Svenson looked steadily into her violet eyes, wondering how much she surmised. "There are worse diversions aboard, believe me. My vice is at least healthier and more laudable than the garbage that a lot of people are shooting in their arms, or shoving up their noses. Agreed?"

Angela looked sharply at him. He had touched a

nerve. She wondered whether Melanie had told him about their cocaine use last evening. "I don't think anything is laudable when you kowtow to despicable people like Onyx Lu."

"Look, Mrs. Clayfield. I didn't know what I was getting into. Lord Hargraves told me that this was going to be some sort of trade mission to drum up business for the Peoples' Republic. Now we're headed for God knows what." Svenson glanced over his shoulder. Sharky was still absorbed in his work. "There aren't enough of us to mutiny. Hargraves is useless, so there's just you and me. That's why I butter up Onyx. At least I can try to find out what in the hell is going on."

Angela smirked. "A great sacrifice on your part."

He grinned back. "It could be worse. By the way, you could do something to help the cause along."

"I'm afraid to ask. What?"

"Quit fooling around with that little lezzie Melanie. She's one of Onyx's zombies. She's so far gone she ain't good for anything."

Only the ominous figure of Sharky beyond the thin glass kept Angela from slapping him. "I have not been fooling around! Melanie has been kind and compassionate. The only clothes I have she gave me. If there is anything sexual, it's in her imagination."

Angela turned toward the door. Svenson grasped her arm and whispered, "Look, I'm sorry. But I'm afraid you and I might be killed if we don't use our wits. You ain't gonna like what I'm about to say, but I'll give you some advice. Why don't you lay a little charm on Gyro? There may come a day when we can use a helicopter. Gyro wouldn't mind if you approach him. He can't keep his eyes off you."

"You are a real bastard, Lars. I really misjudged you."

"Then beat it. Go have another snort and cuddle

up with Melanie. That'll fix everything. I may be a bastard, Mrs. Clayfield, but I'm a pragmatist. Remember that and think about it."

Angela Clayfield left the bridge disappointed. She had hoped for more compassion from Svenson, but it was obvious that he was as pessimistic as she was about getting off the *Lantau Star* alive. Maybe he was handling Onyx Lu the right way. Maybe he would learn some bit of information that might help them.

She walked aft. Gyro was up in the bubble of the helicopter again, working on something. She wondered why he spent so much time there. She considered Svenson's suggestion. All her life she had used men for her own purposes. Why should it be any different now with Gyro just because it wasn't her choice? He waved casually to her as she passed. She smiled back at him and walked on to the stern.

Brigitte was sunning herself. She was without the jeweled belt she had worn while dancing the night before. Her statuesque figure was flawless.

"You are very photogenic, Brigitte. I didn't stay for the whole movie, but you were spectacular."

"Thank you! I'm sorry you didn't stay. We succeeded in driving that old fool crazy. You missed that."

"How did you do it, Brigitte? Did you know you were on camera?"

"Of course. We maneuver our bodies, so we make sure that Lord Hargraves is the star. Maybe you like to try it sometime." Brigitte grinned at her, showing several gold teeth.

Angela couldn't help gaping at her flawless, cleanshaven form. "You are going to get too much sun if you aren't careful."

"Maybe you and I go inside together, huh?" Brigitte grinned again.

Angela pretended not to hear her suggestion. "I think I'll just walk around the deck again." She moved away.

The more Angela walked, the more despondent she became. She came to a passageway leading down a ladder to the engine room. There were two deckhands working around the noisy turbines. They both glanced at her, probably surprised that she was exploring the yacht unescorted.

She continued to walk forward along the passageway until she passed the point that must have been midship. To her left was an exit to the deck she had spotted earlier when circling the boat. Ahead the passageway continued in subdued light. Soon the narrow corridor jogged to the right. She immediately came face to face with another deckhand, one she had never seen before. He was sitting on a chair in front of a closed door that ended the passageway. He had a pistol jammed in his belt, which he immediately reached for with one hand. He held his left hand high with his open palm facing her.

"No! Go back! There is nothing here for you." He had a strong Chinese accent, and seemed to have trouble enunciating.

When Angela didn't immediately move, he leaped to his feet and drew the weapon from his belt. "Go back. Nothing here!"

"Okay, okay!" Angela turned, suddenly fearing she would be shot at. She ran along the passageway and found the exit ladder to the main deck. She reached the top, breathless.

Turning onto the deck, she ran squarely into Lord Hargraves, who caught her in his arms.

"There is a crazy man with a gun down there!"

Hargraves held Angela, trying to calm her. "Yes, yes, my dear. You must have run into Kiki."

"He has a gun. He wouldn't let me pass."

"Yes, I know. You shouldn't have gone forward below deck. They don't even permit me to do that. And I own this boat."

Suddenly Angela realized that Lord Hargraves was actually pawing at her.

"Keep your hands off of me! Dammit! We're all going to be killed! Can't you see that there is something terrible going on aboard this ship? There isn't a decent human being aboard your yacht."

"I know. I know, my dear. Everything you say is quite true." He looked down at her with watery eyes, pupils dilated and nostrils red with abuse. "That's why we have to make every second count, you and I."

He forced his arms around her, fondling her buttocks, until she twisted away and slashed her fingernails across his face. Struggling free, she ran forward to her cabin, entered and bolted the door behind her.

Melanie, curled on the bunk, stirred and turned to look sleepily at her. She bolted upright. "Oh, you've been in some trouble. There is blood!"

Angela looked down to see a deep scratch on the back of her hand. "That fool Lord Hargraves. He's crazy. He had his hands all over me. Melanie, what is going on?"

Melanie, stirring from her self-induced reverie, extended her arms toward her. "Here, let me hold you."

"No, Melanie, I don't want that! I know you mean well, but I want you to go. I want to rest . . . alone."

Melanie fumbled in her purse and produced her cache of cocaine. She offered it to Angela.

"No, Melanie, I don't want that either. Please go

away for a while." Angela wondered how long she would have the strength to refuse the cocaine.

Melanie stood up, ready to leave. "It's too bad about Lord Hargraves. I'll take care of that old bastard for you. He can be handled quite easily, you know."

"Melanie, I don't want to touch him."

Melanie bowed her head slightly, apparently confused. "Yes, I can understand. But don't let it bother you so much. It's part of his contract with Onyx. He has been given rights to all the women aboard. He expects that."

"That's insane."

"Yes, it is. But it is true. Now I am going to go fix that old bastard so he won't want you or anyone else for a while. He is so stupid that he will think he is having fun. May I come back later?"

"Of course, Melanie. To be my friend, if you can understand that."

"I'll try. I haven't had a friend in a long time."

She left the cabin quickly. Angela felt a surge of compassion for the woman. She wanted to call her back and hold her as she might hold a baby. But she didn't dare.

The *Lantau Star* was now plowing her way through rough seas toward the Southern California coast. Sharky emerged from the radio shack and announced that he would take over watch at the wheel for a while.

"Do you know the waters around Ensenada?" he asked Svenson.

"Yes, there is a harbor, minimal for the *Lantau Star*. There is really not much there."

Sharky nodded his head. "Be prepared to lie offshore south of there for a day or so. It will not be necessary to use the harbor. We may just cruise around a bit."

"No problem."

"The yellowtail are running." Sharky spoke those words as if he were going on a fishing trip. "That means the water will be filled with small craft, fishermen. We will rendezvous with one of those tuna boats. He will have two red stars on his flying bridge. He will seek us out, but we must watch for him. I'll fill you in more extensively later."

Svenson glanced at his watch as he left the bridge. It would soon be two o'clock, fun and games time for Onyx Lu. Maybe she would tell him something about the tuna boat.

49

Willy stood on the deck of the *Tashtego*, leaning against the mast. He was there for the whole world to see. Within a hundred yards of him were a half dozen stakeouts, each capable of firing automatic weapons within seconds of any action. Two agents were in the parking lot surrounding the marina, and the others were staked out in various boats in the marina from which they had a clear view of the *Tashtego*. Anyone who came after Willy wouldn't live to tell about it.

Ginny came topside, reading a user's manual on the nine-millimeter Coley had given her.

"Who ever thought I'd be reading up on one of these things?" She curled up at the end of the cockpit and tossed the manual onto the cushion. "What I want to know is, how can you tell when it's time to start shooting?"

"You start shooting before everything gets hopeless. If you come close to having to use that thing, your instinct will kick in and you'll squeeze the trigger." Willy shook his head, realizing that her instinct might be too kind. "The smartest thing would be for you to go on back to Pasadena until this is over."

"Not on your life, baby. It's you and me until this mess is finally done with." She thought a moment. "And then it will still be you and me."

For the past two days the newspapers had featured stories about Willy's departure from New York and the exotic voyage he and Ginny were supposedly taking to escape the terrorism at ConCom. This morning's paper had given specific information about their proposed sail to San Diego in just two days, a tune-up for a globe-circling trip. The stories, of course, were planted.

The phone rang. The FBI had rigged up a phone capable of pinpointing the caller. This call was from Coley Doctor in New York.

"Hey, boss, I have some big news. An old friend of yours is calling the office here, and he insists on being patched through to you."

"Who?"

"It's Max Von Braun. Says he's out in sunny California."

"How do you know it's him?"

"Oh, it's him all right. Here, listen for yourself."

"Willy Hanson?"

Willy recognized the voice instantly. "You dumb bastard, I want Angela Clayfield back right now."

"I haven't got her. But I know where she is, and she's okay. Look, I'm not going to string this conversation out, so the less you talk the quicker you get to Angela Clayfield. Got a pencil?"

Willy motioned for Ginny to pick up the extension. He knew the call was also being monitored and taped by Whitcomb.

"Okay, I got a pencil."

"A black Samsonite utility case, model number
seven-ninety-four, filled with one million dollars in
hundreds. That's what we need. You can buy the
case at any luggage shop. No substitutions. Unless
the money is in that case, your swinging CEO is
dead. Tonight, at exactly eight o'clock P.M., you will
be standing at the last telephone on the left in the
battery of phones just off the lobby of the Hyatt Hotel at LAX. Have the Samsonite with you. No wires,
no homing devices or Angela will die. When the
phone rings, pick it up. There will be a short message and it won't be repeated. If we spot any company, Angela, Ginny and you won't live through the
night."

Von Braun hung up immediately. The message
had been slow and deliberate. The instructions were
crystal clear.

"Coley! Are you still there?"

"Yeah. I heard everything. What are you going to
do?"

"I'm going to buy a black Samsonite, model seven-
ninety-four. And you have plenty of time to hop a
plane and meet me at LAX."

"What about Hawaii? There's lotta little wahinis
waiting for me over there."

"I'm glad you've got your sense of humor, Coley.
We're both going to need it tonight." Willy hung up,
his mind reeling at the possibilities of the evening
ahead.

"God! Willy, what do we do? How will you be protected?" Ginny was asking the same questions he
was asking himself.

Mark Whitcomb boarded the *Tashtego* less than
five minutes after the telephone call from Von
Braun. "Okay, guy. You wanted to play cops and rob-
bers. Here's your big chance."

"Mark!" Ginny seemed relieved to see the FBI

man. "You heard what he said about not bringing any company along. Can't you go somehow, anyway?"

"Go somehow? Look, Ginny, If Willy doesn't have cover, he's a dead man. If we set up unobtrusive protection for him, he may have a chance."

Willy was nodding. "Look, they may still have Angela alive. Let's just get the job done. Mark, you've got to give me a long lead, though—"

"Look, I'm not staying here on the boat," Ginny interrupted. "I'm going to LAX."

"With a very short leash, Ms. Du Bois, with a very short leash.

"We'll let Coley look after you there. He'll get here too late for the briefing." Whitcomb turned to Willy. "You're going to be covered by a dozen good men. You won't see them and the kidnappers won't see them, but they'll be there. We'll also monitor that telephone at the Hyatt Hotel until the call comes through tonight."

"Ginny and I will drive up to LAX to meet Coley." Willy's voice was tight. "Coley will bring Ginny with him to your rendezvous point. I'll go on to the hotel alone. Whoever these guys are, they might tail us right from the *Tashtego*."

"We'll be close, Willy. Let's all keep cool. A lot of cases like this are broken at the drop of the ransom."

By the time Whitcomb left the *Tashtego*, Willy was nervous as hell. He wondered how laid-back their coverage would be in view of his bullish attitude.

Ginny was rattling hangers around the small closet she kept aboard the *Tashtego*. She turned to confront Willy. "What does one wear to a potentially life-ending event? I'd like to know just what would be proper."

"Oh, anything will do. Maybe something unobtrusive, to match Whitcomb's cover."

"How about baggy slacks and a dark baggy sweat-shirt?"

Willy put his arms around her and hugged her for a long time. "That's perfect. I'll help you undress."

As they stretched out on the bunk, Ginny reached under her pillow, pulled out her new nine-millimeter and laid it on Willy's chest.

"Is that thing loaded?"

"I'm not sure I know how to tell."

"Maybe you better leave it here tonight. Whitcomb would have a conniption fit if he knew you had that along."

"No, I want you to take it. Coley says that pea-shooter you carry isn't worth a damn."

"I'm convinced."

"I know," said Ginny, kissing him tenderly on the neck. "You're easy."

At 5 P.M., Whitcomb brought the briefcase stuffed with the $1 million aboard the *Tashtego*. He set it in Willy's lap. "It's unmarked, but each bill has been copied and a numerical list by series generated. It's our job tonight to make sure they never get to spend it. Very generous of your old company, Mr. Hanson."

Willy nodded, painfully aware that he had guaranteed part of the ransom. Deep inside, he still felt responsible for much of this trouble. He should either have left Onyx Lu alone in the first place, or killed her.

"We'll leave here at five-thirty sharp. I'll have a car up front of you someplace and another one behind you. You won't know just where. If anything goes wrong, switch on your emergency blinker." Whitcomb was going down a checklist he had put on an index card.

"After you've met Coley's plane, you'll have time for a short briefing. He knows what to do when you leave Ginny with him. The hotel is about fifteen hundred feet from the terminal. You will start walking toward it at seven-forty. You'll see it on the left where Century crosses Sepulveda."

Willy grinned. "I hope I don't get mugged and lose the million bucks before I get there."

Whitcomb frowned. He obviously didn't like being interrupted. "When you go into the hotel, you'll have cover within a hundred feet. If you get in trouble, fire a shot into the ground. You'll draw a crowd of friends fast. If you want us to close in quietly, scratch the top of your head until you see action. If none of that is possible, push this gadget."

He handed Willy a matchbook-size box with a button on it. "This will get the beepers going and we'll close in. Does anyone have questions?"

"Are you expecting Von Braun here tonight?" Willy asked. "Where did he make the call from?"

"Somewhere in the Bay Area up north. A public phone near Pleasanton. We have a couple of agents in that area now trying to nail the son of a bitch."

"I doubt anything will come of that. Von Braun has proven to be pretty shifty. I would certainly love to confront the old buzzard, though."

The trip to Los Angeles International Airport was uneventful. The heavy traffic on the San Diego Freeway miraculously kept its insane pace without a slowdown. If Whitcomb had an escort in front of them or behind them, neither Willy nor Ginny saw them.

They parked in the garage across from the American Airlines terminal and carefully stashed their weapons under the car seat to ease their move through security.

Coley was the first passenger off his plane. He hugged Willy and Ginny with one sweep of his long arms.

The three of them walked down the concourse to

the Admirals' Club. Once inside, they found a quiet corner and briefed Coley on everything that had happened since the morning phone call.

"Where's the million bucks? I hope you guys didn't leave it back there in arrivals someplace."

"It's in the car back there in the parking lot," Ginny assured him.

Coley put his long legs up on the coffee table and stretched. "Man alive, to be a kid again back in Watts and find a vehicle like that. One car theft, and zoom! Security for life."

Willy glanced at his watch. It was 7:35. "It's time."

The trio crossed over to the garage. Willy opened the car door and grabbed the briefcase and the nine-millimeter. He shook Coley's hand and hugged Ginny. "Okay, guys, no heroics, we'll follow instructions until it becomes impossible."

They walked the first hundred yards together. Ginny and Coley veered off to the United baggage claim to meet Whitcomb. Willy started toward Sepulveda alone, carrying the black Samsonite. He crossed the busy street and walked a half block to the entrance of the Hyatt Hotel. It was 7:52.

He found his way to the row of telephones in a corridor just off the lobby. He set the briefcase down on the ledge in front of the phone at the far left and waited. There were several callers using other phones. He still had five or six minutes.

One man, at the other end of the row of a half dozen phones, was athletic-looking and sharply dressed in a dark business suit. He was holding a phone but not talking. Willy speculated that he might be one of Whitcomb's men. A men's room stood off the same corridor. Occasionally someone went in or out.

It was 7:58. He took the receiver off the hook of the phone Von Braun had specified, but held the cradle down with his finger, pretending to talk. He kept his hands off the briefcase, hoping someone would grab it. But apparently they were not going to make it that easy. The man at the other phone sat tight, still not talking to anyone.

It was 8:01, and Willy was getting nervous as hell. When the phone finally rang, his adrenaline surged as he looked around him and let go of the cradle.

"Willy Hanson here."

"I'll say this one time. Listen carefully." The voice didn't belong to Von Braun.

"Just a few steps away is a men's room. There is a refuse can just inside the door. Reach into it and you will find a small plastic shopping bag. Take it outside the hotel and remove a small tape recorder. Press the play button. Do not touch any other control. That is all I have to say."

Willy glanced at his watch. It was 8:02. He grabbed the briefcase, went into the men's room, and did as he had been instructed. The tape recorder was there. He exited the rest room and headed straight for the door of the hotel. Outside, he removed the cigarette-pack-size tape recorder and pushed the play button, considering all the while that it might be a bomb.

The message began. "Turn left on Century Boulevard, away from the airport. Walk in that direction until you get further instructions. Do not turn the tape recorder off. You will receive further instructions when necessary. . . ."

He held the tiny machine up to his eyes, trying to find a fast-forward button. He wanted to peek into the future. He pressed, but the control had been deactivated. He turned quickly then to walk east on Century, holding the recorder to his ear. He could hear the tape moving, but no voice.

He began to think the machine was defective.

Then, after about four minutes, "Right now you should be in front of a large office building named Airport Center. Keep walking at the same pace in the same direction. . . ."

He was almost in front of the building marked "Airport Center." Whoever had set the tape up had walked through it himself. Willy moved on, picking up the pace a bit.

"Now you should be in front of the Sheraton. . . . Stop before crossing the street beyond the Sheraton and await instructions."

Willy was only a few paces from the street. He glanced around, trying to look casual. If Whitcomb's crew was nearby, he couldn't see them. Century Boulevard was heavy with traffic. It was quite possible his cover was out there somewhere. There were no pedestrians on the sidewalk. He had been standing on the corner for almost a minute.

"Attention . . . Listen carefully, and you will not be shot." Never had Willy felt so alone in the world, even though he had to believe that a dozen of Whitcomb's people were watching him.

". . . Across the street is a parking garage. Cross the street and enter it at the ground level. . . . Go. . . ."

He crossed the street and hesitated before entering the garage. It was not well lit.

" . . . There is a green pickup truck to your left."

There it was. He was practically touching it.

". . . Put the briefcase in the truck bed . . . and then turn around and walk back across the street and continue toward the Sheraton. . . . Wait in front of the hotel for further instructions."

Cars were moving slowly down Century. He stood alone in front of the driveway to the Sheraton. No instructions came from the recorder.

A car slowed down and the window lowered. All he

could see was a pair of long, shiny nyloned legs behind the wheel.

"Want to party, baby?"

He had the distinct feeling he was being set up. As
he drew the nine-millimeter from his belt, the
hooker shouted an obscenity and drove on.

There were still no instructions from the tape recorder. He leaped across a small hedge and rolled
into the valet parking area of the hotel, crawled between two cars and pressed the beeper.

In less than thirty seconds he was pointing the
gun at Whitcomb and Coley. There were men running all around him toward the garage.

". . . Thank you, Mr. Hanson. You did very well . . ."

Coley spun around looking for the source of the
voice. Willy handed him the tape recorder. Whitcomb
was watching it all and talking into a walkie-talkie.

"Blockade the garage!" He repeated the message
several times, then looked down at Willy.

"We've got one of them," he said. "We've got the
woman in the car who stopped on the curb next to
you."

Willy got to his feet, laughing convulsively. "Do
you want to party?"

Whitcomb frowned.

Willy stuffed the gun back in his belt. "She's just
a hooker. She must be scared out of her wits."

Whitcomb groaned, still talking to his men.
"Where is the briefcase?"

"It's in the back of a green pickup truck about fifteen feet inside that entrance." Willy pointed to
where he had emerged from the garage.

"Yes, we've found it," said Whitcomb, still talking
to his men. "Leave it right where it is. Back off a
couple hundred feet and stake out the pickup. We've
probably blown it, but keep out of sight."

Several people had gathered around the threesome, wondering what was going on. Whitcomb led Willy and Coley back to a car now parked at the curb, and they all piled in with Ginny and another agent. They pulled into the valet parking lot of the hotel and parked where they had a clear view of the garage.

"Did you actually see anyone?" asked Whitcomb, his normally slicked-down black hair all askew.

"Just the hooker," said Willy, handing him the small tape recorder.

Whitcomb examined the machine. "Twenty-nine ninety-five at any schlock house," he murmured, trying to rewind the tape.

"The forward and reverse are busted. I tried that," said Willy.

Whitcomb popped the tape out of the recorder and stuck it into the slot on the dashboard. They all sat and listened to the instructions, which completely explained Willy's actions.

"Mr. Hanson, we should have had you wired. After this, leave it to the professionals."

"Hey, look. It's my life, and my money on the line. I think we had to follow instructions. What difference would it have made? They didn't go for the drop."

"We could have had that garage bottled up thirty seconds after you had left the drop. I might as well tell you, Willy, we put a homing device in the brief-case."

"You bastard!"

"Don't worry about it. It's half as big as a small matchbook, fitting into the latch compartment. They'll never find it." Whitcomb was squirming, still holding the handset to his ear. "Okay, repeat that for the folks here in the car."

"Boss, we found the Samsonite about three miles from the garage, in the parking lot of a strip joint in

Hawthorne, the Choo-Choo Club. It's empty. The homer is still intact."

"What in the hell is he talking about?" Willy watched as an agent left the garage carrying the case he had retrieved from the pickup truck. The agent pushed it through the window to Whitcomb.

Whitcomb set it in Willy's lap. "Be my guest. As you say, it's your money."

Willy opened the case. Out tumbled a couple of thousand pages of typing paper.

"Oh Jesus!"

"They pulled it off, right under our noses. They must have switched bags within seconds after you threw yours in the truck. There must have been someone right there, crouched behind the pickup. They must have had almost a full minute to escape in the shadows of the garage. These are smart guys, Willy."

"We'll get them yet," Willy said, but he was no longer so sure that was true.

"I'm going to leave a team here to go over the pickup, and the garage, for whatever it's worth. Maybe they left prints or something else behind. You might as well get back to the *Tashtego*, and get ready for the sail to San Diego." Whitcomb glowered at the agents working in the garage. "It was a peachy scheme, folks, right down to the wasting of the fast forward."

50

Angela Clayfield's timing was perfect. She managed to reach the ladder to the helicopter pad just as Gyro was climbing up with a coil of wire and some tools.

"Gyro, you must love that little bubble. You spend all your time up there."

He gave her his friendly, crinkly grin. "It's not really a bad place. It's up high, like being in a crow's nest."

"Can I come up and take a peek? I've always been curious about these things. How many people can fit in there?"

"It's made for two, perhaps three people if they're small." Gyro paused to survey the length of the *Lantau Star*. He could see Lars Svenson on the bridge. "I guess it's okay. Come on up."

She climbed up slowly, fully aware of Gyro's view of her ample bosom sheathed in the loose bikini top. She looked up quickly and caught him gaping at her.

He extended a helping hand as she scrambled onto the small platform.

He opened the hatch and she peered inside. "Oh! It is small. Do you fly this thing like an ordinary airplane?"

"Oh no. The basic theory is all different. However, like a lot of things, once you know how, it becomes instinctive." He began pointing out some of the controls and trying to explain their function. "It takes quite a while to learn," he told her. "Much longer than it would take you to learn to fly a plane."

He climbed inside the bubble and again extended his hand to her. They sat side by side as he continued to talk about the small craft. Angela watched him as she pressed her bronzed leg firmly against his in the cramped bubble.

There was an awkward pause before he blurted, "You are a most beautiful lady, Miss Angela."

"Thank you, Gyro. You aren't so bad yourself."

"Oh, no, no, I am nothing like you!"

"Gyro! You'd be a funny man if you looked like me." She purposely brushed her arm across him, pointing to the coil of wire he had hung on one of the control knobs. "Now what is that you're doing?"

"Oh, very special project. It's Onyx's idea. This is a remote switch that runs off the altimeter. You know what that is?"

"It tells you how high you're flying."

"That's right! When the helicopter gets to a certain altitude, it will activate the lights on the landing pad. That way, if you come in after dark or in bad weather, the landing pad is all lit up, even if someone on board doesn't turn the lights on."

Angela's thoughts went back several months to a dinner conversation she had had with Charles. An airliner had exploded over India. Charles had ex-

plained that terrorists had rigged a bomb to respond
to barometric pressure, so that the plane would blow
up at a certain altitude.

"Does it work on barometric pressure?"

Gyro looked at her in surprise. He had never
known a beautiful woman to ask such a technical
question. "Oh no. That could be done, but this will
feed right off the altimeter with a special connection."

"How clever, Gyro." She studied him as his interest turned from her back to his project. "Tell me—
you said that three people could get in here. Where
would the other one sit?"

"Back of the seats," he said, pointing over his
shoulder. "It would have to be a small person, like
Onyx, or maybe a woman like you. It would be very
uncomfortable."

"I think you're right, Gyro." She put one leg outside the bubble, preparing to exit the copter. "You
know, Gyro, that remote switch is pretty neat. Actually, you could activate anything on the ground set
up to receive the signal, couldn't you?"

"Oh, yes. I suppose you could. But this is for copter pad lights."

Angela climbed out of the bubble and began to descend the ladder. Pausing for a moment, she called
out, "Gyro, I hope you will join my table for dinner
tonight."

"I would like to do that, Miss Angela." The big grin
returned. She had his attention again.

"Thanks. I'll look forward to that."

Angela walked forward along the deck. When she
glanced back she saw Gyro again working feverishly
at his wiring task, singing.

Angela worked her way back to her cabin. Opening the door, she found a tangle of arms and legs on
her berth. It was Lord Hargraves and Brigitte.

Hargraves looked slowly up at her with bleary eyes, seeming more dead than alive.

"Welcome, my dear. We've been waiting for you, haven't we, Brigitte? You are to be the main course. You should have been here earlier. Poor Brigitte is getting weary, I fear."

Angela was at once terrified and angry. "Look, you raunchy old bastard, get out of here! Brigitte! Get him out of here, now!"

Brigitte looked at her, eyes struggling to focus. "What's the big deal, honey? Melanie comes in here a lot."

"Just get out, or I'll have Sharky throw you out." She didn't know whether invoking Sharky's name would work or not, but she had nothing to lose.

Brigitte looked at Hargraves. "Come on! Let's go. Our kitten is not in a playful mood." Hargraves laughed, and the two of them staggered out the door. Angela locked it behind them and resolved that she would keep it locked.

She ripped the sheets off the berth, spread a large towel on it, and lay down. She looked at the ceiling, tears welling in her eyes. This was indeed a ship from hell and she feared it would carry her to her death. Her thoughts went to Gyro. He was surprisingly normal, considering the strange crew aboard the *Lantau Star*.

Dinner aboard the *Lantau Star* that night was strikingly different from dinner the previous night. The crew was relentlessly pushing the yacht through heavy swells, causing a pitching and rolling that threatened to spill drinks and food again and again.

Lars Svenson was manning the bridge, pointing the *Lantau Star* toward Ensenada, trying to achieve his projected time of arrival at any cost to the comfort of those aboard. Onyx Lu stood next to him, her arms around him. They formed one silhouette in the dim light of sunset that filtered through the unlit bridge. Her body undulated steadily against his as her hands explored him erotically.

"That's hardly fair," Svenson mumbled, both of his own hands committed to the wheel as the *Star* plowed on. He glanced over his shoulder. Sharky had finally retired to his quarters just off the radio shack.

"Fair? Whatever Onyx wants to do is fair. Do you understand that, sailor boy?"

Svenson nodded in the semidarkness as he felt himself becoming an eager recipient of her attentions. He was already convinced that Onyx was crazed, but it was hard to care at moments like these. She had been insatiable that day. He needed sleep badly, and felt certain that Onyx must be on the verge of collapse. Yet she showed no signs of slowing her rhythmic, persistent pleasuring of his body.

All real conversation with her had stopped days before. His only true purpose aboard the *Lantau Star* was to navigate her to Mexico and to cater all the while to her every erotic whim.

Back in the dining room, a much subtler seduction was taking place. The rolling and pitching of the *Star* had finally sent everyone to his or her stateroom. Only Angela and Gyro had stayed behind.

"Where did you learn to fly, Gyro?" She fixed her gaze on the pilot. She locked him in with her beautiful eyes, and he was a willing captive. Western women, especially blond women, were especially intriguing to him. He had never known such lavish beauty except on the cinema screen in Macau.

"I first learn to fly in China."

"The Peoples' Republic?"

"Oh yes. We have Soviet instructors. They were very good. They taught me well, but I had an accident." His eyes dropped as he recalled the event. "One day I took a group of construction engineers to Hong Kong. There were seven of them. Two were killed when we had engine failure."

"That's terrible, Gyro. You must have felt very bad. But engine failure could not have been your fault." She laid an arm across his shoulder as if to comfort him through the bad memories.

"Yes, I know that it was not my fault. It was the equipment. It was not maintained properly. I had told them about it, but repairs were not quickly possible. Parts had to be shipped from far away."

"Does it still bother you?"

"It still bothers me. They still blame me for the accident. They said that I should have been more demanding in my request for repairs. They say I should have refused to fly."

"Why didn't you?"

"If I didn't fly, I might have been shot, or something worse. They lied. I *was* demanding."

Angela grasped one of his hands with both of her own. The pilot's palm was moist. He was staring at her in unabashed admiration. "Gyro, I feel so bad for you. Try to concentrate on the fact that it was not your fault. How did you get your job with Onyx?"

"I was a fool . . ." Gyro hesitated. "I had some savings. I took my money to Macau. I started gambling in the casinos. In less than two weeks I lose two hundred thousand *patecas*. It was all the money I had saved. One of the gambling ships gave me a job when I went into debt, and then I met Onyx Lu in the casino. She offered me a job as her pilot. I agreed that I would do it when she agreed to pay my debt to the casino."

Angela leaned forward to place a gentle kiss on his forehead. He buried his face in the curve of her neck, then looked up at her again.

"You are so beautiful. Why do you do it?"

Angela brushed her hand gently through his hair. "Why do I do what, Gyro?"

"Cocaine . . . Everyone aboard is crazy. Why do you join in all their games?"

"Would it please you if I didn't?"

"Yes."

"Then I won't. You have given me a reason, Gyro. We will support each other." Angela leaned forward to kiss his lips as if to seal their pact. He responded eagerly.

"We are all going to die, you know." Gyro spoke matter-of-factly.

"Why do you think that? Tell me! Please, Gyro."

Gyro looked around to make sure they were alone. "There are enough heavy explosives packed in the bow of the *Lantau Star* to blow up a battleship. The *Star* is like a giant torpedo."

"How do you know that?"

"Kiki told me. He is afraid he will not get off the boat before they set the charge."

"That bastard Kiki. He threatened me with a gun when I tried to go forward."

"Kiki is afraid for his life. Onyx has terrified him. He is really not such a bad guy."

Angela pulled away and held both Gyro's hands in her own. "It's you and me, Gyro. It's you and me. Together we will find a way to get away from all this."

"It is hopeless, I think. But we must try. It will require violence. And Kiki must go with us." Gyro did not sound very confident. "Angela." He looked at her pleadingly. "I have shared a secret with you that could cost us our lives. You must keep a clear head.

Melanie, Brigitte, the ambassador, and Svenson, they are all dangerous because they are totally addicted. They are pawns to be used as Onyx sees fit. They are doomed."

"Do you really think Svenson is committed to her?"

"Of course he is. There are other diversions she uses besides cocaine and heroin."

"He could be using her."

"Not likely. You once asked why I spend so much time in the bubble of the copter. It is possible to have a commanding view of the entire *Lantau Star* from up there. Even now, while Svenson is standing watch on the wheel, Onyx is with him. They are pleasuring each other even while guiding the *Star* through these heavy seas. A short time ago we narrowly missed striking a fishing boat. It is madness. I think Onyx is consuming her own drugs. She is not like she used to be."

Gyro was now holding Angela boldly, one arm encircling her, his hand tentatively exploring her breast.

"Gyro, I think we've talked long enough here. We might be observed. It's better to make them think we're passionately involved than to let them think we're talking about other things."

She moved her lips to his in apparent eagerness. He responded by holding her close, exploring her with uncontrolled abandon.

"Gyro, please show me to my cabin. Perhaps we can talk more there."

The muscular Asian squinted at her, grinning, but his eyes were serious. He was awed by what he regarded as her acquiescence to his attention. "Yes, you are right. We can talk safely there."

"Gyro," she whispered, "you're very good." Her lips

moved to his open shirt and brushed across his chest. "I think anybody watching would be convinced of our amorous intentions." She looked up at him with her wide violet eyes. "I don't think you want to talk right now."

"No, no. Maybe we talk later."

51

Derrick Harrison walked the halls of ConCom freely now. He was alone in the building except for the security guards in the lobby. Those half dozen people authorized to come in rarely did so. The once progressive company had been terrorized so thoroughly that the routine of day-to-day business had ceased.

The aging office manager walked slowly, passing all the offices, pausing to look inside many of them. He tried to picture the person who had last sat in each one. Most of ConCom's employees had been very kind to him, and he had enjoyed the attention paid him as the company's father figure.

He walked into Lois Lin's small cubicle in accounting and sat in the metal chair that faced her small desk. It was here that his seduction by the terrorists had begun.

First there had been the money, more money than he had ever dared dream about. All in neatly stacked bundles of small bills. Lois Lin had carried the bundles around in a big leather designer purse.

Then there was the cocaine. Lois had cajoled and teased him into trying it one night in her small apartment. After that, there had been an endless supply.

And then there had been Lois herself. She had spent countless hours rejuvenating him from what he had come to accept as a state of permanent impotence.

He was shaking now as he looked at her empty chair. He had always given her everything she had wanted; a name, a particular file, an executive's travel itinerary or daily calendar. Addresses and details had been furnished without hesitation. She had seduced him into being her personal slave. She had spotted his loneliness and filled the gap with an all-consuming carnal fantasy world.

Of course, now she had a broken neck. Harrison was isolated in his guilt. There was no one to speak to. His monstrous complicity had resulted in the deaths of all those people, including Lois Lin herself. He knew he was probably next. He was pitifully powerless to defend himself against the terrorists. So . . . he would beat them to their revenge.

He reread the handwritten note he had prepared for Willy Hanson. He looked at his watch. There was still time for overnight delivery service to the West Coast. He called the delivery service, then left the letter with the lobby security guard to be picked up.

The guard, a longtime ConCom employee, was glad to see Harrison. "Just you and me today, pal."

"Who ever thought it would come to this? You and me run the place. Maybe we ought to declare ourselves copresidents." Harrison attempted a chuckle at his own humor.

"You can have that job all to yourself. I'm not

lookin' to get shot, or something worse. All I want is a paycheck and to see my wife and kids every night."

Harrison turned toward the elevators without further comment, his hands shaking again. Charles Clayfield had children he would never see again, he thought.

He strolled into Angela Clayfield's old office and wondered whether or not she was still alive. He pounded his fists on her desk, trying to calm his trembling hands.

In the letter to Willy, he had spilled the beans on Max Von Braun and given away his address in Pleasanton. If they grilled the old pilot, there was a chance they might stop the killing. He started sobbing. All those people dead, all that blood on his hands. "Oh my God, Angela, I'm sorry. I'm sorry." Mumbling and whimpering, he rose from her desk, pausing to line up several papers that he had moved.

He walked to the huge window that looked out on the sea of morning traffic along Fifth Avenue. He slid the window as high as it would go on its track. He climbed on top of the radiator in front of the window, smiling and then laughing at the hum of Manhattan below. He stepped out onto the narrow window ledge.

Harrison paused just briefly, his mind moving back to the days when, as a youth, he and his friends would dive from the jagged rocks of Spuyten Duyvil up in the Bronx. Then with all the spring he could muster, he arched out in a perfect dive, until, still smiling, he splattered across the hood of a taxicab parked at the curb fourteen stories below.

52

Three hundred miles east of Ensenada, on the west coast of Baja, fishing boats dotted the water as far as the eye could see. They were pursuing the albacore, the fine tuna running in large numbers this year.

The *Lantau Star* had slowed to a crawl as it pushed its way among the widely spaced vessels of the tuna fleet. Sharky stood in the doorway of the radio shack. From time to time he shouted instructions to Onyx Lu, who relayed them to Lars Svenson at the wheel.

The *Star* was much larger than the fishing boats, and therefore clearly distinguishable as it proceeded.

All at once Sharky began shouting instructions, leaving the radio shack to point toward one of the boats in the distance, directly abeam at about three o'clock. The boat turned abruptly and moved directly toward the *Lantau Star*.

Onyx instructed Svenson to slow the *Star* until it

was virtually dead in the water. The tuna boat bore on, on a collision course with the *Star*, still a half mile away. As it drew near, the skipper of the fishing boat turned back her engines and crawled to point parallel with and only a few yards away from the *Lantau Star*.

Angela Clayfield crouched on her bunk, watching all this from her single tiny porthole. Remembering the explosives in the bow, she was terrified as the tuna boat came perilously close.

Onyx Lu scrambled alone to the main deck as a line from the trawler was tossed aboard. She grasped the line and began hauling it toward her. A canvas bag dangled from the line low over the water as she pulled it toward the *Lantau Star*. She hauled it over the side and then coiled the rest of the line until it was all aboard.

The two boats remained a few yards apart for several seconds. A strapping deckhand with powerful shoulders waved at Onyx as she signaled that the canvas bag was secure.

"Good work, Pelly!" Onyx gave the seaman a two-thumbs-up salute.

Pelly Kahn turned toward the flying bridge of the tuna boat, adorned by two large red stars, and dropped his arm toward the bow in an urgent motion. The tuna clipper roared to life and turned seaward, toward the fleet of fishing boats in the distance. Onyx watched until the boat was only a dot on the horizon.

She then scaled the ladder to the bridge of the *Star*, toting the canvas bag over her shoulder. Sharky left the radio shack and helped her into the pilothouse.

"We did it, Sharky. We beat those bastards again." Onyx was ecstatic. The usually dour Sharky smiled through clenched teeth, sharing her enthusiasm.

Onyx unbound the tie line and quickly flipped the canvas bag. Neatly banded bundles of hundred-dollar bills tumbled out on the floor of the pilot-house.

"A beautiful sight," Sharky said. He glanced up as Lars Svenson entered the pilothouse. The smell of alcohol entered with him.

Svenson's eyes locked on the pile of money. He was already breathing heavily. He stooped to pick up a thick packet of bills, eyes widening in disbelief.

"Hey, sailor boy! Who said you could touch my money?" Onyx's eyes narrowed and gleamed wick-edly as she drew a tiny .22 automatic from the pack she wore across her belly. "Drop it, and get down on your knees."

He hesitated. Sharky was grinning at him, obvi-ously amused. Svenson moved his hand to rub his reddened nose. The cocaine and the gin were a wicked combination. He stared in disbelief at the re-volver for a moment and then tossed the packet of money back onto the pile on the deck. "Hell, I've never seen so much money. I guess I just had to touch it—"

"Shut up, sailor boy, and do what you are told!"

Svenson looked at her, stunned, not understand-ing what she wanted.

"I said, down on your knees, fool." She waved the automatic menacingly. "You are not so slow to under-stand when we are alone in my cabin."

Svenson dropped to his knees.

"Now, sailor boy, we are going to continue your ed-ucation. Sharky here does not realize that you have already been taught to stay, to heel and to roll over. Now you must learn how to fetch!" She opened the empty canvas bag and held it in front of her.

"Fetch!" she commanded, pointing to the money.

Svenson reached gingerly toward the stack with his hand.

"With your mouth, you fool! Only a very stupid dog fetches with his paw."

The stoic Sharky bubbled with laughter as Svenson groveled in front of them, finally managing to grip one of the packets of money in his teeth. He crawled the few feet to Onyx and dropped the cash into the bag.

She patted his head roughly, making certain he felt the hard butt of the automatic. "Now fetch all the others."

Sharky was still chuckling as he turned to go back into the radio shack. Then he stopped to look again at the groveling first mate. "You might as well shoot him now, Onyx. No man will suffer this kind of embarrassment without seeking revenge later. Just kill him right now, while we are three hundred miles offshore and it's convenient. It would be perfectly safe to dump him here."

"Sharky! That would be premature. Mr. Svenson has so much to tell me about the *Lantau Star*. And he does this trick so well: there must be others we can teach him. Lars! On your feet!"

Svenson dropped the last packet of money into the canvas bag. He struggled to his feet, breathing heavily, reeking of gin, watching Onyx still waving the weapon at him.

"You dare to come to the bridge to stand watch in this condition? Really, Lars, I should have Kiki throw you in the brig. I want you to go back to my cabin and sleep it off. Now go! We'll talk about this when you are sober."

Svenson sighed heavily and stumbled out the hatch and down the ladder, not once looking back.

Sharky and Onyx watched until he had entered

the stateroom. "You know, Onyx, sometimes you can carry a thing too far. He is useless now."

"Don't worry about it. We may need him tomorrow as we approach San Diego, but tomorrow night Kiki will shoot him in his sleep. You worry too much, Sharky."

Sharky shrugged. He would prefer to dump a body farther out at sea.

53

Wispy white clouds floated above most of the Southern California coast. The weak squall line that had moved through was now breaking up, and a fresh, blustery wind was kicking up in the wake of the poor weather, promising fine sailing later in the day. They had decided to leave their marina haven at eleven o'clock that morning. Conditions would be perfect for pointing the *Tashtego* south toward San Diego.

A couple of tuna boats staffed with federal agents would poke along several miles seaward of the lumbering *Tashtego*. A fast cigarette boat, looking very much like a Budweiser ad, complete with bronzed, bikini-clad babes, would run interference nearer the coast.

Coley Doctor stood on the dock, eyeing the colorful crew of the cigarette with interest as they climbed into the high-slung cockpit. He wondered whether they were feds. This was the way he liked to see his federal tax dollars spent.

Coley had cleaned out the post office box and now held a bundle of letters in one hand. He continued to stare at the racing cigarette as the powerful engines rumbled to life. Finally he climbed aboard the *Tashtego* and handed the bundle of mail to Willy, who was just emerging from below.

A big red, white and blue Express Mail envelope seemed to cry for immediate attention. Willy ripped the flap and withdrew two handwritten pages.

"It's from old Derrick. I'd know the handwriting anywhere, but it's not like him to spend nine-ninety-five for Express Mail. He can remember when a six-cent stamp got next-day delivery." Willy started to read, and then slowly sat down in the cockpit as he became totally absorbed by the letter.

Dear Willy:
Of all the people who worked at ConCom, you were the best. I have cherished all my memories of those glory years.
Thanks, Willy.
It was Lois Lin, one of our accounting people, who started the whole thing. She was my lady friend. Hard to believe? I hope you never know what a fool a sharp young lady like that can make out of a lonely old man. That's what I am, Willy, a lonely old man. Please try to forgive me.
Between Lois and Max Von Braun, and with my help, we peddled cocaine and heroin to half of ConCom, including Angela Clayfield. I really never knew what they were after. I never imagined that there would be all the killing. I just thought they were drug pushers.
Lois became an old man's obsession. I gave her

*information now and then. I never knew what she
did with any of it until recently.*

*Of course, Lois is dead. Max Von Braun is living
at the Sequoia Gate Motel in Pleasanton, California. If you act fast, you may catch him. Lois told
me about him and sometimes mentioned a man
named Pelly Kahn. She said that Pelly is a monster.*

*That's all I know, Willy. I'm just a stupid old
bastard. I sure hope Angela Clayfield can be saved.
I guess I loved her, too.*

*By the time you get this letter, I will be trying to
explain my stupidity to my maker. I'd rather do it
my way than wait around for this Pelly Kahn guy
to break my neck.*

*I'm sorry, Willy. I'm going up to Angela Clay-
field's office now and jump out the window. Remember when we used to admire that view?*

Good-bye now.

> *Your friend,*
> *Derrick Harrison*

"Oh Jesus!" Willy tossed the letter to Coley, who
read it aloud to Ginny.

"That old bastard! I knew he was eavesdropping
on the telephone lines back there. And I let him get
away with it." Coley was dumbstruck.

"I'll try to reach Harrison at ConCom and then I'll
call Whitcomb." Willy went below.

A battered old Chevy Malibu pulled up in the
parking area near the *Tashtego.* A tall man carrying
some scuba gear and wearing a Dodgers cap got out
and started walking rapidly toward the boat.

"That's Mark Whitcomb," Coley declared. "No
scuba diver ever had a shoeshine like that. He might
as well be wearing spats."

Ginny nodded. "Willy! We've got a visitor. It's our favorite G-man."

Willy poked his head out of the hatch just as Whitcomb climbed aboard. "Folks, I'm afraid I've got some bad news," Whitcomb said, and found the three staring at him in strange silence.

Willy spoke first. "Derrick Harrison jumped out of the fourteenth-story window at ConCom yesterday morning."

Coley handed Whitcomb Harrison's letter and Whitcomb read it. "I'll have to keep this, if you don't mind. The old man was right about one thing, the Sequoia Gate Motel. Unfortunately, though, Von Braun checked out late yesterday, less than an hour before our guys got there."

Willy groaned. "We've missed him again."

"Maybe not." Now Whitcomb was smiling. "He asked the desk clerk to give him directions to the Sacramento Airport. We've got it staked out and the local police are helping us cover every flight."

"Von Braun is a pilot," Coley mused.

"So what?" Whitcomb said.

"Well, he might fly as a passenger, or he might have friends and slip aboard as a member of some crew. He could even hijack and fly his own airplane. He also could rent a private plane, or even buy an airplane if he wanted to. He might be lugging around a briefcase full of hundred-dollar bills."

"We're covering all those possibilities, Coley."

"So what do we do?" Ginny was getting impatient. The eleven o'clock departure was important if they were to have any chance of reaching San Diego by dusk. "We've got some ideal winds out there. It's time to sail."

"Okay, folks. The skipper says we sail." Willy was just as anxious as Ginny to take advantage of the favorable wind. "Coley, you coming with us?"

"Nope, I'm driving. I'll see you all on Harbor Island." He looked at Whitcomb. "Unless the FBI man here wants me to ride in the cigarette."

"Not a chance, Coley. You'd feel out of place there." Whitcomb broke into one of his rare smiles as Coley turned his attention to one of the bikini-clad policewomen. "Besides, we need someone to cover this operation from the Coast Highway. Stay in close touch, Coley."

"Everyone ashore," Ginny called out.

The big ketch rumbled with the friendly sound of a well-tuned diesel engine. Coley and Whitcomb climbed off, and Ginny backed the *Tashtego* slowly out of its slip. After securing all lines, Willy took his station at the mainsail halyard as Ginny pointed the *Tashtego* down the marina channel to the open sea. The wind was perfect for hoisting sails right in the channel, giving them a fast start down the coastline.

Before they hit the open sea, the *Tashtego* was flying. Willy gave Ginny a thumbs-up salute as he scrambled into the cockpit to stand beside her at the wheel.

"By God, Ginny, this is the way it should be, you and I and the sea. We should going west instead of south, though."

Ginny nuzzled against his shoulder as they stood together at the wheel. "Willy, I've been thinking. They've got their ransom. They've destroyed Con-Com. They've killed everyone but us. What makes you think they won't just disappear? Maybe they won't be interested in us, even if we're sitting ducks."

"Onyx Lu doesn't think like that. I think she has special plans for us. I give her less than a week to show up. If she doesn't, then we'll have to rethink the whole thing. But one thing is for sure. Whitcomb won't give up. There have been too many killings and he's burned up too many man-hours. There's also an outside chance that Angela is still alive."

"Oh well." Ginny smiled and took one hand from the wheel to pull him closer to her. Off to the right they could see the powerful cigarette dashing back and forth along the shore. Seaward they saw the two tuna clippers, far out. The sea was dotted with other boats, some of them occasionally venturing quite close to the *Tashtego*.

"Willy, how in the world can our escorts possibly keep an eye on all these boats?"

"I really don't think we have to worry. Whitcomb probably has the Coast Guard in on this. Keep in mind that the cigarette is never more than five minutes away. It can cover five miles in five minutes."

"I feel as if we're under a microscope. I guess we have to behave ourselves. We wouldn't want to shock Mr. Whitcomb and all his troops."

"I guess you're right. Darkness does come eventually though." Willy kissed her neck. "That's all we get for a while, baby."

The winds cooperated most of the day. They passed a number of military vessels and tuna boats and several luxurious passenger liners.

"Do you envy those people, Willy?" Ginny nodded at one of the sleek liners.

"Nah, all they do is eat, drink and screw. Half of them die within a month of all the exertion."

By seven o'clock they were abeam of La Jolla. San Diego lay a few miles ahead. Just as they were moving along the beach near Point Loma, they both spotted a beautiful luxury yacht far off in the distance. A helicopter was perched atop a pad on the aft deck.

"That would be nice, Willy."

"Come on now, you don't like stinkpots. She flies no sail."

The tuna captain who was their escort called over

to them. "The fancy fellow out there is the *Lantau
Star*. She is registered to a former British ambassador to the Sultanates, Lord John Hargraves." The
escort obviously had a yacht registry.

"Wow, I didn't know ambassadors were that rich."

"Then you havn't studied your history very well.
Governments invariably seek people of means to
serve as their ambassadors because they're willing
to spend a lot of their own money in the social
whirl."

Willy eyed the yacht in the distance quietly.
"Lantau is an island off Hong Kong. Lord Hargraves
must have been assigned to the sultanates in Brunei
or some other part of Malaysia."

Willy's comment passed by Ginny. "I figure we can
tuck up along Harbor Island and drop anchor in
about thirty minutes," she said.

"Great," he replied, forgetting about the yacht.
"Then we can relax and position ourselves as sitting
ducks in the daylight."

Ginny looked at him with tired eyes. "Quack," she
said.

Willy smiled. "Your call is a success. I'm ready to
mate."

"Me too," Ginny said. "In thirty minutes."

54

"You will take me flying today, no?" Juanita Chavez crawled onto Max Von Braun's chest and looked wide-eyed at the captain, who was just awakening from sleep. She moved her body against him, prompting him to wrap his arms around her. He finally opened his eyes and stared into the dark brown eyes of his companion.

"What time is it?" Von Braun's head throbbed, and his mouth was as dry as cotton. The empty bottle of tequila on the bureau reminded him why.

"It is time to make love. See, I remembered. Last night you told me to always answer you like that." She moved her body gently against his again.

"Juanita, I would like to know what the clock says."

The clock on the nightstand did not face them, so she squirmed over to the edge of the bed to look. "It is nine-fifteen. We have slept enough. You must either make love to me or take me flying like you promised." Juanita started a trail of kisses down Von Braun's chest.

"Nine-fifteen, eh?" Von Braun's mind began to come alive. It had been three days since he had heard from Onyx. Today was the day he was supposed to proceed to El Centro and stand ready there with a light aircraft. But Onyx had changed the meeting place from Long Beach to El Centro at the last minute, and Von Braun had expected more details to follow.

All day yesterday he had tried to reach Derrick Harrison, but to no avail. Von Braun felt isolated. Could it be that Onyx was throwing him to the wolves? "Juanita! Stop that. Really, we must take our showers. I will take you flying, but we must hurry."

Juanita bounded from the bed, squealing with excitement. "Oh señor, I have never flown before. It will be so much fun!"

"Yes, it will be." Von Braun gaped at her voluptuous, youthful body. "I will teach you all about the Mile High Club. Memberships are specially reserved for young ladies like you."

"Oh, that will be so nice!" Juanita smiled broadly, without the faintest idea what Von Braun was talking about. She stepped into the bathroom to begin her shower.

Von Braun began to pace nervously. He really shouldn't have waited until the last possible day to depart for El Centro. But Juanita had been a delightful diversion. The pain in his left shoulder was already nagging him as he contemplated the arduous day ahead. Ah well, it would be better to die happy in the arms of this erotic young fireball than to sweat in the desert for three days waiting for Pelly Kahn and Onyx.

Juanita emerged from the shower. She tittered and tried to hide herself behind the towel.

"Ah, you smell like a fresh-cut rose," Von Braun said, feeling like an old fool. Then he made up his mind. He would take Juanita all the way to El Centro with him. Just thinking about it sent another tingling pain through the pilot's arm.

They climbed into the rental car that he had leased a week before in San Francisco, and sped toward the Sacramento Airport. Using a service road, Von Braun pulled up in front of a hangar outside which several light planes were tethered. The Sierra Foothills Flying Service advertised crop dusting, charters, flying lessons and aircraft leasing.

The young man inside eyed Juanita appreciatively as she accompanied Von Braun to the desk. "Good morning, sir," he said to the captain, still ogling Juanita.

"I am Captain Max Von Braun of Trans-Asiatic. I called yesterday about renting that little Cessna over there for the day." Von Braun walked over to the window, looking at the brand-new Cessna, and decided it was just what he needed.

"She's all ready to go, Captain. Now just let me see your papers and we'll get the paperwork out of the way." It was not unusual for an airline pilot to take a busman's holiday once in a while. The attendant glanced up at Juanita, thinking he wouldn't mind spending the day in the sky with her himself. "Your destination?"

"Red Bluff, up north. It should be a beautiful flight today for the young lady. We will probably stop for lunch in Red Bluff. Then we'll just buzz around the foothills and come back in here late today."

"Very well, Captain. If there is any change, you will call us, okay?"

"Absolutely," lied the Captain. It was very likely that this fellow would never see his airplane again.

Once aboard the Cessna, Von Braun produced a bottle of tequila from his briefcase and stowed it in the side keep next to Juanita. "You'll have to look after this. It will keep us from getting airsick."

Juanita eyed him suspiciously. "Is it safe for you to drink that up in the sky?"

"Safe? Of course it's safe. Flying a plane is not like driving a car. There is nothing to run into up there." Von Braun chuckled as Juanita continued to look dubious. "You just have to watch out for mountains, that's all. If you see one right in front of us, give a yell, okay?"

Juanita squirmed uneasily. "Oh yes, I will do that." She broke into a big smile then. "I never know when you are serious, Captain."

Von Braun produced a chart from the briefcase. Of course he had no intention of flying north to Red Bluff. He had drawn a course straight south to Bakersfield, taking him the length of the San Joaquin Valley. Then he would jump the Tehachapi Mountains and hug the west slope of Antelope Valley. This would be the most dangerous part of the trip. He would fly low along the top of the foothills and sneak past Edwards Air Force Base and head south across Joshua Tree National Monument, over the Salton Sea, to the makeshift landing strip near El Centro. He gave himself a fifty percent chance of making it. There was a lot of military surveillance along the way that would end the trip in an instant.

Von Braun taxied the Cessna out toward the airstrip. Their backs were now toward the office of Sierra Foothills Flying Service. Von Braun glanced over his shoulder and nodded toward the bottle of tequila. "Ladies first, señorita. It's time we had a belt of tequila."

Juanita took a small sip and then a larger one before passing the bottle along to Von Braun, who took a long draw and passed it back to be stowed away.

The Cessna paused as Von Braun revved the engines at the end of the runway. He held the controls firmly and started the plane down the small strip, bringing it quickly up into the air. Juanita held on to her seat with both hands as the small plane climbed to 3,000 feet and then banked steeply to point south. "Oh Captain! It's wonderful! I wish I could fly a plane."

"It's easy, kid. I'll teach you." He had her lean over and put her hand atop his resting on the controls. "Now just do that for a while and before we land you will be able to do it all alone."

"This is so much fun." She squealed in delight.

"I want you to slip out of your clothes."

"What!"

"Take your clothes off. There is nothing like flying naked. It's a tradition for first-timers."

Slowly Juanita stripped down to her panties and bra, and then hesitated.

"That's just fine, kid. Let's have another pull on that tequila. Then we'll have another lesson."

In a little over an hour, the Tehachapi range loomed ahead. Von Braun tucked in close to the foothills and flew along at about five hundred feet above the sloping terrain. He had hoped he would be lost in the detail of the peaks to the west as he passed Edwards Air Force Base. He noticed several crop dusters working and decided he could easily be confused with them.

About forty-five minutes later he veered east toward Twentynine Palms. Not long afterward he turned south toward the Salton Sea.

"What time is it?" he asked, curling his arm around Juanita.

She took a hesitant guess. "Time to make love?"

"Good girl!"

"But how can we? There is not enough room."

"I'll tell you what, let's have another pull on that tequila and I bet you will be able to think of a way."

"Captain, you are a very daring and dangerous man."

"I'm sorry, Juanita. But that's the way God made me."

Juanita took a long drag on the tequila. "Don't be sorry, Captain. You are right. I will find a way."

A half hour later, just north of the Salton Sea, Von Braun turned due east, following a desolate desert road. He came to a long stretch that was straight as an arrow. He circled once to make sure of his decision and then gently set the Cessna down, using the straight stretch of road as an airstrip. Pulling to a stop, he let the engine idle.

"Okay, kid. Let's get out and stretch our legs."

"Ah, Captain, you can read my mind." Juanita jumped to the ground and made a dash to a patch of sagebrush.

He pulled the nine-millimeter from his chart case and stared for a moment at the jet-black hair behind the sagebrush. Then he shook his head and jammed the weapon back into the chart case. He just couldn't do it. He never could cross that line. He gathered up her clothes instead and tossed them out the door onto the ground.

He revved the engine and pulled the Cessna into the center of the desert road and roared down the gravel strip. Once airborne, he banked sharply and waved to Juanita, who had run down the strip after him. Then he pointed the Cessna southward toward El Centro.

Cursing himself aloud, he downed the rest of the bottle of tequila. She had a very good chance of mak-

ing it, he told himself. She was less than five miles
from the Salton Sea and the busy campgrounds
there. If she was picked up, it would take some time
for authorities to unravel her story. By then, he
would be hidden away aboard the *Lantau Star*.

The nagging ache returned to his shoulder. This
time it was more persistent than usual. He struggled
with the tight cap on the small bottle of nitroglycerin
and finally succeeded in shoving a couple of the tiny
capsules under his tongue.

The stabbing pain rose to a level that distracted
him from his flying. He wished Juanita were still
with him to help. For a second or two he lost consciousness. Opening his eyes, he saw he was perilously close to the ground. He veered right, aiming at
the narrow road running along the Salton Sea. The
Cessna smacked into the road, bounced along for a
hundred yards or so, then swerved into the heavy
brush, cracking off a landing gear. Von Braun knew
it would be a miracle if the plane did not flip over or
catch fire.

Within minutes, several cars from the campground arrived at the site of the crash. Von Braun
was semiconscious, half aware that a man was at-
tempting to pull him from the wreckage.

"Whoever has a telephone or CB get on the horn.
We need help. This guy looks bad." The man propped
up Von Braun's head with his jacket. Von Braun was
breathing, but did not otherwise move.

Within twenty minutes an ambulance arrived to
join the California Highway Patrol already on the
scene. Von Braun was soon inside and on his way to
a hospital.

Highway Patrolman Lofgren poked around in the
cabin of the disabled plane. He quickly recovered the
briefcase belonging to Von Braun and returned to his
cruiser to use the radio. "You can tell that guy up in

Sacramento that we've found his airplane. And you can tell the FBI that we've got Von Braun. He looks bad. He survived the crash but is on his way to the hospital in Palm Springs. He has no visible wounds. The EMS boys say it looks like a coronary, and they're treating him accordingly. He should be at the hospital within twenty minutes."

55

The *Lantau Star* was now about forty miles off
Point Loma, beyond which lay San Diego Bay. The
big yacht was virtually motionless in the water as
Gyro started the rotors of the copter. Onyx Lu sat
next to him.

Half a dozen of the *Star*'s passengers stood on the
deck watching. Sharky stood on the bridge, a nine-
millimeter jammed into his belt for all to see. Lars
Svenson was nowhere to be seen.

Angela watched as the rotors began to spin rapidly
and chop at the air. The copter rose slowly from its
pad, nosed down close to the sea for an instant and
then climbed swiftly, peeling off to the west for several miles. Gyro returned and circled the *Lantau
Star* at about two thousand feet. Then he began to
descend for his landing. At about a thousand feet, a
battery of floodlights switched on, bathing the landing pad in bright white light. The device Gyro had
engineered was clearly a success.

Gyro brought the copter in, making a perfect, gentle landing on the tiny pad.

Angela breathed a heavy sigh when the copter touched down. It was nerve-wracking to watch Onyx alone in the bubble with Gyro. The only thing that reassured her was the fact that Sharky was still aboard. If Onyx were to escape the *Lantau Star*, Angela believed, Sharky would be the one to go with Onyx and Gyro.

"Hey, love, can you swim?" The voice startled her. She turned to find Lars Svenson, eyes bloodshot, reeking of gin.

"My God! You look a mess. What have you done to yourself?"

"I've been trying to amuse our depraved Medusa, the one in the bubble there." Svenson staggered and held on to the bow rail for support. "I've been trying to find out what in the hell is going on. Now that I have, I don't want to know."

The hatch to the copter had opened. Angela and Svenson watched as Sharky left the bridge to walk aft toward the landing pad. Angela felt her uncertainty return as Sharky scaled the ladder to the copter. He stood there peering inside.

"Don't worry, love, they ain't leaving us yet," Svenson said, reading her mind.

Angela stared at him. For all his disheveled drunkenness, he seemed cogent.

"What makes you think they're not leaving us?" She wondered whether he knew about the explosives in the bow.

"They ain't got their money, that's why. It's tucked away in the radio shack."

"What money?"

"Your ransom, baby. I saw a pile of hundreds that would fill a suitcase. That wasn't fresh tuna the tuna boat delivered. I know. I saw it with my own eyes. In fact I tasted it. Onyx made me play run and fetch."

Angela gaped at him, trying to make sense of what he said. On the stern, the threesome was now climbing down to the main deck.

"Angela, I'm sorry as hell. I tried to play her game to get information. But every time I dozed off, she'd jab me with a needle full of her fuckin' goodies." He paused, trying to compose himself. "Remember, if you get a chance to swim for it, go! We're going to die unless we can figure a way to get off this tub."

Svenson staggered along the handrail toward Onyx's cabin. She couldn't help feeling sorry for him. By the time he reached Onyx's stateroom door, Onyx was waiting for him. She put one arm around his shoulders and pushed him in ahead of her.

Angela retreated to her cabin to await dinner. As much as she hated joining the others, she felt there was no choice. Perhaps Gyro would pass along some news.

Onyx left her cabin and walked quickly toward the bridge. She wore a bright peacock-blue dress that hugged her from shoulders to thighs. Lord Hargraves, dressed nattily in a captain's jacket and sharply creased white duck trousers, appeared amidship to join her. Sharky was waiting for them on the bridge.

"Lord John, you are to be complimented. You have cleaned up very well." Sharky, the man of few words, studied Hargraves approvingly. "You look like somebody, even though we all know that you are nobody."

"Lord Hargraves," Onyx said, "tomorrow's arrival party in San Diego has been confirmed. It will be held at the Coronado. There will be a member of the British consulate, and several city officials. The mayor may attend, and a half dozen members of the yacht club will be there with their wives."

"Oh really?" Lord Hargraves replied, mystified. "Am I supposed to be attending such an affair, after the harsh treatment I've been subjected to on this trip?"

"Yes, Lord Hargraves, really!" Onyx stretched to plant a warm kiss on the cheek of the unsuspecting ex-ambassador. "Lord John, you are a famous man! Your reputation as a statesman and adventurer will guarantee that we receive courteous treatment by customs when we drop anchor near Harbor Island in the morning."

"I . . . I'm stunned. With all the drugs aboard, this vessel can stand very little scrutiny by anyone. I really don't know how you expect to carry this off." Now Hargraves was worried. The *Lantau Star* was registered under his name and everything aboard was his responsibility.

"Don't worry your sexy head about that, Lord John. I think you underestimate your own importance."

Hargraves extended his arms, looked at the gold braid on his jacket and then down at the sharply creased trousers. "But why did you want me to dress like this tonight?"

"Good question, Lord John." Onyx stepped forward again to brush imaginary lint from his lapel. "You see, Sharky here is a thinker. He has prepared for any eventuality. It occurred to him that even though we are considerably offshore, we might get a curious visitor, official or otherwise. In case this happens, you are dressed to handle the situation with authority."

"Yes, that's good thinking." Hargraves actually seemed to be enjoying the flattery they were heaping on him.

"And one more instruction, Lord John: you are not to go pawing and slobbering over any more women aboard the *Lantau Star* until after the dinner party tomorrow night."

The ambassador paled.

"I have assigned Brigitte to you tonight. You may do every perverted thing you want with her tonight, but don't soil those trousers."

"Do the others aboard know anything about tomorrow night's party?" asked Hargraves.

"No, but you may tell them if you wish. I think it will bolster their morale. That's always good aboard ship."

Hargraves turned to leave the bridge. He appeared to be totally demoralized.

Onyx laughed. "He'll cheer up. Brigitte will take care of that."

Sharky broke out in a full fit of laughter. "He is such a fool. Was he really an ambassador?"

"Not a very good one, Sharky. But he is good in bed. And that is even more important than being a good ambassador."

56

Coley Doctor and Mark Whitcomb arrived at the hospital in Palm Springs late in the evening. They were taken immediately to Von Braun's room, where he lay in a deep coma. Von Braun's doctor informed them that there had been considerable damage to his heart. He held little hope that Von Braun would ever regain consciousness.

"His blood is loaded, by the way," the doctor said. "Alcohol and cocaine. I guess the plane couldn't get him up high enough."

Von Braun looked pathetically pale, connected to various tubes and monitoring devices.

"Hey, you old bastard," Coley said to the inert figure. "What in the hell have you done with Angela Clayfield?" Coley moved to the bedside and leaned close to the captain's ear. Then he shouted, "Where is Angela? Is she still in Honolulu?" There was an almost imperceptible flicker of a cheek muscle, but nothing else.

The nurse came in and scowled at Coley. "You'll need to get out of here now, please." She swept the curtain around Von Braun's bed.

Whitcomb grabbed Coley's shoulder and pulled him back. "It's no use, Coley." He turned to the nurse. "If he regains consciousness, I must talk to him at once. Other people's lives might depend on it."

The nurse nodded. "I'll let you know."

Two police officers were waiting for Coley and Whitcomb in the intensive care unit's lounge area. "Which one of you is Agent Whitcomb?" the taller man asked.

Whitcomb extended his hand. "I am."

"Sir, we have a young woman at the police station who claims she was raped by Max Von Braun. She tells a rather mixed-up story. Claims she was aboard the plane that crashed."

There was a sudden flurry of activity down the hall. Coley watched Von Braun's doctor and other staff members rush to Von Braun's room. A quiet tension seemed to overtake the entire unit, even as the monitors of other patients continued to beep and be answered.

About ten minutes later Von Braun's doctor emerged. "Mr. Whitcomb. Mr. Von Braun has died."

When they arrived at the police station, a Lieutenant Rodriguez was completing the write-up of a complaint filed by Juanita Chavez, who was sitting quietly by his desk.

Coley looked at the woman. Very young, he decided. And despite her disheveled appearance, extremely beautiful. She was sipping a cup of steaming coffee.

The police officer addressed Whitcomb and Coley. "The young lady here says that she flew with Max Von Braun from Sacramento to a point in the desert

near the Salton Sea. Von Braun landed the Cessna
on a desert road, where he left her after first raping
her. The plane took off and then crashed a few miles
away. I guess you know the rest of the story."

"That son of a bitch did terrible things to me!" the
woman shouted. "He raped me when we were in the
air! Then when we landed he flew off without me.
My feet are all cut from walking to the campground.
He is a bastard!"

"He's dead," muttered Coley.

"Good!" Juanita shouted. "He's still a bastard!"

"Did Von Braun tell you where he was going?"
Whitcomb asked.

"We were flying to El Centro."

The policeman handed Whitcomb a map. "We
found this when we cleaned out the airplane. There
is a course drawn on it from Sacramento to a point
just north of El Centro."

Whitcomb opened up the map and studied it.
There was another line drawn parallel to Route 8
west from El Centro to Harbor Island, near the San
Diego Airport. Near El Centro, there were scribbled
notes near the indicated landing point.

"We'll have that area staked out," Whitcomb said
to Coley. "Von Braun must have been meeting someone there."

Coley groaned. "The lady's right. He was a bastard. Right about now, the *Tashtego* is picking up a
mooring near Harbor Island."

Coley began to pace the small office.

"Don't worry, we've got them covered." Whitcomb
began to mull over the coverage of the mooring.

"That's easy for you to say. Willy and Ginny are
the bait in your rat trap. And we aren't even sure
who or where the rats are."

"Whoever they are, they don't know Von Braun's
dead. We're keeping that quiet."

"G-man, if you don't mind, I am going to get my ass back to San Diego and help stake out the *Tashtego*."

"I've got a copter due in here any minute. You can hitch a ride with me. Just remember, Mr. Doctor. The whole show might already be over. Your Onyx Lu theory could be all wrong. The ransom has been paid, and it's possible nothing will happen in San Diego."

"You don't actually believe that."

"Of course I don't, Coley. But I've been wrong before."

57

A few miles north of El Centro, between Calipatria and Niland, a dust-laden brown van with two red stars painted on the top veered off the main road and onto a desert trail that snaked eastward toward the Chocolate Mountains. After about a mile and a half, the van came upon a short stretch of road that was as straight as an arrow. In the subdued light of the dashboard, Pelly Kahn squinted at his map and decided that this was the place. The desert trail appeared to stretch straight out for three quarters of a mile. This was to be Von Braun's airstrip.

Kahn looked at his watch. It was about 2 A.M. Von Braun would have no trouble landing by the light of the full moon out here, but it seemed more likely that he would decide to land a little past daybreak.

Kahn got out of the van and began to set up a makeshift campsite. He arranged a few pieces of prospecting gear in front of a small pup tent in case he had to explain himself to anyone.

He climbed back into the van, lowered the seat back and stretched out his legs, nursing a thermos of hot coffee. His part in the project would soon be over. Onyx, Sharky, Von Braun and he would be meeting here in a matter of hours. Then, the fattest of paydays, on to Mexico and eventually Hong Kong. He tapped his right hand lightly on the handle of the nine-millimeter jammed into his waistband.

Kahn looked at his wristwatch again. It was 2:30 A.M. He wished Von Braun would hurry up. They would need the light plane for their escape into Mexico.

Whitcomb's team of agents had arrived late in the afternoon and found no one. The only natural cover, an occasional Joshua tree or a clump of sagebrush, was inadequate, so they had staked themselves out in a broad circle of tiny foxholes in the desert.

Agent Marley had drawn the number one position. He would call the shots for the others. The brown van was now about six hundred feet from where he was dug in. The instructions were not to advance on the van unless the driver tried to leave. Otherwise they were to wait until a rendezvous was made and then close in. The probability of anyone else's coming seemed slim, since Von Braun was out of the picture.

Marley studied the camp and the large van with his night glasses. He could see everything clearly. He felt firmly convinced that there was just one person in the van. That person was stocky. Once, when he left the van, he carried a rifle.

Aboard the *Lantau Star*, Onyx's dinner party continued past midnight. Lars Svenson was the only one not in attendance. He stood watch on the bridge, piloting the boat back and forth in ten-mile legs approximately twenty miles out from Silver Strand beach. He pulled frequently on a bottle of gin that he had stashed in his coat pocket. Off in the distance, he spotted the occasional red slash of a Coast Guard cutter that seemed to rove aimlessly off Point Loma to the north.

Beyond Point Loma, on the other side of the Silver Strand, was the San Diego Naval Base, harboring more firepower than most nations. The odds of their getting into the harbor without scrutiny seemed impossible to him, notwithstanding the reputation of Lord John Hargraves.

Meanwhile, in the dining room, Lord John was dancing up a storm with Brigitte. She had arrived for dinner wearing only high heels and a large topaz affixed to her navel. Nobody objected.

Onyx, Sharky and Gyro, in stark contrast to Brigitte, wore nine-millimeter automatics. Angela noticed that Kiki wore no weapon. The fact that Gyro wore one disturbed her. Was he really one of them? All hope would be gone if she had misjudged him.

There were eleven people in the dining room, including the cook and three deckhands who usually didn't attend evening meals. The room was locked and barricades were set up in the passages that led forward to the cabins. Disco music blared loudly from the intercom, making conversation virtually impossible. Any ship passing by would think that there was one hell of a happy party going on. But Angela, of course, understood that they were all prisoners in that room.

The volume of the music dropped abruptly. Onyx stood up, dressed in a form-molding sheer black dress. She drew the automatic from her thin belt and fired a shot into the overhead. She smiled seductively at her terrified audience and then began to speak.

"Now that I have your undivided attention, I have an annoucement to make." She paused as Lord Hargraves moaned and slumped over the table with his head in his hands. "Brigitte! Attend to Lord John. You are supposed to make him happy, not sad. As for the others, we will entertain you here until after sunrise. I am sorry to confine you this way, but we have endless champagne, cocaine, heroin, scotch and gin to make up for it. I insist that you partake. You also have Melanie and Brigitte. They are at your service, even yours, Mrs. Clayfield. And now they will at last demonstrate their full talents with our friend Kiki."

A portion of the dance floor had been covered with rubber mats. The two giggling women literally dragged Kiki onto the mats and began undressing him, as the music blared again.

Then Angela saw something that both puzzled and terrified her. Sharky drew his weapon and walked toward Onyx. He leaned over her shoulder and pointed his gun all around the room. He was obviously furious, and ended by slamming his fist on the table. Gyro, who was sitting near Onyx, stood and walked toward Angela.

Sharky jammed his gun back into his waistband and walked to a corner of the room to sit alone, staring blankly at the scene unfolding on the mat. Onyx unlocked the door, left the room, and locked it again.

Gyro and Angela walked together to the corner of the room, feigning interest in the seduction on the mat.

"Sharky accused Onyx of being high as a kite. If we were boarded now, everything would be lost."

"Why is Kiki here? Who is guarding the explosives in the bow?"

"The door has been welded shut and booby-trapped."

"That makes me feel wonderful," Angela said sarcastically. "What did you and Onyx talk about when you were aloft today?" She still didn't know whether or not to trust Gyro.

"Just about the lighting on the pad. She insists it be set for one thousand feet. I wanted a higher altitude." He moved closer to her. "I think we'd better stick to the party theme, or we'll look suspicious." He kissed her lightly on the cheek. "Oh, when we were aloft, flying toward San Diego, Onyx got pretty excited. She said she saw a sailboat she recognized moored off Harbor Island. It was a big ketch. She called it the *Tashtego*."

"The *Tashtego*?" Angela stared off into the distance toward the lights of San Diego. "Oh no, it couldn't be."

"That's what she said. I remember the name because I think Tashtego was one of Ahab's harpooners in *Moby Dick*." He brushed her cheek with another kiss; then both stared out the window before turning back to the exhibition.

Kiki was on his back now, straddled by Brigitte, who was dangling her ample breasts over his face as he tried to undress Melanie.

Sharky approached Gyro. "At three o'clock A.M."—he paused to compare Gyro's watch with his own—"I want the copter ready to jump!"

Gyro nodded. "Three o'clock A.M. The rotors will be turning."

Onyx emerged from her cabin. Lars Svenson staggered in front of her, prodded by the automatic she held in her hand. They were making their way toward the bridge. Sharky, gun in hand, motioned for Gyro to follow her.

Sharky turned to Angela. "You'd better get the hell out of this room and hide. Hide in the copter."

Angela was stunned, but decided not to question his advice.

At the mat, the deckhands were gleefully joining in the action. One of them rolled toward Angela and grabbed her ankle to drag her into the orgy. Angela kicked him away and stepped back.

"The minute I leave," Gyro said, "you get out of here. Climb up to the copter and crawl in behind the seats. If you're fast, you might make it before we all reach the bridge."

"What about him?" She nodded toward Lord Hargraves. He had finally removed his sharply creased trousers and was hanging them over the back of a chair.

Gyro looked at him and shrugged. "It is hopeless. He has lost his sanity. Quick! Go!"

She followed Gyro to the door, then walked aft into the darkness.

A few moments later the diesel rumbled to life and the *Lantau Star* accelerated to full speed and pointed straight toward San Diego.

58

The *Tashtego* had rounded Point Loma about 10 P.M. and proceeded north for several miles. Ginny had received clearance from the harbormaster for her radioed request to pick up a mooring near Harbor Island. It was located about a thousand yards from where they would move into their slip in the morning. Whitcomb had suggested this so that the stakeout plans could be completed before they took the slip. After all, the stakeout might last several days, or even weeks. He wanted to make one last sweep of the area in the daylight.

Ginny and Willy welcomed their isolation at the mooring.

"How about a couple of martinis?" Willy called out to Ginny, who had gone below to advise the harbormaster that they were now lashed up at the mooring.

"Good idea! Give me a minute, Willy." She came up a short time later with the drinks and joined him behind the wheel on the aft deck. San Diego's spectacular waterfront sprawled before them. Party boats, harbor cruise boats and tuna clippers all moved against the skyline in the distance. Here and there in the distance they could see the gray silhouettes of aircraft carriers and battleships.

"Maybe we made a bad choice," said Willy. "Only a fool would cause any trouble here."

"Who cares, right now," Ginny said, handing Willy his drink. "This mooring feels like heaven. Let's not spoil it, Willy."

Willy shrugged.

"The dockmaster said we're going to have a visitor," Ginny said, taking a sip of her drink.

"Who?"

Ginny looked off her port side. "Take a look."

A small launch was motoring toward the *Tashtego*. Coley Doctor was standing tall next to the pilot.

"Oh Jesus," muttered Willy, "I'm glad to see him but he isn't going to stay out here all night, I hope?"

"Hey, boss! I heard that. I had planned to stay all night, but I won't stay where I'm not wanted."

"Good idea, Coley. Three's a crowd on the *Tashtego*. Ginny and I have to catch up on our sleep."

"Your what? I never heard it called sleep before. I've got to bring you guys up to date on a few things." Coley climbed aboard and slipped the launch pilot a couple of bucks. "Come back in a half hour, pal. Got that?"

The young fellow grinned and nodded. Willy scrutinized him closely and decided he was probably one of Whitcomb's men. The launch putted slowly off toward the marina as the three of them watched.

Coley told them the details of Von Braun's crash and death near the Salton Sea. He then told all he knew about the stakeout in the desert.

"And then, of course, there is Juanita." Coley paused, waiting to be prompted.

"Okay, Coley, who is Juanita?" Ginny shook her head and smiled.

"Juanita is a pretty little desert flower. She claims Von Braun dumped her in the desert after initiating her into the Mile High Club. The doctor said Von Braun's coronary came a little later. Now that's the way I want to go."

"Thanks for sharing that, Coley." Willy patted him on the back. "Here comes your launch."

Ginny poured the rest of the martini from the small pitcher into their glasses.

"Whitcomb wants me to join the stakeout in the desert. You two are certainly safe here for now. There are more feds around than real people."

Coley climbed into the launch. "Ta-ta, lovers. Get your sleep!"

The launch moved away, then circled slowly back toward the *Tashtego*, Coley still standing amidship.

"By the way, boss. I ain't gettin' paid so good since that funny company of yours all took a simultaneous vacation. See what you can do about that, will you? It's no way to run a company." The launch putted back toward the marina, leaving a wake on the flat, gleaming water for the whole distance.

"So who do you think will show up in the desert?" Ginny's question was a good one, with no obvious answer.

"I would say that whoever is in that van is waiting for Von Braun, who we know will never show up. If I were running the show, I would pick that guy up now and find out who in the hell he is, or beat him to death trying."

"Great. Then I'd have to come visit you in San Quentin, given the caliber of justice these days."

Willy offered a toast. "To our Pacific crossing. May it start next week!"

The two clinked glasses. They finished their drinks and went below.

Ginny never had any difficulty sleeping aboard. Willy had never mastered the art, especially on an open mooring. Wakes from distant boats moved the water, tide changes, and harbor noises that seemed to be amplified across the open water combined to make him restless.

He finally managed to doze fitfully for a couple of hours before being awakened by the heavy swells caused by the passing of a large vessel. He fished around for the nine-millimeter in the side keep and slipped on a pair of jeans, moving slowly and deliberately so as not to wake Ginny. He pushed the automatic into his waistband and fetched a pair of binoculars from the chart table.

"I need a kiss before you leave me," Ginny mumbled, barely audible.

"I'm sorry I woke you. I'm just going topside for a while."

He leaned over to kiss her softly and pulled the sheet up around her. She fell asleep again immediately.

Topside, he saw a destroyer escort making the bend to point toward the towering Coronado bridge and the massive naval base on the other side. Its heavy wake was what had interrupted his sleep. He followed the landing lights of a big jet lumbering over the skyline, barely audible as it approached Lindbergh Field to the north.

Willy propped himself up against the cabin and extended his legs along the seat extending toward the taffrail. This was better. Maybe he could doze for another hour or so before daylight broke.

A couple of miles away he could see another sizable craft moving up the channel. He lifted the binoculars strung around his neck and focused them on the vessel. It was the British ambassador's yacht they had seen in the open water earlier in the day. One of Whitcomb's agents had identified it from a yacht registry. Willy recalled the name, the *Lantau Star*.

He let the binoculars fall to his chest after watching the boat proceed up the channel. His eyelids closed as the surface of the water became motionless once again.

When he opened his eyes, the *Lantau Star* was a thousand yards away, still inching its way up the channel. He again trained his binoculars on the yacht. There was no sign of life aboard. The bridge was dark to accommodate the vision of whoever was at the wheel. Once he saw some movement on the port side. Someone was walking aft toward the helicopter pad near the stern.

The vessel had come to a virtual halt in the water. His heavy eyelids fell shut again. He hoped the darkness would last a good while longer.

59

Lars Swenson stood at the wheel of the *Lantau Star*. His instructions were to proceed directly toward the large ketch dead ahead and pull up alongside. Even in his drunken state, he felt sure he could do that. Onyx had given him a little pick-me-up that would make the simple assignment a snap.

The party aboard the *Lantau Star* had ended the way Onyx had planned. Everyone had passed out on the mats in the dining room.

"Where is Angela Clayfield?" she asked Gyro with sudden alarm.

"Probably collapsed in her cabin. That's where I last saw her," he lied.

"We'll see, Gyro. If she is not ... How could you lose sight of her?" Onyx was waving her automatic wildly.

Sharky entered the room and glared at Onyx. "Where is Mrs. Clayfield?" he asked, his eyes sweeping the room.

"We don't know," Onyx replied.

Sharky shrugged. "If she is so difficult to keep track of, then she must die." He looked sharply at Gyro. "You come with me to the copter." Sharky drew his nine-millimeter weapon. He reached out and pulled Gyro's weapon from his belt and slid it along the deck into the corner.

Sharky looked down at the naked, dormant orgy. He kicked at Lord John Hargraves. Hargraves groaned. "You old fool!" Sharky said. "It's a good thing it's almost over. You have failed on your last diplomatic mission. I'll bet you failed all the others."

He looked back at Onyx. She was rocking unsteadily on her feet. Then he noticed a Coast Guard cutter moving slowly toward them from under the towering Coronado bridge. If they were boarded now, they were doomed.

"Gyro! Fire up the copter!" The hint of daylight was rising in the east.

The pilot raced toward the copter.

"Onyx," Sharky ordered, "get the money. Now!"

Onyx ducked below, too drugged to inspire confidence.

Sharky raced to the copter pad, then scaled the ladder as the big rotor started to turn.

As he climbed aboard, he reached behind the seat and shoved Angela Clayfield down as far as he could. If Onyx saw her, they would all die.

Gyro and Sharky both looked over their shoulders and saw the *Tashtego* looming perhaps a hundred fifty yards ahead. They could see rapid movements aboard the ketch.

"Where in the world is Onyx?" Sharky muttered under his breath. The Coast Guard cutter was now less than a quarter mile away.

Then Onyx appeared with the small duffel bag slung over her back and began scaling the ladder, holding the nine-millimeter in one hand as she climbed.

Now on the top rung of the ladder, she flung the bag onto the floor of the copter.

Picking his moment carefully, when Onyx's hand gripped the top rung of the ladder, Sharky slammed his boot onto her fingers. Onyx screamed and fell heavily to the deck below. To Sharky's amazement, the duffel bag, tied to her wrist, was jerked out of the helicopter and fell onto the deck with her.

Onyx moaned, then moved, scrambling for the automatic, which had tumbled from her hand in the fall.

"You bitch! You drunken bitch!" Sharky howled as he glanced across the water to see the cutter closing in.

"Up, Gyro! Now! We have no more time."

The big rotors dug into the air and the copter rose first slowly, then rapidly into the sky. "Higher! Gyro, higher!"

The needle on the altimeter spun on the dial: 700 ... 800 ... 900 ... 1,000 feet.

Then a sheet of flame rose from the bow of the *Lantau Star*, followed by a deafening roar that must have awakened most of San Diego.

The small helicopter bounced wildly in the sky as a concussion wave rocked it. Gyro held steadily to the controls and sped the copter low over the water, climbed the hills around Old Town and picked up Interstate 8 below. It had all happened breathtakingly fast.

Sharky breathed heavily and stared at the empty highway about a thousand feet below. "We made it! But we don't have the money. That crazy bitch. She took the money to the bottom of the bay with her."

Angela struggled to sit up in the cramped space

behind the two men. She was terrified, but elated to be off the *Lantau Star*.

"Where are we going?" she asked Gyro, but Sharky responded.

"My dear, we were going to set you free. But we can't do that yet, can we, Gyro?"

There was no response from Gyro, who was trying to keep the copter tucked in close to the hills so that they would not be seen.

Sharky turned to look into Angela's eyes, only a few inches away. "Our friend Onyx has lost our money. But luckily we still have you. Lovely as you are, you are what Americans like to call a cash cow. Since we have lost your ransom, it will be necessary to milk our cash cow again."

Sharky laughed loudly in the confines of the small copter. Angela slumped to the floor, wondering what had been gained by leaving the *Lantau Star*. Gyro was no ally, after all.

Sharky sat wide awake with a tight grip on the nine-millimeter. Then she realized that Gyro was sweating profusely.

60

Willy Hanson awoke with a start. He opened his eyes to the heavy chopping sound of a helicopter, and saw the *Lantau Star* less than five hundred yards off.

Ginny appeared at the hatch. "What's going on?" The thumping chop of the blades digging into the air became more rapid and echoed noisily across the water.

The helicopter hovered over its pad for a moment and then moved vertically, fast. Then came the blinding flash and a deafening roar. A shock wave buffeted the *Tashtego*, turning her sharply on the mooring. Willy, knocked tumbling to the deck, groped for a rail stanchion and hung on for his life as the main boom jerked and tossed the loosely gathered sail on top of him. He heard Ginny yell something unintelligible from below.

Across the water, the *Lantau Star* was a cauldron of fire and steam. The luxury yacht was tilted crazily toward the bow and was slowly sliding from view under the churning water.

The *Tashtego* soon stabilized. Willy crawled out from under the mass of sail and loose rigging and made his way to the cabin hatch. Ginny was pulling herself to a standing position.

When she saw Willy, she forced a faint smile. "Are we okay?" Obviously in pain, she was rubbing her left arm and shoulder.

Willy hadn't taken stock of himself yet, but he too began to rub at a shoulder.

Black smoke rolled across the *Tashtego* from the fire aboard the *Lantau Star*. The Coast Guard cutter was approaching them now. Ginny pushed debris away from the hatch and climbed up on deck.

"Willy! Look! Look! There is someone in the water!" Ginny stumbled aft over fallen rigging to grab a life ring from the clamp on the taffrail.

Willy followed and hurled the ring as far as he could in the direction of the swimmer, the thin line trailing in an arc. It fell short, but the strong swimmer closed the distance quickly to grasp the floating life preserver.

"Anyone else, Ginny? Do you see anyone else?"

She scanned the water, shaking her head. The yacht was sinking fast. Not a soul was visible.

Then, off the sunken bow, the Coast Guard cutter came into full view. The crew was pulling aboard another survivor who had been hidden behind the sinking vessel. It appeared to be a young man.

Willy pulled on the lifeline, urging the swimmer to hang on tightly. She was clutching a bag.

Ginny hooked a ladder over the transom of the *Tashtego* and reached down to pull the swimmer aboard. At first she thought the tiny swimmer was a child.

When the swimmer climbed aboard, she tossed the

sodden duffel bag to the deck. Then she turned to
face them, brushing a mane of jet-black hair away
from her face. The hair tumbled down her back far
below her waist.

Willy gaped at the woman, whose startling green
eyes were fixed in a wild-eyed stare. It just couldn't
be.

"Onyx!"

Onyx kicked at the duffel bag. "Willy, darling, I
bring you your money."

The woman looked down at the blood gushing
from an open wound below her knee. She was
breathing hard and no doubt had lost a lot of blood.
Onyx grasped the handrail behind her and started to
say something, but no words came as she slumped,
unconscious, to the deck of the *Tashtego*.

Willy put his arms around Ginny, hugging her
tightly to his chest. Off the starboard beam, the
stern of the *Lantau Star* slipped beneath the water
with a last sizzle, leaving the pall of smoke and
steam over the flat, still water.

Police boats quickly circled the *Tashtego*. Within
minutes Whitcomb had pulled alongside with a
launch holding several of his team.

"She needs attention right away." Willy, still holding Ginny tightly, nodded at the survivor huddled
unconscious on the deck. "That's Onyx Lu. And
that's ConCom's million dollars in the duffel bag."

Whitcomb knelt to feel her pulse and then called
for medics to board the *Tashtego*. He brushed the
long black hair from the small woman's face and
studied her for a moment.

"It's Onyx Lu, all right."

The radio crackled aboard the police launch now
lashed alongside the *Tashtego*. One of Whitcomb's
men came aboard to report the grisly news.

"They have one other survivor aboard the cutter.

Calls himself Lars Svenson. Says he was first mate on the *Lantau Star*. He claims there are at least a half dozen people still aboard, including Lord John Hargraves. We have to get Svenson to a hospital right away."

Willy touched Whitcomb's shoulder. "Tell him to ask this Svenson guy about Angela Clayfield."

He came back with an answer almost immediately. "Svenson doesn't know for sure, but he thinks she left in a helicopter over a half hour ago with Onyx Lu."

Whitcomb eyed Onyx, now being strapped to a stretcher. "Well, we can only hope he's half right. We know he's half wrong."

61

A hundred miles away, Gyro skimmed along the desert less than a hundred feet above the sand and rocks. They had had amazing luck escaping detection by sticking close to the surface in the sparsely populated area.

Sharky was the first to spot the van with the two red stars on the roof. It was the only vehicle visible in the barren landscape for several miles. Gyro circled once at high speed as Pelly Kahn emerged, waving a bandanna tied to the barrel of a rifle.

"Thank God!" muttered Sharky. "But where in the hell is Von Braun's plane? I guess we'll have to land. How's the fuel?"

"We'll have to land," confirmed Gyro.

"Okay, set her down as close to the van as you can. Von Braun should show up any minute. If he doesn't, we may have to use the van." Sharky slammed his fist on the dash panel. "That son of a bitch! Von

Braun was Onyx's idea, not mine. That son of a bitch!"

Sharky climbed down from the copter as the rotors slowed to a stop. He ordered Gyro and Angela to follow him.

Suddenly a bullhorn blasted forth in the cold morning air. "Drop your weapons now! Now!"

Pelly Kahn spun around and fired a hail of shots toward the sound of the bullhorn. Before the echoes died away, a return of fire from half a dozen positions ringing the van dropped Kahn on the spot where he stood.

Sharky tossed his nine-millimeter to the ground and put his hands in the air. Angela and Gyro stood frozen in each other's arms.

Another helicopter thumped into view, banked steeply and then set down close to the ring of agents surrounding Angela, Gyro and Sharky. Coley Doctor stepped out and ran to Angela. "Angela, you are the most beautiful sight I've ever seen!"

Coley turned to one of the agents holding a handset. "Tell the boys in San Diego we've got Angela Clayfield."

It was over. The ambush had worked perfectly.

Papeete

It was about a month later. It had been three days since they had lost sight of Diamond Head to the north. The South Pacific stretched in all directions like an endless pond, not a ripple on the surface. The *Tashtego* lay somewhere between the equator and Tahiti. The jib had been secured and the big mainsail fell limp, catching not a breath of air.

Ginny and Willy welcomed the break. Their sail to Hawaii had been an exhilarating ride with favorable winds that had pushed them along at a fast pace.

A big chart covered one wall of their cabin. A heavy marker zigzagged a course across the entire length of the chart. It went southwest from San Diego to Hawaii; south to Tahiti; west to Samoa; north-northwest through the Solomons; then east along the Bismarck Archipelago, into the Suva Sea, south of the Philippines. Finally the course entered the South China Sea and then veered almost straight north to Hong Kong.

There would be no speed records set along this course. It was the long way around. When they arrived didn't matter. Getting there eventually did matter in some vague way.

Ginny and Willy rarely spoke about the harrowing climactic day off Harbor Island. The newspapers they had brought aboard in San Diego were already yellowed from dampness and the sun. But Willy was reading through them now as the *Tashtego* sat motionless on the flat water.

"You know, if Angela Clayfield weren't such a seductive wench, we would probably be history now, and Onyx Lu might not be facing kidnapping charges and ten counts of murder."

Ginny nodded, stretching her bronzed legs out on the bench along the cockpit. "I hope she can get off the drugs. I think she can. She has a strong will."

"You know, Ginny, if Gyro hadn't been interested in her she would never have gotten Onyx's place in the helicopter. And Onyx would have made sure the *Lantau Star* was a lot closer to the *Tashtego* before detonating the charge. I guess being seductive pays off sometimes."

"Sometimes? Try all the time. How about me turning into your seductress until the wind blows us into Papeete?"

"Ginny, that's what I like best about you. You're a mind reader."

THE BEST IN MYSTERY

<table>
<tr><td>☐</td><td>51388-6</td><td>THE ANONYMOUS CLIENT
J.P. Hailey</td><td>$4.99
Canada $5.99</td></tr>
<tr><td>☐</td><td>51195-6</td><td>BREAKFAST AT WIMBLEDON
Jack M. Bickham</td><td>$3.99
Canada $4.99</td></tr>
<tr><td>☐</td><td>51682-6</td><td>CATNAP
Carole Nelson Douglas</td><td>$4.99
Canada $5.99</td></tr>
<tr><td>☐</td><td>51702-4</td><td>IRENE AT LARGE
Carole Nelson Douglas</td><td>$4.99
Canada $5.99</td></tr>
<tr><td>☐</td><td>51563-3</td><td>MARIMBA
Richard Hoyt</td><td>$4.99
Canada $5.99</td></tr>
<tr><td>☐</td><td>52031-9</td><td>THE MUMMY CASE
Elizabeth Peters</td><td>$3.99
Canada $4.99</td></tr>
<tr><td>☐</td><td>50642-1</td><td>RIDE THE LIGHTNING
John Lutz</td><td>$3.95
Canada $4.95</td></tr>
<tr><td>☐</td><td>50728-2</td><td>ROUGH JUSTICE
Ken Gross</td><td>$4.99
Canada $5.99</td></tr>
<tr><td>☐</td><td>51149-2</td><td>SILENT WITNESS
Collin Wilcox</td><td>$3.99
Canada $4.99</td></tr>
</table>

Buy them at your local bookstore or use this handy coupon:
Clip and mail this page with your order.

Publishers Book and Audio Mailing Service
P.O. Box 120159, Staten Island, NY 10312-0004

Please send me the book(s) I have checked above. I am enclosing $ _____
(Please add $1.25 for the first book, and $.25 for each additional book to cover postage and handling.
Send check or money order only—no CODs.)

Name _____
Address _____
City _____ State/Zip _____
Please allow six weeks for delivery. Prices subject to change without notice.